Carlina

PNW Syndicates 1

Carlina

PNW Syndicates 1

Flo Journey

Table of Contents

Chapter One

I could hear my stepsisters, I mean *sisters*, running to the door. Through the window, I could see a black SUV with blacked-out windows pulling up to the door. As I watched, a man stepped out and walked toward the door, handing Annabelle something while Beatrice tried to grab it from him before her sister could touch it.

It had always been this way with those two. Supposedly, from the day they were born, they'd fought each other to be the first, the prettiest, the lightest hair. You name it, they fought about it.

Thankfully, I'd only lived with them for five years, but those five years were enough to make me want to pull out my hair. They moved in when they were 15 and I was 13.

In the beginning, I looked up to them. They were my new sisters, and I wanted to be like them. For two years, it was like this.

My mother, Celeste, married their father, Baron Teller, after their respective spouses had passed away. From the very beginning, my mother and stepfather wanted us to act like family, so I was to call Annabelle and Beatrice sister versus stepsister.

"Carlie, come down here at once!" The great Baron was requesting my presence.

I'm sure it was for something he needed done. It was never for dinner, a guest, or even an outing. I knew better than to make him wait a second longer than necessary. The last time I dallied wasn't well received. I threw my book on the bed and rushed down the two flights of stairs to the main parlor.

"Yes, Father?" Even though he was my stepfather, my father having died not long after I turned 10, I was to call him Father since the day they had married. It rolled off the tongue, even if there was always a taste of acid on my tongue after saying it.

"Thank you for *joining* us, Carlie. Please sit near your sisters."

How interesting. They usually prevented me from sitting on the same furniture they occupied. Maybe he had turned a new leaf and was going to be nicer to me? If he had turned a new leaf since this morning, then maybe, but it was highly unlikely.

My mother stood next to him, shadowed by his height and presence.

I was in such a rush to get downstairs I didn't notice Baron holding an envelope, nor both girls silently waiting for me to sit.

Usually, they would have something negative to say about my clothing or hair. While I was from as wealthy of a family as they were, I was never on the same level in their eyes. Realistically, I think my father had been worth much more than theirs, but I'd never said it out loud. They would run to Baron, and I would have to hear about all he'd done for my mom and me over the years. According to conversations I've overheard, his wealth had been faltering, but he still lorded it over our heads every chance he had. More like my mother had taken him in, considering it was *our* house he was living in.

"As you know, several of my companies do a lot of business with the company owned by Mr. Wessex. It appears his son, who was away at a private school, is returning home. He's looking for a wife before he joins the family business. It would seem Mr. Wessex wants you three to meet for lunch," Baron boastfully said.

I rolled my eyes but made sure no one saw. I couldn't care less about Mr. Wessex or his son. His name came up frequently. Whenever Baron had a meeting with Mr. Wessex, he would be sure to bring news about how *great* Chad, Chris, or whatever his name was, had been doing and how much he would help his father's company when he returned. I was tempted to tell Baron if he liked what's his name so much, he should marry him. All I knew was he was my age, and he went to a private school in the mountains of Oregon.

Annabelle and Beatrice sat up straighter. "I heard he was ugly and deformed," they said at the same time. "Send Carlie. She'll fit right in."

"Girls, stop. This will be a great opportunity for you to not only marry someone wealthy, but also to ingrain yourself into the Wessex family." Baron's eyes were glimmering with excitement at the prospect of getting his hands on some of the Wessex fortune.

The comment caused the twins to whisper to each other while I watched my mother's face. She wouldn't meet my eyes, which always meant something I wouldn't like was about to happen.

I knew what my father would have said if he were still alive. "Carlie, you are the last of our line. You're smart and beautiful, and you're destined for so much more than this life."

I didn't want to marry for money or fame, but for love. If I was going to marry at all. Honestly, I was content with my books and my third floor. But it wasn't great. It was too hot in the summers and too cold in the winters. Not to mention, I knew my father had left me a large inheritance. Unfortunately, I couldn't claim it until I turned 19.

My 19th birthday was only three weeks away, and then I'd have the money to leave. I didn't know where I would go, maybe to see some of my mom's family in the Midwest, or maybe my father's family in Canada. Either way, I was going to leave, and there was absolutely nothing Baron or his daughters could say or do about it. I would miss my mother, but ever since she married Baron, she wasn't the same woman who had raised me.

"His father is requesting a sit-down lunch with the three of you to determine if one of you should marry his son. If his father chooses one of you, you'll be married in two weeks. The meeting is tomorrow."

Annabelle was the first to screech about how she would never marry someone without seeing them first. From what she'd heard, he went to a private school because he was a criminal. No way would she marry him.

Beatrice, unlike her sister, sat for a minute, thinking over what had been said. When it clicked, she then ran around the main parlor like her hair was on fire, screaming about how it wasn't fair, and she didn't want to marry 'some stranger'.

I chuckled to myself at the visual because Annabelle and Beatrice had blonde hair while I had reddish brown. In the sun, the fiery red really came out, but cooped up in my room reading, it was usually more of a mousey brown.

"Settle down, girls. You must listen to the rest of the letter." Baron finally remembered I was there. "Carlie, this applies to you as well."

The twins focused on me at the same time. I knew I wasn't invisible, but I could usually sit and listen for a while before any of them remembered I was there.

"Wait, she's invited too? I thought it was for *your* daughters, Daddy," Annabelle mock whispered. Her air quotes were laughable.

Baron sighed. "Yes, since neither of you seems like you want to marry him, Carlie can also attend, and since I'm her rightful stepfather, she's also technically invited."

And there it was. My mother didn't know he'd already planned to push me on Wessex's son. She stared at him before opening her mouth to speak.

"Baron, you didn't tell me Carlie had to attend. I thought this was because of your —"

Baron looked as if he was about to slap my mother, but his face grew red instead. "Celeste, mind your words in front of the girls."

I wondered what this was really about because arranged marriages weren't much of a thing anymore, especially in the

United States. I'd heard sometimes different cultures would still do them, but we lived in Oregon and weren't part of those specific cultures.

While Baron talked about the legitimacy of me going, and the twins cried about how they shouldn't have to go, I was wondering how I could skip it altogether.

I didn't have nice clothing, so it was an easy excuse. I'm sure I could fake an injury. Baron and the twins worked me so much, no one would think twice. I could be mean or rude or something the father would hate. Maybe I should send a letter to my father's family now and move out after the meeting. Even if I'm not selected, I should have plenty of time to prepare and move out before the wedding. It would be harder for me to get my inheritance when I turn 19 a week later, though. I knew they probably missed me, since they hadn't seen me since my father passed away. Either way, I was going to send them a letter asking them if it was okay for me to come visit and stay with them for a while.

I was so busy daydreaming about what I would do once I left, I didn't hear Baron say my name until he hit me on the forehead with the envelope. The twins both laughed as I rubbed the spot where he'd hit me.

"Did you not hear a word I said? Are you deaf or just dumb?"

"Neither, Father. I was busy thinking about what I would wear to the meeting."

"Yes, if you'd listened to what I was saying, you'd know I was talking about this very thing. Now, the rest of the letter speaks about what the ladies must wear. You are to wear a pair of black pants, gold shoes, and a lightly colored top. All three of you must each wear a different color top. The only color choices are blue, green, and red."

The twins immediately called blue and green and smirked at me.

"I can't wear red. It doesn't work with my skin tone or my hair."

"I don't care what does or doesn't work for your skin tone. The twins are older and already called their colors." Baron beamed at the girls for their quick thinking.

"I'll make it work. However, I don't have gold shoes." I didn't want to go, and now they found it funny what color I was stuck wearing. This was getting better by the sentence.

"I'm sure either Annabelle or Beatrice has a pair. If not, your mother can take you shopping out of the stipend she gets."

Annabelle spoke up, "We don't have shoes to fit her enormous feet."

I knew it wasn't true, but her saying it meant the small amount of money my mom received from caring for my inheritance needed to be used to buy me new shoes.

"Two more things, girls. The son will not be there. It'll only be his father. His car will pick you up at noon tomorrow for lunch at their estate. Celeste, you need to take Carlie to get shoes now." He opened his wallet and gave my mom a debit card, one I knew was only in her name. But why did he have it?

"Carlie, get your shoes and let's go." My mother grabbed her purse from the coat rack by the door.

"Take the pickup, and I better not see any damage to it when you get back," Baron called over his shoulder as he walked into the kitchen with the girls.

I heard him say he'd take them to the store in the Mercedes after we left. Like they needed anything else. Their closets were so full, they took up pretty much the entire second floor for themselves.

Putting on my sandals, I caught up with my mom as she started the pickup. Baron mostly used it to haul stuff for business, so it was dusty and dirty. The seats were worn, and the glove box door was hanging on by a single screw.

"Mother, why are you letting him make me go to this lunch?"

"Carlie, I don't have a choice. I assume he already RSVP'd for all three of you, and there's a lot you don't understand."

"Oh, I understand you won't stand up to him in the house dad built. And apparently, he's controlling your money, which is supposed to be to help me. What am I not understanding?"

She wouldn't look at me and really hadn't since she married Baron. I heard them fighting early in the marriage, but for the last two years, the fighting had stopped. I wish it meant their marriage had improved, but I knew it was really because my mom was broken and had given up.

"It's safer if he holds on to it than if I do. You know how often I lose things."

"Yeah, I'm sure." It made me sick to even look at her. I was confused by why my father put in the stipulation to make me wait to receive my inheritance until I turn 19 instead of the more traditional 18. He probably couldn't have imagined my mother would turn around and marry what seemed like the first man who'd paid her attention.

She was beautiful, with bright red hair and freckles across her cheeks. After my dad's death, I don't think she saw herself as the same person she was before. Baron came along with two teenage girls and said all the right words, so she jumped at it. She relegated me to below the twins, and into the attic like the unpaid help in the process.

It looked like she was going to say something, but we arrived at the store before she could.

"Here we are. You need a red shirt and gold shoes, right?" She acted like nothing had happened in the car.

"I have a nice red sleeveless shirt already, and it fits well. It's the one with the crisscrosses in the back."

"Oh yeah, I remember it. You haven't worn it before, have you?" I doubted my mom knew what I was talking about since I'd bought it before my senior year of high school. She didn't even go shopping with me. Instead, I'd gone with one of my friends.

"No, I was going to wear it to graduation, but we both know what happened there."

High School graduation was supposed to be special, a coming-of-age celebration of sorts. However, at the last-minute Baron had something happen at one of his businesses. Because he couldn't go, my mom nor stepsisters would go, and then no one could take me, so I wasn't able to attend, and spent the time sitting in my room reading instead.

Instead of saying anything about graduation, she continued like I had said nothing. "Okay, so you have a shirt... what about gold shoes?"

"Why does he want us to wear gold shoes? So random."

"I have no idea why most people do what they do, but let's humor him, alright?"

"Sure, whatever. It's technically your money, anyway." I rolled my eyes as I sulked toward the shoe section.

My mother rushed to catch up, barely doing so by the time I got to the shoes.

It was summer, so not only were the summer shoes still in stock, but fall and winter styles were being put on display.

I held up a pair of black booties I loved. "You think he would notice if I spray painted these?"

"I'm sure a man of his wealth would notice if something had been spray painted. Not to mention I'm sure it would still smell tomorrow."

"Yeah, you're probably right. Gold shoes it is."

The clerk said the store only had two pairs of gold shoes in my size, and I immediately hated the first pair. They were gladiator sandals, and even if you could see them with pants on, I didn't want to wear something that seemed so uncomfortable.

While I was looking for shoes, I kept thinking of a way to get out of the lunch.

"Mom, what would happen if I didn't go to the lunch? Like just left?"

Absently looking at shoes, she faced me. "Why would you? I'm sure Baron and Mr. Wessex would be very upset."

"How would you feel about me leaving, though?"

Tears welled in her eyes, but she blinked them away swiftly. "I would be sad if you left and didn't follow through on your commitments."

I wanted to scream at her, "*my* commitments?". Meeting a rich man for his son wasn't in my plans. She didn't even seem bothered by it, only the fact I wouldn't be following through with my commitments. Instead, I did what I always do when my mother and I argued; I smiled and carried on with whatever I was doing.

The only other pair of gold shoes were ballet flats with a small gold bow. Flats were okay as I was already five-seven, while the twins were barely five feet tall. Okay, I was being mean. They were like five-two. Except for a few things, most of their clothes fit me. I knew because they would give me their old clothes every time they went shopping, which was frequently.

"Carlie, can you please find a pair of shoes? We need to get home soon."

"Why? Baron's going out with the twins. I'm sure they'll be shopping for hours."

"Because I told Baron we wouldn't be long, and dinner needs to be ready soon."

I knew Baron would probably take the girls out to dinner. He always did after they went shopping. Instead of arguing with her, I agreed and put the shoes back into the box. Walking to the front of the store, I kept thinking about how I never wanted to get married. Being married to Baron had changed my mom, and I liked who I was. I didn't want to change for some guy.

As the cashier rang up the shoes, I thought about the earlier conversation where my mom looked genuinely surprised Baron was including me.

After she paid for the shoes, which I was happy to find out were on sale, we walked to the pickup.

"Mom, why were you surprised when Baron said I had to go as well?"

"Oh, nothing. Baron and I already knew about the lunch. We didn't know the specifics, but only that it was going to happen. When we'd spoken about it before, and you weren't to be included."

"Then why was I?"

My mom looked at me sadly. "I don't know, but it'll be a good thing, I promise."

The last time she promised me something, it was right after my father had died. She'd said nothing would ever come between us, but she broke those promises the minute Baron and the twins moved into the house.

Chapter Two

13 Days Until the Wedding - Preston

"What are you doing, Preston? You aren't supposed to be here."

Victoria shooed me out of the kitchen. I knew what my father had said about me being here during the lunch with the ladies. Who I married should be my decision, especially under the circumstances.

"I know, but I was hungry, and I should be there."

"Preston, I'll bring up something for you to eat. According to your father, you are not to be here when they arrive."

"Fine, I'll go back to my room, but I expect food."

Victoria smiled, knowing I was joking about being stern. "And you shall have it."

After my mother died, leaving my father and me alone, Victoria helped raise me. She was the chef and housekeeper, but to me, she was a surrogate mom. I knew she didn't like this situation any more than I did. I hoped this whole thing would have a favorable outcome, especially now I was close to 19.

Hugging her before I jogged upstairs, I threw a 'Thank you' over my shoulder.

Father had said I couldn't be in attendance, but it didn't mean I couldn't watch them arrive.

Since coming home after graduation, which shockingly, my father did not attend, it had been 'Preston keep out of the public,' and 'Preston, why didn't you come home last night?'. He claimed there was a situation he had to take care of but hadn't clued me in to what it was about. My father was one of the most controlling individuals I'd ever met, and I went to a private academy full of pretentious families who all wanted a leg up on their competition. I understood, given his position, why he wanted to 'protect' me, but I'd been training to take over for him for as long as I can remember.

All I wanted was freedom, which I found in my classic Ford Mustang. I drove the winding roads behind our estate every chance I got, which wasn't often enough. I rarely drove it. It felt good to let the car hug the turns. It was especially freeing at dusk as I watched the sun disappear beyond the horizon. I hadn't been able to bring my car to the academy because, "We don't want students to leave without permission." So, it had been almost two years since I'd driven it. I was glad Victoria's husband, Freddie, was handy with a wrench because he'd kept my car in running shape. I would have to get them something nice when I eventually received my inheritance from my mom's side of the family.

Thinking about my car and driving it around, I almost missed the knock on the door to let me know my food had arrived. I knew Victoria was far too busy getting lunch ready for my father to stand around and talk, so I waited a moment before opening the door and retrieving the plate of cheese, crackers, and grapes.

Ever since I was a kid, my mother, and then Victoria, gave me this snack when I was withdrawn or preoccupied.

With the way I knew my father treated the staff, I didn't know why Victoria stayed around as long as she had. Freddie could easily find a job in the city working on cars, but he chose to work in my father's garage, maintaining our vehicles and anything else needed on the property.

Victoria was in charge of everything inside the house. They must have been doing something right because my father hadn't fired them yet, or even yelled at them, as far as I could remember. Yelling at the staff was one of his favorite hobbies after making money and making people bleed.

As I nibbled on my cheese and crackers, I heard the gravel crunch under the arriving car. I knew it was my dad's Denali SUV. He always used it for important matters. He thought it impressed people.

I hope the girls liked Seth, my father's chief bodyguard and driver. He could be a handful at times, but he knew how to drive.

I made sure the thin curtain was blocking anyone from seeing me as I looked out my third-floor window. Father had said Baron's twins would be the two he selected from. While I waited for Seth to open the back door, I thought about how one of these two girls would be my future wife.

All this pomp and circumstance so I could take over the company the day my father decided he was done. It was what I had not only trained for but also educated for. The great Wessex legacy. Oh, and the nice inheritance I would receive when I turned 19. My grandparents on both sides only had one grandchild, me. While they were all very wealthy, they only had me to leave their fortunes to. I was destined to receive millions in about a month. I couldn't believe they added a stipulation saying I must marry to receive it. With the stipulations, I needed to make sure my father had a prenup drawn up for my intended bride to sign. Recently graduating from the academy and still young, I wasn't ready for marriage. Why must they force me to marry so soon? I guess they didn't foresee me being sent to the academy because I got into trouble at home, or the trouble I'd gotten into at the academy. Thankfully, I'd been able to smooth out both those problems.

I still thought the reason I had to pick between these specific girls was horrible, but the deal was between my father and theirs, and I had no say in any of it. Getting involved in Charles Wessex's business affairs was something I had no intention of doing. Being his only child and heir to everything, I should have known there would be conditions to my becoming an adult. Why must everything be on his schedule? Until I got my inheritance, there wasn't much I could do, so why fight it before I had to?

I heard voices carry to my window, and I looked down at the women leaving the SUV. I knew nothing about Baron Teller other than he had blonde twins and owed my father a lot of money.

The first out of the car looked high maintenance with her blue pirate shirt with puffy sleeves and ruffles. She had her hair pinned up in such a way I could not only see the pins from here, but I'm sure a tornado wouldn't move it.

I'm sure Father will love her.

As the second girl stepped out of the SUV, I noticed she was wearing a low-cut, tight green shirt. Her pants were looser than her sister's, but not by much. I noticed her shoes, also gold, were wedges. At least this one had her hair down.

Father must have given them instructions on what to wear.

I wished I could go down and meet them or at least know what they were saying. I'm sure it was something about how nice the house was, or how they couldn't wait to meet my father. Same old, same old I was used to hearing whenever I went out with him.

They looked like most of the girls I went to school with. Blonde, wealthy, could get any guy they wanted, and usually did. They were plain in a pretty way, and I'm sure both were boring to be around. Right as I was about to step away from the window, I saw someone else step out of the SUV. Knowing my father had said it was only supposed to be the twins, I stepped closer to the window.

The first thing I noticed was how the sun caused her loosely braided hair to look like it was on fire. She was taller than the twins, even wearing gold flats.

I rolled my eyes at the fact my father requested they wear gold shoes. They would have to take them off as soon as they got inside. It was a waste if they'd bought new shoes for this lunch since my father never let anyone step foot outside of the entry foyer wearing shoes.

This girl was wearing a pair of loose-fitting black pants and an open-backed red shirt with a criss-cross pattern. It wasn't tight, and it had a V neck front collar.

Yeah, my father would never pick this one.

Since she was obviously related to the twins somehow since she was here, I'm sure she was as boring and pretentious as the other two. There was something about her I couldn't pinpoint, but I couldn't take my eyes off her.

Stepping back from the window, I realized she was looking right at me. I knew she couldn't see me because of the curtains, but it felt like her eyes were meeting mine. She had beautiful, piercing green eyes.

I realized she was nothing like the other two. I still didn't want to get married, but I did want to get to know the redhead. She seemed interesting, and I liked interesting. Something about her drew me to her in a way no one else ever had.

Knowing there was no way I could see them up close, I decided to take my car out for a spin. I may even kick up some gravel leaving, to prove to my father I wanted nothing to do with this shell game he was playing. Checking the calendar I shared with my father to see if there was anything scheduled, I saw there wasn't, so I picked up the phone and called down to the garage.

"Freddie, hey it's me, Preston. Can you have the Mustang out back in about 10? I'm thinking about leaving for the day since, you know, Father doesn't want me around during his lunch."

Freddie laughed before responding. "Let me gas her up, and she'll be ready for you. Be careful, okay? I know how you like to speed through the mountains."

My father never told me to be careful. It was like I had two sets of parents, the ones who loved me and the one who was in charge of me. Not for much longer, though. "I always am. I wouldn't want anything to happen to such a beautiful car."

"Do you want Victoria to pack you something to eat?" Whenever Freddie spoke of Victoria, even in a mundane sense, you could tell how much he loved her. If I was to ever get married for real and have a family, I'd want a marriage like theirs. Full of love and laughter. Not some prearranged crap, making a means to end for my father, but something real.

"Great, thank you." I hung up and changed out of my sweatpants and workout shirt. I put on a pair of jeans and a t-shirt of my favorite band, Sumo Cyco.

They were a metal band out of Canada, and I loved their music. Their lead singer was cute, but her voice was what had really drawn me to them. Hopefully, I was stuck marrying enjoyed music as much as I did.

I had two more weeks of freedom before I had to marry a complete stranger, and I was going to make it count. Unless my father had a task for one of his businesses before the wedding.

I jogged down the back staircase to make sure no one saw me. I knew this estate like the back of my hand. It had kept me from getting caught many times, right up until the day I got caught and sent to the academy. I still didn't understand why my father chose this as the final straw. Now, I can say I'm a graduate of a prestigious academy, even if I'm sure my father's sizeable donation helped grease the wheels for my academic success. I wasn't dumb. I was quite smart, in fact, but I didn't care before I went to the academy, and I didn't care while I was there, either.

As I approached the Mustang, I saw Freddie step out from the driver's side.

"The food's in the trunk, and it's all gassed up. I also checked the tires because I noticed one was a little low."

I patted him on the shoulder. "Thank you, and please thank Victoria for me."

I knew he and Victoria would be listening in on the conversation my father would have with the girls, but they wouldn't tell me anything. Probably out of fear of losing their jobs.

I resigned myself to my fate as I got behind the wheel.

"To hell with it." Throwing the car into first gear, I slid around the house, spraying gravel all over the place. I knew where they were having lunch, so while they wouldn't be able to see me, they would definitely see the car and hear the gravel pinging off the windows. If I could make it to the pass before they left, my father's phone call would have to wait. There was no service through the pass, so he wouldn't be able to reach me until I was at the top or came down.

Chapter Three

13 Days Until the Wedding – Carlina

Of course, they fought to see which one would be first out of the SUV. Not like it mattered, since we were all going to the same place. Annabelle and Beatrice were both rude to the driver. Every time he tried to start a conversation, they would giggle and talk to each other instead.

He had introduced himself as Seth, and when he looked at me, his smile was somewhere between amusement and pity, as if he knew I had to put up with them every day. I would smile back and go back to daydreaming about what I was going to do after I received my inheritance. I couldn't wait to see the look on the twin's faces when I packed up and left.

Pulling up the driveway, I took in the mansion. The house my father had built, and we lived in, was nice. It was three stories and had enough rooms and bathrooms for everyone. It even had a library, which he had loved.

Baron had removed the desk and chairs and put in a pool table, but thankfully he kept the books. He may not be a great person, but I had to give him credit for keeping the books. They were my one escape.

I marveled at the building as we got closer. It was three stories with columns along the front holding up the roof of the porch. Sheer curtains allowed light in through each window but still gave privacy. The windows along the front side were stained glass, and it looked like there could be a garden off to one side. From an architectural point of view, it was beautiful, but it didn't seem welcoming. Maybe the reality of what was on the other side of the doors was what caused me to think a certain way.

As the car stopped, Annabelle and Beatrice bickered again about who would get out first.

I sat back, not wanting to be involved in their fight, nor did I care.

Seth parked the car, got out, and walked around to open the door.

Annabelle elbowed Beatrice right before the door opened and slid out. Beatrice composed herself and joined her sister, both preening like male peacocks as they approached the front door. I knew they would wait for Seth or someone else to open the front door, so I didn't know what the hurry was.

It was finally my turn, and I considered staying in the car. Seth would have understood, and maybe he could have taken me home while the twins fawned over Mr. Wessex.

I knew neither of them wanted to marry his son, but they would do their best to outdo each other. If Mr. Wessex picked one of them, I'm sure they would do it, but they would take all his money and probably come back to the house to live with their father.

Not me. I wanted nothing to do with the Wessex family or their delinquent son.

Seth looked at me while he held the door open.

I took a deep breath and stepped out. Tilting my head at Seth as a thank you, I walked toward the large, ornate door.

A woman wearing a traditional maid's outfit opened the door, but instead of a skirt, she wore pants.

Out of the corner of my eye, I saw fluttering in a window on the third floor. I looked up and saw the silhouette of a what looked to be a young man. I couldn't make out much other than he had dark hair and ice-blue eyes which seemed to look right through me. Catching myself staring, I looked back toward the door to catch up with Annabelle and Beatrice.

The woman, who I learned was named Victoria, let us know lunch would be served in the garden room.

From the minute we walked through the door, the twins pointed out paintings and furniture and were sure to mention they were each worth more than my entire wardrobe.

Victoria kept walking, briefly telling us what one doorway or another lead to.

I looked around, trying to see if maybe I could see the person I saw earlier, but it was only Victoria, the twins, and me. I almost ran into Beatrice when Victoria stopped at two large wooden doors.

Pushing a button, both doors slid into the wall, revealing a room whose stained-glass windows I'd seen from outside. The other two walls, made of standard, clear glass, showed a pond, fountain, and a small gravel path barely wide enough for a vehicle. Victoria explained during the heat of the summer, the glass doors could be moved to open the entire room to the summer breezes.

"Ladies, please sit. Mr. Wessex should be down any minute. Can I get you anything to drink?"

"I'd like a lemonade." Annabelle blurted.

"I want one too, but make sure it's fresh squeezed." Beatrice was next.

Victoria's smile didn't reach her eyes as she stood there.

I said nothing because I didn't feel right having someone wait on me.

"Miss, would you like something?" Victoria asked me directly.

"I'm fine with the water already on the table. Thank you, though."

With a soft smile and a nod, she left the room to get the twin's drinks. With any luck, she would open a carton of store-bought lemonade and give that to them instead.

"Wonder what they're going to serve us. I'm sure they want to impress us, even though there's no way I'll marry him." Beatrice sat at the table, playing with one of her forks.

"I heard Mr. Wessex's son had to go to boarding school because he killed someone. No way will I marry a criminal." Annabelle walked around the room looking at the paintings on the interior wall.

Silently, I walked toward the glass walls to look over the garden with the fountain. It was a small fountain with three ducks encircling the outside edge. The fountain was almost level with the pond, so it looked like the ducks were floating on the water. I could see a small path leading from the pond into the garden and thought about what losing myself in a book near the pond would be like.

"—at do you think?" I realized Annabelle was asking me a question.

"Can you repeat that?"

"God, you don't listen to a word I say, do you? I asked you what you thought about this place." The look Annabelle and Beatrice gave each other meant I had missed more than a simple question.

"It's gorgeous. Did you notice the flowers and monarch butterflies in the stained glass? The ducks in the pond are also in the glass." I figured if I kept it about what was around us, I couldn't walk into saying something that would get me in trouble. It wouldn't be the first time they tried to get me to admit things without realizing it. I was older now and knew their game.

Seeing I wasn't going to fall for whatever it was they were trying to do, the twins went back to what they'd been talking about, clothes or shoes, or whatever. Annabelle and Beatrice sat in the two chairs with their backs to the glass.

I took the chair overlooking the garden, but my back was to the stained-glass windows. I figured Mr. Wessex would want the chair looking out through the three glass walls.

Moving the napkin to my lap, Mr. Wessex and Victoria walked through the door.

I got up to help her, but Victoria motioned for me to sit back down. She was carrying a platter with four glasses on it. Two looked like the twin's lemonade, and there was a clear glass and a black glass.

"Here are your lemonades." Victoria placed a glass in front of each twin.

Mr. Wessex had stopped right behind his chair, with both hands on the chair back, as if waiting to see what was going to happen. He was probably around the same age as my mother, with small wrinkles forming near his eyes. His dark brown hair showed some stray grays. As he looked over the table, I couldn't help but notice the same piercing blue eyes from earlier. He wore dark slacks and a gray button-up shirt, leaving the top button undone.

I was sure he was more comfortable than I was, but then again, he wasn't at lunch to be assessed like cattle. He was the one doing the assessment.

"This is fresh squeezed, right?" Annabelle sneered.

"Yes, I squeezed it myself before bringing it to you. If you wish to add sugar, there's some in the middle of the table." Victoria smirked.

It was absolutely from a carton.

"Here's a water for you." She placed the red glass near me.

"Thank you, Victoria."

"You're welcome." Victoria walked back toward Mr. Wessex before placing the black glass near his empty spot.

Mr. Wessex thanked Victoria as she left the room. Once she was out the door, he sat.

"Thank you for coming to lunch." Mr. Wessex's voice was deep and did not sound sincere.

One twin muttered, "Like we had a choice," but the other one coughed quickly to cover it up. If Mr. Wessex heard, he didn't act like it.

Since I assumed neither twin would be polite, and even though I didn't want to, I knew I should keep my manners. "Thank you for the invite. I hope you're doing well today?"

"I am. Thank you for asking. I'm not sure I know you, though. Did Baron have three daughters?"

The twins giggled rudely.

"No sir, I'm Carlie, Baron's stepdaughter. He married my mother, Celeste, five years ago right after my 13th birthday."

A flash of shock appeared on his face but quickly disappeared. "I'm glad you could join us, Carlie. Please call me Charles. Mr. Wessex is for business, not for future family."

I smiled before looking down at my hands. I wanted nothing to do with his family.

"So, ladies, before Victoria comes back with the lunch she planned for us, can you tell me a little about yourselves?"

Annabelle and Beatrice sat up straighter.

I knew he was talking to all three of us, but when they sat up, I knew they were about to take over the conversation. It happened every time any attention was directed at us equally. They completely shut me out, which suited me fine; the less he knew about me, the better.

It was interesting he didn't know I would be attending. Didn't the invitation state for all three of us to join him?

The twins introduced themselves and rambled on about trivial things and what they liked while I looked back at the pond.

Sitting near the center of the pond was a mother duck with six ducklings. The hen swam in a wide circle, ending near a small cluster of cattails. She turned to watch all the ducklings follow her. When they were all next to her, she showed them how to get bugs near the waterline. All six ducklings wiggle-swam into the cattails while the mother stayed on the outside edges.

I wondered what it was like to have a parent who protected her young the way this duck did.

The twin's laughter brought me back to the conversation. As I focused, I realized Mr. Wessex had asked me something. I didn't answer, and the twins giggled about it.

"My apologies, Mr. Wessex. Your pond is quite lovely." Might as well tell the truth. What could I lose? A marriage I didn't want and wouldn't do?

"Oh, that thing? My wife loved waterfowl, so when I had this property built, I had them build the pond for her. She loved it and spent much of her time out there. In fact, the day before she passed away, she was out at the damn pond instead of inside with her family."

The bitterness was coming off him in waves. I don't know if it was toward his wife, the pond, or maybe both. How you could marry someone and be so bitter toward them, I'd never understand.

"I'm sorry for your loss, Mr. Wessex."

"No need to be sorry. You didn't make her sick."

This was a man I did not want to have to associate with more than necessary.

"What was your question?" I wanted to focus his attention back on the lunch and his question versus his wife. As I thought it would, his attitude changed back to the almost jovial individual he was when lunch first started.

"Yes, I was wondering what you do in your free time?"

The twins wore matching smirks, waiting for me to respond.

I considered if I should answer honestly and figured it really didn't matter.

"I read, mostly. My father had an extensive library. I try to get some sewing in when I have time."

Mr. Wessex's expression changed slightly into a grimace before he smiled again.

"My wife loved having a library. She would sit in there and sew, especially after she got sick. You're very different from your sisters, aren't you?"

Right as I was about to tell him they weren't technically my sisters and were just freeloaders who lived in my house, Victoria came through the door with a cart full of food.

I smiled as she came to the table.

She placed four covered plates on the table, one in front of each of us. After setting the last one in front of Mr. Wessex, she circled around and removed the covers.

As she removed mine, I could smell the fish before I saw it. On the plate was a piece of salmon with broccoli and rice. It looked and smelled divine.

"Thank you, Victoria. It smells wonderful."

She smiled at my compliment, and I couldn't wait to dig in. Looking at the other plates, I noticed the twins and I had been given fish, while Mr. Wessex's plate contained a steak with roasted red potatoes and steamed baby carrots.

I wasn't a huge fan of steak, so I was glad Victoria had served us fish. I would need to thank her again for her unintentional thoughtfulness before we left. Fish wasn't the twin's favorite food, so we rarely had it at home. The fact not only was it my favorite but also something the twins didn't like, made my day.

Not surprisingly, Annabelle nor Beatrice said anything about the fish and instead stared longingly at Mr. Wessex's plate while Victoria walked out with the cart.

The minute the door closed, Mr. Wessex raised his glass to us. "To the future pairing of my son with one of you wonderful young ladies."

I wanted to gag, but I focused on the fish while we clinked glasses.

We waited for Mr. Wessex to take his first bite before we did. I could tell the twins were pushing their food around. I savored every bite of the perfectly cooked salmon. Even the rice was the exact consistency I preferred. I made sure I didn't eat faster than Mr. Wessex, but by the time I'd finished, the twins had barely eaten their rice and maybe one bite of broccoli.

Mr. Wessex looked from my plate to the twins' plates. "Are you two not hungry, or do you wish for something else?"

I wanted them to say no, to say they weren't hungry, but knowing them, it wasn't their way.

"Sorry, Mr. Wessex. It smells great, but neither myself, nor Beatrice, likes fish. Unlike Carlie over there who ate everything on her plate like she was starving."

There was no point in defending myself, because if I did, it would get back to Baron, and my life would exist in my room for a week or more.

"I'm sorry to hear. Is there something else you'd like? I want to make sure you two eat as well." It was the first truly nice thing he'd said to us, which surprised me. He didn't seem like a man who cared much about what guests, or those he was trying to force into a marriage, wanted.

"If it wouldn't be too much trouble, I think we would like a dish similar to what you had. We love beef." Annabelle smiled sweetly, the smile she regularly used to get her whatever she wanted.

I hated their "sweet" smiles because when I tried to do it, it made me look insane.

"Of course. Let me get Victoria to prepare two dishes for you both."

As if Victoria was listening to the conversation on the other side of the door, the minute he spoke, she appeared with the cart to whisk away their dishes. "I will prepare those dishes shortly. Miss, do you or Mr. Wessex want anything while we wait?"

"Just more water, thank you." I didn't want to impose any more than we already were, especially with the twins making her create new lunches for them.

Victoria nodded with the slightest smile before she turned to Mr. Wessex.

"Can you please bring a coffee for me?"

Victoria bobbed her head slightly before turning around with the cart and leaving the room.

"While we wait for your meals to be prepared, do you have any questions for me regarding my family or my son?"

I wanted to ask him why he needed to find someone to marry his son. Everyone says he's attractive, wealthy, and educated. Since I didn't really care other than a passing curiosity, I didn't ask.

Annabelle, always wanting to be in the spotlight, asked about his son.

"What are you looking for in a wife for your son?"

Inwardly, I was both interested but also horrified she'd asked outright. With the pause Mr. Wessex took, I assumed he wouldn't answer.

Finally, he sighed and spoke softly, "Ever since my son's mother, my wife, died, he's never really been the same. He's sullen, impulsive, reckless, and not quite dangerous, but he could become dangerous if left unchecked. I need to find him someone who can keep him on track, keep him working toward the family's goals, and keep him out of jail."

If I hadn't been taught better, my jaw would be on the floor. I guess he's honest, but how could someone speak about their son in such a way? I looked over at the twins to see their reactions, but I couldn't tell how they were feeling, which was slightly terrifying.

They looked like they were thinking, which usually meant they were up to no good.

Victoria quietly walked in with the water and coffee.

"Thank you."

Victoria bowed her head before speaking. "Your lunches should be ready soon, Misses. Is there anything else I can bring for you?" No one responded, so she turned and left the room.

Beatrice watched Victoria walk out before speaking. "While your son's wife would need to keep him in check, what would she get from the arrangement?"

"The last name of Wessex, a small stipend per month to help pay the bills until my son starts making money with the company, and one housing staff of your choosing, whom I will pay for the first year of marriage. After about a year, Preston should be making enough money to pay your own staff. I expect the wife to maintain a classy appearance and host events to provide networking for the Wessex family. Oh, and she must sign a prenup agreement."

I closed my eyes so he couldn't see how hard I rolled them.

He wanted a babysitter for his son and someone who could elevate his family's name in the best ways possible. It sounded like a recipe for disaster. Had I not already agreed to be part of it, this would be a deal breaker. I wonder if his son even knew what his father was trying to do. The fact he hadn't even mentioned his son's name made me feel gross. It was as though his son was a piece of property he could sell off.

I guess the twins and I weren't in a much better position, attending a lunch with a man who was picking his son's wife. At least if there was a prenup, and I was chosen, I could add my own stipulations.

Before either twin could ask the question reflected in their eyes, which I knew would be something about how much their stipend was, Victoria returned with two plates. Placing them in front of Annabelle and Beatrice, I could see they were eager to start eating.

Victoria wasn't out of the room before the twins dove into their food. I was expecting Mr. Wessex to ask me questions, but he alternated between looking at his coffee cup and looking outside.

Victoria had barely been gone a minute or two when she was back with a tray full of small desserts and a carafe of coffee.

I looked over at the twins, and their plates were clean. I must have zoned out again.

"Ladies, please enjoy Victoria's specialty, cheesecake."

I wasn't a huge fan of cheesecake, but I knew the twins loved it, so I took one small piece and a cup of coffee. I was ready for this day to be over. It was exhausting, and I was ready to get home and read a book in bed with my fuzzy socks. I had to have fuzzy socks and maybe some tea.

I again thanked Victoria for the dessert while I pushed it around my plate.

The twins had each taken two or three pieces. I couldn't keep track because it seemed like once they put one on their plate, it was gone.

Mr. Wessex seemed amused by the fact they were eating so much cheesecake, but he didn't comment on it.

"Mr. Wessex, when do you think you'll make your decision regarding your son's wife?" I was okay with the silence, but I wanted this lunch to be over as soon as possible. I figured it was the last question he was waiting to discuss.

"Thank you for asking, Carlie. I'll decide tonight, and then I'll let your father know who I've chosen."

"What if the person you choose doesn't want to marry your son?" I knew I was walking into what could be a danger zone, but I wanted to know what to expect, even if I wasn't the one chosen.

From the way he looked at the twins, he was absolutely going to choose one of them.

I almost felt bad for them because they were definitely not going to want to marry his son.

"This is not optional. The individual I pick will be the one my son marries, whether they like it or not. I've already discussed this with your father, and he understands the consequences of refusing my offer."

His tone was of finality, and I knew something more than simply finding a wife for his son was going on.

I looked at the twins, who either didn't understand what was happening or didn't care because they had something up their sleeve.

They were sitting back nonchalantly, drinking their coffee, and watching the interaction between Mr. Wessex and me.

"Thank you for your time and the wonderful meal. I believe it's getting to be time for us to return home and let our father know how it went." I stood, hoping Annabelle and Beatrice would take the hint it was time to go.

Only when Victoria arrived less than a minute later to tell us Seth was ready to drive us home did they stand.

Mr. Wessex stood and followed us to the front door. "Please send your father my regards, and let him know I will contact him in the morning with my decision. Until then, please have a good night."

The twins didn't respond, but my parents raised me to be polite. "You as well, Mr. Wessex."

Just then, Seth arrived in the SUV. He stepped out and opened the door for us.

The twins got in first, elbowing each other slightly for the best seat, as usual.

I nodded at Mr. Wessex and glanced up at the window where I'd seen the individual earlier. There was nothing but the curtains, and I didn't know if I was hoping to see him again or not. Shaking my head, I got into the back seat next to Annabelle and Beatrice.

They were already talking about Mr. Wessex and what they thought.

I looked in the rear-view mirror and caught Seth looking back at them, knowing he was listening to every word.

The ride home went faster than the ride to the house, or maybe I was more excited about getting home than I'd been to go to lunch in the first place.

"Thank you for driving us, Seth. I hope you have a nice evening."

"You as well, Carlie."

I don't remember having told him my name, but considering how many times Annabelle and Beatrice had used it in the SUV, he'd probably heard it from them.

Chapter Four

13 Days Until the Wedding- Preston

It took much longer than I'd expected for my father to call to yell at me for my gravel stunt. I'd almost thought he'd forgotten as I parked at the lookout high on the pass. Sitting on the hood of my car, I opened the basket Victoria had made while I looked out over the valley.

The phone in my pocket vibrated, and I rolled my eyes. I knew it would only get worse if I didn't take the call, so I begrudgingly answered, "Yes, Father?"

"What did you think you were going to accomplish by throwing gravel everywhere, other than making me mad?"

"I was trying to stay out of the way of your luncheon."

"You could have done it without driving like a maniac."

"Did you need anything else? I was about to eat my lunch. Since you weren't interested in having me there for yours, even though it was about me."

"You knew you couldn't be seen at the lunch. It was understood they couldn't see you until the wedding date, otherwise this whole plan could crumble, especially if Mr. Teller sees a picture of you."

"Why can't I be seen? Why did you make them wear different color shirts? That's weird."

"Because I don't want your intended bride or her sisters to know what you look like. Your name is already in the news, but nothing with your face. You know how young women love taking pictures. We can't afford for your face to be in any state or federal databases. Cameras could capture your image and connect you when returning from doing what you do for the company. The shirts are so I don't have to remember their names."

"Real classy, Father. I don't know why I have to be a pawn in your game."

"You need to grow up, and getting married will help accomplish your growth. It also keeps Teller firmly under my control, which is necessary."

"How does marrying someone I may not even like help me grow up?"

"Don't back talk me, Preston."

He sounded irritated, but I was tired of all this crap.

"It's a real question. I don't understand how getting married will automatically make me more mature."

"It's similar to running a business. Negotiation, compromise, even interacting with someone you may not like, which gods know I do a lot of."

"Owning a business will teach me more about that than being married to some random stranger."

"You're doing it. End of discussion."

"So, I shouldn't drive fast, and I should go along with whatever you want me to do? Great, so the same conversation we've had over and over. Is there anything else, or can I get back to my lunch?" Even though I wasn't feeling especially hungry anymore.

"Nothing other than to remind you to stay out of the public's eye until you transition to working aboveboard for my companies. So, stop driving the hot rod, and let Seth drive you."

"Don't worry, *Father*. I plan to stay on the property for the next two weeks. I wanted to get out one last time before I'm forced to marry." There was nothing for me in town other than the family business. I didn't have any friends, and being the son of Charles Wessex didn't help. I didn't want or need anything right now. Well, not entirely true. I wanted one thing, but I knew it couldn't happen for a while, if ever.

Hanging up the phone, I laid back on the hood, eating the food from the basket and thinking about my life. Regardless of how I felt, it was going to fundamentally change in two weeks' time.

If nothing else, at least all three women I'd seen were attractive, but I couldn't get the image of the redhead out of my mind. She wasn't like the other two. I assumed my father would set me up with one of the twins. In his eyes, they're exactly the type of woman the son of Charles Wessex should marry. Some short, fake, annoying blonde who was nothing more than arm candy.

I knew my father was trying to marry me off, thinking it would force me to stay local. Even though I knew he wanted me to take over the businesses, I liked what I did for the company, and being a figurehead was not in my plans. My father even shied away from the things I did, but it kept me in the shadows, which is how I liked it.

He also wanted part of my inheritance. What he didn't know, and I had no intention of telling him, was I already had plans for it. Those plans did not include financially propping up his companies or lavishing a brand-new wife with money. No, I had a plan, and there was nothing my father or new bride could do to change it. I needed to wait it out. In two months, I'd be one of the wealthiest people in the nation, if not the world, and I was going to enjoy the look on his face when I walked away from everything, including my bride.

As I reclined on the hood of my car thinking about what I planned to do with the money, I realized my father was more than likely choosing my future wife as I laid here. I figured I should probably get home before he sent the police to collect me. I laughed because I knew if he sent someone for me, it would have to be someone he'd paid off. There was no way he'd allow the police to search for the son of the largest criminal in Oregon, if not the entire Pacific Northwest.

Chapter Five

13 Days Until the Wedding – Carlina

After being dropped off at the house, I did my chores and lay in bed thinking about the lunch with Charles Wessex. He was exactly what I expected him to be. The stereotypical wealthy man who thinks his money can manipulate and control those around him. I saw Baron do it every day, even though Wessex's wealth was far vaster than Baron's would ever be.

As I contemplated how I was going to leave this town and my mother behind, I heard a faint knock on my door. The only person who ever knocked was my mother. The twins, and even Baron, would barge right in with no hesitation.

"Come in." I sat up straighter in bed and pulled a book from my desk, so it looked like I had been reading. As anticipated, it was my mother. I put my book back on my desk and looked at her. "Did you need something?"

"I wanted to know how lunch went. Did the twins behave themselves?"

"It was interesting. Yes, they did, for the most part, anyway."

My mom cocked her eyebrow at my statement.

"What do you mean 'for the most part'?" Something about the way she asked made me feel as though she was digging for something.

"They didn't like the fish we were served, so they asked for steak."

"But they eat fish all the time?"

"I know, but you know how they can be."

She agreed.

"So, what did Mr. Wessex ask you girls about?"

"Just basic questions about ourselves and what we liked to do. Then Annabelle asked what he was looking for in a wife."

"She did what?" Mom clutched her chest.

"Yeah, and he answered. He wants someone to essentially babysit this grown man, but he said the person chosen as wife will get a house, a housekeeper and spending money for a year. After which time, he assumes his son will be making enough money to support the household. Oh, and we have to not only be arm candy for events but also be able to do, I guess, normal rich wife things, like hosting parties and stuff. Don't worry though, I'm sure he'll pick one of the twins. They're the standard arm candy he seems to be looking for."

Mom said nothing, so I asked, "Everything okay?"

"Yeah, well, you get to sleep. I'll see you in the morning, bright and early." She reached over and hugged me before leaving.

I couldn't tell if she wanted to know how it went or if Baron wanted to know, and he'd sent her to get the answers. Either way, I didn't want to think about it any longer, so I turned off my light, curled up in bed, and hoped sleep would find me faster than usual.

Chapter Six

12 Days Until the Wedding - Preston

"Preston, your father is requesting your presence downstairs." Victoria knocked on my door.

Rolling over, I checked to see what time it was, and thankfully it was after 9.

Father would routinely wake up at all hours of the night and expect the entire house to be awake with him.

Throwing on a pair of basketball shorts and a T-shirt, I went down to his office. As I walked through the door, I could hear him on the phone yelling at someone about something.

Thankfully, Victoria was standing there with a large cup of coffee for me.

I mouthed 'thank you' to her as I went to sit in front of the large wooden desk. Sitting in one of the two high-backed chairs, I sipped the perfect latte while I waited for him to finish his call.

"I don't want any excuses. I want you to find more avenues for these imports. We need to move this product. Otherwise, you'll be buying it yourself, you understand?"

My father ran many businesses, but one of the largest was his wholesale company. He imported millions of dollars' worth of goods every week and sold them to drop shippers and stores around the world. His other businesses made as much, if not more, so I didn't know why he was still doing it. I knew roughly what his legal businesses made, but I had no idea exactly how much the illegal business did in a year. My goal was to do my job, get paid for it, and don't ask questions.

Finally, he slammed the phone down and directed his attention to me. "Good, you're up. I've chosen your bride. I want you to know the stipulations, and I have a job for you."

"When did you add more? I thought the only stipulation was I had to marry." Of course, there were more. Charles Wessex could never have just a single stipulation. Growing up, there were always multiple things required to satisfy him if I was in trouble. There was always something else. I ignored the job comment for right now. I needed to keep a low profile, and most of the jobs he'd tried to give me made the news.

"Well, of course you must marry, but you also need to remain married for at least a year. During which, you'll get the house on the edge of the property, you'll have a paid housekeeper, and you'll have to go to at least six events with your wife. You must also take a prominent role at the company of your choice. If you divorce before a year is up, you will lose the complete inheritance. As a layer of financial protection, your future wife will sign a prenup, so she can't divorce you for your money once you have it."

I scoffed. "Do you also want me to get her pregnant so we can have an heir?"

"Not a terrible idea, you know."

"I was joking. I don't even want to marry, but I absolutely don't want to have a child with someone who I'm hoping will be out of my life after a year."

"Fine, you don't have to have a kid, but we need to talk about how your inheritance will be used for the businesses." Although he never explicitly stated his intentions regarding my inheritance, I always suspected he would try to exploit it for personal gain.

"Can we talk about this after my impending wedding? You know I'm still two weeks away from being able to collect on it?"

He waved his hand at me when his phone rang again. Answering, he stated, "Just a minute. I need to finish up this meeting." He muted the phone and looked at me. "Where are you going to be in" — he looked at his watch — "say 30 minutes?"

"I'll be in the pool unless Victoria needs something."

"Okay, I'll find you for the job I need you for." He shooed me away as he unclicked the mute button. I'd been dismissed and assumed we'd talk about it later. There was no way he would be touching my money, but I wasn't going to tell him while I was still essentially under his thumb.

Walking out the door, I realized I hadn't found out which of the ladies from the lunch was going to be my wife. Part of me was hoping it was the redhead. I couldn't get her out of my head last night, but I also didn't want it to be her. The way she carried herself, I was immediately much more attracted to her than her sisters. She was probably just like every other rich girl I'd ever met. They wanted someone with money, like their father. Someone who could continue to support their wealthy lifestyle. Even though I was going to be rich, I wasn't planning to blow it all on some chick who would up and leave me the minute she found someone at the country club she thought was better. Assuming she even stayed with me after she found out what I did for my father's business.

On my way back to my room to change to go swimming, I saw Victoria motioning to me.

"Do you need something? I can go into town for you if you do."

Sometimes Victoria would run out of something while cooking, and I would run out and get it for her if I was home. This way, she wouldn't have to leave the kitchen or get Freddie to drive into town for her.

"No need. I wanted to talk to you about what happened during the lunch."

"Why? I mean, I'm grateful, but you don't normally discuss what happens during my father's lunches with me."

"This time, since your life is being directly affected by a decision out of your control, I thought I should share what was discussed."

"I could leave, get out of town."

Victoria patted my arm. "You could, but you won't."

"How do you know?"

"Because the money will go a long way to soothe some of the trauma from the last 19 years."

While I wanted to scoff at what she'd said, she was right.

"So, what do you have for me?"

"Three girls, supposedly sisters, but they aren't. The twins are used to wealth and getting what they want. The third, however, is polite, respectful, and loved my fish."

"Well, your fish *is* amazing." I smiled at her to continue.

"Thank you, but you're biased. Anyway, I expect your father will pick one of the twins. They're blonde, short, thin... you know, the typical rich girl look."

"But?"

"Why do you think there's a but?"

A timer went off in the kitchen, so Victoria held up a finger and walked into the kitchen, and I followed.

"Oh, something smells good. What is it?"

"I'm making chicken and dumplings for dinner tonight. Are you going to be here?"

"Yeah, I have to be. Now back to the three sort-of sisters."

"The redhead, she's smart, but it also looks like she works hard. Her hands aren't as soft as the other two, and she carries herself differently."

"Thank you, Victoria. I'm going to swim until Father assigns me the next job, unless there's something else?"

"Nope, enjoy your time alone."

I gave Victoria a quick hug and started for my room. She didn't tell me much I hadn't already known from watching them enter the house.

"Preston, one more thing."

I turned around. "What?"

"All three are older than you. I didn't hear it from them; I overheard your father on the phone. The twins are two years older, but the redhead is only a week older."

"So, he's probably going to marry me off to one of the older twins. Fantastic."

Victoria shrugged and chuckled. I laughed and continued to my room.

Knowing my father the way I did, he wouldn't choose the one I wanted him to, but a year wasn't too long. She wouldn't know about the inheritance, and once the year was up, I'd get a divorce. Two weeks, I had two weeks until I would be married at 18. I wonder what my mom would think about this, me being married so young like she was. There must be someone I could find who would love me the way my mom loved my father, faults and all.

Not wanting to think about my mom or the fact I grew up without her, I changed into my swim trunks and jogged down to the pool. When I didn't want to think about something, I'd swim until my body was so tired I'd fall asleep, at least for a while. It was a coping mechanism from the past, and it still helped during times like this.

45 minutes later, my father came out to the pool deck and stood there until I noticed him. It must not have been long because it was well known he had a temper if not acknowledged immediately.

I got out and grabbed a towel before I went up to him.

"You said you had a job for me?"

He handed me a folder. "Yes, I need you to go to Port Angeles and convince the individual in the folder to sell me his business."

"Any means?"

"You need to be home in time for your wedding, so make it quick." Without saying it, my father meant even if the purchase contract was signed in the owner's blood with his lifeless hand, it was to be completed before I returned home. Now, to research the individual and figure out when I need to leave in order to get back in time for the wedding.

Chapter Seven

The next morning, I worked on my normal chores.

Annabelle and Beatrice never had chores. I've never seen them doing anything other than lounging around and spending money. The doorbell chimed as I cleaned the table after lunch, and the twins jumped up and ran to the door.

From the dining room, I could see the twins race to the door, but they couldn't see me.

Seth, the driver who had driven us yesterday, stood on the porch holding an envelope.

"Is Mr. Teller here?"

Annabelle beat her sister to answering, "No, but you can leave it with me. He should be here soon."

He shook his head. "No, I have strict orders to deliver this only to Mr. Teller."

Knowing Annabelle wouldn't just accept his reply, I wasn't surprised when she sauntered up to him, twirling her hair.

"My daddy trusts me. Why can't you?" she asked in her sickeningly sweet voice.

Seth stepped back and placed the envelope in his jacket. "I'm sure he does. But I like my job, and I was given orders, which I will follow. I'll be waiting in my vehicle, so I'll be sure to greet him when he arrives." He turned sharply and returned to his car.

Huffing, the twins flopped onto the couch, playing on their phones.

Finally, Annabelle looked up from her phone and turned to Beatrice. "Why do you think he wouldn't give it to me?"

Baron walked in, letter in hand, before Beatrice could answer.

The twins jumped up to meet him while I stood in the doorway of the dining room.

I was curious about who he'd chosen, and if he explained why. I was more interested in the tantrum to follow once one of the twins was announced.

"Daddy, open it. Who did he pick?"

"No, we're going to wait for your stepmom. She should be here for this as well."

Usually, Baron had no issue with doing stuff without my mom around, so his response surprised me.

"Why does she have to be here? It won't change who was chosen," Beatrice commented.

Baron stopped, wondering if she could be correct.

I stepped out of the doorway.

"I'd like my mother to be here when it's read, just in case it's me. Can we please wait? She's in the shower and will be down in no time."

All three looked at me as if I had multiple heads. "Why would he have chosen you?"

"I don't think he did, but I still think we should wait. Is that acceptable, Father?" I spit out the words.

Baron looked at me for a minute before deciding. "Yes, we'll wait for Celeste to come down. Carlie, can you please go check on her and let her know?"

"Sure." As I got closer to their room, I could hear the shower was no longer running, and my mom was humming to herself. It was something she'd always done when she brushed or braided her hair. She used to hum to me years ago while she brushed my hair.

I smiled at the memory as I knocked.

"Come in."

I saw her sitting in front of her vanity and brushing her strawberry-blonde hair. Turning to look at me, she waited for me to speak.

"Seth, Mr. Wessex's driver, has brought a message from Mr. Wessex. I got Bar- I mean, Father, to wait until you came down to open it, but the twins are eager to get this over with."

Putting her brush down, she stood and followed me from the room and down the stairs.

The twins were on the couch, and Baron was pacing between the front door, to the doorway, and back to the dining room. Seeing us come down the stairs, he stopped pacing. "It's about time. Come sit with your sisters."

I sat on the loveseat near the couch. I didn't want to be too close in case they started throwing things.

Baron opened the letter and read aloud, "Before I announce who is to marry my son, I want to make the ground rules regarding the marriage clear. This is very important, not only for the Teller family but also for the Wessex family. You must accept the following stipulations in writing within 48 hours of this delivery, or I will cancel the arrangement."

Baron's eyes roamed the page before reading again. This time, his voice was higher in pitch. "You must stay married for at least 12 months. There is a house in the Wessex name for you to live in. Should a divorce occur before the year is up, you will have no claim to the property. The married couple must attend at least six events, and my son must approve all clothing. You will receive a small stipend for which you are to purchase both personal and household items. A paid housekeeper will be provided for one year, after which point you can either continue paying if you choose or learn how to keep house yourself. Finally, you are not to become pregnant during the first year unless it's an agreed upon decision between my son and yourself. All of this will be in a prenup you must sign the morning of the marriage."

At his last statement, I looked between him and the twins.

The silence was deafening before they both exploded.

"There's absolutely no way I'll abide by those rules if I'm picked." Beatrice tried to snatch the letter from Baron to see who Charles had chosen.

"Over my dead body will I buy household items with a stipend. Not to mention, is there even time to have your lawyer look at the prenup before the wedding?" Annabelle hung back but still complained.

"Both of you need to stop complaining. If you're chosen, you *will* marry him."

"Well, who is it?" I asked, trying to piece together whatever game Mr. Wessex and Baron were playing.

Baron shuffled the papers in his hand and looked at the second page before looking at us. He looked like he was going to be sick. Maybe he didn't want this marriage to happen after all.

"Daddy, read it already." Annabelle stood.

"Fine." He stood next to my mom as she looked between the paper and the three of us girls.

"Annabelle, he wants you to marry his son." Baron's eyes never left the paper as Annabelle yelled and stomped around the room.

Beatrice looked both happy and sad at the same time. She was likely sad for her sister but happy for herself.

"There is no way this is going to happen, Daddy. Do something. Pay him, give him your car, whatever you need to do."

"Annabelle, there's nothing your father can do. He agreed to this and must follow through. Right, Baron?" my mom finally spoke.

"Listen, I will not marry this man, and there's nothing you can do to make me. In fact, I'll go tell him myself." Annabelle went for the front door.

"Annabelle, stop. Let me think about this for a minute. Don't go anywhere yet because you'll make things worse," Baron said, finally. He handed the paper to my mom.

"Worse for who, Daddy? You don't have to marry some criminal." Annabelle was on a roll, and Beatrice and I watched as she stalked around the living room like a caged tiger.

"Baron, we need to start planning for the wedding." My mom folded the paper and put it into her pocket. "Girls, why don't you go to your rooms while your father and I discuss this?"

I headed for the stairs without question while Beatrice grabbed Annabelle's arm and pulled her out of the room.

On my way up the stairs, I could hear Baron yelling about the letter. Since I wasn't chosen, I didn't need to worry about the second part of my plan, which was to leave as soon as I could for Canada. I still planned to leave after I got my inheritance, so I sat at my desk to write a letter to my family there. I'd kept my father's address book hidden all these years, and I didn't know if my mom knew I still had it or if they even still lived at the address I had for them.

Flipping through, I found my father's brother and worked on writing the letter. Before I knew it, Baron was yelling at me to help mom cook dinner.

Putting the letter and address book into my hiding spot, I walked downstairs to find my mom in the kitchen. "What are we having for dinner?"

There was a variety of ingredients on the counter as she stared at a cookbook. She looked up as if in a daze. "Oh, I was thinking meatloaf with corn on the cob."

"Sounds good. I'll shuck the corn." I'd gone into the pantry to get out five ears of corn when I heard my mom come closer.

"You know I love you, right?" She had tears in her eyes.

"Of course I do. What's going on?" I hugged her, confused by what was happening.

"Nothing, I don't think I tell you enough." She turned to the island and put the meatloaf ingredients together in a bowl.

Shaking my head, I grabbed the corn and walked to the sink.

My mom and I worked in silence as we got the corn and meatloaf ready. While the corn boiled, I set the table.

"Dinner's ready. Will you call them in? Baron's in his office," Mom called from the kitchen.

I went upstairs and knocked on the twins' doors. "Dinner's ready."

Knocking on the door to Baron's downstairs office, I could hear him talking to someone. He didn't respond, so I knocked a little harder.

"What do you want? Can't you tell I'm busy?"

"Father, dinner's ready."

"I'll almost done. I'll be there soon."

He returned to his conversation.

Shaking my head, I went back to the dining room. "Father said he'll be here when he's done with what he's doing," I told the three sitting at the table.

We were almost finished with dinner when Baron finally joined us. "Why didn't you wait for me?"

"Baron, it's been over thirty minutes since Carlie told you dinner was ready. We were hungry."

"No excuse! You should have waited for me, and what is this anyway? Meatloaf, again?" Baron whined as he put the meatloaf onto his plate.

No one said anything until he put the first forkful into his mouth.

"Yes, with everything going on today, I figured something like meatloaf would be filling, and I know the girls like it as a comfort food." My mom moved the leftovers toward the center of the table.

"You know I don't, so you should have asked me what I wanted."

I wanted to scream. We had repeatedly tried asking him in the past what he wanted for dinner, and he always got upset and told us to think for ourselves. Then we didn't ask him, and he got upset with us for not asking him. I also knew for a fact he liked meatloaf and regularly asked my mom to make it.

Keeping my mouth shut, I got up to remove the dirty dishes.

"Do we have dessert?" Baron asked between bites.

My mom answered, "Yes, we have pineapple upside-down cake."

"I don't want pineapple upside-down cake. Do we have any ice cream?"

"Yes, Father. I'll get you a bowl. Does anyone else want ice cream?"

The twins and my mom declined ice cream, so I went to the kitchen and dished out a bowl for Baron.

As I walked in, Baron was talking to Annabelle about the wedding.

"It's in two weeks, so we need dresses, shoes, and to figure out where we're going to have it. Mr. Wessex and I will discuss who's going to pay for what, since we don't have the kind of money he does."

Putting the ice cream in front of Baron, he sneered at it before pushing it aside. "I don't want ice cream."

Looking at my mom, I raised my eyebrows as I reached for the leftover meatloaf to take it into the kitchen.

"Baron, you said you wanted ice cream, not pineapple upside-down cake." My mom placed her hand on his arm.

"Oh, yes. Sorry, I had a stressful phone call before dinner and haven't been able to stop thinking about it. Sorry, Carlie. I do want ice cream. Please continue cleaning the table."

I was surprised he'd apologized, but I wasn't going to mention it. Instead, I took the leftovers into the kitchen and watched through the doorway as Beatrice and Annabelle went into the living room.

Returning to the dining room, I paused when my mother asked Baron what was going on.

I could barely understand his mumbling, but I think he said he was working on a problem.

Not wanting to involve myself in Baron's problems, I focused on wiping down the counters. I'd finished cleaning the kitchen when my mom brought in Baron's dishes.

"Is everything okay?" I asked, not expecting an answer.

"Yes, Baron's tired. I don't think he's ready for one of his daughters to get married. He's trying to get out of the agreement, but I doubt he'll be able to."

"I see. Well, I'm done for the evening. Is there anything else you need from me before I go to my room?"

"No, thank you for helping me with dinner. I'll finish up these last few dishes. Have a good night." My mom hugged me before turning back to the sink.

Given Mom and Baron's earlier behavior, I couldn't see how Baron could get out of the agreement. It sounded like the agreement was set in stone, regardless of Baron's dismay at the terms he'd personally agreed to.

Chapter Eight

12 Days Until the Wedding – Preston

After my father handed me the folder, I couldn't go back to swimming. I sat on a pool chair and looked over the information inside. I got about halfway through reading when I heard the bell indicating dinner would be ready soon. Closing the folder, I knew I only had about 10 minutes before I needed to be at the table.

In this house, if we were home, we were expected to be at dinner. It was a rule my father had set up before Mom died. I hated it when I was younger, but now that I was older, I thought it was a nice tradition. Thankfully, Father didn't require a dress code unless we had guests.

In the dining room, I only saw two place settings. Jogging up the stairs, I figured I had time to shower quickly and get dressed before dinner.

During my shower, it hit me. I realized my father would probably want to talk to me about the wedding, the job, or my inheritance and suddenly wasn't hungry anymore. Regardless, I knew I had to be there. Quickly drying off, I dressed and mentally prepared myself for whatever he was going to say.

My father was leaving his office and heading to the dining room just as I reached the bottom of the stairs.

I sat in my designated spot in the dining room. It was the same seat I've had since I was a kid.

"It's nice seeing you for dinner." My father took his place in his usual spot at the head of the table.

"I was here, and it's a rule, right?"

The moment he sat, Victoria came through the door leading to the kitchen with a cart holding two drinks and two covered plates. She placed all four items on the table before we lifted the lids.

The smell of the chicken potpie immediately made my mouth water.

Victoria's cooking wasn't only delicious, but it reminded me of the past. Back when I believed everything would be okay. Before Mom got sick, and Father started working day in and out, trying to push her memory out of his mind.

"Did you send the letter to Mr. Teller yet?" I really didn't care, but I pretended to just to get through dinner faster.

"I had Seth deliver it to them personally. Baron has been on the phone ever since, trying to negotiate a way out of our deal."

"Are you going to tell me which girl you picked?"

"Do you want to know? If you do, I'll tell you."

"Yes, I think I do."

"Okay, you'll be marrying Annabelle, one of the twins."

"Do you remember what she was wearing at the lunch they came to?"

"No, they looked and acted the same, Victoria told me she was the one wearing the blue shirt."

"So why her?" I'd hoped my father had a valid reason versus randomly picking the woman who would be my wife for a year out of a hat or something.

"Drew out of a hat, honestly. Mr. Teller doesn't have a choice, and this is happening whether he likes it or not."

He really drew my future spouse from a hat. Fantastic. I'd always known my life wasn't my own, but this was taking it to an extreme. Knowing better than to fight his decision, I simply agreed.

"Is there anything specific you want for the wedding?" At least he was giving me a choice in something, which I guess I should be thankful for.

"Can we have it here? I know this is an arranged marriage, but I'd like to have it here near the pond. This way, it feels like Mom is here with me."

I swore my father's eyes teared up before he blinked them away. "Yes, of course we can. It'll help cut down on the expenses by having it here."

Always looking at the financial aspect of everything.

"Thank you. Also, can it please be small? I don't really have many friends who could stand with me on such a short notice, so the smaller, the better."

"Yes, I agree, especially with this being an arranged marriage. I'm sure Mr. Teller will agree."

"What if he doesn't? I mean, it *is* his daughter being married."

"I'll have to convince him it's for the best. We could have a large party at the one-year anniversary."

Like there will actually be an anniversary party.

"Okay, so what do I need to do to prepare for the wedding?"

"You'll need to get a tux. I'll have my guy come to measure you tomorrow morning. Will you be available?"

He was asking if I would have the job done before then.

"I really don't have a choice, do I?" I didn't want to sound bitter, but I was bitter.

"Not really, but I'm trying to accommodate your schedule."

"With the tux fitting happening in the morning, if I have your permission to leave the property, I can travel after. If there isn't time after the fitting, I can study on the plane. It's not like I have much else to do other than swim."

"Don't be a smartass. I meant leaving the property where someone local could see you."

"You weren't very clear, Father."

"I'll call my suit guy, William, after dinner. Unless he's busy, he'll be here around 10 tomorrow morning."

"Let me know."

Victoria came in with a strawberry rhubarb tart as I finished dinner.

"Mr. Wessex, Preston, would you like coffee with your tart?"

"No, thank you, Victoria." I dug into the tart. "This is delicious, thank you."

"I would like a cup, please. Thank you, Victoria."

As I ate my tart, I thought about what he'd said. "I'm going to bed to read over the information you gave me about the job. Please let me know what time my fitting will be if not at 10. Also, I need to take the jet to Port Angeles."

"Okay, have a good night. I'm working late, so I'll get everything scheduled for your trip and for the fitting."

Leaving the dining room, I made my way upstairs. Not that I hated my father, but he hadn't been much of a father since my mom died. Marriage was a means to an end, but that didn't mean I wanted to get married. If marriage was what I needed to leave this life behind, then marriage it would be.

Chapter Nine

11 Days Until the Wedding - Carlina

The sound of Baron, my mom, and Annabelle, all screaming at each other woke me the next morning. My mom rarely yelled, so when I heard her, I rushed to put my clothes on and ran downstairs.

Mom and Baron were sitting on the coach while Annabelle was pacing back and forth, yelling.

Not wanting to get involved, I went straight to the dining room. Beatrice was already sitting at the dining room table eating, so I went into the kitchen and got something to eat before returning to sit across from Beatrice.

"What's going on in there?"

"Annabelle's trying to argue about why she shouldn't have to get married, and she's throwing both of us under the bus in hopes they'll agree. So far, they haven't budged, so she's continuing to argue."

"Why would she be trying to get you to be the one who has to get married?"

"Apparently, being twins doesn't mean anything when it comes to Annabelle being forced to do something she doesn't want to do."

"I'm sorry. I fully expected her to throw me under the bus, but I'm surprised she's doing it to you, too."

"Meh, it's whatever." Beatrice went back to her breakfast as I half listened to them fighting.

I'd always thought Annabelle and Beatrice were inseparable, but apparently Annabelle only looked out for herself. Never having had siblings until the twins moved in, I didn't know what it was like growing up with someone around my age. When the twins first moved in, I'd originally thought we were going to be best friends, sisters, and do stuff together. But the twins only saw me as a servant.

The fighting stopped after a couple minutes, and Annabelle stormed into the dining room.

"Where's my breakfast, Carlie?"

"In the kitchen. You can get it yourself."

"What? Absolutely not. You need to go get it for me." She scraped a chair across the floor and threw herself onto it. She crossed her arms and stared at me.

"I don't know what you're expecting, but I have other things to do." I stood and placed my dishes in the dishwasher before going to the living room.

Annabelle huffed as I passed the dining room, and Beatrice finished her breakfast.

"Mom, is there anything you need me to do? I planned on working out in the garden today."

"Good idea. No, I don't have anything for you. Do you, Bar—"

His phone rang before she could finish his name.

He jumped from the couch and practically ran to his office.

"What was that about?"

"I think he was waiting for a call from Mr. Wessex about the wedding day plans. Speaking of which, Annabelle wants you to be her bridesmaid."

"She does?" After all the yelling earlier, and the way she had treated me for years, I didn't believe it.

"Yes, of course she does. You're one of her sisters. Beatrice will be her maid of honor."

"Of course. Thank you for letting me know." I was still confused by Annabelle wanting me to be part of her wedding, but I didn't put too much thought into it as I walked outside and started in the garden.

My mom used to love being out in the garden. We would sit with my dad and watch the butterflies land on the milkweed. We'd have picnics and plant things together every spring.

After my dad died, my mom stopped coming out as often, and I worked on it by myself. It was one of my happy places. I was pulling weeds when I heard someone screaming inside the house. I waited to see if I'd heard right when I heard another yell and a door slam.

Looking up, I saw my mom with tears streaming down her face. I stood quickly and went over to her. "What's wrong? What happened?"

"It's Baron. He got Mr. Wessex to agree to a change."

"What kind of change? What's going on?"

"He got Mr. Wessex to agree to have you to marry his son instead of Annabelle."

"What? I can't get married. Mom, you can't let him do this. I'm less than a month—"

"She doesn't have a choice. If Carlie wants to keep this house in the family, she will marry him. You have less than a month until what?" I heard Baron say from behind my mom.

My mom was quick to answer him before I could. "Until her birthday. You know the house goes to her on her 19th birthday."

"Celeste, do you want to tell her, or should I?" His smirk told me he knew something I didn't, and it was something I wouldn't like.

"Carlie, after Baron and I got married, he needed money to help with a business he was starting, so I mortgaged it for money for him."

"You did what? This was supposed to be my house! How could you do this to me? Your name isn't even on the deed. You have no claim to it."

My mom looked down at her feet as she responded. "Baron has a friend who works at a bank, and he made it work so we could get a mortgage on it."

"So, the house was leveraged for one of Baron's businesses?" I couldn't believe my mom could do something like this. I thought she was smarter than this.

"Yes, but it's almost paid off again. Well, sort of."

"What do you mean, sort of?" I didn't like the sound of this one bit.

"If Baron keeps his job with Mr. Wessex, it should be paid off in about six months."

I looked at Baron. "Is this true? Will it be paid off in six months?"

"As long as I keep Mr. Wessex happy, then yes, it will be paid off." Baron smiled and put his hand on my mom's shoulder.

"How do I know you're telling the truth?"

Mom looked back at Baron. "I've seen the paperwork. I know it's true. Please Carlie, think about the house."

I looked around the garden. "You know what? No. Screw this house. I'm not going to go through all this so Baron can continue doing whatever, or whoever, he does every day. He gets mysterious calls and disappears for days at a time. Yeah, not suspicious or anything." I looked at my mom. "Do you even ask him? Or do you just go along with it because he's your husband?"

Baron stepped closer and grabbed my shoulders, pushing me against the wall. He looked down at me as he spit out, "You will do what I say, you little bitch. I am the man of this house, and you WILL obey."

I swallowed back the insult I had on the tip of my tongue. "Father, I would like to speak to my mother alone, please."

"Of course you can, since it doesn't make a difference. In less than two weeks, you'll be married to Mr. Wessex's son."

I forced a smile as he turned and walked back into the house.

I waited until he walked inside and then waited to make sure he was out of earshot before I spun back to my mom. "How could you do this to me?"

"I didn't have a choice. He needed the money to keep his business going, and I loved him."

My eyes welled with tears, but I refused to let them fall. "You knew it was mine. How could you not even think about what I would've wanted? What if it isn't paid off in time? Then what?"

"Then you can use the money you're getting on your 19th birthday to pay off the rest." My mom grabbed my hands in hers. "It was to protect you and your future. I thought it would help."

Snatching my hands away from her, I stood. "How? How does any of this help anyone but Baron? Is it in both of your names or only his? Even if I pay it off, how can I be sure I'll get it back? What's the wording on the inheritance? Do I have to be here to collect?"

The realization of what I was asking showed on my mother's face. "I only have his word. The paperwork is here somewhere, and I haven't seen it in years, but I believe you must at least be local to inherit the money. Where would you go, anyway? You would leave me?"

"It's almost worth leaving at this point. You're putting your husband ahead of your own daughter. Which, it appears you've been doing the whole time. You didn't even say anything when he slammed me against the wall. I don't know, but I'm going to have to think about this." She was standing there with her mouth open, about to speak as I left.

Going into the house, I intended to go to my room, when I saw Annabelle and Beatrice on the couch giggling over something on their phones. When they saw me, they stopped and looked at me.

"OMG, thank you so much. I can't believe you would do this for me." Annabelle ran up and hugged me.

I pushed away from her. "Do what?"

"Agree to marry an ugly criminal, so I didn't have to."

"Excuse me?"

Baron was in the doorway of the living room watching the conversation.

"Daddy said you agreed to marry Mr. Wessex's son because you knew I didn't want to. He said you're better at household chores, so you would know what to do to make him happy."

Before responding, I saw Baron shake his head.

I took a deep breath before spitting, "You're welcome." I lowered my head and went to my bedroom without another word.

Flopping on the bed, I couldn't believe how today was going. I'd been enjoying the sun, gardening, and now I'm stuck getting married so Annabelle could have her own way. Over my dead body. I'm leaving, even if it means losing the house.

I went to my closet, pulled out a suitcase, and started packing. At this point, I didn't care where I went, as long as it wasn't here.

Zipping the suitcase, I heard Baron's heavy footsteps on the stairs right outside my room. Throwing the suitcase into the closet, I laid back on my bed.

Baron stepped into my room without knocking, as usual. Looking up, I knew he was angry, but I didn't know why. His daughters weren't the ones being forced to marry. Maybe it's because he knew if he didn't pay off the house, then he would have nowhere for his precious daughters to live.

"Yes?"

"Your mother said you were thinking about leaving, but I would advise against it."

It somewhat surprised me she'd told him, or he may have been listening to our private conversation. I wasn't going to give anything away, though. "And I would advise you to stay out of my business. You are not my father."

Faster than I could move, he pushed me against the wall, his hands digging into my upper arms.

"Let me go before I make you regret touching me," I stammered.

His face turned red with anger.

"You *will* stay here, and you *will* marry Charles Wessex's son, even if I have to handcuff you and drag you there." He let me go and stepped back.

I rubbed my arms where his fingers had dug in.

"I mean, why not? You and the twins will be living in this house. I don't need it."

"It isn't just about the house." Baron paced the room.

"What then?" Feigning ambivalence, I played with the hem of my shirt.

"If you leave, your mother will lose this house, and I will leave her."

"You would leave my mom, the person you married and supposedly love, if I left?"

"Yes, because I made a deal with Mr. Wessex promising you would marry his son, and you shall marry his son. Mr. Wessex is not someone you want to upset."

"Why should I care if you leave my mother? If I left, one of your precious daughters can marry him. It's not like there aren't two other options."

Baron looked like he was about to slap me, so I stepped back.

He stepped close enough to where his nose was touching mine.

"No, YOU will marry him. Not only if you know what's good for you, but if you want your mom to keep this house and stay happily married." Baron slammed the door on his way out.

I sat on the bed and thought about what I was going to do. I didn't necessarily need the money, but I didn't want my mom to be hurt. If I left without going through with the marriage, I knew she would be. There was no doubt Baron would keep his word and leave my mom the minute I wasn't present at the wedding. As much as I hated the twins sometimes, I didn't want them to be forced to marry some random man, especially if the rumors about him were true.

It wasn't my job to protect anyone other than myself, since no one else ever had, but does getting married protect my mom? From what Baron had said, it would. I knew what I needed to do, but I really didn't want to. Either way, someone was going to get hurt. Are other people's lives always full of these types of decisions, or is it just mine?

Regardless, I couldn't do anything until morning, so I stayed in my room until bedtime. After everything I'd learned, I wasn't hungry, and I wasn't about to face the four of them.

Later in the evening, my door opened quietly, and Beatrice stuck her face in. "Is it okay to come in?"

I sat up straighter in bed. "What do you want?"

"I know you didn't volunteer to marry him. I know Father made the decision for you."

Before I could respond, she continued, "Don't worry. I won't tell Annabelle. I wanted you to know if you decide not to marry him, I understand and will respect your decision."

"Thank you. I haven't decided yet, but I appreciate you."

As if unsure of what to do next, Beatrice stood there awkwardly before we heard Annabelle yelling for her. "Well, I should go. Father ordered something for dinner, and I'm sure it's here. Are you coming down?"

"No, I think I'll stay up here by myself, but go enjoy dinner."

Beatrice nodded and walked out the door, softly closing it behind her.

Not bothering to change out of the clothes I'd been wearing all day, I laid in bed considering my options for the next weeks. After staring at the ceiling long enough to know the pattern of the paint, I finally closed my eyes. Sleep didn't come fast, as visions of the house being torn down and Baron laughing played on repeat.

Chapter Ten

11 Days Until the Wedding – Preston

Knowing I had nothing scheduled until the tailor was due to arrive at 10, I woke up at nine and checked my emails. I also did some research into a project I had been working on while at school before coming home. I'd graduated already, but I'd been brought on as a TA of sorts to help some underclassmen with a couple of projects.

At 9:30, I walked down to the kitchen to eat before he arrived. I'd been fitted for a tux before, so I knew it could take a while to get everything measured and started.

In the kitchen, I found Victoria finishing up scrambled eggs. Slices of ham and biscuits were already on the counter.

"Are we going to eat in here, or do you want me to set the table?"

"Where's Father? Will he be joining us?"

"No, he had an important call this morning."

"Always a businessman, right? I'll eat in here with you … assuming you're staying?"

"Yes, I have to start preparing lunch and then dinner."

"Do you need me to run to the store for anything?" I asked as she made a plate for me.

"No, we're going to have simple salads with salmon for lunch, and I was thinking pork chops with applesauce and smashed potatoes for dinner."

"Delicious. My schedule has me here for lunch but, unfortunately, not for dinner. I'm definitely going to have to get in some laps if you keep feeding me like this. This figure won't keep itself."

Victoria rolled her eyes at my comment while I finished eating breakfast. "You won't be here for dinner?"

"No, Father needs me to go to Washington for something, but I'll be back tomorrow, hopefully."

"Be safe. Is Seth driving you to the airport?"

"I hope so. Father said everything would be scheduled for me. All I need to do is show up." I put the plate into the sink and heard the door chime. I kissed Victoria on the cheek. "Thank you for breakfast. The tailor's here for my tux fitting."

"Enjoy your fitting. I'm sure you're going to look very handsome."

I turned back to her as I heard Freddie open the door. "Victoria? Am I doing the right thing? Getting married to a total stranger for money?"

She looked up at me before answering, "Preston, you do what you need to do to get out of this house, to be free and become your own man. You deserve everything, and your mother would be happy to know you're doing what you need to in order to become the person she wanted you to be."

"How do you know, though? What if she would be upset I'm not marrying for love?"

"We talked a lot after she got sick. I know she wanted what was best for you, no matter how you got there."

"Excuse me." Freddie walked into the kitchen. "The tailor is ready for you in the library. Love, could you prepare a hot black tea for him and an iced green tea for his assistant?"

Victoria wiped her hands on a dish towel. "Of course. Preston, enjoy the fitting. You never know, this could be the only marriage you have."

I laughed as I left the kitchen and headed to the library. I knew this marriage would last the year; it had to. I wasn't sticking around any longer. When I closed my eyes and envisioned my wife, I didn't see a short blonde with daddy issues. No, I saw someone closer to my height of five feet, eleven inches, who was smart and could keep up with me. Possibly with red hair. I needed to get her out of my head, especially since I was stuck marrying her sister.

"Good day, Mr. Wessex," the tailor greeted me when I entered the room.

"Please call me Preston. Mr. Wessex is my father."

"Very well, Preston. You can call me William. Are you ready to be fitted for your tux?"

"As ready as I'll ever be. What do I need to do?"

"Please sit, and we'll go over choices. My assistant, Tony, will show you several tux styles, and you'll choose the one you like before we measure."

After an hour of questions and being measured, I was ready to be done.

Finally, William put the pen down. "Okay Tony, we're done. Do you have any questions, Preston?"

I put my clothes back on. "Will I need a final fitting before the wedding?"

"No, we have enough measurements for your tux to fit perfectly. Tony will drop it off the morning of the wedding."

"Thank you for your time, William and Tony. Can I help you take anything out to your vehicle?"

"No, thank you. And please thank the lady who brought us the tea. It was very good."

I watched Tony put the clothes back on the racks and zip up the covers. It felt strange not helping.

"I will. I should leave to get to work on your tux. Have a good day." Tony smiled while William shook my outstretched hand. "You as well, Preston."

On my way out of the library, I stopped by the kitchen before heading up to my room to get dressed to swim.

I knocked lightly, seeing Victoria talking to Freddie.

"Did the fitting go well?" Victoria asked as Freddie kissed her forehead and walked out through the kitchen door.

"It did, and they wanted me to thank you for the tea. Oh, I didn't grab the glasses. Do you want me to go get them?"

"No, thank you. I'll grab them after they leave. Have you packed, or are you going to swim first?"

"How did you know?"

"You've been a fish since you were little. Why would anything have changed?"

"It didn't. Do you remember if the house my father is giving me for the wedding has a pool or not?"

"I don't remember, but you could ask Freddie. He was out there recently getting things ready. If not, you could always put one in." Victoria was preparing a salad.

"The less money I spend on the house, the better. Can you ask Freddie the next time you see him? The pool is calling my name, so I think I'm going to get into the pool before flying out. My father probably set a later flight for me, assuming I needed to do hours of research. With what's for lunch, I need to get in a few laps in anyway." Looking at the watch on my wrist, I saw it was almost noon.

"You can have lunch whenever you want since your father is still in his office. I'm making the salad for him right now. He decided he didn't want salmon. Take all the time you want; I can throw it together whenever you're ready."

I smiled at her. "Well, if you need anything, let me know. You know where I'll be."

Victoria nodded as I left the room and went upstairs. I changed and headed to the pool.

Downstairs on my way past my father's office, I could hear him on the phone even though the door was closed. Whatever he was talking about made him angry.

Since I was holding up my end of the arrangement, at least for now, it couldn't be about me. I needed to know what time I flew out, so even if he wasn't happy about the interruption, I knocked and turned the doorknob.

He lifted his head while on the phone and held up a finger.

"No, our agreement was clear. We don't have flexibility on this, and I will not discuss it further. My son walked in, so I must let you go." He hung up without giving the other person the opportunity to respond.

"How did the fitting go?"

"Well, I'm pretty sure they measured every single part of my body."

"Yeah, William is very thorough. What can do I for you?"

"I plan on getting in a swim before lunch and then eating before I leave, but I didn't know if you had a set time for the jet to take off. I'm still leaving tonight, right?"

"Absolutely, and this is time sensitive because the owner is now talking to other companies. Here, let me check." He scrolled through a couple pages on his computer before turning back.

"You'll be flying out at four today from Redmond, directly to Port Angeles. Timothy will be there with a car to take you to the hotel or directly to the owner. Your choice."

"Is he expecting me?"

"No."

"Does he have a family?"

"Does it matter?"

"Yes, I've told you before. I want all the information included in the packet, even if it seems trivial. If he has a family, he could be there with them versus if he's single and lives alone."

"Fine, let me look." He went to the large filing cabinet taking up much of his room. Keying in his code, he found the folder he was looking for and brought it back to the desk.

"He's separated from his wife, lives in an apartment, and has a teenage daughter who visits him sometimes but should be at her mom's tonight."

"See? Not so hard, is it?" I hate it when he doesn't give me all the information, and I walk in partially blind. It makes it more dangerous because there are so many unknown factors. I'm very good at what I do, but I don't want to hurt those who aren't involved in whatever my father has going on from one day to the next.

"No, I just don't feel it's necessary. In the past, we never worried about background details."

"Well, Father, we aren't in the past, and I don't enjoy killing a whole family unless it's absolutely necessary."

"This new generation is soft. At least you're good at what you do."

"You mean, I'm good at what you've been training me to do since I was old enough to walk?"

"I did what I had to in order to prepare you for your future." My father sat back with his arms crossed.

This was not the first argument we'd had regarding how I did the job. It shouldn't matter since I always did it, did it well, and never got caught.

"Is Seth taking me to the airport?"

"Of course. This is very important, so make sure you don't mess it up."

One time. I 'messed' up one time, and now he can't let it go. No one remembers the name of the person who died, and I served my time. He sent me to a fancy academy away from media and anyone who may remember. For the record, it wasn't even my mess up. It was a situation of wrong place, wrong time.

"Wouldn't dream of it. I'm going to swim and have lunch. The brief will be ready when I return, as always."

He didn't respond, considering he was already picking up his phone to make a phone call.

***

There was a moment as I slid into the pool where I thought about what my future wife was doing. Was she being fitted for her dress? Would she even wear a dress? I really didn't know anything about her aside from her name and who her father was. I still didn't know how I was going to be married to someone for a year. Someone I probably wouldn't even like.

At least I'd have all my money in two months, which only gave me ten months to hide it from my future wife. It wouldn't be hard. What would be is keeping my money from helping to boost one of my father's companies.

As I swam, I thought about how I could keep my money safe from not only my future wife but also my father. Soon, the constant strokes gave way to freeing my mind and not thinking about anything. I swam with no thoughts until Victoria came out.

"Preston, you've been in the pool for over an hour. You need to eat."

Treading water, I knew she was right, so I got out and dried myself. "Do you need me to change before eating, or is this okay?"

"You're fine. Come eat. You father left for an errand, so it's just us."

"Do you think he'd be mad if I took the car out to the mountain before I leave?"

"Absolutely. You know he has a tracker in the car, right? So, he'd be alerted if it left the property."

"What? He does?"

"I heard him talking about it after lunch the day the young ladies were here. He knew where you'd gone."

"Is nothing private in this house?" I stormed into the kitchen, dripping water on the floor.

"Preston, dry off before you make more of a mess. Stop pouting like a toddler."

"I'm not pouting like a toddler. Give me at least a five-year-old tantrum." Even though I was pouting, I still went back and cleaned up the mess I'd made before I went back into the kitchen. "I'm sorry, but I hate it. I'm 18 years old and still feel like I'm under his thumb."

"He wants to protect you for as long as he can. You're all he has left of your mother."

"He has a funny way of showing it."

Victoria rarely talked about the relationship my father and I had, but if she did, I knew I should listen, even if I didn't agree.

"He's trying. I know sometimes the result isn't good enough for you, but I truly believe he's doing his best."

"You may be right, but for right now, forcing me to marry a stranger, pulling me from school when I wanted to stay the summer to help finalize a project with the undergrads, and telling me I need to work in one of his businesses does not seem like 'the best.'"

"I don't totally disagree with you, but you'll be 19 soon, and you'll be able to do what you want, when you want, and with whom you want."

"Yeah, you're mostly right. I may have to be married for a year, but I can stick with it knowing the end result." I handed her the towel I no longer needed.

"You sound like the Preston Wessex I raised. Now, get into the kitchen and eat."

"Yes, ma'am."

Victoria swatted me with the towel I'd just handed her. She hated being called ma'am, especially by me.

"Oh, and can you please ask Freddie to remove the tracker from the Mustang?" Putting my hand up at Victoria's attempt to argue.

"I'm not planning to go anywhere, but in less than two weeks, I'll be married. He doesn't need to know everywhere I go. Have him put it on the Supra since I'll be driving it to work anyway."

Victoria bit her lip as she considered my request. "Okay, I'll have him move it to the Supra, but please don't do anything to make your father suspicious. I don't want Freddie to be fired."

"You know I would never put your and Freddie's job at risk for my own personal whims."

"Will you please go eat now? I don't want you getting hangry."

"Hangry? I'm always a ray of sunshine." Even though I was joking, I knew she was right. If I didn't eat for a while, especially after swimming, I had a tendency to become angry and snap at things quicker than normal.

Victoria followed me in, so I thought it was a good time to ask her about the wedding. As much as I didn't like the idea of marrying a stranger, I was somewhat excited about it. While I didn't think about it like little girls supposedly did, I knew I wanted to get married and have a big ceremony with family and friends. Shaking my head, I figured after I got divorced and found someone I truly wanted to be with, I could have the big ceremony. Even if her family couldn't pay for it, I knew I'd have enough money to pay for whatever we wanted.

In between bites, I asked, "So, do you know anything about the wedding? I know it will be here, but that's it. Anything else I should know?"

When I was growing up, I would often ask her about marriage because I saw her and Freddie together so often. Their relationship was so much different from that of my parents.

"It'll be here. You have your tux taken care of, but I don't know what the bride will wear yet. We're getting Louie's to cater."

"Louie's was my mom's favorite, wasn't it?" I couldn't remember ever going there with my father, but I remember my mom talking about it.

"It was. I think your father feels the same way you do about wanting your mom here, at least in spirit."

"Or were they the cheapest?" I knew I was bitter, but after years of being treated like a commodity, it was second nature.

"No, I would have been the cheapest. For all his faults, he loved your mother, and I know he truly misses her."

It was then I realized I'd stopped eating during the conversation. Looking down at the rest of the fish, forcing myself to eat it. "You know I want to believe you," I said. "But it's hard, and it'll take time."

"That's understandable, but don't forget what I said about him trying his best."

Standing to change out of my swim trunks and get ready for my flight, I walked through the doorway before turning around. "Is there anything I can do to help? Pick flowers, colors? Something? Anything?"

Smiling, Victoria answered, "Yes, be there on your wedding day with your tux on. Let those who care about you worry about everything else, okay?"

"If you say so, but please let me know if there's anything else I can do."

"I will." Victoria's smile showed just how much she truly cared about me, even if we weren't blood.

In my room, I opened the closet and pulled out a duffle bag. It was the same duffle I'd used for as long as I could remember, but it held more weapons now than it used to. The older I got, the more weapons I would bring with me on jobs. When you're young, you think one weapon would do the job, but as I aged, it became apparent more options were necessary. I pushed a button on the side of the closet door. The clothes moved aside, and another door opened. Many women would kill to have a walk-in closet like this; however, I used mine to kill. Lining the walls were cabinets full of weapons and ammunition.

Knowing what I did about the target and what the goal was, I passed by most of the guns. I wasn't personally a fan of guns, as it took away the personal nature of torturing and killing. They also tended to create a bigger mess for the cleaners to deal with. It was easier to clean a pool of blood than a wall of blood spatter.

I grabbed my Glock 30. It's the same one my father gave me for my eighth birthday. Even though I rarely used it, it felt like an extension of me, and I felt unprepared if I didn't have it on me.

I opened a lower drawer and pulled out a box of .45ACP ammunition, two 10 round mags, and a second barrel. What was unique about this handgun was my father modified it to have an interchangeable barrel, which made it so the police could never trace it back to my weapon. The used barrel was melted down or thrown into a large body of water, depending on the target and location.

Opening my wallet, I made sure my national concealed carry license was in it. Even though I flew privately, I didn't want to get stopped or be seen to have the handgun on me without my license. Walking back to my bedroom with the gun, I put it into the duffle bag. I went back for my favorite weapons.

Ever since I was a child, I'd felt drawn to knives. It didn't matter how long, short, curved, or straight they were, I wielded them with deadly accuracy. Knowing I wouldn't need any throwing knives for this job, I passed those by. My father had hired others in the past who focused on showy knives like a switchblade or a butterfly knife, but I wasn't like them. After working with others and seeing their injuries, not to mention I didn't want to leave my blood at a crime scene, I wanted no part of those weapons. Paranoid? Yes, especially since I knew my father had paid off enough police agencies to ensure my blood wasn't in any database.

Running my hands over the knives, I pulled down the ones I wanted to take for this specific mission. It was one man in his 50s who looked overweight and likely had a heart condition, so I didn't pull any of the long blades. I also hated cleaning hidden and collapsible blades, so I passed those. I chose a five-inch tanto and a seven-inch KABAR, popular with the US Marines. Both were easy to handle, easy to clean, and I could carry them on me if I needed to. Placing those two on top of the handgun, I threw in some clothes and the folder with the target's information before zipping the bag and carrying it downstairs.

Looking at my watch, I saw it was 2:30, and the doorbell rang right on time. Seth was nothing if not punctual, especially on my father's orders.

"Afternoon, Seth. How are you?"

"Good, Preston. Taking you to Redmond, right?"

"Yes, I have a flight leaving in over an hour."

"Do you know when you'll be back? I can be there to pick you up."

"I'm not sure yet. Hopefully in the morning, but it may even be tonight, depending on circumstances."

"Completely understand. Call me when you leave for home from wherever you're going, and I'll be sure to be there."

Seth wasn't only my father's driver; he was also part of our organization. If I was flying out with a simple duffle bag, he knew it would most likely be a very short flight. He also knew there was a chance I'd need help cleaning up before I arrived back at the house.

No matter the mission, father expected us to arrive back at the house in perfect condition. This way, if the police ever asked for video of us leaving or returning to the house, he could show us without a speck of blood on us. Not that he'd ever had to show the police anything anyway, but it was better to be safe than sorry.

I got into the passenger seat. Being driven somewhere didn't mean I wanted to sit in the back. I thought of Seth as an equal, not simply a driver.

Seth got in, and we took off to the airport.

"So, you drove the ladies to lunch, right?"

"You know I did, Preston. What do you want to know?"

"Saw through me pretty quickly, huh?" I chuckled.

Seth had been my father's driver since before my mother died, so he'd watched me grow up.

"I mean, it's your life and future. I assumed you'd be curious."

"Anything you want to share or can tell me about the three?"

"Well, I'm sure you know two are twins, those are the blondes. The third, Carlie, is related to them, but I believe it's by marriage. The twins are driven by money and prestige, but I don't know what drives Carlie. She was polite and respectful, even though she didn't need to be."

"Victoria said similar things. The twins were pretty much the same, but Carlie was different."

"I wouldn't say the same. Annabelle is definitely a gold digger who would stab her own father for money, but Beatrice seemed different, almost like she wanted to be more like Carlie but couldn't because of Annabelle. It seemed like she at least tried to be courteous at times."

"Interesting. Thank you. I'm sure my father told you not to tell me anything."

"Actually, he didn't say anything about it at all. I didn't have much interaction with them. I drove them here and delivered the letter to them but not much else."

"What, if anything, can you tell me about their father, Baron Teller?"

"I can tell you he probably beats his wife and is *at least* emotionally abusive to the daughters. He's also shady, and I wouldn't trust him to follow through with anything he's agreed to."

Something for me to remember as I moved forward with my plans. I already knew Baron wouldn't be an ally. I held out hope he wasn't everything Seth had said. It seemed he knew exactly what he was doing and was potentially worse than we thought. I doubt he understood who he was dealing with, though, and it would be his downfall.

"Anything about his wife?"

"Her name is Celeste. Nice lady from what I can tell, protective of the girls, at least Carlie, anyway. She seems plain and subdued and is definitely under Baron's thumb."

"Thank you for your observations. I think I have all the info I need now."

"Listen Preston, I know you didn't ask my opinion, but I'm going to give it to you anyway."

"I'm all ears."

"Regardless of which woman you marry, I want you to protect the ones he didn't choose. Your father hasn't told me who he's selected, but I'm concerned. I know the twins are probably snobs, but I don't think they deserve what could be coming to them if Baron crosses your father."

"I agree with you. Thank you for seconding my thoughts."

"Anytime, and we're pulling up."

Arriving at the company jet on the tarmac, I opened the door before Seth could walk around. "You don't need to open the door for me. I'm a grown man."

Seth laughed as he closed his door again. "I keep forgetting." He winked.

"Haha, very funny. I'll give you a call when I'm on my way back."

"Sounds good. Have a safe trip." Even on the most dangerous missions, Seth always wished me luck—and I always came back safe. I'm not normally superstitious, but in my last almost four years of doing solo missions, nothing had ever gone wrong.

I climbed the stairs to the jet and sat near the front. Even though there were ten seats on each side, I preferred to sit closer to the door.

The pilot returned from his final outside safety checks and saw me.

I gave him a thumbs up, and he entered the cockpit. Within 30 seconds, we were taking off. Having Charles Wessex as a father often had benefits, and flying privately was the one I enjoyed the most.

The co-pilot came over the speaker to let me know it would be a 70-minute flight. He said if I needed anything, push the call button, and he would come out from the cockpit if it was safe to use autopilot.

50 minutes later, the pilot came across the speaker again, waking me. "We'll be arriving in Port Angeles in 20 minutes."

Removing the folder from my bag, I looked over it one last time to make sure I had everything I needed before we landed. My goal was to get to the dealership right after it closed. According to the folder, they closed at five pm. I could be back on the plane by seven, assuming everything went as planned.

The wheels bumped the tarmac, so I put the folder back into the bag and waited for the door to open. When it was time to deplane, I stepped down onto the tarmac to see Timothy waiting with a black sedan. "Evening, Timothy. We'll be going to Torx Auto Imports. Do you need directions?"

"I don't, but thanks. I've driven past the location multiple times. Don't worry, always with different vehicles."

"I wasn't worried. I know you're good at what you do."

Timothy was the point guy, the one my father sent out to make initial contact with business owners or individuals my father wanted to do business with. Even though he was a six-foot one inch Italian and looked like he could break bones with his bare hands, he was one of the nicest guys I'd ever interacted with. He was strictly talk, and I didn't think he even carried a weapon.

"Oh, your father also sent over the purchase agreement. He said you would be acquiring the signature." Timothy handed it to me, and I placed it in the bag before I got into the car, placing the bag at my feet.

"Yes, I will."

"One other thing, Mr. Wessex. Will I need to be calling in the cleaning crew?"

My father routinely had a cleaning crew ready for locations I needed to have "conversations" at. They weren't always needed, but they were efficient and paid well for their time and effort.

"I hope not, but let's keep them on speed dial."

Timothy laughed because I said the same thing every time, and my average was around 50% needing them versus not.

Arriving at Torx at 5:45 pm, Timothy drove us around to the back staff parking lot. I noticed two cars, a Nissan 350Z and a Nissan Altima. "Timothy, do you know those cars?"

"Yeah, the 350Z is the owner, Mr. Hudson, and the Altima is the secretary's, who he's been banging for the last year. She usually goes home around six. The cameras are only in the front. They cover the lot and not the main road or the side street, but that's it. There are no cameras in the back."

"Great, thanks. Drop me off here, and I'll go in through the back. I'll beep you when I'm done."

On my cell phone, I had a two-digit code I put in, automatically beeping whoever picked me up. It was a program I'd set up when I was 13, and it saved a lot of time when jobs were done. Looking down at my bag, I debated taking it or just the knives and the purchase agreement. Thinking I may need the gun, I grabbed the bag and walked up to the back door without looking back. By the time I was at the door, Timothy and the sedan would be gone, leaving me alone for however long I needed.

Opening the door, I noticed most of the lights were off. I slowly creeped toward the one light I could see. Based on the plans in the folder, I knew this would be the owner's office.

The door was closed, but from the window next to it I could see a blonde bent over the desk with her skirt hiked up around her waist. As I got closer, I could see the heavy-set man I knew to be the owner plowing into her from behind. Not wanting her to see me if it could be avoided, I stayed in the shadows for two minutes before he grunted and stopped.

As he pulled back, I heard the young lady say, "What about me, Jake?"

"What about you, Tina? My daughter is supposed to be at my house tonight because her whore of a mother is having her boyfriend stay over. I need to leave soon to pick her up."

"But you said we would talk about our future the next time I stayed late. I thought you were divorcing her."

"We're separated, Tina. As for our conversation, not tonight, and maybe not ever if you keep pushing me."

"But..."

"No buts, get the fuck out. I need to take a shower before I get home so my daughter doesn't smell you on me."

Great, he's a cheater and a jerk. This will make my conversation with him less gentle.

I saw her pull her skirt down and walk out into the hall with her head down.

Even if I'd been standing in the light, I don't think she would have seen me with the tears trailing down her face. I watched as she went to her desk, grabbed her purse, and moved toward the door to the staff parking lot.

When I heard the door shut, I moved quickly and quietly, so if she came back, she wouldn't see me. There was a moment where I almost felt sorry for her. Almost, but she had to know he was married and had a kid when they started sleeping together.

When I heard the back door close, I walked over and waited near it until I heard her drive away. After waiting for a minute to make sure she hadn't forgotten something and came back, I walked back to the office.

I could hear the shower going, so I sat in the chair furthest away from where Tina was getting railed. Some dealerships had showers for their employees, but those were usually in the service area. He must have had one installed for exactly this reason.

I put my bag down and pulled out the contract. I didn't want to jump straight into the knives even though they were my preferred method.

As I waited for him to finish his shower, I sat and thought about how my life was going to change once I got married. Would I still go after targets? Should I tell my wife? Absolutely, and absolutely not, were the answers my brain immediately gave.

The door opened as I was internally debating my dilemma.

I looked up and smiled sweetly at Jake Hudson, owner of Torx Auto Imports, who imported a lot more than vehicles.

He was wearing nothing but a towel. He'd left his clothes on the floor near his chair, but I'd moved them as part of my plan. I put his tie and Tina's panties on top of the desk in case I needed them.

"I'm sorry. We're closed."

"Oh, I know. I saw Tina leave." I put my feet up on the desk, pissing him off a little more.

"Who the fuck are you?"

"You can call me Mr. Wessex, and I'm here hoping you'd reconsider Wessex International's generous offer to buy your company."

"You're not Charles Wessex, and whoever the fuck you are, you can go tell *Charles* I am *not* selling to him. Now or ever."

"I was hoping you'd reconsider given I came all the way to Port Angeles to meet with you, but I understand you have a pressing dinner date with your daughter."

"Fuck no. The bitch won't talk to me, just like her mom. I only said that to get rid of Tina."

And just like that, his words cut the only strings I'd been worried about, leaving me to do whatever I wanted. I reached into my bag and pulled out my tanto. I placed the short, straight blade with double edges ending in a sharp, angular point in the sheath behind my back.

I cracked my neck before standing. "Well Mr. Hudson, can I call you Jake? Mr. Hudson seems too formal for what's about to happen." I stalked closer with one hand behind my back.

"You can get out of here before I call the police."

"Oh Jake, that won't be necessary. We're going to have a friendly conversation." I cocked my head to the side. I wasn't ready to show my favorite knife yet because it tended to scare people.

"The hell we are." He reached for the top drawer of his desk, but I'd already removed the gun. It was so predictable I could almost write a 'How to Not Be an Idiot' guidebook with how many people did the same things.

"Oh, were you looking for the Smith and Wesson you had in there? Don't worry. I put it somewhere safe. We wouldn't want someone to get hurt, now would we?" I pulled my hand from behind my back, and Jake cowered in front of me. "What are you doing? It's the contract I need you to sign."

Confidently standing straighter and now thinking I wasn't planning to hurt him, he puffed out his chest again. "Like I said earlier, I'm not signing it."

"Well, we have all night, so I'm sure you'll sign it at some point. So, let's get started, why don't we?" This time I pulled the tanto from the sheath. "Why don't you sit? I'm sure after the long five minutes you spent horribly banging your secretary, you must be tired."

"Why you—"

"I said sit." I pushed Jake down into the chair.

His towel fell as he sat against his will.

Thankfully, the chair was leather, so the blood wouldn't soak in. I hated it when they were cloth. It made the clean-up crew's work so much harder.

I put the knife behind my back as I casually strolled around him.

To stop him from moving, I used his tie to bind his hands to the sides of the chairs.

"You can't do this! You don't know who I—" I stuffed the panties Tina had left behind into his mouth.

"I know exactly who you are. You're the man who's going to sign over his business to Wessex International."

He mumbled something I didn't care to decipher as I held up the knife so he could see it.

"Nod if you understand."

Jake nodded.

"Perfect. Now this is going to go one of a couple different ways. They all end in you signing the contract. Do you understand?"

His eyes widened as I put the blade of the knife against his pinkie finger.

"Again, nod if you understand."

He nodded again; this time I could see the fear in his eyes.

"Great, now I usually start with the fingers, but since you like putting your prick into things you probably shouldn't, I think I'll start there."

He tried to push me away, but his bindings kept him tied to the chair.

"All you need to do is sign the agreement. I won't have to make a single cut if you sign it." I slid the edge of the knife up his thigh, the tip pushing into his balls. He winced as it made contact. "Do you want to sign voluntarily?"

I looked up, and he shook his head.

I didn't know if he thought I wouldn't do it, but I'd done a lot worse to people who weren't running a multi-million dollar importing company and bringing in not only cars but people and drugs as well.

"Fine, now remember, you could have stopped this." I skewered one of his balls but stopped short of touching the other one.

He screamed through the panties, but I knew no one would be close enough to hear him. Another of Timothy's jobs was to keep random passersby from interrupting my work.

"I'll give you one more chance to keep what little you have left. Will you sign the agreement?" I looked up to see this grown man in tears but nodding.

"Exactly what I like to see. Let me grab a pen." I left my knife embedded in his testicle while I pulled a pen out of the desk and handed it to him.

I tilted the contract so he could sign it while still tied up. After changing pages to make sure he signed all three lines, I put it back onto the desk. Slowly, I pulled out the knife, watching him the entire time.

He took a deep breath in relief as I pulled the knife the rest of the way out.

"I appreciate your cooperation. You will receive the agreed upon purchase price in three to five business days. Oh, and for cheating on your wife and not picking up your daughter, I'll leave you with this parting gift." I swiftly cut off Jake's penis before going into the bathroom to clean my knife.

He signed the paperwork after all, so I didn't have to kill him, but I'd wanted to leave him with a little something extra to always remember me by.

After the blade was clean, I walked back into the office and put everything back into the bag, not sparing him a second glance as I worked quickly. I could hear him mumbling and crying, but I grabbed my phone and entered the two-digit code.

Before I left the office, I looked back at him, bleeding all over the place. "Don't worry about bleeding out. There will be a crew here soon to get you all bandaged up and sent to another country. Your family thinks you left, because it *is* what you tend to do, isn't it? Leave to get out of something you've done? If you ever set foot in this country again, what I did tonight will look like a kiddie ride. Do I make myself clear?"

I smiled as he dipped his head in agreement.

"Perfect. It's been a pleasure doing business with you. I'm sure no matter where you end up, you can have surgery to fix your *injury* right up. Hey, maybe this time you can get something to actually please a woman." I smirked at him as I left the office.

Opening the employees only door, I saw a tan SUV waiting for me.

"Do we need to send in the clean-up crew?"

"Yes, and I'd make it at least somewhat fast since there's a decent chance he could bleed out."

"Did you get the contract signed?"

"Have I ever not completed the job?"

"Good point. Is there anywhere else you want to go before we head to the plane?"

"No. Please take me to the plane. I need to get home to continue planning my wedding."

"Oh yeah? You're getting married? Congratulations, I guess."

"Timothy, that is the most apt thing you've said all night."

We laughed as he drove me back to the plane.

***

As I sat on the plane, I messaged Seth to let him know I was on my way home, and he could meet me in 70 minutes, give or take. He sent me a thumbs up, and I sat back in my seat. I was asleep before the co-pilot even announced takeoff. I woke when the wheels hit the tarmac as we were landing.

"Did your trip have a happy ending?" Seth asked as I slid into the SUV.

"It did. At least it did for me. Can we listen to music?"

"Absolutely, I'll get you home." Seth hit the gas. I reclined my seat and lost myself to the music.

***

Arriving at the house, I opened the SUV's door before turning to Seth. "Do you know if my father is home?"

"Yes, he should be in his office."

"Perfect, I'll brief him. Thank you for the ride." I got out and shut the door before going up the steps to the front door.

While I enjoyed my work, it could be draining. Probably because I hadn't been as active while at school aside from once or twice during vacation when my father requested my help with an issue.

The door to his office was wide open. I could see him going through documents, so I went straight into his office.

I sat across from him and pulled out the contract. Waiting for him to acknowledge me, I set the paperwork on the desk in front of him.

"Timothy called while you were in the air."

"Oh?" Usually, he didn't unless something had gone wrong.

"He called to confirm the package has been sent via ship. It's not likely to arrive safely, however. The cleaning crew thanks you for the work."

"I do what I can," I answered as he looked through the contract.

"Will the signatures hold up in court?"

"They weren't made under 'duress', and I checked them against other signed documents before I left. They're identical."

"Words every boss loves to hear. This should be the only thing I'll need from you until after the wedding unless something comes up last minute. Thank you, Preston. You added millions to the Wessex name."

"Anything to serve the company, Father." I swallowed back bile.

He went back to his paperwork, and I went to my room. I could have gotten Victoria to make me something to eat, but I wanted a shower and to pass out, even though it was still early. Maybe I would watch a show until I fell asleep.

Chapter Eleven

9 Days Until the Wedding- Carlina

It was early when my mom knocked on my bedroom door. I didn't have the energy to tell her to come in, so she opened the door after a few moments. I'd feigned being sick all day yesterday so I wouldn't have to deal with her or look Baron in the face.

The audacity to threaten to take my house and leave my mother if I didn't help him with his own business issues still pissed me off.

"Are you feeling better?" My mom sat next to me on the bed.

I'd pulled the blankets up so only my eyes and the top of my head were showing. "How would you feel if you not only were being forced to marry someone against your will so you don't lose the only house you've ever known, and also found out your own mother had planned and agreed to it?"

"Don't be such a grouch. We'll get it paid off. The mortgage will be gone, and you'll have your house back for the future if you ever need it."

"What do you mean 'for the future'? It becomes my property the minute I turn 19."

"Of course it does, but Baron assumed you would let us live here until we no longer want to, and I mean, the twins have their rooms."

Sitting up, I looked at her. "He *assumed*, huh? Well, maybe I should have been part of the conversation before they moved in."

My mom looked sad. "You were young, and I didn't want to bother you with the specifics, especially after losing your father."

"So, now you assume I'll let you keep living here after all you've done to me?" I shook my head. Eventually, I'd crumble and let them live here, at least until I could get my money and my divorce. But for right now, I wanted her to squirm.

I sat up a bit. "I don't know. After what Baron has done, maybe it would be best if you all found another property."

I heard her softly sniffle.

"If you're feeling better, today we need to go pick out your dress."

"Do we have enough time? I mean, we have what? Nine days until the wedding?"

"We do if we buy something off the rack. Baron said we can spend up to 500 dollars on the dress."

"So, what? Something cheap? Because *that's* what I've always really wanted for my wedding. Ever since I was a little girl, I envisioned my dress to be some tacky, cheap, off-the-rack dress. This will be the wedding of my dreams, Mom." I rolled my eyes. I'd never really thought about getting married, but I knew I didn't want a cheap wedding dress.

My mom put her arm around my shoulders. "I know it isn't ideal, but once you get your inheritance, you can have a larger wedding with the money. One with everything you want, it can be spectacular."

If I ever get married again after divorcing in a year.

"I doubt I will. Maybe someday I'll meet someone I *want* to marry instead of being forced into it like some ancient arrangement."

"I know, but let's make a day of it. We can go shopping together and find you a dress."

"This isn't over; I'm still not happy with you. But since apparently this is happening whether I like it or not, I may as well get fitted. Let me get up and showered, and we can go."

"Okay, and we can get a coffee on the way."

I could tell she was excited. I wasn't sure why, since she was forcing me to do this. Well, her and Baron.

After my shower, I dressed and put on a skirt and tank top so I could change out of it easily while trying on dresses. For a moment while I dressed, I wonder what Mr. Wessex's son would wear for the wedding. Knowing his father, I assumed he would wear a tux, but who knew after the things I'd heard?

Downstairs, I saw Annabelle and Beatrice were both waiting by the door with my mother.

"Where are you two going?" I asked them, instantly suspicious.

Beatrice looked at the floor while Annabelle answered, "With you, of course. You can't get a dress without your bridesmaids, can you?"

"Who says you two will be my bridesmaids?"

"Well, it's not like you have any other friends who are willing to be your witnesses, do you?" Annabelle was practically beaming while she said it.

"I wasn't planning to have anyone stand up there with me. This is a small wedding. Why do I need someone up there with me?"

"No, you must let us join you. It may be the only wedding you ever have."

I could tell Annabelle was having fun with this, while Beatrice didn't seem to want any part of it. I almost felt bad for her.

"Well, since you're ready, let's go. Did Father give you money for your dresses?" I asked, because apparently, I was on a budget, so they should be as well.

"No, silly. He gave us his card and told us to get whatever we wanted. Do you have any specific colors in mind?" Annabelle opened the front door to leave.

"Of course he did." Closing my eyes, I saw the colors of flowers and leaves. "Yes. You can pick whatever color and style you want as long as it's the same color as one of the flowers in our garden."

Beatrice looked up at me, and a small smile crossed her face.

"Really? You want us to look like a flower?" Annabelle scoffed.

"No, I want colors matching one of our flowers, and you can choose whatever style you want. One request though."

"What?"

"You can't both have the same color or the same style. Understand?"

"Why does it matter?" Annabelle opened the door to the SUV my mom and Baron had recently bought.

"You know how much I like the garden, and I want you two to be colorful and unique. Please?"

"We'll do it." Beatrice answered before Annabelle had the chance to say anything else.

My mom got in on the driver's side, and Annabelle sat in the front passenger seat. Beatrice and I sat in the back like we usually had to when the four of us went anywhere together.

The first stop was at Dutch Bros, a coffee shop known for their delicious coffee. I ordered my normal Vanilla Latte while Annabelle got a large Vampire Slayer, and Beatrice got a Caramelizer. Both were cold drinks, but I preferred mine warm.

"Okay, do you want me to pay for it?" I'd brought extra money, even though I didn't want to spend a dime.

"No, it's my treat, girls." My mom paid for the drinks.

"Thank you." Beatrice told my mom before kicking Annabelle's seat.

"Yeah, thank you," Annabelle ground out.

"Thank you, Mom. Where to first?"

"I was thinking we should go to the bridal store first and see if we can find your dress before getting dresses for the twins. How does that sound?"

"Great," Beatrice replied as Annabelle opened her mouth.

"Perfect, off we go."

The bridal shop was a small store in the middle of downtown. It had been there for as long as I could remember.

I didn't remember ever going inside before, but I remembered walking by during the trick or treating events the community hosted downtown during Halloween.

We found a parking spot right in front of the shop.

I followed my mom into the shop, and a small bell rang as the door opened.

"Hi! I'm Nancy, and welcome to 'I do'. What are we looking for today?"

"My daughter, Carlie, is getting married in nine days, and I'm hoping you'll be able to help us." My mom placed her hand on my arm to show I was the one getting married.

"Oh, you'll find wedding gowns right around the corner. Having such a close wedding date doesn't give you enough time to order one or make any major modifications. Let me think."

"Please, take all the time you need. We can sit over here?"

"Yes, please sit over here. Would you like something to drink?"

Beatrice, Annabelle, and I all held up our drinks.

Nancy smiled before turning to my mom. "For you?"

"No, thank you. Well, maybe some tissues."

Nancy nodded before leaving the room.

"Do you think this place will have something? It's so small." Annabelle pretended to pick at something on her pants.

"I'm sure they will." Mom was ever the optimist.

Nancy walked back in with tissues and five dresses. "These are the only dresses we have around your size, so we have time to make small alterations if necessary.

"Thank you. How much are they?" My mom asked.

"They range in price from $250 to $750. What's your price range?"

"If possible, I'd like to keep it under $500."

"Okay, only one of these is too expensive. Do you want to try on the remaining four?"

"Yes, please." Hopefully, I'd find something I liked out of these four and was flattering. I didn't want to get married in the equivalent of a burlap sack.

"Okay, let's go this way to the dressing room. You three can stay here, and we'll be back after getting Carlie into her dress."

I stood and followed Nancy back to the dressing room.

"I'll give you one at a time and help you into them if you need me to."

"Thank you." I reached for the dress she was offering.

As I put the dress on, I looked into the mirror. It made me look like I was wearing a nightgown. It had no shape and long sleeves. There was no way I was showing them this dress.

"This is a no."

Nancy chuckled. "I figured. Here, this one should be better."

Hopefully, or else I was going to look like a 90-year-old getting out of bed to chase off the coyotes.

"Thank you."

This one fit much better and was a halter style with a long train. The back had a corset style bodice with a zipper below, and the subtle boning and beads in the front were a shade darker than the dress, so it made the flowery patterns pop in the light.

I loved the blush pink undertone, but I didn't know what my mom would think. "Can I try on the other two first and come back to this one?"

"Absolutely. I'm here for you." She handed me another dress that I immediately knew I wouldn't like.

I realized I didn't want a dress with sleeves. "Not this one. I don't like the sleeves."

"Ok, at least we're getting somewhere. So, the last dress doesn't have sleeves, but it's more like a tank top."

"Oh, let me try it on."

Nancy handed me the dress around the curtain.

Looking at it before I put it on, I knew I would like this one as well. It was also a blush color but with thin straps and a decorative bodice with small stones. The train was shorter, and the skirt was a little fluffier than the other one I really liked. It was pretty, though, so I figured I would have my mom and the twins look at this one too.

"Okay, I'm ready." I stepped out from behind the curtain.

"You look so good! Ready to show the ladies?"

"As ready as I'm ever going to be."

Nancy chuckled again as we walked out to the main room.

Annabelle and Beatrice were deep in conversation when I walked out, so my mom saw me first.

"Oh, you look so beautiful." My mom sniffled as she held a tissue to her eyes and dabbed at her tears.

"This is the first of the two Carlie liked. This dress is your classic corset bodice with thin straps. The train is shorter, which is popular with weddings where there will be dancing."

"But it's not white?" Annabelle snottily commented.

"No, most wedding dresses aren't stark white anymore. Most modern brides choose an ivory color. The blush color is very pretty, too."

Standing a little taller. "I think so too." Turning around in the mirror, I looked at myself.

"I like this one," my mom said.

"I want to see it up close before you go back. Is that okay?" Annabelle asked.

"Sure." I held still as Annabelle stood and stepped toward me.

After she circled around the back, she stopped in front of me and stepped closer. As she did, she tripped, her drink going all over the front of the dress.

"Seriously?" I didn't even know what to say.

"Oh no, that's going to leave a stain." Annabelle smirked as she returned to her seat on the couch.

Nancy came up to me while I was on the verge of tears.

She looked at the dress. "We'll be back, you and I Annabelle will have a conversation about you paying for the little *mishap* that just happened." She led me to the back.

"That was going to be *the* dress."

"I know, but that stain has already set. Why don't you try on the other dress?"

"Okay, but why would she do that?" I asked out loud.

"People can be crappy. Let's get the other dress on." Nancy helped me get it on.

I walked back to the dressing room to put on the other dress. After I had it on, I looked into the mirror. This was the dress, at least for this wedding.

"Okay, I think I'm ready."

"This is definitely your dress. You practically glow in it." Nancy said.

"I absolutely love it." I liked the first one, but I didn't think I would find two dresses I loved this much within my price range. When I walked in this time, they were all paying attention.

"Oh, this one's really nice too," my mom said.

Annabelle scoffed at the dress, and Beatrice looked like she was going to tear up.

"It looks great, Carlie. You look like a princess." Beatrice turned to my mom. "Can I get one of those tissues?"

My mom handed her one.

"Gross, it isn't white either." Annabelle said as she went to stand up.

Nancy took her comment in stride. "Yes, this one has a longer train and a slight blush undertone, so it doesn't appear as blush as the other, unless it's in the right light. Then it has the same blush hint. The longer train looks great in photos."

"Mom, I really like this one." I turned to Nancy. "How much is this one?"

"It's $400 and comes with a veil."

It seemed like it should be much more, but I wasn't going to complain.

"Nancy, I think this is the dress. Do you have time to do minor alterations?" My mom reached into her purse for her credit card.

"Yes, we won't need much. Maybe adjust the length depending on what shoes Carlie plans to wear? Do you have them picked out yet?"

I looked at my mom. I hadn't even thought about shoes.

"We'll have shoes figured out by the time we come back for alterations. What day can you do?" My mom followed Nancy toward the front of the store where the cash register was located.

"Let me look at my schedule." Nancy reached the front desk and flipped through the pages of her planner. "I have a couple of dresses I need to finish before I can get started on hers. It looks like I can see her in two days for an alteration fitting, and then in another four days for the final fitting. It should give you roughly three days before the wedding. Can that timetable work for you?"

I couldn't wrap my head around the fact I was going to be married in nine days, so I stood quietly while my mom answered for me.

"Will three days be enough for you to make any alterations needed?"

"Yes, I only have two other wedding dresses in for alterations, and I can push them back to push this through."

My mom handed her the credit card, and Nancy ran it while my mom talked. "We'll all be back in two days."

"You don't all need to come. Carlie obviously needs to, and you can, but her sisters won't need to."

Internally, I was happy because I was tired of Annabelle's comments. I didn't mind Beatrice, and of course, I wanted my mom with me, but Annabelle could stay home for all I cared.

Nancy handed my mom her card and had her sign the receipt.

"Oh, okay. I can come back with her. I guess the twins can stay home."

"What? But I want to see the fitting." Annabelle pouted.

I was so tired of Annabelle. "Do you, or do you want to mock me some more?"

"I wasn't mocking you. I was giving you my opinion."

"Well, it's not needed anymore, at least not for my dress."

She opened her mouth to argue, but my mom spoke up, "Okay girls, let's get to the next store for the twin's dresses. Thank you, Nancy. See you in two days."

Nancy smiled as we left.

I was glad she spoke up. I didn't want to get married in the first place, but it was nice to have at least one person on my side, even if it was practically a stranger.

We piled into the car with Annabelle again in the front and Beatrice and I in the back.

"You looked really pretty in the dresses, Carlie," Beatrice quietly told me as we buckled in.

"Thank you," I whispered in return. I didn't need Annabelle to say anything else about my dress.

"Where do you ladies want to go for your dresses?"

"Let's go to Angela's. I saw some dresses there the last time we were in town." Annabelle spoke up before Beatrice could.

Angela's was a great store, but it was one of the most expensive in town, catering mostly to the elite and tourists who traveled through.

So, *their budget* was *much higher than mine. Freaking fantastic. Why am I not surprised?*

"Sounds good. Let's see if there's any close parking."

Luckily, there was a spot only two buildings down from the storefront.

I didn't really want to go into the store, but they had gone into mine, so I felt I had to. At least for Beatrice because she had been kind.

Mom opened the door for the twins, and we were met by a young woman wearing a two-piece suit outfit.

Her hair was pulled back into a sharp bun, which made her face look harsh. After looking us up and down, she turned up her nose. "What can I do for you today?"

"We're here to get bridesmaid dresses for these two," my mom offered.

"I don't know if we'll have anything in your... price range." The saleslady looked down her nose at my mom.

I opened my mouth to say something when Annabelle stepped forward.

Pulling out Baron's black credit card, Annabelle showed it to the saleslady. "Maybe don't be so quick to make assumptions? Is there someone else here who can help us? I'm not really comfortable working with you."

At the sight of the card, the woman's attitude completely changed. "Welcome to Angela's. Please have a seat, and we'll be with you shortly." She went behind a curtained partition, probably to call the police to check if someone's black credit card was reported as stolen.

Annabelle turned back toward us, smiling. "I knew it would work."

I rolled my eyes as I sat. My mom sat on one side of me while Beatrice sat on the other. Annabelle sat next to Beatrice, as far away from me as she could get.

A young lady came out with glass flutes filled with water. "Would you like lemon or lime in your water?"

"Nothing for me, thank you," I said.

My mom also declined the offered fruit.

Annabelle and Beatrice asked for limes. Having handed them their waters, the young lady left, leaving us sitting there looking around.

Upon taking our first sips, the first woman returned with another lady.

"Oh, now that you know we have money, you think we're worthy of your attention?" Annabelle sneered.

"I'm sorry about before. My name is Meg, and Julie and I will assist you. What are we looking for?" She looked shocked by Annabelle's comment but quickly turned on the charm.

I hated people like her. Some people only saw someone for how much money they seemed to have versus who they were as a person.

"We're looking for two bridesmaid's dresses."

"Do you have any specifics we need to consider, like color, length, or style?"

"No," Annabelle quickly replied.

"Yes. Any style, any fabric, but the colors need to be a color of a flower," I said before the women could walk off.

Annabelle glared at me, but I smiled back.

"So, the only thing is it needs to be the color of a flower? It would surprise me if we had a dress that didn't match the color of a flower." The lady looked confused.

"Yes, we have a very large garden at home as well as at the wedding site. So, I would like my bridesmaids to be dressed in a color representing one of the flowers from *our* garden," I smiled as I politely responded.

"Do you have any pictures of the flowers for reference?"

"No, but my bridesmaids have lived there for years. I'm sure they know what the flowers look like by now, and I'll have the final approval, anyway."

Annabelle looked like she wanted to argue, but Beatrice put her hand on Annabelle's arm.

"Very well. Ladies, do you want to come over to the dresses with me so we can see your options?"

"Absolutely, thank you." Annabelle stood while Beatrice looked back at me and shrugged her shoulders.

"Did you have to be so rude?" my mom asked me.

"Me? Rude? Are you kidding?" I couldn't believe my mom would ask me such a thing after everything I'd been through with Annabelle.

"Yes, it seems like you're being unnecessarily rude to Annabelle. Why not let them choose their own colors?"

"Mom. Because it's not their wedding! I don't even want to get married, and now you're saying I'm being rude by having one small request? You're more worried about them having to choose a color than me being able to choose the groom. Our garden has over 20 different kinds of flowers they could choose from, not including all the greenery. Why not the purple or yellow of the milkweed flowers? I think it would be harder for them to find a color *not* found in our garden. Which, I'm sure Annabelle will try to do anyway."

"I understand, but this is hard on them."

"Hard on them? How? Please tell me how this is 'hard on them' when they aren't the ones being forced to marry a complete stranger." My patience with her was at its limit. To say this was hard on them while I was the one being forced into marriage was as insulting as it was ridiculous.

The saleslady returned in time to save her from having to reply. "The ladies have each chosen five dresses to start with. I have someone helping them try them on." The lady pulled over a small stool. "While they're getting dressed, why don't you tell me more about your wedding?"

I looked at my mom to see if she was going to say anything. She didn't, so I spoke up, "It will be in my fiancé's family's garden." The location was the only thing I knew for sure.

"How quaint. I'm sure it will be a beautiful wedding."

I don't know why, but her attitude and fake kindness bothered me. It wasn't quaint. His family owned damn near the entire town we lived in.

My mom sensed I was getting angry and put her hand on my knee.

"Yes, it will be a small affair with only close family and friends," my mom responded before I could.

"With two bridesmaids?"

"The twins are her sisters. They wanted to be part of it. You know how it is with sisters. They always want to be involved with each other's big moments." My mom laughed.

The lady also laughed, so it seemed the tension from before wasn't as thick as it had been.

"Oh, I completely understand. Sisters can be both a blessing and a curse."

Annabelle and Beatrice walked out together.

Annabelle was wearing a short, strapless, bright neon pink dress with a ruffled skirt.

I groaned inwardly. Not only was it not a color we had in the garden, but it was also something you would wear to the club, not to a garden wedding during the day.

Beatrice, on the other hand, was wearing a knee-length lavender dress with a halter-style top.

We had a lot of lavender in the garden because my father had loved it.

"Beatrice, that dress is perfect. It looks so good on you," I said it loud enough to make sure Annabelle heard me.

"Thank you. I know how much lavender we have, and I remembered it also has a special meaning to you because of your father." Beatrice spun in her dress.

I looked over at my mom and saw her tear up a little.

"What about my dress?" Annabelle asked with a sneer.

I remembered my mom's early comment about me being rude. I tried to think of a way to tell her it wasn't appropriate for the wedding.

"It looks good on you, but I don't think we have a flower that color in the garden. You should definitely get it for the club, though."

"Ugh, I thought it would be perfect." Annabelle stomped back to the dressing room.

"I'm sorry. I told her it wouldn't work, but she thought you would say yes to make her happy," Beatrice said.

"Am I asking too much? Also, do you like your dress? I'm serious about you looking beautiful in it."

"No, you're not asking too much. You know how Annabelle can be. I'm not used to this type of fabric, but it's so soft. I really like how it looks when I spin." She spun again and laughed.

"Great, I think it'll be perfect." I suddenly had the urge to hug her.

With tears in her eyes, she hugged me back. "Thank you for including us. It means a lot to me."

"It's what sisters do." I realized the words were true in regards to her. I was happy she would be there with me. Annabelle, not so much, but I could see Beatrice and I becoming closer as we got older, and I moved out.

Beatrice turned to the lady and gestured to the dress. "I'm going to get this one. I'll put it back in the dressing room after I change, so you can package it up."

"Great choice." The lady got up and went to the front of the store to help another customer.

Beatrice turned to my mom and me. "I'll be right back, and we can see what else Annabelle has to show us."

"Sounds like a plan." I sat back in the chair.

When Beatrice left, I looked at my mom. "Better?"

"Yes, but you should have let her get it. It would have been easier." My mom looked sad.

"But I'm only asking for this one thing. I want one single thing, and she knew what it was. I'm tired of catering to her all the time. You never take my feelings into consideration, so why are you so dead set on catering to hers? Why are her feelings so much more important than mine?"

"Catering to who?" Beatrice re-entered the room.

Before my mom could stop me, I told her, "Annabelle."

"Even before our mom died, Annabelle always got whatever she wanted. It's nice seeing someone tell her she isn't always the priority. It won't do any good, but I like seeing her put into her place once in a while."

I turned to my mom and cocked my eyebrow at her, daring her to say something.

She didn't, and Annabelle walked out in another short dress.

This one was light green, which was an improvement. It was tighter than the last one, but the small straps and color were at least more acceptable.

"What's wrong with this one?" Annabelle cocked a hip as she asked.

"Nothing. The color is great, and I think it looks good on you." I smiled as the lady came back.

"Really? Nothing negative to say?" Annabelle glared at me.

"No. If you like it, I like it."

"I do. Are you sure it isn't too short? Or not the right color green?"

"Do *you* think it's too short or not the right color? Annabelle, I promise you, it looks good on you, and the color is fine. I think it will complement Beatrice's dress nicely."

Looking defeated, Annabelle turned to the lady. "I'll take this one."

"Great choice. Leave it in the dressing room, and I'll have the attendant bring both dresses up to the register."

Annabelle walked back to the dressing room without another word.

"Don't you think the dress is a little short for a wedding?" my mom asked me.

"Yes, of course I do. But *you* told me not to fight with her. The style didn't matter, but the color did, and she knew that. At least this dress's color is in the garden." I sighed, knowing I would never win against Annabelle, so why fight more than I needed to?

"I think it'll look good with my dress," Beatrice answered as Annabelle returned.

"Ready?" Mom stood.

"Yes, I guess. Daddy said we could get dinner, but I'm not feeling it right now. Are you hungry, Beatrice?" The look on Annabelle's face told Beatrice even if she was hungry, the answer was no.

"I'd like to. But if you aren't feeling it, I guess we can go home."

I could tell Beatrice was having fun, but it was less stressful to not anger her sister.

"Well then, let's pay and get home. I'll whip something up once we get home if anyone gets hungry." Mom led us to the front of the store.

As we got closer to the register, Annabelle sped up to get there first. The lady was already standing there with the dresses in bags.

"Your total is two thousand, four hundred and seventy-two dollars."

I felt my coffee threaten to come back up. Over 2000 dollars for two dresses? Glad it wasn't my money.

Annabelle handed over the card. "Put it on all this, please."

"Of course. These dresses are not refundable and are dry clean only. If you get something small on them, a spot clean will prevent it from staining unless it's coffee. In that case, it's ruined." The lady handed the dresses over to Beatrice as Annabelle signed the credit card slip.

"Thank you for shopping at Angela's."

I still couldn't believe how much they'd spent on their dresses. Walking toward the exit, I kept my eyes focused on the door. Even after receiving my inheritance, I didn't plan to spend that kind of money on a single dress. Their bridesmaid dresses each cost over twice what my wedding dress was. I reached the door first, so I opened it to allow my mom, Annabelle, and Beatrice with the dresses to walk out.

"Thank you for driving us to get our dresses. I had fun," Beatrice thanked my mom as she got into the SUV.

"You're welcome. It was my pleasure. We don't do this sort of thing enough, and now, with Carlie getting married, we won't be able to in the same way anymore."

Annabelle grumbled something under her breath I didn't catch as I was getting into the back, but I didn't care enough to ask her to repeat it.

The ride back to the house was quiet, which I was grateful for. I was lost in my thoughts, and I also didn't really want to interact with my mom or Annabelle.

***

Getting home, I hugged my mom. "I'm tired. I think I'm going to shower and take a nap."

She smiled. "Of course. I'm so proud of you. You'll be a beautiful bride."

"Yeah, I wish Dad was here to see it."

"You know he would be proud of you as well."

"I do, thank you."

I went up to my room to get my robe. From inside the bathroom, I could hear Beatrice and Annabelle fighting, but I didn't care enough to listen to what they were saying. Sometimes they were best friends, and other times they fought like they hated each other. Not my problem, and they were exhausting sometimes.

Chapter Twelve

7 Days Until the Wedding - Preston

The next morning, I realized it was still too early for breakfast, so I checked the status of the projects I was working on with some of my former classmates. Seeing everything was on track with them, I settled in to look over my bank statements.

Even though I couldn't access my inheritance until I was 19, I could manage them after I proved to the executor that I was financially literate enough to not lose it all. The trustees were good. I'd never had a complaint with them. They managed it well at a conservative five percent increase each year, but I wanted more.

I didn't just *want* more. I *needed* more to do what I had planned. In the year I'd been managing the funds, only one had less than ten percent growth, which was a little more aggressive than most. I always kept back enough so if something happened to my investment, I could restart and make it all back. Seeing all the zeros helped calm the snake tightly coiled in my chest since moving back home. I smiled knowing my father had no idea how much I had in the multiple accounts or how I'd been managing it. Closing the tab, I searched for Annabelle Teller.

The first thing I found was an article with pictures of her at a club. She was in the middle of dancing with some guy who had his hands on her ass.

Fantastic.

I kept scrolling through the search results, and only to find more of the same. She was a rich brat who spent her daddy's money. I then looked up Baron Teller to see if I could find more information about his family. On the second page, there was an article about him marrying a widow, but that was it. No matter how I searched, I couldn't find a single picture of him. His businesses were frequently in the news. Once or twice is one thing, but it seemed like he pushed to have them front and center as often as he did. That just brought unwanted attention, especially because some of them no longer existed. The name itched a part of my brain, but for the life of me I couldn't remember where I'd heard it.

No wonder he owes my father as much money as he does.

I was tired of reading article after article about how Baron couldn't keep a business running longer than six months.

Where did he get the money to keep starting new businesses?

On a whim, I searched for myself to see what the newest rumors were about me.

Son of tycoon Charles Wessex forced to attend private college due to criminal record.

Various versions of this had been published over the years. This type of article could easily be determined to be true or not. I wasn't worried about what people thought, so I didn't send it to Evan. I tried not to use his hacking skills any more than necessary.

After a deforming accident, Preston Wessex hides awaiting plastic surgery.

That's a new one. Looking at it further, I noticed the author had written the article the day after I got home from the academy.

Knowing Annabelle was probably a fan of these types of sites, considering she was all over them, I had an idea, but I needed to run it by Victoria and my father first. Closing my laptop, I dressed and went downstairs. I was giddy over my plan, and I hoped they liked my idea.

I found my father and Victoria sitting at the kitchen island talking. They turned to look at me as I cleared my throat.

"Good morning. Are we having breakfast in here this morning?"

"You can, but I need to get back to my office soon. I was confirming some last-minute wedding details with Victoria. Was there something you wanted to talk to me about?"

"Yes. You know how we're having the wedding near the pond with the garden? I was thinking about having it in the mid to late afternoon on the lawn with fairy lights and have masks."

Victoria's eyes lit up. "You mean like a masquerade wedding?"

"Yeah exactly." I knew she'd like it. Years ago, she told me about the time Freddie took her to a masquerade ball. I didn't know how my dad would feel about it, though.

He looked between Victoria and me before standing. "If Victoria is willing to add this to her list of things to do, I don't see a problem with it." He looked at Victoria for confirmation.

"It won't add much. Do we have a final count on how many people will be there?"

"I have 45 RSVPs."

"You have 45 people coming? I told you I wanted to keep it small. We have five on our side, and what? My bride will have five. I meant our immediate families only."

"Yes, between the two families, there are also some community leaders, business associates, and the media." My father looked at me, confused.

Victoria spoke up, "Charles, can you please let the bride's family know? They'll need to be prepared for a masquerade, but let them know we'll take care of the masks if you're okay with the change of plans."

"I will. Use the card you usually use for groceries to buy the masks."

Victoria clapped while smiling.

I shared her smile because she seemed so happy to help me. I wasn't ready to clue her in on my ulterior motive for wanting the masks just yet.

"Thank you. I'll add that to the list. Don't forget to let them know."

"I won't. Thank you, Victoria. Anything else, Preston?"

"No, but is there anything you need from me? I feel like I should be doing more."

"I'll leave the planning to Victoria and Freddie. If they need you, I'm sure they'll let you know." My father took his coffee and left to go to his office. I could hear his shoes clicking on the tile as he walked down the hall.

I turned back to Victoria. "Are you really okay with adding another task? I know you have a lot going on."

"Absolutely. I'm excited you're helping. Which, speaking of, can you check with Freddie to see if he needs anything? I know he'll need help the day before the wedding to set up the canopies and chairs, but he may need help with the lights, too."

"Sure. Thank you for helping. I really appreciate it." I hugged her as I saw her eyes fill with tears.

"Of course, Preston. Like I said earlier, you're as close to a son as Freddie and I have ever, or will ever, have." She sniffled into my shirt.

Hugging her tight, I let her go. "Victoria, I know the next couple of days are going to be stressful, but I want you to know how special you are to me."

She smiled as I grabbed a pastry and the coffee from the island.

"I'm going to go eat this and take a swim before I head out to talk to Freddie. Or do you think I should speak to him now?"

Victoria looked over at the large clock hanging on the wall. "He's working in the back fields, so later would probably be better."

"Sounds good. Lunch at normal time?" I asked as I walked out.

"Of course."

I was going to miss Victoria and Freddie when I moved out. Maybe I should ask if they wanted to come to the new house. I knew I couldn't pay what my father paid, but they may still be interested. I would rather they both retire, but I knew they wouldn't for a long time. Maybe I could persuade them to retire sooner rather than later.

My thoughts were filled with ways to help Victoria and Freddie so they wouldn't have to work for the rest of their lives.

I opened my laptop to check my emails while I drank my coffee. Other than the underclassman worrying about their final project, everything else was pretty useless. Closing it, I sat looking out the window.

I knew my father would ask about my inheritance every day once I got it. How was I going to hide it? Right now, it wasn't something I wanted to dwell on because I didn't have an answer. Maybe I should talk to the trustee about how to disburse the money in a way that didn't show a lump sum for him to see and think he could take. I could worry about it after the wedding.

I changed and headed back downstairs with the empty mug, dropping it off in the kitchen.

"Yes, he wants the guests, as well as the bride, to be masked." I heard him pause to listen. "No, you don't have to buy one." Another pause, and I heard his chair hit the desk, so I knew he was upset.

"Yes, I know this wedding is draining but remember two things: you're barely spending anything on this wedding, and you owe me." He slammed his hand on the desk before responding, "No, *you* listen! If you don't follow through with what we've arranged, I *will* take the house."

I stepped closer, hoping I could hear the other side.

"Oh yes, I know how you came by it. Why would I tell her?"

I wanted to stay and listen to the rest since it was obviously about me and the family I was marrying into, but I could hear him pacing. When father paces on a call, he could come out of his office at any moment, and I didn't want to be caught eavesdropping if he opened the door. I shook my head at the games wealthy men play.

***

Swimming laps normally helped clear my head, so I took full advantage of the opportunity as I dove in.

This is why I never wanted to be wealthy, or at least not the type of wealthy my father was. You can have money and not be like my father. At least I hoped I could be.

Chapter Thirteen

7 Days Until the Wedding - Carlina

"Mom, we need to go. The appointment is in 20 minutes," I yelled as I ran down the steps. It was the day of the dress fitting, and I was nervous.

What if it didn't look as good as I thought it did? What if the Wessexes hated it?

I didn't see her in the kitchen, so I searched the rest of the house. I could hear Baron yelling, so I crept closer to his office to listen.

"We have no money. This wedding will bankrupt me if you keep asking for more."

"Dinner will not bankrupt us. Just give me the small amount I get as executor of the trust," my mom responded with a meek voice.

"You used any remaining money to buy her dress."

"Then maybe you shouldn't have let your daughters spend over $2000 on dresses."

I heard a door slam, so I pretended to be looking for something in the kitchen.

My mom stopped short when she saw me standing there. "Carlie, I didn't know you were downstairs. Did you find your shoes? We need to go."

"No, let me go grab them. I'll be right back." I ran upstairs to get the heels I planned to wear with my dress. They were simple two-inch kitten heels with straps around the ankle. I didn't normally wear anything with a heel, so I wanted to make sure I didn't fall in them. I ran downstairs with the shoes in hand. "Got them. I heard yelling. Is everything okay?"

"We can talk about it in the car. Did you get something to eat before we leave?"

"I'll grab a banana. Let's go."

What Baron had said spun in my brain as I grabbed the banana. I followed my mom out the front door.

"What happened?" I asked as my mom backed the car out of the driveway.

"Charles called and said his son wanted to have a masquerade wedding now, and Baron was worried we'd have to buy the masks."

I loved all things masquerade, so I felt excited for the briefest moment. Then I realized it was my wedding, and it brought me back to the present.

"I mean, they shouldn't be too expensive, right?"

"No, I think Baron is worried. He owes a payment on equipment or something, and it's stressing him out."

I wish my mom was more involved with Baron's businesses because it seemed money was always going out but never coming in.

"Mom, can I ask you something?" I'd never really asked her about it, not wanting to cause issues, but with me getting married in seven days, I figured, why not?

"Sure, Carlie." Mom glanced over at me as we drove to the dress store.

"Do Baron's businesses actually make any money? The twins always have everything they want, so I assumed his businesses do well. But it seems like we're always having to go without."

"I don't involve myself in much of his business dealings. I know they make enough to pay the bills we have, since the house is paid for." She winced as she made the comment.

"No, it *was* paid for. I still can't believe you allowed him to do what he did with my house."

"I didn't know what else to do. But it'll be paid off soon, and then it'll be yours after the twins move out."

"Yeah, what if they never move out? What if they decide to stay in the house forever? It's not like anyone's going to want to marry Annabelle anytime soon with her attitude."

"Carlie, don't say such things."

"Mom, you and I both know she's difficult. Now answer my question."

"I don't know. I'm sure at some point they'll leave, and you'll be able to do whatever you want with it."

Instead of arguing, I went along with it to keep the peace.

My mom found a parking spot right in front of the bridal store.

Opening the door to the store, I saw Nancy helping a young lady try on a flower girl dress. She looked up and saw mom and me before whispering something to the girl.

"Carlie, Celeste, it's so nice to see you. I'm almost done with this dress fitting, and then I can work on yours. Do you want to sit over there while I finish up?" She gestured to a couch across from the front desk.

My mom and I went over and sat on the couch. I watched Nancy finish up the fitting, and the girl twirled in her dress. I wish I could be as happy as she looked as she giggled and twirled.

"Okay, ladies. I'm ready," Nancy called from over by the mirror.

I noticed a young woman who had been sitting near where the girl had been. She had a matching smile, so I guessed it was her older sister.

"Your dress is hanging in the dressing room if you'd like to go back and put it on. Marie will help you if you need it."

I noticed the young woman stand and smile. "Hi, I'm Marie, and I'm here to help you with whatever you need. Are you ready to try on your dress?"

I barely acknowledged my mom. "As ready as I'm ever going to be."

"Good. Let me get Darcy out of there, and we can go back." She went to the back, and I heard her calling for the young girl. I heard running, and the young girl ran into Nancy's arms.

"Grandma, I love the dress. Thank you so much."

"Of course, Darcy. Now be good and sit there while we get Miss Carlie here into her wedding dress. Is it okay if she sits with you, Celeste?"

Mom smiled down at the little girl. "Of course. We can talk about how lovely she looked in her dress."

Marie walked back out. "I'm ready if you are."

"Yes, thank you." I smiled at my mom, who was already talking to Darcy.

Walking into the small dressing room, I saw my dress hanging on a clothing hook opposite the mirror.

"I'll stand outside the curtain. Holler if you need help."

"Thank you." I took off my clothes as I looked at my dress. This was one of the last steps before walking down the aisle, and I guess I thought it would be different.

"Are you related to Darcy?" I took the dress off the hook.

"Yeah, she's my cousin. I work here with my grandmother sometimes."

"I thought I noticed a resemblance. Okay, I have the dress on. Can you help me do up the back?"

Marie stepped around the curtain as I turned away so she could zip up the lower back before she tightened the corset ribbons. Looking at myself in the mirror, I felt like a little girl pretending to be a grown-up.

"Okay, are you ready?" Marie asked as she finished the back.

"Yes." I stepped into the heels I wasn't used to wearing, usually going for flats before anything else.

On our way out to the front of the store, Marie held the back of my train so it would be easier to walk in. The heels were higher than I was used to, so I was a little wobbly on my feet, but managed to keep from falling. I should have practiced wearing them.

I stepped up onto the little box in the middle of the room like I did when I first tried on this dress. This time, however, instead of Annabelle and Beatrice sitting on the couch, it was my mom and Darcy.

"Now that we've seen what it looks like while wearing your shoes, is there anything else, like jewelry or gloves you want to try on before we start adjusting the dress?" Nancy circled me, looking me up and down.

"No, I think I'm wearing everything I plan to wear for the wedding."

"Great, so all you need to do is stand there, and when I ask you to raise your hands or move a certain way, please do, okay? I don't want to poke you with a pin if I can help it."

"Sounds good. Thank you for doing this."

"Of course. It's one of the reasons I own a dress shop. I love helping make sure brides look their best on their wedding day."

Darcy spoke up, "And flower girls on their day too, right Grandma?"

"Yes dear, flower girls too." Nancy chuckled as she pulled the dress tighter.

I looked over at my mom, and she was unsuccessfully trying to blink away the tears.

"Are you okay, Mom?"

"Yes, I just…"

"It's a big day for the mother of the bride, and it can be sad," Nancy answered for my mom. "Okay, step down and raise your arms. I'm going to make sure the bodice fits right."

Doing as she asked, I felt it tighten, and it stayed tight as Nancy pinned the dress.

"How's this? It's not too tight, is it?"

"No, it's tight, but I can still breathe."

"The last thing to adjust is the length. Can you step back up?"

Stepping up, I made sure not to snag the dress on my shoes.

"Do you want your shoes to show, or do you want the dress to touch the ground?" Nancy looked at my mom and me.

"I don't know. Mom, what do you think?" I had no idea if one was better than the other.

"Personally, I like the toe of the shoe to be seen. This way, you're less likely to trip on the dress by accident, and it'll be easier to walk. What do you think, Nancy?"

"I completely agree, especially if you're not used to wearing heels or will be on uneven ground."

"Both things are true, so I think it's a great idea, Nancy. Toes showing it is."

"Perfect. Please stand still while I mark where I'm going to hem the dress."

"Are you going to have to cut it, Grandma?" Darcy looked worried.

Nancy continued to mark the dress. "No, dear. It doesn't need much, so I won't have to cut it. I'll hem a little in the front."

"Good, I've seen her have to cut dresses, and it always makes me sad."

Nancy chuckled as she finished pinning. "Okay, we're done. Marie, can you help her take her dress off without pulling out any of the pins?"

"Let's get you out of this dress, Carlie." Marie walked to the back.

I followed her and stood there while she unbuttoned the back of the dress.

"I'm going to lift the dress over your head. Hold still so the pins don't poke you."

"I won't move." I didn't want to get poked, and I really didn't want to get blood on the dress.

In one quick motion, Marie had lifted the dress over my head, and I was standing there in my bra and underwear. Marie was the first person outside of my mom and the twins who had ever seen me in my underwear. Normally, I would have felt self-conscious, but oddly enough, I didn't this time.

"Okay, got it. You can get dressed, and I'll get this back to the sewing table for the alterations to be completed."

"Thank you for your help. I hope she has enough time to get it done. I know it's on a tight schedule."

"It will be. If anything, she'll have me come in and do fittings and consultations while she works on your dress, but Grandma is one of the best in the state for alterations."

"Really? And she lives here, of all places?"

"She used to live in Portland and worked with the high-end designers. After she had my mom and aunt — they're twins — she thought it was time to slow down and move here. My aunt died, so my mom and my grandma are raising Darcy."

"Oh no, I'm sorry."

"It happened when Darcy was very young. She wasn't even a year old yet, so she doesn't remember, so I became a sister to her."

"That's sweet. Do you want to take this to the sewing room while I get dressed?" I laughed as I realized I was still standing there in my underwear having a regular conversation.

"Yeah, I probably should before Grandma comes looking for us. Or worse, she'll send Darcy." Marie laughed as she went toward the back room marked with a "Sewing Room" sign.

I turned in the other direction and went back to the main room where Nancy, Darcy, and my mom were standing and talking to each other.

Well, Nancy and my mom were talking. Darcy was standing near them, listening. Nancy paused her conversation when she saw me come in.

"Did Marie help you?"

"Yes, she took the dress into the back."

"Perfect, as I was telling your mom, it'll be ready in four days, which still gives us time to fix it if anything's wrong at the final fitting."

"Thank you so much for doing this. I know it's your job, but I appreciate you taking the time to do this for me."

"It's what I love doing."

"I heard. Marie was telling me how you worked with top designers in Portland."

My mom was shocked and looked at Nancy for confirmation.

"Yeah, not only in Portland, but Seattle and Los Angeles as well. I was well known for being the person you called if you needed last-minute alterations during a fashion show, so I traveled around the world."

"Wow, incredible. We're so happy you're here in our small town," my mom said. "Is there anything else you need before we leave? What about the veil?"

"I don't need anything else from you for the dress. What are you thinking for a veil? Long or short? And is there a particular style you're looking for?"

"Something that lays around the middle to lower back, I think. What do you think, Mom?" I turned to see my mom looking through various veils hanging on a rack.

"I think this one is the perfect length." My mom pulled out a veil.

"Let's try it on then. Do you want to get back into your dress?" Nancy unhooked it from the hanger.

"No, it's okay. I can picture what it'll look like." I didn't want to bother them with getting the dress back out.

Nancy placed the veil on my head, using the little combs along one edge to secure it to my head. She asked me to get back onto the box so I could see how it looked.

It was much lighter than it looked, with little crystals lining the edges.

"Will this be the actual veil?" I looked at it from various angles.

"No, this is just a store sample. We have stock in the back."

"I love it. I think it'll be perfect."

"Great, then I don't need anything else from you today. If you could not broadcast my past, I'd appreciate it. I'd prefer to only take on jobs I want. I don't accept everyone who has decided they want something. I don't have time or energy to deal with prima donnas."

"I completely understand, and we won't say a word," my mom affirmed.

"Well, thank you. I'll see you in four days, okay? Oh, and remember to bring your shoes."

"I will, thank you." I held out my hand, and Nancy shook it.

As we got into the car, I turned to my mom. "If she's so well known, how was the dress so cheap? She could have charged almost anything."

"I thought the same thing, but I'm not going to question it. You got the perfect dress for a great price."

"True, maybe it's the universe's way of telling me I should get married."

"I agree. Time to head home."

"Mom, what were you and Baron arguing about earlier? Do we not have the money for the dress? I thought for sure my inheritance would cover it."

"Oh, he's been waiting for some payments to come in from clients, so we're stretched a bit thin, but it'll be fine. The Wessexes are covering most of the wedding expenses."

I knew it was more than that, but I let it go, partially because I didn't care and partially because I didn't want to start what would likely become a bigger fight. Instead, I changed topics.

"I was thinking about asking if we could stop at the bank. I'd like to find out if I could get a printout of how much money is actually in the account."

"We could try, but I don't think they'll give it to you until you're 19," my mom said.

"True, I'm sure you're right, but what could it hurt to ask? Do we get monthly or yearly statements? I'd like to be prepared."

"I don't think so. Baron doesn't know about your account, and I'm the only one it would have come to."

"Oh, the man who knows everything wouldn't know. It's strange, but how would I know?" I knew I was being sarcastic, but I didn't care anymore. I also didn't believe he didn't know.

"I'll look around Baron's office next time he's gone and see if maybe he's been keeping them somewhere, unopened."

"Yeah, I'm sure he's holding a bunch of my mail without opening it. I guess it isn't a big deal, but it's something I've been thinking about a lot lately."

"I understand, and I'm glad you're thinking ahead. Your marriage will be good, I'm sure of it. You won't need to worry about it."

I'm glad my mom thought so, but I absolutely did not expect it would go well at all.

"We'll see."

We rode the rest of the way in silence as I thought about what she had said.

***

The minute we walked into the house, Annabelle and Beatrice jumped up from the couch. "Did you hear?"

"Did I hear what, Annabelle?"

"You're going to be wearing a mask during your wedding because your soon-to-be husband is horribly disfigured, and he doesn't want you to run away from the wedding."

"What?"

"Yeah, Daddy told us you're having a masquerade wedding, and Preston was the one who wanted it."

"So how does that translate into he's disfigured, and why should I care?"

"Annabelle, I told you she wouldn't care." Beatrice tried to get Annabelle to stop talking by putting her hand on her shoulder.

"Because he's disfigured and ugly! That's why. There was an article about how he was in a horrible accident, see..." She turned her phone to show me a picture of a man with bandages covering his face.

You couldn't even tell what color his eyes were.

"The picture proves nothing, and I don't care; it isn't like I even have a choice to marry him, is it?"

The look on Annabelle and Beatrice's faces showed they'd thought I'd volunteered to marry him so Annabelle wouldn't have to.

"What? But Daddy said—"

"Girls, what do you want for dinner?" My mom's interruption kept the conversation from spiraling into yelling and tears.

Mentioning dinner did exactly what she'd intended, and the girls listed off what they wanted.

Finally, my mom looked at me. "Is there anything in particular you want?"

"Remember Carlie, you need to fit into your dress, so don't eat anything with a lot of carbs," Annabelle gleefully offered.

"Yes, Annabelle. I remember. I was there today for the fitting. How does Halibut with broccolini sound? I can help make it."

"Annabelle and Beatrice, how does Halibut and broccolini sound to you?"

Beatrice quickly answered, "Sounds great. Do you need any help?"

Annabelle, pursed her lips as she thought about it. "Yeah, whatever, but I'm not helping."

My mom ignored her comment. "Great, I'll get it started, and no, Beatrice and Carlie, you don't need to help in the kitchen. Beatrice, can you please let your father know dinner will be ready in 20 minutes?"

"He isn't here." Beatrice offered.

"What do you mean, he isn't here?" Mom asked.

"He left and said he had to do something at the bank. Do you want me to call him?"

"No, it's okay. I'll save some for him if he doesn't get back in time for dinner."

I could tell my mom was worried about something, and I wondered if it was about the argument they'd had earlier in the day

"Go rest before dinner, Carlie. You've had a busy day. If I need any help, I'll ask Beatrice."

"Thank you." I yawned.

I went up to my room and opened the door. Looking around, something felt off, but I didn't see anything out of place. Likely it was that this was one of the last nights living here in this room. Not wanting to think about it, I laid down and stared at the ceiling. In a week, I would no longer be living here, and the thought felt weird.

Chapter Fourteen

3 Days Until the Wedding - Preston

"Freddie, do you need help setting things up for the wedding?" I'd spent the last three days swimming and trying to help Freddie and Victoria, even though they said they didn't need it.

"I'm going to, but first I need to work on the cars for a bit."

"Oh, speaking of cars, were you able to switch the tracker?"

Freddie looked around before answering, "Yes, but don't say it too loudly. I don't want your father to know what I did."

"Don't worry, I won't tell him. In fact, I don't even know why it's being tracked. I'm an adult."

"You may be an adult, but you know how your father is. I moved it from your Mustang to your Supra."

"Thank you. Let me know if you need my help with setting up, and I'll come out."

"Will do," Freddie replied on his way to the garage.

Knowing I had a couple hours to waste before Freddie would need my help, I decided to take a walk around the pond before everything needed to be set up.

Father had called and had chairs dropped off earlier along with the canopies. The only other things were the caterer, who would be here on the day of the wedding, the cake Victoria said she was handling, and the music, which would be set up the morning of the wedding along with the lights.

"Mom, I don't know if you can hear me, but I'm getting married in three days. It's not to someone I love or even know. I know you married my father without really knowing him, since your families arranged it. You loved him. At least toward the end, if nothing else. Married life may not be for me, though. With everything I do and how busy I am, can I even be a good husband? It wasn't like Father was a great example. Hell, after you died, he wasn't even a good father. I'm getting my inheritance in a month, and don't know if I want to even stay in Oregon, let alone here. Father expects me to use some of your money to pay for his businesses and thinks I'll be happy about it. I'm not happy about it at all."

I paused, knowing I wouldn't get an answer but always hoping for one. She would tell me what I should do or at least how to navigate this whole thing.

A mother duck walked toward the pond with her ducklings following as I watched them.

Freddie didn't need me yet, so I decided to swim until he did. I texted to let him know I would be swimming. I walked back inside from the pond and through to the double doors that led outside to the pool deck.

Freddie came in after I'd swam for about a mile. I stopped and got out of the pool. "You ready for me?"

"Go get dried off and changed, and we can put up the canopies and set up the chairs."

"Sounds good. Give me ten minutes."

***

"I'm here. What do you need?"

"I'm going to grab the forklift so we can raise the canopies, lay out the dance floor, and get the chairs ready. We also need to set up the archway, but Victoria is going to have a friend of hers come help put the flowers on it, so we don't have to do it."

"Sounds good. Let's do it." I read the directions for raising the canopies while Freddie went and got the forklift. We probably could have done it without the forklift, but it made things a lot easier having it available.

Over the next three hours, Freddie and I put up the canopies and put out the chairs. Thankfully, it wasn't too hot, so we didn't need many breaks.

On my way back to the pallet of chairs, I saw Victoria walking toward us. I paused as she stopped near Freddie.

"It's time to stop for the day. Freddie, Charles needs you to look at something, and Preston, William, the owner of the suit company, called and will be in here about 30 minutes for your final fitting."

"I didn't know I had a final fitting. Let me take a quick shower, and I'll meet him in the library. Freddie, I'll help you finish setting up tomorrow. Let me know when."

"Sounds good. See you tomorrow." Freddie went around to the front of the house with Victoria while I walked through the house to my room. After a quick shower, I went to the library and waited for William to arrive.

It was another ten minutes before the doorbell rang, and Victoria directed William into the library. In Tony's arms was a garment bag.

"Good afternoon, William. I didn't realize I had a final fitting until Victoria mentioned it earlier today."

"We didn't initially plan to, but I wanted to have one in case. I would hate to bring the tux on your wedding day and have it not fit. Even if it was to happen, I know one of the best seamstresses in the state, but I don't really want to call her in if I don't have to."

"I appreciate your attention to detail. Let's get to it." Tony unzipped the bag while I took off my shirt and shorts. He pulled out the tux and handed me the pants, the shirt, and jacket as it was time to put each one on.

After I put everything on, William and Tony both walked around me as I stood there.

"Can you raise your arms?"

"Sure." I did so, and they did another circle.

"I don't mean to toot my own horn, but this tux looks like it was made just for you." William and Tony both laughed.

I knew it was a lame joke since the tux was literally made for me, but their laughter caused me to laugh as well.

"Everything fits well, so take it off, and Tony will put it back into the bag. Do you have any questions?"

"Not that I can think of."

"Perfect. Take the tux off, and we'll be out of here."

I handed the items to Tony as I removed them for him to put back into the garment bag.

After zipping it, he handed the bag to me before he and William headed to the door.

"Wait, do I need to pay you for this?" I hadn't thought to ask him how it was being paid for.

"No, your father is taking care of it. I hope you have a great ceremony." William waved and walked out of the house to his vehicle.

Looking at the garment bag in my hands, I shook my head before heading to my room to put it away. I wish there was something else I could help with. I thought about how there was still so much to do. After hanging my tux in the closet, I went back outside to continue setting up the chairs even though I said we would do it tomorrow.

Chapter Fifteen

3 Days Until the Wedding – Carlina

As I looked at my clock, I realized today was the day of my final fitting. I was oddly nervous about the wedding now. Probably because it was in three days away, and I wasn't ready to be married. There was nothing I could do unless I left, but I still hadn't received anything back from my family, so I didn't know if they even got the letter. I couldn't worry about it now with the wedding in three days.

Looking at the clock, I saw I had about two hours before we had to be at the store, so I got dressed and went downstairs for breakfast.

The house was quiet, so I assumed the twins were still sleeping, and Baron was at work, but I wondered where my mom was. She was usually somewhere in the house. I didn't see any notes or anything in the kitchen, so I got some cereal and sat at the island.

After finishing my cereal and banana, I wandered around the house. Still not hearing anyone, I made my way down the hall toward Baron's office.

He usually kept it locked if he wasn't home, even though he and my mom were the only ones who ever went in there. Heads would roll if we were ever caught in his office.

Putting my ear to the door, I didn't hear anything, so I tried the doorknob. Unexpectedly, it opened. For another ten seconds, I held my breath, listening. Once I realized no one was going to jump out and see me going into the office, I crept inside and closed the door quietly behind me. There was a wall of books I knew Baron had never read on one side of the room. Paintings and other memorabilia he kept were on the other side of the room. Two filing cabinets along the back wall flanked his large wooden desk, which occupied most of the room's center.

I glanced over the paperwork on his desk. Most of it looked like invoices, bills, and other mail. My eyes landed on a plain envelope with my name on it. It had been opened roughly, so I couldn't tell who it was from. My fingers had barely brushed the envelope when I heard my mom's voice coming from the kitchen. Snatching the letter, I ran to the door and peeked out. Not seeing anyone, I slipped out and put the envelope into my pocket. Near his office, I made my way into the bathroom and made a presentation of washing and drying my hands.

Beatrice and my mom were talking in the kitchen.

"Oh, I didn't know you were up. Where were you?"

"I had breakfast and needed to go to the bathroom, so I used the bathroom near the office."

"Sorry, I didn't make you anything to eat. I was out working in the garden because I didn't realize you were up, and Beatrice has only been up for a few minutes."

"Where's Annabelle?" I really didn't care, but it seemed like the right thing to say.

"Baron wanted her to go to work with him today," Mom said, while Beatrice shrugged.

"Since we have about an hour before we need to leave, Beatrice, do you want to come with us to the final fitting? This way, you aren't all by yourself here at the house." I asked. Not only did I want her to come, but I also didn't want to leave her in the house by herself. Sometimes I get lonely when I'm alone in the house, so I could imagine she did too.

"Really? Are you sure you don't mind?"

"Yes, please come with us." I could tell Beatrice really wanted to join us, but with Annabelle always demanding to be the center of attention, she was afraid to ask.

"Okay, I will. I'm so excited! I'll get changed so we can go." Beatrice practically floated to her room.

"I'm glad you invited her. She needs to get out of the house more," Mom said as she got ready to go.

"That's what I was thinking. So, what's going on with Annabelle and Baron?"

"I don't know, and I didn't ask. I know he yelled for her to come down and told her she was going to work with him." My mom shrugged.

"Does it really matter? I'm gonna go change, and I should be down close when we need to leave."

"Okay, I'll be ready."

***

I waited until I got to my room before I pulled the envelope from my pocket. I turned it over, hoping to see an address, but there was no return address. My name and address were on the envelope, but the return address appeared to have been ripped off. There was nothing else even on the other side. I'd never seen a stamp like the one used on the envelope, but since I didn't get much mail, I didn't know if the stamp meant anything special.

It had been refolded, so someone had read it and put it back into the envelope. I read the two short paragraphs.

Carlie,

It's so good to hear from you. I'm sorry we haven't been in contact sooner, but when your father died, we tried. Your mom was receptive in the beginning, but when she met her new husband, we stopped receiving any correspondence from her.

You're more than welcome to come visit or live here if you need to. I would caution you not to move before your 19th birthday to ensure you get your full inheritance. As you may not know, when your father died, all the paperwork was mailed to us. We have the original deed to the house, as well as his Will. Please call or visit soon.

Love,

Aunt Margaret and Uncle Matthew

If Baron hadn't known about the inheritance before, he did now. I can't believe he opened my mail. Never mind, I could totally believe he would do such a thing.

I placed it in the hiding spot under my bras and underwear where I normally put things I didn't want anyone to find and changed before heading downstairs.

I almost forgot Marie had told me to wear the undergarments I wanted to wear on the day of the wedding, so I changed again and left my room.

As I reached the bottom of the stairs, Beatrice jumped up from the couch, holding a box in her hands.

"Celeste said she was going to finish up on something she was doing upstairs and would be ready to go soon. Oh, and I got your shoes, you left them by the front door."

"Thank you for grabbing them; I probably would have forgotten them otherwise. I really am excited you're coming with us."

Beatrice rushed up and hugged me before I could say anything else.

I hugged her back and hoped this was a pivotal point in our relationship. I could have at least one sister, like I always wanted.

Ten minutes later, my mom came down and grabbed her purse. "Ready to go?"

Beatrice and I answered at the same time as we walked to the door, "Yup."

Beatrice climbed into the backseat, so my mom and I sat up front. We knew how to drive, but Mom liked to drive. I didn't mind because it gave her a chance to get away from the house, so I sat back and watched the trees and buildings pass by.

Arriving at the dress shop, all the parking spots were full, so we had to park almost a block away. Beatrice held my shoes as we walked side by side, with my mom leading the way.

"You know you don't have to hold my shoes."

"I know, but I should at least do something since I'm one of your bridesmaids."

I smiled as she skipped along. Holding open the door, my mom and I walked in, with Beatrice following behind. Not seeing anyone around, we walked to the center of the room. Marie came out with Darcy a short time later, both smiling. "Welcome back. You're here for your final fitting, right?"

"Yes, is Nancy here?"

"Yes, she's on the phone with a friend of hers, so she'll be here shortly. Carlie, if you want to come to the back with me, Darcy will sit up front with Celeste and..." she trailed off as she hadn't met Beatrice during my first fitting.

"This is Beatrice, my sister."

"Nice to meet you, Beatrice." Marie offered her hand for Beatrice to shake.

"Beatrice and Celeste, you can sit here with Darcy while I take Carlie to the back to put on her dress."

They sat as I followed her.

"Are you ready?"

"As ready as I'll ever be."

"Did you bring the undergarments you plan to wear with the dress?"

"Yes, I hope they'll work."

"Unless they're a weird pattern or solid black, I think they'll be fine."

"Wait? Has that happened?"

Marie laughed. "Oh, the stories I could tell. Short answer is yes, I've had my assortment of wild and crazy patterns trying to blend in under a wedding dress."

Laughing in response, I couldn't believe it. Even with how upset I was at getting married under these circumstances, it would never have even occurred to me to consider wearing something other than plain white under my dress. Even if the marriage didn't last, I still wanted the pictures to look good.

Removing my clothes, I stood there in my bra and panties while Marie held out the dress for me. Carefully, I stepped into the dress and turned so she could fasten the back. The dress was much tighter than the last time I tried it on, but it wasn't uncomfortable. Since it had only been a couple days, I knew it was my nerves causing me to feel like I was constantly out of breath.

"Okay, I'm done. Are you ready to see yourself?"

"Not really, but let's take a look." I moved so I could see in the mirror. I looked so much older than my 18 years, and I was really surprised by how much I liked how I looked. "Ready?" I asked Marie.

"Yup, I'm ready if you are. Let's go show your mom."

I took a deep breath and followed Marie out to the front of the store. I heard a small gasp from Beatrice, and I could see my mom's eyes tear up as I stepped into their view.

"How does it feel?" Nancy asked as she stepped out of the back room.

"Really good. It's tight but not too tight." I smoothed my hands down my sides.

"Perfect, exactly what we want. It should be form fitting but not so tight you can't breathe. How's the length?"

"Let me get my shoes." I realized Beatrice was already holding them and had brought them over.

Beatrice handed me the shoes before hugging me. "You look so pretty."

"Thank you." I hugged her back. Putting the shoes on, I straightened out my dress again before standing up straight.

"How is the length with your shoes on?"

I walked back and forth, trying out the shoes with the dress. It was perfect. "It's perfect, and I have no issues walking." I twirled a little, the skirt of the dress lifting in the breeze my twirl created.

"Great. So, I have your veil but changed it slightly to suit the theme. I heard from a friend it was a masquerade. If you don't like it, let me know, and I can take the mask off. Instead of having a veil and a mask separately, I've incorporated a mask into the veil, so it's one piece. Let me grab it." Nancy went into the back and brought out a box.

Opening the box, she pulled out a white veil with a white mask attached. While wearing, it would only cover the top half of my face.

"It's beautiful. What's it made of?"

She handed it to me, but I was afraid to take it. It looked so fragile.

"Don't worry, it isn't fragile. The mask itself is papier mâché, painted, and then coated with a thin layer of resin." Nancy knew exactly what I had been thinking.

I held it out, inspecting the fine blue filigree around the eyes and nose. I placed the mask on my face while Nancy helped adjust the veil.

"All done. Are you ready?" Nancy stepped away from me.

"Sure." Opening my eyes, I saw myself. I was a vision in the mirror. The mask felt perfect, as if it was made for me, but I guess it had been.

"Mom, Beatrice, what do you think?" I turned toward where they were sitting.

"You look beautiful." My mom dabbed at her eyes.

Beatrice covered her mouth with her hands. "Perfect. You look absolutely perfect."

I smiled before turning back to Nancy. "I guess we're good?"

Nancy smiled as I took the mask off and handed it back to her. "Yes, let's get you back into your normal clothes, and I'll pack up the mask and dress."

"Okay. Wait, can I have something added to the mask? How much do I owe you for the mask?"

"Of course, I can get it done now, what did you want to add?"

"Can you add a Monarch Butterfly, maybe here?" I pointed at a place above the right eye.

"Absolutely, let me just go back and get it done now. Also, you owe nothing. I told you the veil was part of the cost, and the mask is part of the veil."

I smiled before walking back to change out of the dress, with Marie following me.

"We'll put your dress into a cloth bag you can take with you. Remember to ask someone to help you fasten it and give yourself plenty of time to get dressed so you aren't rushed."

"Okay, thank you. Can you unfasten the back for me, please?"

"Of course."

I turned around for Marie to unfasten the back. When she finished, I slid it over my head, and she took it with her when she left the dressing room.

I changed back into my clothes and joined Nancy at the front of the store, where she was talking to Beatrice and my mom.

Darcy ran up to me. "You're so pretty in your dress."

I bent down to hug her. "Thank you, Darcy."

Marie handed me the garment bag containing my dress while Nancy handed Beatrice the box with my mask and veil. I could see my mom holding my shoes.

Double checking I had everything, I turned to Nancy.

"Thank you for everything." I awkwardly hugged her because of how big my dress was. She hugged me back.

"It was our pleasure. I hope your wedding is everything you hope it will be." Nancy watched as we left, with Darcy and Marie waving.

***

The entire ride home, all Beatrice could do was talk about how good I looked and how she was a little jealous of my dress. Her excitement was contagious even though I still didn't really want to get married, especially to someone I didn't know.

I carried my dress into the house, while Beatrice had my veil.

My mom had grabbed my shoes from the car.

Annabelle jumped up from the couch as soon as we walked through the door.

"Where have you been?"

"Carlie had her final dress fitting," my mom replied as Beatrice and I headed for the stairs.

"Why did you go, Beatrice?"

"Because I wanted to, and there was no one here, so I figured why not?"

Instead of responding, Annabelle flopped back onto the couch.

Beatrice shrugged, and we walked upstairs.

"Why was she all upset?" I asked Beatrice, stepping into my room.

"No idea. She doesn't usually care what I do, and she was busy, anyway. What was I supposed to do? Sit around waiting for her and doing nothing?"

"I don't know, but I'm glad you came with us." I smiled.

She placed the box and shoes she had taken from my mom on the bed.

"I'm glad I went too. Well, we should see what's for dinner."

"I'll be down in a bit." Beatrice gave a little wave as she left my room, softly closing the door behind her.

Sitting on the bed looking at the dress hanging on my closet door, I pulled out the letter I'd received from my aunt and read it again. Maybe I should leave and go to Canada. It could mean I'd lose everything, but it would be worth it, especially if anything Annabelle had said about the man I was supposed to marry was true.

Returning the note to its hiding spot, I stood and looked at the dress one more time before going downstairs.

Our nightly dinner was unusually quiet.

Annabelle was still upset Beatrice had gone with me but never explained why.

When my mom asked Baron why Annabelle went to work with him, he brushed it off as wanting to have her learn the business.

Even Annabelle wasn't forthcoming with what had happened, and she usually talked nonstop. She liked to brag about all the things she'd gotten to do if we hadn't.

Chapter Sixteen

1 Day Until the Wedding - Preston

"Preston, I need you to get in here right now," I heard my father yell from his office.

I rolled my eyes and left the kitchen, where I had finished breakfast. In his office, he was sitting behind his desk with his fingers steepled in front of his face.

"What's going on? I was finishing breakfast." Standing in front of his desk, I was tired of being controlled by him, but I had less than a year before I could carry through with my plans.

"Baron is sniffing around about the disappearance of Jack Hudson. He used one of his daughters as a lookout as he dug through files in the office at the warehouse."

I knew Baron was not a great person, and I had my own folder on him from the minute he'd started hanging around my father, but I didn't expect him to be this much trouble. Now that I remembered who he was, I was also worried about which daughter my father had chosen because she could also be a liability. I'd hate to marry someone to only have to kill her before the honeymoon was over.

"Did he find anything?"

"No, the office had initial files, but I guess he asked around. He called me this morning asking about Torx."

"Did you tell him anything?" I knew my father wouldn't, but I needed to be sure.

"Of course not, but he may become an issue."

"Father, he's already an issue. He has been ever since he offered up one of his daughters to pay off a debt."

Rubbing the bridge of his nose, he sighed. "I know, but right now, we need his connections for one of our businesses. The minute it's up and running, he's expendable."

I didn't know what type of relationship Baron had with his daughters, but I doubt they'd be happy to learn their new husband or brother-in-law had killed their father. I caught myself. What did I care what some rich bitch thought? Other than Victoria and Freddie, I had no one I cared about. Well, not entirely true. I had formed some friendships at the academy, but I didn't know if I'd kill for them. For Victoria and Freddie, I would in a heartbeat.

"Do you need anything else?" I wasn't sure why he'd yelled for me to tell me about Baron. The paperwork was still processing, so it wasn't like Torx was making us money yet. If we had to, we could cut it loose.

"No, I got confirmation the package arrived unable to communicate what had happened. The local police are writing it off as a transient who got stuck in a box."

I released a breath I hadn't realized I was holding. I was always careful, but there was always a small part of my brain wondering if I'd ever get caught.

"Good to hear. I strive for perfection. If there's nothing else, I need to get out and help Freddie finish setting up for tomorrow." My father waved as I walked out the door.

Chapter Seventeen

1 Day Until the Wedding - Preston

I laid in bed, one day before I'm to be handed off like livestock. The more I thought about it, the more I realized I didn't want to run from the wedding. I didn't want to be married, but the money I'd receive in less than a month would be enough to go anywhere I wanted. I could buy myself as many houses as I wanted.

We didn't have any family coming to the wedding because we really didn't have anyone to invite.

I finally got out of bed and ambled downstairs to see Annabelle and Beatrice sitting on the couch playing on their phones while I could hear my mom in the kitchen.

"What are you doing in here?"

"I wanted to make you your favorite meal for dinner. Your last day as a single woman," Mom said over her shoulder as she worked at the stove.

"It's okay, you don't need to go to the trouble. We could have anything for dinner." I knew she was making stuffed cabbage rolls, and it took a good part of the day to prep. It was a lot of work for only us to eat since the twins and Baron didn't like it.

"I wanted to, okay? You missed breakfast, but do you want something to eat? Why don't you go outside and sit in the garden? I'll bring you something to eat. Oh, I almost forgot, you need to pack tonight. Mr. Wessex's driver will be here tomorrow morning to pick up your belongings to take to your new house."

"Wait, what? Why can't I keep my stuff here? I could come back and grab it."

"I'm not sure. I guess Mr. Wessex offered and Baron accepted. Sorry I didn't tell you sooner. I only found out late last night."

"Can I at least go with him? I want to know where my stuff will be since I am getting ready at Charles' house."

My mom looked at me for a minute before answering, "I don't see why not. He could bring you to the main house before you need to get your stuff for the wedding."

"Thank you. I'm going to go back upstairs and start packing now. This way, I can make sure I have everything."

"Okay, I'll bring up something for you to eat in a few minutes."

"Thank you." I hugged her and went upstairs.

Getting into my room, I closed the door and sat on my bed. I looked around and realized I needed to figure out what I wanted to bring. Did I need furniture? Probably not, but maybe I would need my blanket. I didn't know if the new house was brand new with nothing or if it had everything I would need. I was pulling out my suitcases when I heard my door slowly open.

"Here's your snack. I also got some boxes for you in case you need them." My mom placed a plate of fruit and cheese on my desk.

"Mom, do you know if I'll need my furniture?"

"Doubtful, and if there isn't furniture, they have enough money to buy you anything you may need."

"I don't want to spend their money. I don't even want to leave this house."

Mom sat on the bed and watched me pull out the rest of my suitcases. "I understand, but this is something you need to do for the family."

"Why am I always the one being asked to make sacrifices. I don't see Annabelle being asked to do anything. No, the only thing I need to do for my family is to keep this house and not get married."

My mom was getting angry. "Carlie, you don't have a choice right now. Stay married, get your money, and live your life. There's no point in you staying in this house of sad memories. Go make new, wonderful memories."

The memories in this house were my memories of my family. Why didn't she understand? I wanted to keep the memories I had of this house and my father. The memory of my mom and dad laughing during Christmas and us watching a movie together in the living room where the twins were now always lounging around instead. I wanted my memories back. My life was more than appeasing some rich guy.

"Yes, Mom. Well, thank you for bringing me something to snack on. I should get to packing." There was no use telling her how I felt, considering she'd proven she didn't care.

She bowed her head before walking out of my room, shutting the door behind her. I thought I had heard her sniffle as she walked away, but it was too late for her tears. She had gone through with this, all of it, including essentially giving my house to Baron. I loved her, but right now I don't know if I liked her much.

It took me most of the day to pack everything. Beatrice was helpful and brought up boxes when the ones I had were full.

It was then I realized I wanted her as my maid of honor, but I wasn't going to tell her until tomorrow at the wedding. I had no energy to deal with Annabelle complaining about how I didn't choose her or some other nonsense.

Whatever my future looked like, I was determined to make the decisions myself and not allow others to dictate what happened.

After I finished packing, I looked around my room, realizing tonight might be the last night I saw this room. At least, the last night I might sleep in it. A tear slid down my cheek as I heard my mom yell up the stairs to let me know dinner was ready. I swiped it with my hand and walked downstairs with my head high. I wouldn't let anyone see how much this was affecting me.

***

Entering the dining room, I saw everyone was there except Baron.

Of course, the twins had ordered Chinese because they couldn't be bothered to eat what my mom had made.

As they dished up, I saw Beatrice take one of the cabbage rolls and put it on her plate.

"Thank you for making this, Mom." I took three cabbage rolls. This had been one of my favorite meals my father used to make. He would make it every Sunday for as long as I could remember. It was a family tradition and one I decided I wanted to carry on after this disaster of a marriage was over. Maybe I should start now to see how far I could push my future husband.

I saw Beatrice take a bite of the cabbage rolls and her close eyes in delight.

"This is incredible. I'm sorry I haven't tried them sooner." Beatrice finished her roll and reached for another.

"Thank you. Carlie's father used to make them all the time, and after years of waiting, I finally learned the recipe."

I smiled at her. I knew she was trying, but she could have done more, and sooner. As I finished eating, Baron walked through the door carrying a box of paperwork.

"You got here in time for cabbage rolls. Do you want one?" My mom walked over to take the box from him.

He stepped back from her so she couldn't touch the box before he went straight to his office.

My mom trailed behind him.

Annabelle and Beatrice looked at him strangely before returning to their food.

I wanted to know what was in the box, but at the same time, I didn't care. It was probably work stuff. Shrugging, I finished my food. Right as I was getting up to take my plate into the kitchen, I saw my mom leaving Baron's office, rubbing her arm.

She looked up and saw me staring at her, so she put both arms behind her back and returned to the table.

"I'm going to my room to finish packing and read some before bed. Tomorrow is a big day, and I'm kind of tired." I knew I'd already finished packing, but I didn't want to do something inane like watch TV with the twins or talk to my mom. I wanted to go to my room and space out.

"Baron said the driver will be here at 10 am to move your stuff, and you're welcome to go."

Oh, I'm welcome to go? Wow, thanks Baron. You're so generous.

Instead of saying it out loud, I nodded.

Up in my room, I tried to memorize every room in the house because part of me knew I wouldn't see it again. Deep in my heart, I knew I wouldn't be back.

I finished packing and laid in my bed, looking at my bare room. I realized after I left there would be nothing in this room to remind the others of who had slept here. It was strange but also freeing in a way.

Chapter Eighteen

0 Days Until the Wedding – Carlina, morning

"Carlie, you need to get up. Seth is here to move your stuff to your new house."

I blinked and pulled my blankets over my head as my mom threw my curtains open.

"I thought you said he would be here at 10?" I mumbled from under the blankets.

"It's 9:50, and he's here a little early, so get up." My mom was bright and cheery.

I looked for my clock only to realize I'd already packed it away. I didn't know what time it was. Hearing it was almost 10, I jumped out of bed and threw clothes around, trying to find where I put the clothes I'd planned to wear before the wedding.

"Don't rush. Your clothes are on your dresser, and I made breakfast for you. We can eat while he's moving your stuff."

I quickly put my pj's into the closest box I could find and closed it. I followed my mom down to the kitchen and saw Seth and two men standing in the living room.

Seth had a small smirk while the other two looked bored to be there.

Silently, I walked into the kitchen where my mom had made French toast and bacon. It was my favorite breakfast, so I knew she'd make it for me one last time. Sitting at the island table, I watched Seth and the other two go upstairs.

"Did you tell them which room was mine?" I asked around my French toast.

My mother may be many things, but at least she could make great French Toast and crisp my bacon perfectly.

"Of course. Did you expect them to go through the rooms until they found the one full of boxes?"

I hadn't thought about it and maybe exactly what they would do.

Finishing the second slice, I saw the two guys walking down with two boxes, followed by Seth, who had a large box. I knew I hadn't packed them light, so it surprised me to see them each carrying two of the boxes.

Over the course of the next 30 minutes, I watched my life go out the door two boxes at a time. I was standing by the back door looking over the garden when I heard someone clear their throat.

"Miss, if you're ready to go, we're ready to leave." Seth stood with his hands clasped in front of him.

"Thank you, I guess I am." I smiled as I looked at the garden one last time.

"Miss, please forgive me if I'm overstepping, but would you like to show me the garden before we leave?"

"I would love to. Thank you, Seth." Even though I know we were on a time crunch, the fact Seth wanted to check out the garden showed me he was a good person, even if Charles may not be.. I tried to memorize exactly what the garden looked like because I knew no one would take as good care of it as I did. I swept a tear away before Seth saw it.

"This was the garden my father and I built years ago. I think I was five when we started it. We planted all these flowers. See how the colors change gradually? We did it together."

Showing him around, I stopped at my favorite flowers and explained what the unique plants were. "It's very nice, Miss. Thank you for showing me. Are you ready to see your new home?" Seth opened the door for me to walk through.

"Sure, will you have time to take me to the main house? That's where I am getting ready, I think. We can't stay long okay? The wedding is today, there is so much to do. I don't—"

Seth held up his hand as I rambled.

"You're going to see your new house because your belongings are going there. Victoria, I believe you met her? She'll be there to help you get ready, as will your seamstress, Nancy, in case you need anything. You'll also need to sign the prenup, which I have waiting for you at the house."

Confused by why my seamstress and Mr. Wessex's housekeeper would be at the house, I stumbled on my words, "Why? Who? Why?"

Seth stepped closer. "I'll explain everything in the car. Shall we go?"

I followed him out the front door to see two black SUVs. Unsure which SUV to get into, I stood at the bottom of the steps while Seth walked to the one in the back first. The two men had been standing between the two SUVs said something before getting into the rear SUV. Seth moved to the passenger door of the first one.

"Do you want to sit in the front with me or in the back?"

"Can I sit in the front? I don't want you to feel like you're driving me around. Wait, did everything fit into the SUVs?"

Seth laughed. "Yes, it did. The other one doesn't have back seats, so there was plenty of room. I'm driving you around, though."

I moved my head to hide my smile. "Yes, but I don't want it to feel like it, though. Can we agree on those terms?"

"Fair enough." Seth opened the front passenger door, and I climbed inside. I watched him walk around the front of the car before I looked back at the house. Instead of watching it as we pulled away through the side mirror, I faced forward. It's where my life would be, not back in the house my father built.

I turned to Seth. "Okay, so what's happening?"

He didn't take his eyes off the road. "Preston felt you would want to know where your stuff was going to be, so he wanted you to see the house and be comfortable with it before going to the main house for the wedding. Yes, Victoria is the cook and housekeeper, but she's close to Preston. She thought maybe you'd be more comfortable with her there, at least for a bit, before she goes back to the main house to finish preparing the desserts. Nancy's a good friend of Victoria's and wanted to be there, again with your permission, in case you need any alterations on your dress day of."

"That's very thoughtful of Preston. Please thank him for me. Do my mom and stepsisters know the change of location for where I'm getting ready? I was supposed to get ready at the same house as the wedding."

"Yes, your mother and stepsisters do, but Baron is not welcome at your new home. Heck, after I drop off all your stuff, I don't know if I'm welcome there." Seth laughed.

"Why wouldn't you be welcome?" I couldn't figure out why Seth couldn't come to the house.

"Oh, no, sorry. Just a small joke, I'm saying after Preston sees you, I don't know if he'll allow another man anywhere near you with how beautiful you are."

I didn't have a response to that. After hearing all the things from Annabelle and Beatrice, I was slightly worried about what type of man Preston was. But, I also had butterflies jumping around in my stomach. I'd never had a man be protective of me since my father had died. Instead of putting my foot into my mouth more than I felt I already had, I mumbled, "Oh."

The rest of the ride was quiet, and quick updates came from the radio Seth had hooked up to the dash.

After about 30 minutes, we pulled off the main paved road onto a gravel driveway. On both sides were large trees which blocked the view of the house from the road. As we turned a corner, the house came into view. It was a two-story brick house which resembled the large house I had met Mr. Wessex in those short two weeks ago, but it was smaller and looked more rustic. Vines climbed for the upper windows, and the large, dark brown double-doors stood out against the lighter brick. The round, gravel driveway was wide enough for three cars, which was good because two cars, a red SUV and a blue pickup sat near the stairs.

Seth pulled up past the two cars and backed into the space in front of the pickup until he was almost touching the bumper while the other SUV parked next to him but in front of the red SUV. The second SUV that loaded my stuff backed up, facing away from the front door.

I waited for everyone to get out and start unloading, but no one did. I looked at Seth with confusion.

"Preston wanted you to choose your room, so you need to go in and decide before we bring things inside. Are you ready to see your new home?"

I took a deep breath before nodding.

Seth jumped out of the SUV and opened the door for me. "They'll be moving Preston's stuff into his room during the wedding."

"Wait, we won't be in the same room?" I was confused. Married couples always slept in the same bed, right? Does he already not want me? My emotions were all over the place.

"He'll explain why he felt having separate rooms is best. It's not my story to tell."

I felt my chest fall. Great, he doesn't want me. I don't even know if I wanted him, but maybe there was a small inner voice hoping this whole thing would be a blessing in disguise.

"Okay."

As we walked inside, I could hear familiar voices behind a set of matching doors, but I ignored them as I followed Seth upstairs.

The staircase was dark wood with a red and black runner.

I ran my hands over the shined railing. This was going to be my home in less than 12 hours. No, it was already my home.

"There are four bedrooms and three bathrooms. The two main bedrooms have separate full bathrooms, and the other two bedrooms share a bathroom in a Jack and Jill configuration."

"I want one of the bedrooms with the ensuite bathroom, please."

"I had a feeling you'd say that, so here's one of the main bedrooms." He opened the eggshell blue door to a large room with a light-wood canopy bed. There were matching dressers and nightstands.

I moved around the room, inspecting everything. There was a high-backed chair next to a window overlooking a large field. I opened the door to the walk-in closet and went over to the bathroom. The tile floor continued under a free-standing tub and a large shower. Across from the shower, there was a double sink with a silver countertop and faucet. Two round silver mirrors hung above the sinks.

"Will you please show me the second room?" It was a beautiful room, but I didn't want to choose it without seeing the other one first. The little power I felt by being able to choose the room first made me giddy. I wasn't used to being allowed to make my own choices.

"Right this way."

We walked through the blue door and took a right down a short hallway to a light green door.

Looking back at the blue door, Seth answered before I could ask. "The bathrooms are next to each other. It helped with installing the plumbing when they built the house. The other two bedrooms are just there on the other side of the stairs."

I considered looking at the other two also, but I didn't want to share a bathroom with anyone if I didn't have to.

Seth opened the green door for me.

The room was the mirror opposite of how the blue room was set up. The furniture was a darker wood, but otherwise the rooms were arranged the same. I went into the bathroom expecting to see the same thing, and mostly it was, except the tile countertop was gray with gold flecks, and it had a built-in bathtub. Leaving the bathroom, I stopped by the window with a matching high-backed chair overlooking the same field. Out of the corner of the window, I could see another building.

I pointed at it. "What's that building? Does Preston have a barn?"

"The old carriage house is now Preston's, and now your garage."

"Oh, I don't have a car."

Seth smirked. "I'm sure Preston will remedy that soon."

"Oh. He doesn't need to buy me a car. I want to buy my own things."

"I can respect your wishes, Miss, but if Preston says he's buying you a car, I suggest you let him buy you a car." He clinched his jaw, as if to mean if Preston wants something, Preston gets it.

Against my better judgement, I asked, "Why?"

"Preston is used to getting what he wants."

"Oh, okay."

He still hadn't answered my question, but I could tell he didn't really want to, so I was okay with it.

"Do you know which room you want?" Seth changed subjects as we walked back into the hall.

"Maybe you should show me the other two, just in case."

"They're much smaller and have terrible views. These are the two best rooms."

"Yes, but they're so close together."

"You're assuming Preston will pick the other main room?"

"True, but as you said, the other two are much smaller and have terrible views."

"Touche. I still think one of these would be better."

"Okay, if you insist. I want the one with the blue-door."

"Great, let's get you downstairs to get ready for your wedding, and I'll get everything moved in."

Seth smiled as he turned to go down the stairs. "Miss, your life is about to change, and only in the best possible ways."

I didn't respond because I didn't quite believe him. I was hoping so, but I had my doubts.

At the bottom of the stairs, Seth stopped in front of the doors I'd noticed earlier. As they opened, Victoria, Nancy, Darcy, and Marie all stood from the couches they'd been sitting on.

"Well, I'll get the men to work on carrying your boxes in. Oh, before I forget, can you sign this prenup so I can get it back over to the Wessex house?" Seth sat the document on the coffee table.

I read the draft twice, so I could be sure I knew what it said. Scribbling my name on the last page, I laid the pen down.

"Thank you. Please let me know if you need anything." Seth backed out of the room and slid the doors closed.

"We won't, but thank you," Victoria answered as the doors slid shut.

Nancy and Marie giggled at her response as they looked at me.

"Are you ready?" Nancy asked.

"No, but it's happening either way. What are you doing here?" I walked over and hugged her before hugging Marie and Darcy.

"Well see, Victoria is my best friend, and she mentioned the other day while we were doing flowers how this wonderful young woman was marrying our Preston, and I couldn't believe it was you. So, when Victoria asked if I wanted to help get you ready, I jumped at the chance."

"You didn't have to help." The fact these women I didn't even know were willing to help me settled some of my nerves about the wedding.

"No, we didn't. Victoria said you probably didn't have a flower girl, and well, we couldn't let you get married without one, so we twisted Darcy's arm."

"Grandma, you didn't hurt me. You asked me if I wanted to get dressed up."

Nancy smiled down at Darcy. "It's a figure of speech. We're joking about twisting your arm."

"Thank you, all of you. Was the dress I saw Darcy in at the store her flower girl dress?"

"It was. Grandma wanted to make sure it fit just right." Darcy beamed at my question.

"Now I need to wait for my mom and stepsisters to get here, and I can get ready."

"I have something for you to snack on while we wait." Victoria pulled out a cart full of small sandwiches and a carafe filled with light yellow liquid. "You need to eat because there's a long time between now and dinner, which will be amazing."

I smiled as I looked at the women around me. They weren't family, but they treated me better than mine ever had.

"Oh, one more thing, I'm going to ask Beatrice to be my maid of honor. This could cause issues with Annabelle."

"Don't worry, if she causes any issues, I'll handle her." Marie popped her knuckles.

I laughed, but based on how Victoria was looking at her, I thought she might be serious.

It took an hour for the movers to finish, and it was another half an hour before my mom and the twins arrived.

Mom looked around at all the women in the room before hugging me. "Sorry it took so long. Annabelle couldn't find her shoes."

I mumbled under my breath that maybe she should have left her behind, but I made sure no one heard me.

"So, this is your new house? It's nice. Do we have time to look around?" Beatrice held her dress bag over her arm.

"My dress! I forgot it!" I yelled. Things were so rushed this morning I forgot to grab it from the closet where I'd hung it the night before.

"It's okay. Seth grabbed it for you." Nancy opened the kitchen door, and both the dress and the box containing my veil were there with my shoes on top of the box.

"Oh, I need to send him thank you chocolates or something." I put my hand over my frantically beating heart.

"Trust me, he doesn't need chocolates." Marie's eyes twinkled.

With the potential dress disaster resolved, I looked at Victoria. "Do I have time to show Beatrice the house? I don't know much about it or my way around yet, but can I show her my room?"

"If you want to run up and show her your room, you have time, but make it quick. We're on a tight schedule."

"Perfect, let's go." I hauled Beatrice out of there before anyone could say a word. Even Annabelle just stood here, dumbfounded.

I practically ran up the stairs. "I have something to show you and to ask you."

"She said we didn't have much time, but I don't think we need to run," Beatrice said as we reached the top of the stairs.

"Sorry, I wanted to get up here before Annabelle tries to join us. This is my room."

I opened the door expecting to find boxes, but there were only three on my bed. I opened the closet and saw Seth had hung all my clothes. At the dresser, I opened the drawers to find all my clothes neatly placed.

Worried about the note from Aunt Margaret and Uncle Matthew I'd hidden, I rushed to open the box labeled 'intimates' to find my underwear and bras, along with the box I kept important things in. Inside, I found the note exactly as I had left it. I took a deep breath and pretended nothing was wrong. If Beatrice had noticed, she didn't say anything.

"Wow, this is your room. Like, just yours?" She wiggled her eyebrows at the comment.

"Yes, Preston decided he wanted me to have my own room for now. He'll be choosing his later, I guess."

"Wow, maybe the things Annabelle found out about him were wrong?"

"What was I wrong about?" Annabelle came through the door.

"Nothing, we were talking about how this is Carlie's room, and Preston will be in another room."

"I'm sure he told you a lovely story, but knowing what I know of him, he'll be in your room tonight, whether you like it or not."

Beatrice gasped. "Annabelle, stop."

"It's okay. Since you're both here, I have something I'd like to ask. Beatrice, will you be my maid of honor?"

Beatrice ran up and hugged me. I could see she was tearing up as she said yes.

I could practically see the steam coming out of Annabelle's ears.

"Perfect, let's go get ready." I didn't give Annabelle a second glance as she stormed out of the room. Beatrice and I followed her downstairs.

Downstairs, I told the group about Beatrice being my maid of honor. Not like she was really doing anything, anyway. Hell, I didn't even know if she felt bad for me having to get married or if she was just happy it wasn't her marrying someone she didn't know.

Marie did my hair and makeup before I was sent to my room with Nancy to put on my dress.

"Look, I know you don't know me well, but I want you to know something; Preston isn't a bad guy. He isn't a good guy, but he isn't a bad guy," Nancy said quietly.

I was about to ask what she meant, but my mom came in asking if I needed help.

"No, I think we're almost done. Are the twins ready?" I asked my mom.

"Annabelle said she forgot something at the house and is running back to grab it, but Beatrice is ready."

"Then I think we're ready. Thank you for helping me, Nancy." I hugged her again before going back into the living room.

Marie and Darcy were waiting for me to come in.

"Let's get your mask and veil on before we leave. Unless you want to wait until we get there?" Beatrice asked while she held both her mask and my mask with its connected veil.

"Can we wait? I would hate to sit on the veil or something and ruin it."

"Victoria had to go back to the main house to finalize a few things." Marie handed me my bouquet.

"Should we wait for Annabelle? I don't want to make everyone wait for her."

Nancy made a face. "If she isn't back, then she isn't back. The bride waits for no one."

"Then let's go get married." I held the bouquet up as I looked at the women surrounding me. I smiled at Beatrice as she waited for me to go before her to the car.

Ready or not, the wedding was happening.

Chapter Nineteen

"Preston, are you ready? The wedding is starting in an hour," my dad yelled from downstairs.

I'd finished putting on my cufflinks when I wondered if I should carry my knife during the wedding. There would be enough security at the wedding, so I decided against it. Peering at my reflection in the mirror, I realized I was too young to get married, yet here I was about to marry some spoiled rich girl. Shaking myself out of it, I heard the door as it opened, and Evan walked in.

"Evan, what are you doing here?" I hugged my friend while patting him on the back.

"A little birdy told me you were getting married, and there was no way I was going to miss you tying the knot. So, I had dad fire up the jet and got here about 20 minutes ago." Evan stood in a sleek dark suit, his longer hair in a ponytail.

I'd met Evan at school, and we became fast friends. He was a very talented computer hacker, and there had been times our skills worked well together. He also happened to be the son of a crime boss in the southwest states, so our family lives were similar.

"I little birdy, huh?" I tried to think of who knew Evan was a friend of mine who also knew I was getting married.

"Well, since you're here, which I'm grateful for, will you stand by my side as my best man?"

"I thought you'd never ask." Evan laughed. "So, who's the lucky lady? One of the girls from school?"

Sighing, I explained to Evan the plan my dad had concocted.

"Wow, I'm sorry. That sucks, my friend. Well, I saw a blonde flying down the road on my way here. She almost hit me on the last corner before the house. Maybe there won't be a wedding after all?"

Interesting, wonder what's going on.

"Most likely her sister. Did I tell you they're twins?"

"You're marrying a twin? I'm sorry. I dated a set at one point, and it wasn't worth it. Well, it was very worth it for a while, but then it became boring, and there was too much drama."

"Thanks for the reassurance." I looked out the window at the canopy I would soon be married under.

"Hey, not to talk business on your wedding day, but my father has a job he needs you to do."

"Oh? Yeah, let me get married, get her settled into the house with her allowance, and then I'll get ahold of you."

"Sounds great. You ready for this?" Evan and I made our way downstairs.

"As ready as I'll ever be."

"First to marry out of us three friends, doesn't surprise me with your bad boy looks." Evan smirked as I tried to punch his arm.

Turning the corner at the bottom of the stairs, I almost ran into Victoria. I was used to seeing her in skirts and plain dresses, but today she was all dressed up with her hair and make-up done.

"Do you need anything? Evan and I can help if you do."

"No dear, we're all good. The food is ready to be brought out for the reception, and Mr. Teller is in the office with your father discussing last-minute details, at least from what I heard as I came in from the other house."

"Speaking of which, I should probably introduce myself to Mr. Teller. Did the bride's wedding party get settled? Victoria, do you know if Seth had time to show Annabelle around before she needed to get ready?"

A brief look of confusion came over Victoria's face before I heard my father calling my name. Not letting her answer, I kissed her cheek. "I need to go see what Father wants. Evan, can you help Victoria if she needs anything?"

Evan bobbed his head before offering the crook of his arm to Victoria, who smiled at him as they walked out toward the garden.

I watched them walk away before turning toward my father's office. Knocking lightly, I opened the door to find him sitting at his desk with another man sitting across from him.

They stood as I entered. The minute I saw Baron Teller's face, I knew who he was, but I kept my face neutral to see if he recognized me.

His facial expression never changed as he introduced himself.

My father subtly nodded when I looked at him. He knew I recognized Baron, but Baron had no idea who I was.

"It's nice to finally meet you, Preston. You father was telling me about you." Baron offered me his hand, and I shook it.

It felt like a snake was sliding through my stomach as I shook his hand.

I could tell by my father's reaction he had not told him much, if anything, about me, but I kept up the ruse. "I hope nothing but good things."

"Of course, even though my daughters have been digging into your past for the last two weeks. Your father has assured me everything online is fake, and I shouldn't be worried about you marrying my ste— my daughter."

The slip caught me off guard. What was he about to say before he corrected himself?

Biting my tongue, I cleared my throat. "I'm glad everything's working out then. I look forward to this wedding and bringing our two families together."

Baron smiled broadly at my father. "So do I. Well, I best get out there to walk the bride down the aisle. I'll see you later." He shook my hand one more time before he walked out, humming a tune.

Waiting a couple minutes, I went out into the hall and looked both ways to make sure he was gone before I came back to finish speaking with my father.

I stepped closer to my father. "You didn't tell me it was *that* Baron Teller."

My father smugly replied, "How many Baron Tellers do you know? I only know of one, and if I had connected the dots for you, what would you have done?"

"What deal did you make behind my back, Father?"

"I don't know what you mean. You know everything."

"You and I both know that's a lie. My marriage for a business? Carte blanche to continue trafficking? Does the daughter I'm marrying know about her father's businesses?"

Father grabbed my arm and pulled me away from people who had started paying attention to our conversation. "Listen, this marriage didn't give him permission to do anything, and it doesn't give him a business. It keeps him in line, do you understand? He currently owes his bosses millions of dollars. I have floated some, but if he keeps it up, I won't be able to help him. There is no way he wants to go against the Bartone Syndicate. He cares about his daughters more than anything else, so by us having one with our last name, it keeps him in check. It's not like knowing who it was would have changed anything."

"It could have. Maybe instead of agreeing to your conditions, I could have killed her during the honeymoon, so he knows what it's like to lose someone close to him. But no, I have to be married to her and share a house with this filth for a full year."

"Preston, please calm down. Everything will work out in the end. Can you please trust me?"

I realized I was pacing. "Trust you? You should have told me."

"And have you start a fire before the kindling was prepared."

I hated my father's idioms sometimes. I understood what he meant, but it was still annoying.

"The fire was lit when we had to rescue Marie, and her friend was killed. I was the one who had to see the bodies of all the girls who we weren't able to save, not you…"

"If you say so, but you need to remain neutral and get through this wedding. Do you understand?"

Grinding my teeth, I slumped into the chair opposite him. "Yes, I do, but I don't like it."

"I'm not asking you to."

"Fine. Are you ready to get this sham of a wedding started?"

My father walked around the desk and put his hand on my shoulder. "I only do what's best for you. Please don't ever forget that."

Shrugging it off, I stood. "Yeah, I remember."

His words were hollow, especially knowing who my future father-in-law was. With what I knew, I was going to have to be careful about what I told my future bride. I couldn't risk her running back to Baron and telling him what I had planned. This day got a lot more complicated.

***

Walking out to the lawn with my father, I greeted and shook hands with people I knew. Most of the attendees were business acquaintances of my father's or community leaders. I saw Freddie and Victoria sitting in the front row on my side, Victoria already holding a tissue. Even with their masks on, I knew most of the people here.

Evan stood next to the officiant with a huge grin on his face. Despite our pasts, he was one of the happiest guys I knew, and it made me smile. I also knew he would be by my side no matter what, and the reassurance helped. Not only in life, but as I walked down the aisle.

Shaking hands with the officiant, I hugged Evan again and faced the audience. Not only was every seat filled, but there were guests standing near the back. So much for a 'small' wedding. The wedding of the heir to my father's companies was apparently a monumental event. It should be, but it didn't feel special to me. It normally was something to get through and get past.

Evan leaned over, whispering in my ear, "I saw one of the bridesmaids. She is *hot.*"

Assuming he was talking about the redhead, I wanted to punch him for even looking at her, let alone complimenting her beauty. Knowing he didn't mean disrespect, I nodded and whispered back, "Yeah, they're all really pretty."

Before he could respond, the officiant asked everyone to please settle down, and the music started. Everyone grew quiet as I saw Baron and his wife walking down the aisle to find their seats. Baron's grimace turned into a smile when he caught me watching.

I smiled at him before looking at the next person walking down.

Marie's little cousin, Darcy, was the flower girl. Her pastel pink dress fluttered as she jumped down the aisle with a basket of flowers. Her mask was white and covered with little flowers. Every few steps, she threw out a handful of multi-color flower petals.

She ran up to me after her basket was empty. "Preston, Marie told me to tell you to close your eyes when the bride music starts playing." She hugged me and jumped over to the other side.

I didn't know Marie and Darcy were going to be here, so I scanned the crowd for Marie. Even with the masks, I finally found her standing next to Seth as she finger-waved. I rolled my eyes and tipped my head back as someone else began their walk down the aisle.

I almost choked on seeing the bright pink mini-dress. This was a wedding, not a nightclub.

The dress barely covered the blonde's ass, and the way she sauntered down the aisle trying to get every man's attention made me sick. Her mask only covered the top half of her face, so I saw her smirk at me as she leaned in to give me a half hug, making sure her chest rubbed against my side before standing on the bride's side.

The next woman down the aisle wasn't the red head like I expected but the other twin instead. She was wearing a lavender dress, and Evan leaned in.

"Isn't she perfect?"

All I could do was mumble, 'huh uh' as the bridal procession music started.

I looked over at Darcy, who had closed her eyes. Knowing I would never hear the end of it if I didn't close my eyes, I did as she'd asked.

After about 30 seconds, Evan tapped my shoulder. I opened my eyes and saw the flaming red hair cascaded across her shoulders as she walked down the aisle by herself.

The dress fitted her perfectly, and her hair highlighted the blush color. She had on a half mask, so it shielded me from seeing her face. A large monarch butterfly was painted above the right eye of her mask. The presence of the butterfly almost brought a tear to my eye, it was like my mother was there. I couldn't see her eyes as her head was down. The smug look on my father's face told me he'd known I was marrying her the whole time. But why didn't he tell me?

As they got closer, the blonde smiled at me before taking the spot next to her twin. I could see her eyes narrow as she looked at her sister, but she didn't say anything.

I heard the bride gasp as she looked up and saw the twin in the pink dress before she composed herself and stepped up across from me.

All I could see was her, and I felt like my vision was blurring around the edges. I could see her eyes were glassy.

I leaned down and asked her, "Are you okay?"

"Yes. Let's get this over with." She blinked back the tears, and whatever was going on with her caused me pain.

I caught myself thinking I wanted to take away her pain and bring her happiness for the rest of my days as I heard the officiant start the ceremony.

Chapter Twenty

0 days Until the Wedding – Carlina - Afternoon

"Where is Annabelle?" I asked, not really caring but not wanting to cause more drama.

"She called and said she's pulling in. Let's get you back into the room so Darcy and the twins can go out first, while you wait for Baron," my mom said as she stood around, fretting.

"Mom, I'm going to walk alone. I don't need, or want, someone to 'give me away'. Beatrice will walk in front of me, and you can go first with Baron and sit."

I could see she wanted to argue, but I wasn't budging. At this point, I would rather there be no wedding at all than walk down the aisle with Baron. It was supposed to be my dad, not some man who pretended to be my father only when it suited him.

Instead of arguing, she walked out the door and left Nancy, Beatrice, and I.

"Are you sure you want to walk alone? I mean, it's your choice, but..." Beatrice quietly said.

"Yes, I want something to be what I want, and we both know Annabelle is up to something."

Beatrice was wringing her hands. "I hope not, but you're probably right. Maybe I should go out earlier to check?"

I gently grabbed her arm. "No, please stay here with me."

She smiled. "Okay, I will."

Nancy cleared her throat. "Okay, your veil and mask are ready to go on. Are you ready, soon to be Mrs. Preston Wessex?"

"As I'll ever be."

Nancy placed the veil on my head and adjusted the mask.

Looking in the mirror, I couldn't believe I was seeing myself.

Nancy went to sit with Marie after hugging me one more time.

I was nervous to finally be face to face with Preston. I knew the eyes I saw the day of our lunch with his father were his, but to see the rest of him, I didn't even know how tall he was.

Beatrice looked at me from behind her mask with lavender sprigs painted on. "Ready?"

"Let's go." I took her arm, and we approached the doors. She helped me walk through to the canopy. She stopped and hugged me again before turning and stepping forward. Waiting for her to get to the altar, I didn't look up and waited for the music to change.

The music changed, and I slowly made my way up the aisle, focusing on the floor until I looked up. Immediately, I saw was Annabelle in the bright pink dress I'd told her not to wear.

The smirk she wore in addition to the god-awful dress caused me to see red. I couldn't believe, of all days, she would do this to me. Then again, I could believe it, but I'd hoped against hope she wouldn't.

I looked into the blue eyes which had kept me up at night since I first saw them two weeks ago. Standing next to him was a man of almost the same height. If I didn't know better, they could have been brothers.

Feeling him enter my personal space, his deep voice vibrated. "What's wrong?"

I didn't want to tell him. If I told him, I'd start crying and everyone would see. I had to be strong. "It's nothing."

He took a deep breath as he nodded before he leaned back.

His eyes were frost blue, and I couldn't tell what he was thinking. It looked like compassion or maybe concern, but from everything I'd heard, compassion wasn't in his vocabulary.

My eyes were glued to Preston as the officiant spoke. Even though I couldn't see his entire face, I saw the visible part was chiseled. Suddenly, I wanted to run my fingers through his hair. *What is wrong with me? I'm marrying him to save my house.*

The officiant asked, "Do you, Preston Charles Wessex, take this woman as your bride...", and I zoned out as I watched his lips form the word "Yes".

I realized I'd been holding my breath, hoping this was all a joke. It was my turn.

Chapter Twenty-One

I couldn't believe I was marrying this beautiful woman. The officiant asked if I took her as my bride, and I couldn't say yes fast enough.

The officiant began my bride's section of the vows, but my brain didn't fully register what he was saying until he said, "Do you Carlina Antonia Bartone take this man as your husband?" I looked at my father sharply when her last name was spoken.

His eyes showed the same sense of surprise as mine did.

I forced my face to be neutral as I watched her look up at me as she quietly said, "Yes".

I felt my heart jump as she said it, and I knew I was done for. No matter what, Carlina was mine, and I was going to do everything in my power to keep her mine.

I couldn't stop staring at her eyes as the officiant went through the rest of his speech until I heard him say, "By the power vested in me by the state of Oregon, I now pronounce you husband and wife. You may kiss the bride."

I'd never wanted to do something more than I wanted to kiss Carlina right now, but I didn't want to spook her.

I leaned in until our noses were almost touching. "May I kiss you?" I saw the heat in her eyes before she simply consented with the smallest tip of her head.

I took a breath and pulled her close. Even with the mask on, she was the most beautiful woman I'd ever seen. I leaned close and softly kissed her, pulling her closer. I heard her moan slightly and smiled against her lips before I stepped back, admiring her.

Oh, she was going to be so much fun, but I wanted to go slow. I didn't want to scare her and have her leave me.

I felt Evan slap me on the back as I turned and gave her my arm.

She grasped it, and we walked down the aisle while the guests clapped. Reaching the house, I saw Seth standing there with Marie.

"It was such a beautiful wedding. So now you and Carlie will have some time alone together before the photographer comes in to take your photos. She'll knock when it's time." Nancy and Marie each hugged us before leaving to go back to wherever everyone else was.

I sat on the couch and gestured for her to sit next to me.

She moved her dress around so she could sit facing me.

"I guess I should introduce myself?" Laughing, I was suddenly nervous. Her beauty had me tongue tied, which was new for me.

"Considering the fact we're married now, I think it's a little late for introductions, but sure. My family calls me Carlie, but my full name is Carlina as I am sure you are aware of."

"Preston Charles Wessex, people just call me Preston. Some people call me PC, as in 'Prince Charming' as a joke."

I saw a slight roll of her eyes.

"Oh, I wanted to thank you for allowing me to choose my own room. I hope you're okay with the room you have."

I honestly had no idea which room had Seth put me in. I know one of the smaller bedrooms was going to become my armory and office, but other than those rooms, I didn't know what he had planned.

"Of course. I want you to feel welcome. It's your house too, after all."

I saw a sense of sadness in her eyes, but she smiled. "No, it's our house now, since we're, you know, married and all."

"So, before the photographer gets in here, will you tell me why you were so upset earlier?"

"My stepsister, Annabelle, the one in the pink? She wasn't supposed to wear what she did."

"Oh, the dress which was more suited for a nightclub than a wedding? I did wonder about the clothing choice."

She laughed lightly, and I knew I'd made her feel better.

"Yeah, I wanted one thing, well, two things. You'll probably think they're silly, though."

I lifted her chin as she looked down at her hands. "I'm sure you'll say many silly things over the course of our marriage. It isn't like I had a choice to marry you either, after all." The moment it left my mouth, I knew I sounded like a dick. It wasn't intentional... or was it?

I saw fire in her eyes at my comment before she responded, "Well, I've decided I don't want to tell you now."

I took her hand from her lap. "Your choice. Tell me or don't, but I won't beg for you to speak to me."

She bit her bottom lip like she didn't want to say what she was thinking.

The sight of her biting her lip went straight to my cock. Hopefully, she didn't notice me straining against my pants.

"What do you want to say? Trust me, I've probably been called worse."

Not saying anything, she pulled her hand back and stood. She didn't look at me as she walked to the door, as a knock came from the other side.

"Look Princess, you can dislike me, you can even hate me, but we're married, and you're living in *our* house. So, let's pretend for the cameras, okay?" I regretted my tone, but the fire in her eyes made me want to do it more.

I could see she was about to cry, but she brushed the tears away before they could fully form.

I stood and walked behind her to the door, placing a hand on the back of her neck as I opened it.

The photographer stood there smiling. "Ready?"

"Yes, and can we make sure we get photos by the fountain?"

"Absolutely."

For the next hour, we took photos with and without our masks on. Nancy had done something allowing the veil to detach from the mask, so Carlina chose what she wanted. Most were mundane, boring images with family members. I really wanted to exclude Annabelle and Baron, but with the way my dad glared at my suggestion, I let it go.

Those photos would be burned, anyway.

I made sure Carlina had photos with the people she wanted without me, so if something happened to me, she would still have photos of good memories. At least I hope she considers this wedding to be a good memory.

In my opinion, the best photos were of just us. Even though I could tell she was mad at me, there were images where she truly smiled, and her eyes lit up. I wanted nothing more than to make sure she always smiled, no matter the cost.

By the time we finished having our pictures taken, the caterer announced dinner was ready, so I helped Carlina walk to the head table.

I thanked Victoria for thinking ahead and having a head table for only Carlina and I. I couldn't bear to look at the bride's family table because even in the darkened space, I could still see the pink dress which had upset Carlina so much.

The musicians played through dinner and people continued to come up and wish us well. It felt never-ending. We were exhausted by the time they announced the bride and groom to the cake for the traditional cake cutting. I knew the traditional dances would need to be done soon, but I hoped to get Carlina to myself soon so we could both rest. Or fight, whatever she was up for because the entire night I could tell she was thinking about all the things she could call me. Before the couple's first dance, I'd gone up and talked to the musician.

"Hey, I'll give you an extra hundred if you don't have a father of the bride or mother of the groom dance, please?" I slipped him the 100-dollar bill.

After pocketing it, he looked at me. "You didn't need to pay me to do less, but I'm okay with it."

I smiled before going back to the head table.

"What did you just do?"

"I figured you were getting tired, so I talked to the musician about shortening the list of songs to play."

"Oh, great. You're right; I am getting tired. Thank you. But I hope you don't have any ideas about tonight. I plan to go back to the house and straight to sleep."

I held up my hands in mock defeat. "No plans whatsoever, Princess." I smirked as she glared at me for calling her a pet name already. I didn't know what was sexier, the glare or the smile, but I was committed to seeing both as often as possible.

Chapter Twenty-Two

0 Days Until the Wedding – Carlina—Evening

After the forced dancing, I was elated to get off my feet for the drive to the house. My mind was still reeling from his comments from before we took the photos.

Who the hell does he think he is? Some rich kid who thinks this is all fun and games? Preying on people in desperate situations?

The more I thought about it, the madder I got. This marriage was for convenience, a necessity for me. I'm sure it was something to tell his buddies about the next time he went skiing or something.

"What are you thinking about?" Preston asked.

I could tell Preston was smirking as he took his eyes off the road to look at me. He had driven for the ceremony, and he'd brought out his classic Mustang to do it. I had to admit it was a nice car, but the company could have been much better.

"How much of an ass you are."

"Oh Princess, you wound me with your words. You haven't seen me be an ass yet. Trust me, I can be much worse."

I was pissed. He didn't need to talk down to me, and the way he said princess made me want to strangle him. It wasn't endearing, but more mocking.

As we pulled up to the house, I realized I didn't have anyone to help me get out of the dress, and I could feel the panic setting in.

"What is it this time?" Preston rested his hand on my thigh right above my knee.

I liked the warmth because it felt good, but I also wanted him to take it off because he was a jerk.

Sliding my hand over his to remove it, I knew I was red in the face. "I don't have anyone to help me out of this dress."

"Oh, I can help you out of the dress."

"I'm sure you could, but if you think you're getting a free show, you're sorely mistaken."

"I paid for the wedding. Is it really free?"

I gasped at his comment. Could he really be this callous? "Maybe I should give your father a free show, since I'm sure he was the one who actually paid."

I heard the hiss of air come out of his mouth while his hand found my thigh again.

This time, he applied more pressure.

"Don't ever say that again. Ever. Do you understand me?"

His anger caused me to realize maybe I'd stepped over the line. Considering his behavior, I'd never undress in front of his father, or even him, at this rate.

Meekly, I responded, "Yes, I understand. I'm tired of this dress. While beautiful, it's quite heavy."

"It's a good thing I asked Victoria to come over to help you then, isn't it?"

"You did?" I was surprised. He went from hot to cold to fast so quickly it made my head spin.

"Yes, I'm not a total animal. Well, maybe sometimes." He winked. The bastard winked at me. For the rest of the drive, I looked out the window, trying to get my mind off the fact his hand was still on my thigh and his thumb was doing light circles.

I jumped out and practically ran to the front door the minute he stopped in front of the house. I was hoping to get away from him and out of this dress.

Opening the door, Victoria was standing there with a cup of tea.

"Here, I made you a cup of tea to help you sleep tonight, but first, let's get you out of your dress." She was so thoughtful, I almost cried.

"Thank you. I don't know what I would've done if you hadn't come to help." I told her once we made it upstairs.

"If you'd needed help, Preston would have called me." She held my bedroom door open.

I glanced toward the other main bedroom door to see if Seth had given him that room. The door was closed, and there was no indication it was his room. It made me wonder where he planned to sleep.

"I doubt it. At least he's not acting like he would have." I wanted to flop onto the bed and sleep for an entire day.

"Yeah, he can be a jerk, trust me, but deep down, he really isn't."

"Well, it must be real deep down after the way he acted tonight."

Victoria laughed as she helped me out of my dress. "There, we're all done. Do you need anything before I leave?"

All I could think about was sleeping. "No, thank you. Will I see you again?"

"You'll see me tomorrow morning." Victoria smiled.

I didn't even think about why she would see me tomorrow, but as I crawled into bed, all I could think about was how soft it was.

"That's good. I'll see you then." I laid my head on the pillow and was out before Victoria turned off the light and closed the door.

Chapter Twenty-Three

0 Days Until the Wedding – Preston – Evening

"What did you say to her?" I heard Victoria ask even before she was in the room.

"Nothing."

"Nothing, my ass. She thinks you're a jerk."

"Maybe I am a jerk." I took a small sip of my whiskey before putting the glass down. I was thinking of all the things I had said wrong, and how I didn't start the relationship, or, I guess marriage, off on the right foot.

"You're not a jerk, but you can act like one sometimes. Grow up, Preston. This may be the best thing that has ever happened to you, and yet you sit in the dark. Did you even notice that she had a monarch butterfly on her mask?"

"Yes, because being forced to marry is such a great thing," I scoffed as I picked the glass back up.

"Preston Charles, you look at me right now." Victoria almost never used my full name, so I knew I was in trouble. I placed the glass back on the side table and looked at her.

"I don't know what's wrong with you, but you need to snap out of it. No matter what, you need to stay married to get your money, so please don't screw things up."

"I won't, I promise, I'm sorry. I couldn't stop thinking about how my mom wasn't here, and it was a really nice wedding, and then she walked out with the butterfly. You did a great job, and I'm sorry." Stepping up Victoria. I hugged her and held her as I sniffled.

"I know, I wish she was here too, but you can't take it out on Carlie; it's not her fault, and she deserves better." Victoria held me.

Composing myself, I stepped away. "Did I tell you I talked to Father about you coming here for part of the day?"

"Yes, he told me himself. I'm supposed to make his breakfast, and then I can come over here and help until it's time for me to go back over there for dinner."

"I'm glad, and I'll make sure you're paid well."

"Your father said he'll be paying me what he always does, regardless of where I'm at, so you don't have to worry about it."

"Oh, I'm glad, especially since I have to leave soon."

"Where are you going?" Victoria stepped back, looking me up and down.

"Evan's dad has a job for me down south, so it's I'll probably be gone for a couple weeks. It'll be nice to have you here for Carlie."

"Is it, you know... *that* kind of job?" Victoria asked.

"Probably, but I don't know for sure yet. I know you don't like it, and I want to get out, but right now I have to bide my time."

"I know, but I don't want to lose you too, Preston." She picked up her purse and went to the front door.

"I don't want to lose you either," I replied as she turned at the door to give me a small wave.

"You don't need to worry. I'll see you in the morning."

I nodded, not knowing what to say.

It had been relatively easy to get my father to allow Victoria and Freddie to come over and help around my property. He'd even offered to pay them, which I'd known he'd planned to pay a housekeeper, but I didn't think he would pay for Freddie. Surprisingly, Father also told me I could have personal security guards from the company he normally uses versus using his like I have been. Of course, I picked Seth. It made me slightly suspicious that he readily agreed to everything I asked for, but I couldn't worry about it now.

I considered refilling my now empty glass, but with me leaving tomorrow, I figured I should get some sleep since I needed to pack in the morning.

I quietly creeped up the stairs.

While I knew which room Carlie had chosen, I didn't know which room Seth had given me. Walking first to the other main bedroom, I saw it was bare of any personal touches. I chuckled at Seth putting me in one of the smaller rooms.

Before I could stop myself, I knocked gently on Carlie's door before opening it.

The light from outside illuminated her face as she slept, with her hair all over the place. She was beautiful sleeping. Hell, she was beautiful all the time, but I didn't deserve her. I had to keep my distance; I wasn't going to ruin her with my life. One year of pretending to be married, and I would have everything I needed and more.

Closing the door, I went to the other side of the hall, past the stairs. I opened the first door to see my room looking exactly the same as it had at my father's house, except my desk and everything on it was missing. There were two doors, both to my left.

I opened the first to see a modest closet with all my clothes hung. The next door was the bathroom. I walked in and opened the door leading to the other room. I had forgotten this was a Jack and Jill bathroom. It helped to have the bathroom between my office and the bedroom.

Seth had arranged my desk and computer against the wall near a window, while the rest of the room was dedicated to my armory.

Guns lined the walls, and a cabinet with drawers and an open glass top sat in the center of the room. I knew the drawers held my knives. I ran my hand over the top of the case before going back into my room. Stripping down and getting into bed, all I could think about was the redhead down the hall.

Chapter Twenty-Four

1 Day After the Wedding - Carlina

I woke to the sun shining on my face. At first, I was confused about where I was, but I remembered the wedding, the new house, and the jerk probably still sleeping somewhere in the house. The bed was so comfortable I didn't want to get up. My bladder took a moment to protest. I swung out of bed as a light knock sounded at my door.

"Who is it?"

"Carlie, it's Victoria. I wanted to let you know breakfast is ready if you wanted to come down and eat."

"Give me a couple of minutes, and I'll be down. Thank you."

Why was Victoria here? She'd mentioned she was coming over the night before, but I was so drained I didn't remember if she'd said why.

After using the restroom and putting on some loungewear, I slipped my feet into my slippers and went downstairs. I could smell the food as I got to the bottom of the steps. Not watching where I was going, I ran into a thick wall of muscle, who chuckled.

"Ma'am, you need to watch where you're going." I took a step back and looked up at Seth with a bagel in one hand and a cup of coffee in his other.

"Seth? What are you doing here?"

"Preston will explain everything over breakfast. I need to go out to the garage. It was nice seeing you." He tipped his head slightly on his way out the door.

In the kitchen, Victoria and an older man were going over paperwork, and Preston sat at the small kitchen table.

"Morning," I greeted Victoria. "Can you show me where the plates are so I can fix my plate?"

"Oh dear, you don't need to. I already have a plate ready for you. If you want more, let me know, and I'll get you more. There's jam, honey, and peanut butter on the table. I also put orange juice on the table, but if you want something else instead, let me know."

The man I didn't recognize stood smiling beside Victoria.

"Thank you. I really appreciate it. I'm not used to this type of breakfast."

"Get used to it. Victoria makes our breakfast and dinner most nights." Preston answered as I sat. "Victoria will be our housekeeper, at least for the foreseeable future, and Freddie, her husband, is our handyman."

"Nice to meet you, Freddie."

"Nice meeting you, Mrs. Wessex."

"Please call me Carlie. I'm not ready to be a missus yet." I glanced at Preston. "No offense."

Preston finished his piece of toast before brushing off his hands and looked at me with a small smirk. "No offense taken. You'll be Mrs. Wessex for at least a year, so you can take your time getting used to it."

I looked up with the fork halfway to my mouth. "A year?"

"Yes, remember the deal? We're expected to be married for a year. After that, we're free to go our separate ways." He looked at me like I was dumb.

Everything suddenly came crashing down. My inheritance in two weeks, being married for a year. If he thinks our marriage will last a year, he's fooling himself.

"Oh yeah, I remember now. Things were crazy before the wedding."

"Preston, you need to tell her about your upcoming trip while she eats." Victoria stepped closer to the table.

Smiling at her, I returned to eating.

Preston looked at his phone for a second before placing it face down on the table. "Do you remember my best man? His name is Evan. I need to travel to help him with something. I should only be gone for about a week if everything goes according to plan. In the meantime, Freddie and Victoria will be here during the day, and Seth, along with another security guard, will be here on and off all day and night."

I almost choked on my orange juice. We just got married, and he was already leaving? What was I supposed to do in this huge house all by myself?

"Thanks for letting me know. If I need to leave to go into town or go see my mom, will I have Seth drive me?"

"He can, or you can drive yourself, assuming you have a driver's license."

"Yes, I may not be worldly like you, but I do have my driver's license." I drank the rest of my juice and placed the glass on the table as I saw Freddie and Victoria go into the other room with the paperwork they'd been looking at.

"I didn't know, since you don't seem to have any electronics either. Do you have a cell phone?"

"No, Fath- I mean, Baron, didn't feel I needed one since I never left the house except with my mom or stepsisters."

"Okay, I'll have Seth get you one today." He smirked. "Since you have a driver's license, can you drive a manual transmission?"

"Yes, my father taught me a little in his car before he died. I was really young at the time, so I practiced with a friend's car a few years ago."

"Great, if you're comfortable with it, you can drive my Supra around if you need to go anywhere. I'll leave a credit card for you in case you need to buy anything."

"I may be your wife, but I don't need your charity." I fumed as I slathered jam on my toast.

"So, you have your own money?"

"Well, no, but I don't need anything. I have everything I need, and I don't want to use your money."

"Stop being stubborn, and let me give you access to stuff, okay?"

"Why? So I have to repay you later in other ways?"

"What? No, I mean, if you wanted to." Preston wiggled his eyebrows at me.

I almost threw the knife I had used for the jam.

"No, thank you. Don't you need to pack since you're leaving soon? Do you need me for anything else?"

"Yes. While I'm gone, there will be some construction around the house, so your window may be partially blocked. Also, if you want, Victoria or Freddie can take you to my father's house so you can use the pool during the day. If you know how to swim, that is."

I was tired of his snarky remarks and stood with my toast. Without responding, I went to my room, eating along the way. I was hoping maybe his attitude from the night before was because of stress from the wedding, but no. Apparently, he was always like this. Little did he know, the minute I received my inheritance, I was taking his car and leaving.

Chapter Twenty-Five

1 Day After the Wedding - Preston

"Did nothing I say to you last night register in your thick skull?" Victoria walked back into the kitchen popping me on the back of the head.

"It did, but something about her makes me want to either strangle her or kiss her until her lips are bruised, and I doubt she'd be okay with either of those things right now."

I could hear Freddie laughing from the other room.

"Try to control yourself and not kill her before your one-year anniversary." Victoria cleared the dishes from the table.

"No promises." I jumped as she threw a napkin at me.

As much as I joked about being a jerk, I felt slightly guilty about what I'd said.

I called out to Seth on my way up the stairs, "Hey, can you get Carlina a cell phone and bring it to the house when you come get me later?"

"She doesn't have a cell phone?"

"Apparently not." Something about what she'd said about her financials after getting married tickled the back of my brain, but I couldn't worry about it now. Evan and I needed to prepare. From what Evan had sent right before Carlina had come down for breakfast, I needed to be on my A game. I usually was, but this was going to be a longer job than most.

Instead of turning into my room, I walked over to her closed door. Knocking, I waited for the slight, "come in" before I opened it.

"Come to harass me some more?" Carlina was sitting on her bed with a book. Her hair was in a bun, and she was wearing short shorts. I adjusted my view from between her legs to her face, where the sunlight was making her freckles pop.

"No, I came to apologize. I didn't mean to assume or make you feel bad."

She looked at me through slitted eyes, as if looking for signs of a lie.

"Victoria told you to come up and apologize, didn't she?" she smugly asked.

"No. I really wanted to apologize, but she told me I should be nicer to you." If I had to live a year with this woman, I needed her to not kill me in my sleep.

"Thought so. She seems to have all the brains around here." She smiled as she looked down at her book.

"Before I start packing I want to apologize. I'll be leaving in about two hours, so if you need anything, please let me know."

"There is nothing I need, but thank you." She didn't even look up from her book as she went back to reading.

Shaking my head, I shut the door softly before going to my room.

Carlina had me tied up in knots. Half of me didn't want to be married and didn't want someone living with me. But the other half wanted to go back into her room, toss the book on the chair, and show her what she was missing.

I felt my cock grow hard and looked at my watch to see how much time I had. If I showered quickly, I would have plenty of time.

Tossing my clothes into the hamper, I entered the bathroom naked. The bathroom wasn't as big as the two with the main bedrooms, but it was big enough. A mirrored wall hung over the double vanity opposite the shower. The shower had a toilet to its left and a bathtub to its right. I started the water and looked at myself in the mirror.

I was in good shape, strong, but not overly defined. As the water heated, I ran my hands down my sides and across my chest, wishing it was Carlie doing it.

Testing the water, I stepped inside and leaned against the wall, peering at my reflection in the mirror.

I closed my eyes to picture Carlina running her nails up my legs to my dick. Envisioning her touching me, I spit in my hand before slowly running my hand down to my cock and pumping my hand up and down. Stroking, I thought about all the things I wanted to do with her, to her. This time, I wouldn't push. I wouldn't force my desires on her, at least not in the beginning. In my mind, Carlina's hand was making the motion on my shaft, while I pictured myself running a stiletto knife over her collarbone and bringing a bit of blood to the surface. The thought of using a knife on her quickened my hand. Getting close, I slowed down to enjoy it, thinking about her hot mouth around my dick as I gently but firmly held her in place by her hair. Cumming, I leaned against the wall of the shower and opened my eyes, realizing the water was cooling, which in this house meant it had been at least 20 minutes since I got in.

Once I caught my breath, I washed my hair and body before I got out to get dressed. This was going to be the longest year of my life.

I pulled on a pair of boxer briefs and pulled clothes from the closet.

Evan had said I'd need to be there for a week, so I planned for a week and a day. If I needed to stay longer, I could always get my clothes laundered or buy new ones. Normally, I wouldn't take a job like this, but Evan was a good friend, and my future relied on keeping a good relationship with him and his family.

Satisfied with what I'd selected, I folded everything and put it into a suitcase. I grabbed my duffle and added weapons. Having everything out in the open and sorted helped a lot when I packed. I'd have to thank Seth later for his help.

My Glock-30, the additional barrel, and ammunition were added to the bag before I opened the knife drawers. I ran my hand over the hilts until I found the knife I was looking for. I wasn't exactly sure what the job entailed, so I also added the KBAR and Tanto. As I placed the last knife into the bag, I knew it would be the one I used, if I needed to use one at all.

Before I closed the drawer, I looked over the slender knives and thought about how I'd asked a couple of ex-girlfriends if I could use the steel on them, and they always freaked out. Thankfully, the NDAs my father had insisted they sign kept me out of the media's crosshairs. Using a knife for something other than death would be nice.

I wondered if my father had made Carlina or her family sign the NDAs. I guess I should've asked, but I didn't really care. With how Carlie looked at me, there was no way anything resembling knife play was in our future. Pity because the blood would match her hair.

Shaking my head, I zipped the bag and made sure the office door to the hall was locked before going back to my room. With the security I had, I knew no one would come into the house, but I didn't need Carlina to find my weapons before I had the chance to talk to her.

I heard my phone ping, so I checked the screen. Seth's text said he would arrive in 10 minutes. Not needing to reply, I grabbed my bags and went downstairs to wait.

I left my bags near the front door and went in search of something to read during my trip. After getting a book from the library, I leaned against the door, waiting for Seth to arrive. I opened the front door and carried my bags outside after I saw the headlights from the SUV pulling up.

"Did you get the phone?" I asked as I opened the rear passenger door to put my bags inside.

"Yes, I added it to your service plan as well. I got a white phone with three cases because I have no idea what she'd like."

"I gave her my credit card so she could have bought her own cases, but I'm sure she'll appreciate it. Let me take it up to her, and then we can leave."

Seth handed me the phone and cases.

I jogged upstairs, not wanting to make Seth wait any longer than necessary. I heard a soft "come in" after I knocked on Carlie's door. She was still sitting on her bed with her book, but this time she looked up and didn't seem as mad, which I took as a good sign.

"Yes?"

"Seth got you a phone and three different cases because he didn't know which one you'd like. I hope the phone's okay. If you need help getting used to it, Victoria has the same one."

Carlina smiled a real smile as she reached out for the phone and cases. "Can you please tell Seth thank you? And thank you for having him do it. I'm sure I can figure it out, but if I can't, I'll definitely ask her. Have a good trip."

"Thank you. If you need anything, Seth programmed my number, his number, and Victoria's number into the phone." Not knowing what else to say, I awkwardly turned around to leave.

"Preston, wait." I faced Carlina.

"Sorry I've been so rude. I really do appreciate everything you've done."

"Everything's new and strange, so I get it. Take this week to get comfortable, and I'll be back soon. We can do something fun together when I get back."

I jogged down the stairs and out the front door I'd left open in my haste to give Carlina her phone.

"Everything good?"

"Yup, let's go." I hopped into the passenger seat as Seth started the car and pulled away from the house.

"So, how are things going with Carlie?"

"Well, it's only been a day, and I'm leaving to go kill probably at least one person, so you know, same ole, same ole."

Seth laughed. "Are you going to tell her?"

"What? I kill people for a quasi-living? No, I don't think she'd love the idea."

"Maybe, or maybe over time, it won't be as big of a deal. Look at your mom. Even Victoria, while not married to someone who kills, is relatively fine with it as long as the circumstances warrant it."

"Yeah, well, I don't intend to stay married to her past the year requirement, so there'd be no point."

"Famous last words, Preston, famous last words." Seth's words hung in the air as he turned on the radio, and the rest of the drive to the airport was quiet.

***

As usual, the flight to Vegas was quick, and I read most of the way there. Normally, I had little time to read. Reading was enjoyable, and I was thankful someone had filled the library with books, or maybe they'd always been there. I tried to remember the last time I'd gone to the house Carlina and I were now sharing and realized it had been before my mother's death.

Stepping off the plane, I saw Evan and his driver, Todd, waiting on the tarmac. I hugged Evan before shaking Todd's hand. I waited until we got into the town car before speaking to Evan.

"So, nothing has changed with the job, right?"

Evan looked at me before patting my shoulder. "You haven't been to Vegas in a long time. Tonight, we have dinner with my family planned, and then we're going out to one of the casinos. Tomorrow we can talk about the job."

I agreed with a smile. It shouldn't always be about work, and I enjoyed spending time with his family. Where my family was quiet, small, and all about tradition, Evan's family was loud, large, and every day was a surprise. "Sounds good. I'm up for some family bonding time."

"I knew it."

We spent the rest of the night enjoying delicious food and good company before heading to the casino. I didn't gamble much, at least not against the house, but I figured why not throw a couple of thousand down and see where it takes me. When I walked out of the Casino at 2 am, I was 35,000 dollars richer, and Evan had found himself a pretty blonde.

All in all, it was a good night, but part of me wished Carlina could have been by my side so I could be the talk of the town with her as my arm candy.

Chapter Twenty-Six

1 Day After the Wedding - Carlina

After Preston brought me my new phone, I went back to reading. I should have been learning how to use my phone, but I was in a good spot in the story. So engrossed in the book, I didn't realize darkness had fallen. I pulled myself out of bed and put on my slippers to find something to eat.

The silence on my way down the stairs was unsettling. This was a relatively big house, and it sounded like I was all alone. I wasn't used to things being this quiet.

Walking faster, I opened the door to see Victoria dancing to music only she could hear between the island and the stove. Whatever she was cooking smelled amazing.

Sitting at the kitchen island watching Victoria, I smiled.

She seemed in her element in the kitchen, and somehow she hadn't seen me yet.

It was another 15 seconds before she saw me for the first time and jumped. She removed one of her earbuds.

"Sorry, I didn't see you there." Victoria chuckled as she put the lid on a pot.

"Don't be sorry. I didn't say anything. I watched you dance around for a minute."

"Oh, you saw?" Victoria turned back to the stove, sheepish.

"I did. It looks like you really enjoy cooking."

"I do, and Mr. Wessex and Preston allow me to make what I want, within reason, so it's nice having the freedom. Speaking of which, I don't know what you normally eat or what you like, so I made a chicken casserole with a tart for dessert. In the meantime I was making a jam."

"Sounds delicious, and I'll eat most things. My mom cooks Middle Eastern dishes sometimes, but normally we ate what you would consider 'American' because of Baron and my stepsisters. I'll eat pretty much anything, especially if I don't have to cook it." I laughed as I did air quotes around 'American'.

"Perfect. For the next week, I can experiment on you with some new dishes I've been working on."

"I'd be happy to be your guinea pig; let me know what time to show up." I liked Victoria; she was down to earth and really seemed to want me to be comfortable.

"Do you have anything planned for after dinner?" Victoria asked as she placed a plate of chicken and rice on my plate.

"No, I'm in the middle of a book, so I think I'll finish it tonight. Preston had Seth buy me a phone, so I may play with it for a little while since I've never had one before. With it being dark now, I don't think I want to be exploring the house or outside alone."

"You should. There's no reason for you not to. There are plenty of lights and a fence around the entire property. This house isn't very big." Victoria laughed.

"Do you want to go with me?"

"I would, but Freddie's going to be done soon, and I think we're going into Redmond to have dinner. At least the house had been cleaned before you and Preston moved in."

"It had been empty?"

"Yes, for years before you moved in. This was the first house Charles and his wife lived in after they got married. When he started making more money, he wanted something slightly closer to town that was bigger. Preston came home from the hospital to this house. They moved to the other house before he was old enough to walk. The only thing really remaining from before is the library. Those stayed throughout the years because the library is climate controlled, and Mr. Wessex made sure to keep it dusted and clean."

"There's a library? Why didn't they take the books to the new house? Will you show me tomorrow?"

"I'm not really sure. I think the books were Preston's mom's, and Charles didn't think to take them. She came out here often before she got sick. And of course I'll show you the library, dear. I'm going to clean up while you eat. No rush on dessert. If I leave before you're ready for it, it's in the oven."

"Thank you, Victoria." I thought I heard her say, "No. Thank *you*," but I couldn't be sure as she was walking out through one of the far doors, and I was so engrossed in my food.

What could have been five minutes or 15, Victoria was back and gave me a tart with a fruit jam she had been making when I came in earlier.

I savored the tart as much as I did the casserole and realized if I wanted to keep eating this much food, I should probably be more active during the day. Between her cooking and reading all day, I was ready for bed.

But first, I wanted to read more of the book I was reading. "Thank you for dinner. What time is breakfast?" I didn't want to be rude or make her wait for me.

"It's whatever time you want. I'll be here in the morning after cooking Mr. Wessex's breakfast and can stay as long as needed until you wake up."

"I don't want to mess up your schedule."

"Dear, your schedule is my schedule. I get paid to sit here and do cross-stitch, crossword puzzles, or cook while I'm waiting, so whenever you feel ready for breakfast, you can message me, and I'll get it started it."

"Message you? Oh yeah, on my phone. Okay, I'm going to go read some more before bed."

"Okay, dear, have a good night. I'm about done here, and then I'll leave, but I'm going to keep the kitchen light on so if you get hungry, or decide to explore, there will be at least one light on downstairs."

"Great, thank you. G'night." Reaching my room upstairs, I grabbed my book and decided I'd read in the large bathtub. Hopefully, there would be some bath salts or bubble bath in the bathroom somewhere. If not, I'd survive but made a mental note to buy some if there wasn't.

To my delight, there was an entire cabinet full of different bath and shower things, and another cabinet held the softest towels I'd ever felt. There was even a robe with my name on it. I don't know when they'd had time to make it, but I wasn't going to complain. I'd thank Victoria in the morning because I knew Seth and Preston wouldn't have done something this thoughtful. They weren't the bubble bath type of guys.

As the water ran into the tub, I chose the bubble bath I wanted to use, a lavender soothing blend promising to help me sleep. Sliding into the warm tub full of bubbles, I closed my eyes and relaxed. It had been a long time since I'd really done anything truly for myself like this. By the time I got out of the bath, I'd finished my book, and it was well into the evening. I ambled over to my bed and slid under the covers, not noticing my phone sitting on the nightstand notifying me I had a message.

Chapter Twenty-Seven

5 Days After the Wedding - Preston

Since arriving in Vegas, things had been going non-stop. Evan had me meet with his father the night after we went to the casino to go over the job. It was time-consuming but relatively easy, so for the next two days we scoped out the locations we had discussed and laid around Evan's pool.

"The plan starts tonight; are you ready?"

"This isn't my first rodeo. Of course, I am. Why are you so worried?"

"Because if all this goes right, it puts you one step closer to our end goal."

"You know I won't have the money until after I've been married for a year, right?"

"Yeah, it's a stupid stipulation, but it's fine. It'll take roughly a year to get all our ducks in a row, anyway. Have you thought about what will happen after?"

"No, but I'm sure your father has." I smiled as I took a sip of my lemonade. I drank alcohol occasionally, but never during a job, even lying around a pool.

"Yeah, he's going to take a year-long trip with my mom. She can't wait."

"A whole year? Where are they going?"

"Back to the home country, see different places in Europe, go to the middle east, I have no idea. I think they plan to throw a dart at a map after they tire of wherever they are."

Evan's parents were in their 50s, so it didn't surprise me they wanted to travel. His father, Carlos, worked long, hard, dangerous hours and had for as long as Evan had been alive, at least according to Evan's mom, Nancy. He must not have worked too many hours because they had six kids. Evan was the only son and the heir to Carlos' business.

The only problem was Evan didn't want it. He was happy enough to be behind his computer, living off the interest of the trust fund his grandparents had set up for him. None of Evan's sisters wanted the business either, which was why I was sitting beside Evan's pool waiting for a flight to come in.

I normally didn't mind coming and hanging out with Evan in Vegas, but I was itching to get home. Even if it meant seeing Carlie glare at me. Maybe it was me counting down the days until my inheritance was mine, and I could take the next step in my plan. I'd always figured I would do it alone, but there was a small voice in my head telling me Carlie would be a good partner in the future. I tried to shut out the voice because being married, especially to someone you loved, complicated things. Thinking of Nancy and Carlos, though, their love didn't complicate anything, at least not from what I'd seen.

"How's married life?"

"Well, since I've been with you for most of it, even though my wife is hotter than you, I wouldn't know." I laughed as Evan clutched his chest.

"You wound me. But really, do you think you'll be able to live in the same house together for a year?"

"Yeah, I think she hates me, but this wasn't a great situation you know? Okay, maybe not hate, maybe loathe with every fiber of her being would be more accurate."

"I doubt it's that bad."

"No, it probably isn't, but she thinks I'm a jerk."

"Well Preston, my friend, you *are* a jerk."

"And you still love me, so what does that make you?"

"A golden retriever." Evan laughed as he jumped into the pool. He was a great friend, someone who didn't care who my family was, how much money I may or may not have, or I did for a living.

Laying back on the chaise, Evan's phone beeped. I grabbed it and looked at it.

A message from an unknown number popped up. *The plane landed.*

"Hey, get your laps in while you can. The plane landed," I yelled at Evan while I laid back to get more sun before we had to leave.

Chapter Twenty-Eight

5 Days After the Wedding - Carlina

Since Preston left, I slept in every day. The morning after he left, I checked my phone and saw Preston had messaged me and said he'd landed in Vegas. Not knowing what, if anything, to reply, I left it on read. I messaged Victoria and let her know I was up and ready for breakfast.

I sat at the kitchen table while Victoria told me about herself and how she and Freddie met. It was a sweet story and how relationships should form, not by being betrothed against your will. They met in high school where Freddie was the pitcher on the baseball team, and Victoria was a softball catcher. I hadn't dated or played sports in high school, and I wonder if my life would be different now if I had. Would I be where I'm at now, or somewhere completely different?

After breakfast, Victoria showed me around the house. I was so excited about finding out there was a library, complete with reading chairs and a perfectly sized couch for lounging while I read during cold or snowy weather. Victoria had explained last night it was the only room they'd maintained while the house was vacant. The room had floor to ceiling bookcases with ladders to get up to the top shelves.

I had expected to see all old books like in movies and in photos of large estates. However, the books were a mix of new and old, and they looked to be separated by genre.

Other than the library, the first floor consisted of the kitchen, an attached dining room, the living room, and a small guest bathroom.

Walking around, I was pleasantly surprised to find the house wasn't overly fancy. It meant less work for Victoria, and eventually me, to clean. If I stayed long enough to need to clean. While Victoria put a roast for dinner in the oven, Freddie showed me around the property, at least the parts worth looking at.

Most of the property was empty fields and trees. They had cleared the area around the house to build the house, a garage, and a shed. The shed didn't hold much other than some gardening supplies. The garage was much larger, and I saw the Supra Preston had told me about.

Handing me the keys, Freddie explained where I could normally find them.

The garage also held the Mustang I'd seen the day I had lunch with his father. Wanting to look at the Mustang, I started walking toward it, but before I could check it out, I heard what sounded like a convoy coming up the drive.

"Oh, I forgot. They're moving the vehicles in today for the construction project." Freddie looked outside the garage before turning back to me.

"Preston mentioned it. What are they building?"

"Don't rightly know. Preston was pretty tight-lipped about it, honestly. Did you ask Victoria? He tends to tell her things she then tells me. I live by the motto, 'If she doesn't tell me, I'm not supposed to know.'" Freddie laughed at his own comment.

"Can't blame you there." Smiling, I pat his shoulder.

After getting back into the house, the rest of the day was listening to the crews set up the equipment in the back and paper the windows. The lack of a view didn't bother me, as there wasn't much to see anyway.

I sat in the library and read before dinner, and I took the book back to my room to read after I'd finished eating.

***

The next day, I asked Victoria if I could take a swim in Mr. Wessex's pool, so she drove me over. Still getting used to the area, I didn't want to get lost. Especially when it was with someone else's car. Well, apparently half mine now.

When we got to the house, I helped Victoria prepare lunch. After having lunch with Victoria, I spent the rest of the day in and out of the pool. It was nice, and I thought maybe I would talk to Preston about putting a pool in. Even though I could get used to this, I was feeling a little stir-crazy.

When I thought about calling my mom, I realized I didn't know her number. Thinking about it, I realized I didn't know anyone's numbers other than the ones programmed into my phone. Looking up I saw Freddie coming into the room.

"Hey Freddie, would it be alright if I took the Supra to my mom's tomorrow? I'm going stir crazy and haven't seen her in days. I'm used to seeing her every day, so it's been strange not speaking to her these last few days."

"Preston told me the Supra is your car until he comes back and buys you a new one."

"Thank you. What do I do if I need to get gas?"

"If you need to get it while you're out, Preston left you a credit card. If it isn't full, I'll take care of it when I fill up the other cars."

"I'll make sure it's as close to full as I can. I don't want you to have to fill it for me." This level of help surprised me, as I'd always been pretty independent.

"It's what I'm paid to do. If anything is weird about the car, let me know, okay? I'll get it fixed if I can't fix it myself."

"Thank you, Freddie. I really appreciate it." And I did. It was nice to have someone willing to help. Yes, he was being paid for it, but just because you're being paid to do something doesn't mean you'll go the extra mile like Victoria and Freddie have.

Finishing my book before dinner, I grabbed another from the library as I returned to my room for bed. As I reached the second floor, I looked over at the double doors across the staircase from mine and resisted the urge to walk over there. The voice in my head was interested in seeing how Preston lived away from the eyes of other's, but I didn't want to invade his privacy.

***

After breakfast, I set out to see my mom. I hoped she'd be home because otherwise I had no way to contact her.

Arriving at the house brought a sense of sadness. Yes, the new house was nice, but it wasn't home yet. This was home, at least for my entire life so far. I parked in Baron's usual spot in the driveway and walked to the house. It felt odd, like should I knock? Should I go in? I knocked since I wasn't sure.

"Coming."

I heard my mom's voice.

Opening the door, I saw a flash of shock on her face before she rushed out to hug me.

"How are you? Is everything okay? How did you get here?" She started throwing questions at me so fast I only heard a couple.

"Everything is fine. Do you want to go to lunch? Or we can go inside."

"I just finished putting some pot pies in the oven, so let's go inside. I can get you something to drink."

Sitting in the kitchen, I remembered all the times when I was a kid and would watch her and my father cook together.

"So, how is everything?"

"It's good, Mom. I drove here in Preston's Toyota Supra. The house is nice. You saw some of it at the wedding. There's a full library though, like ours but bigger."

"Is he treating you right?" I could see the concern in her eyes. It really didn't matter since she's the one who let me be married off like cattle.

"Yes, he's away on business right now, so I've been swimming, reading, and relaxing."

"Well, good." She was fumbling with a napkin, which was her tell something was bothering her.

"What's wrong?" I realized the house was too quiet. I knew Baron was gone, but I expected the twins to be lounging around. "Where are the twins?"

She looked around before answering. "Baron has been having Annabelle go to work with him. Something about her taking over if something happened to him. It's strange because she doesn't know anything about what he does, but she seems to be fine with going anyway."

"Why did you look around? No one else is here. What about Beatrice?"

"Habit, I guess." She nervously laughed. "She went to the store to get some ingredients for dinner. Ever since you left, she's been stepping up and really helping me around the house. I haven't even had to ask her, but she's been happy to do it."

"That's good." I pulled out my phone. "I almost forgot; Preston gave me a phone to use so he could contact me, and I could contact others. Can you put in yours and Beatrice's numbers please? I want to be able to contact you if I can't come over very often."

Taking the phone, she punched in the numbers. "What do you plan on doing after this weekend?"

"This weekend?" Her question confused me.

"When you get your inheritance. Do you plan on helping us with the house?"

"Honestly, I haven't thought about it with everything else going on. I don't know, it depends on the amount of money and the terms of Baron's deal with Mr. Wessex. Do you know what the full terms were? With everything going on, I didn't really think to ask, and now I wish I had?"

"The deal?"

"I'm sorry Carlie. I don't know any more than you do."

Sure, you don't. It was another nail in the coffin of our relationship.

"Before we leave, can I see the garden?"

"Sure, I haven't been out there as much as I would like, but it's still doing well. In fact, Beatrice has taken over some of the work."

We walked to the back doors, and I stepped outside. The garden looked much the same as before I left, which made sense since I'd only been gone five days, but it felt like home. I wanted to lie on the grass and soak in the sun with the flowers and butterflies all around me.

For the rest of the afternoon, I sat and visited with my mom.

Beatrice and I sat on the couch and talked after she came home. I believe Beatrice and I had things in common and could be friends in the future. Realizing how late it was as my mom prepared dinner, I was about to tell her I need to get back to my house for my own dinner when I heard the front door slam.

"Whose car is in my spot?" Baron yelled.

My mom rushed into the living room with Beatrice, and I followed close behind.

Baron was red in the face and stomped off to his office.

Annabelle was standing in the living room with a smug grin on her face.

"Ran home already? What? Preston didn't like you?" Annabelle remarked as my mom explained my presence to Baron.

"No. We're great. Thanks for asking. How's work going?" I replied.

She grimaced before she replied, "It's great. I'm going to be rich, probably richer than you and your *husband* with the changes I'm going to make."

I resisted the urge to roll my eyes because money didn't mean much to me. Yes, it was a means to an end, and I wanted what was mine, but I didn't need to spend all my time concerning myself with it.

"That's great. Well, I was about to leave. I have dinner waiting for me." I hugged Beatrice while Annabelle glared at me.

My mom and Baron came out of the office as I was about to walk out the door.

His face wasn't as red, and he smiled at me. "Why don't you stay for dinner? I'm sure Preston won't mind you spending time with your family." He tried to usher me into the dining room.

"No, it's okay. I need to go. But thank you for the offer."

"Has he said anything about the family business? Do you know if his dad has done anything?" Baron pushed as I moved closer to the door.

"No, I've mostly stayed out of the business talk, and I haven't seen Mr. Wessex since the wedding."

"A shame. When you see him next, could you speak to him about it? Oh, and did your mother tell you we need to redo the plumbing in the entire house soon?"

"No, she didn't, but thank you for letting me know. I'm sure you'll get figure it out. I'll tell Mr. Wessex you said hello. It was nice to see you all again, but I really must be going now." As Baron continued to ask me questions, I walked out the door.

Backing out of the driveway, I relaxed as soon as I was off the property. The way Baron treated me made me sick. He wasn't the same man my mom had married, or maybe he was, and I hadn't seen it. It was like he wanted information from me, but I wasn't going to give it to him.

The drive home was relaxing, and I sat in the car for a minute after arriving at the house. I was exhausted, but I didn't know why. No, I knew why. Baron was draining, and pretending to be even vaguely nice to Annabelle took everything I had. I left the car parked in front of the house.

I could smell a savory combination of mouth-watering spices as soon as I opened the door. I saw Victoria and Freddie were in the kitchen, so I joined them.

"How was your visit?" Victoria asked as she placed a plate of food in front of me on the island.

"It was good but exhausting. I spent time with my mom and Beatrice. Then Baron and Annabelle got home, and it became strange."

"Before you answer, did you leave the car out front?" Freddie asked as he stood.

"Do you want me to move it?" I went to stand.

"Sit down, eat, and tell Victoria all about your day. I can move a car." He was halfway to the front door when I realized I had the key in my purse.

"Wait, let me get you the key." I tried to get him to stop, but he was already out the door.

"Don't worry, he has extra keys for all the Wessex vehicles. For practical things like this, and for when one, or both, of them loses their keys or lock themselves out."

"He isn't upset I didn't park it in the garage, is he? I can from now on if I need to."

"It's okay. He would rather you didn't, but he'll never tell you. He likes the garage to look a specific way, and let's just say Preston isn't great at listening." Victoria laughed as she sat across from me.

"I've noticed." I laughed as I looked over the spread she'd prepared. Boneless Pork chops with applesauce and fried squash. "This looks delicious. I hope I didn't keep you waiting."

"Not at all. If you had, I would have put a plate in the oven with a note. I've done it before, and I wager I'll do it again."

I smiled at her. She really was a good person.

"So, what happened after Baron and Annabelle got home? If you want to talk about it."

I explained to her what they'd said, and how it made me feel.

"I hope I am not imposing, I think Annabelle was trying to make you jealous, and Baron was trying to get insider information."

"That's what I thought as well, and it made me feel gross. I already don't like Baron, never have, and I think he hits my mom, but I've never seen it firsthand. I just—" I didn't finish because she placed her hand on my free hand not holding the fork.

"You don't have to explain yourself; I understand. We have gut feelings, and if yours is screaming at you, then you need to listen to it, good or bad. Now eat before it gets cold."

"Yes, Ma'am." I chuckled as I lifted the fork to my mouth.

After Freddie came back to tell me he had moved the car, he and Victoria left for the evening.

I went upstairs and started the shower to hopefully wash away some of what I had been feeling. By the time my shower was over, I was so tired I didn't read. I went straight to sleep instead.

***

The next morning, I woke to a hazy film on my bedroom window from the construction crew the day before. I checked my messages to see if Victoria was already here cooking for the day.

She'd arrived and was making breakfast, so I hurried to get down there.

I was definitely being spoiled, and I was okay with it.

"Freddie and I are going to be busy for the next two days, so if you need anything, message me, okay? Charles is having a gathering, so I need to prep the food for it, and Freddie has to make sure the property is tidy."

"Do you need any help? I know my way around a kitchen."

"Thank you, but no. I'm sure Charles would have a fit if I had his brand-new daughter-in-law cooking with me for his business associates. I'll make Freddie help me."

"Okay, but if you need help, please let me know. I'm going stir crazy, and I have no idea when Preston will be home."

"I haven't heard from him either, so I don't know. Relax and enjoy the time you have while it's quiet."

"Thank you, I will. I'll see you in what? Three days then?"

"Yes, I put some leftovers in the fridge with the reheating instructions—" Victoria explained.

"Victoria, I'm not one of the guys. I can function in a kitchen."

She sheepishly looked at me.

"Sorry, I'm used to Preston, Charles, and Freddie. They couldn't tell the difference between a soup spoon or a regular spoon without someone telling them."

"I get it. Go cook and I'll see you tomorrow." I walked her to the front door and waved as she got into the truck with Freddie.

Walking back into the house, I debated what I was going to do for the rest of the day. I could read another book or maybe take a drive into town.

Not wanting to really get dressed, I plodded upstairs toward my room.

The sound of the construction wasn't as bad today. The sound had become constant, so I didn't notice it as much as I had before. The one time I tried to look at what was being built, they had a wall of plywood blocking the view.

As I got to the top of the stairs, I looked at my room and then at the two doors opposite. Curiosity got the best of me, and I wanted to see what type of person Preston was when he was in his room, alone.

Turning the knob, I opened the door, looking down the stairs to see if anyone had heard me. Knowing no one was in the house but me, I still laughed nervously. There was no one here who would see me. Before I realized it, I was in Preston's bedroom. It was plain and didn't look like anyone lived in it yet. He'd been gone most of the time since we'd been married, so maybe he wasn't always like this.

There were two doors in the room. Opening one of the doors, I saw a closet full of clothing.

The second door led to the Jack and Jill bathroom, which was much smaller than mine. I wonder why Seth gave him this room, or did he request it?

I reached for the door leading to the other bedroom when I heard my phone chime from my room. Not bothering with the other room, I returned to my own.

Picking up my phone, I saw a text from my mom wanting to know if I was going to come see them again.

I sat on my bed and thought for a minute. Did I want to go back to the house, or should we have lunch somewhere else? I knew there was more than enough food in the fridge to feed me for days, so maybe I should have her come over instead.

Not knowing exactly what to say to her, especially with how she'd never supported me against Baron, and her already asking for money even though she knew I had none until my birthday, I threw my phone onto the bed and went back to check out the room on the other side of Preston's bathroom. The handle turned easily, and I debated if I really wanted to go in there or not before I fully opened the door.

"What the hell." I took in the entire room. The room had only one window, and there was a desk with a laptop, monitor, and printer. Along the rest of the walls were guns of every shape and size. I'd didn't interact with guns much growing up. I couldn't believe what I was seeing.

Dresser-like cabinets were situated beneath the neatly hooked guns. It was like my body was on autopilot as I opened each of the drawers to see pieces and parts of guns and ammunition.

Closing each one so no one could tell I'd been there, I turned toward the middle stand. In each of the drawers, I saw knives. Hundreds and hundreds of knives. I could barely breathe. I couldn't even imagine why Preston would need this type of weaponry, especially since he was supposedly planning to take over his father's businesses. Did Charles know about this? Did he have a similar room?

As I looked around one more time, I saw two things; there was an empty space for a missing gun. Which, seeing how everything else was organized, it didn't seem like an oversight. The other thing I noticed was a half-open drawer on the filing cabinet.

I made my way over to the filing cabinet against the wall near the computer. I wanted all the information I could find, so I could decide what I wanted to do. As I opened it completely, I saw files with names on them. Removing one, I opened it to see a picture of a man with basic information.

I took the file and returned to my room, making sure all the drawers and doors were as I found them. Grabbing my phone, I went to my internet browser and searched for the man's name, Jake Hudson.

Scanning the results, I saw a news article about him from the Port Angeles Times, so I clicked it. As I read through, I developed an uneasy feeling in the pit of my stomach. The title of the article should have been enough.

Local Man and Business Owner missing.

As I kept reading, the more I knew why there was a gun missing from the room.

The article described him missing, and a tearful secretary explaining how she had just seen him the previous evening when they closed. The police declined to comment other than it was an ongoing investigation, but there was no sign of foul play.

No sign of foul play, my butt, I thought. Closing my eyes, I realized what I needed to do. I took the file back to the room and returned it to where I'd found it.

Getting back to my room, I grabbed a bag and threw some of my stuff into it. I took only the things I knew I would need for the near future. A man with so many weapons was not someone I wanted to be around, especially after the article I'd read. I may be naïve in some things, but I knew danger when I saw it. With my bag in hand and my phone in a pocket, I went down the stairs and out the front door.

No amount of money is going to force me to live in a house like this, especially with a man with that many weapons.

Opening the door to the Supra, I threw my bag in the back. Regardless of my inheritance, I decided then and there I was leaving. I was going to Canada. If I went back to my mom's, Baron would want to know what happened, and he would hand me right back to Preston the minute he returned from his trip.

Thinking about the missing gun and the fact Preston had said he had to go away on business, I almost gagged thinking about what he could be doing. I took off after the thought, watching the house get smaller in the rearview mirror as I pressed the gas pedal. The GPS on the phone said it would take nine hours to get there without stopping. I knew I'd have to stop at some point because I'd never driven that far by myself before. I set the GPS and started driving. Hopefully, my aunt and uncle would be home because if they weren't, I didn't know where I'd go, but I knew I couldn't stay here.

Chapter Twenty-Nine

7 Days After the Wedding - Preston

The first part of the job was done. Two days ago, Evan and I had picked up Mr. Martin from the private airstrip and took him to one of Carlos' casinos, The Zephyr. Yesterday, we drove Mr. Martin around Las Vegas, showing him the different areas. We even took him to Lake Havasu and Hoover Dam. Apparently, Jeff, as he asked to be called, had never been to Nevada and wanted to do a dime store tour. Today wouldn't be as easy, though.

I woke up at seven and saw Evan through the window, already in the pool doing his morning laps. Whenever there was a job or a test, Evan would swim at least a mile in the morning to calm his nerves.

Down in the kitchen, I saw Carlos and Nancy eating while Carlos read the paper.

"Are you ready?" Carlos put the paper down.

"I'm always ready."

"Preston, please eat first. I don't want you to work on an empty stomach." Nancy got up to get me a plate of food from what was on the stove.

"Thank you."

Nancy returned with a plate. "I'll let you two talk while I get Evan."

We watched her leave before either of us spoke.

"So, Evan briefed me, but is there anything else I need to know?"

"Jeff, the man we escorted to The Zephyr last night is here to negotiate a large supply of dirty money he wants us to clean. However, I have heard there's a prospective player in town who's new to the area. Evan's going to show Jeff the businesses, unlike the sightseeing you've been doing, while you find out who the new player is and take care of those trying to encroach on our business."

"Are the newcomers looking into laundry services, or are they also looking into protection?" Using non-specific wording was a habit, even though Nancy and everyone in the house knew what Carlos did and how he got his money.

Evan told me his mom had been pushing Carlos to leave the life for their safety, especially with how much Las Vegas had changed since Carlos started his business. He wouldn't even consider it until he found someone who could help Evan and take over.

"They're looking into all aspects, even the more unsavory things."

Great, meaning I'd have to deal with drug dealers and sex traffickers, two of the lowest of the low in the organized crime hierarchy.

"How many are we talking?"

"It sounds like from everything I've been hearing, it's only the leader of a group. His name is Ryan Daniels. Supposedly, he has minimal security with him."

As dangerous as Las Vegas was, it was also a haven for criminals, so high-level meetings and deals went down in casinos with little fanfare or security. I benefitted from it because if I left a trail of bodies, it could come back on Carlos or me, and I would never want it to happen.

"Okay, let me know if you come across any other information on them."

"I can do you one better. We have a guy, Todd, who works security at The Zephyr where they're staying. I set up a meeting for the two of you in an hour."

"Do you trust this Todd guy?"

"He's planning to marry my Maribelle."

"Well then, I hope these are congratulations on their upcoming wedding." I really hoped we could trust Todd, because if not, I knew what I would have to do to protect Carlos and the business. I didn't want to see Evan's sister go through the heartache if she didn't have to.

Carlos nodded in understanding as Evan came into the kitchen. "Anything I need to know before I get changed?"

"Nothing I can't tell you in the car. You have anything, Carlos?"

He shook his head, and I turned back to Evan.

"Okay, let's get ready. We can get there early, so I can check things out."

Evan rolled his eyes. "You've been there at least a hundred times. You should know it like the back of your hand by now."

"I want to be prepared. You'll live."

Knowing I would need to get information from the men before I killed them, I added my knives to my inner jacket pockets and my gun to my hip. To the unsuspecting eye, I looked like a businessman looking to lose some money after work, which is exactly what I was going for.

Giving Evan twenty minutes to get ready, I started down the stairs looking at my phone to see if I had any missing messages. It stung a little that I hadn't heard from Carlie, but I didn't really expect to.

Putting my phone into the pocket of my slacks, I straightened my jacket as I approached the front door.

I could hear Evan rushing down the stairs behind me, trying to catch up.

Like clockwork, a car pulled up in front of the house to take Evan and me to The Zephyr and to accompany Jeff and Evan around town.

The ride was quiet. Even though Evan was a talker under normal circumstances, in situations like this, he was usually in his own thoughts, much as I was.

Pulling up in front of the main doors of The Zephyr, Evan and I got out while the driver went to park the car and await our return. The Zephyr was Carlos' jewel, the largest, cleanest, and most prestigious of the casinos he owned. It was clean and smelled good and brought in hundreds of millions, if not more, a year. He took pride in his businesses, both the front facing and the less than legal ones.

I could spot security as we walked in, and we received a few subtle head nods from them.

I checked the time. "Evan, you have about 15 minutes until you're supposed to meet with Jeff. I'll sit over in the lounge area since I can see the front door and the elevators."

"Okay, in the meantime, I think I'll play some blackjack." Evan enjoyed gambling, but he wasn't very good at it.

I was, but I tended not to bet against the house, especially Carlos' house.

"Sounds good." As soon as I sat in the lounge, a young woman asked if I wanted anything to drink. I asked for a diet coke, and pretended to play on my phone, watching the comings and goings.

Right on time, Jeff Martin left the elevator, straightening his tie.

Evan saw him almost immediately, tipped the dealer, and walked toward him. Reaching Jeff, he shook his hand, and they started toward the front lobby doors.

I sat up straighter to make sure I could see everything going on around me.

No one was paying attention to the two men as they left, but as soon as they stepped outside, a young man with a shaved head and tattoos wearing a white tank top broke from the roulette table and started walking toward the front.

Initially, I thought it could be someone who simply wanted to leave. As he neared, I could see the white supremacist tattoos, causing me to reach for one of my knives. Knowing the security wouldn't blink an eye if I needed to handle something, I palmed the knife.

The numbers 88 were on the back of his neck, and a German war eagle was on his wrist. Carlos mentioned the individual looking to encroach on Carlos' business was a racist piece of shit and had white supremacist tattoos. It could still be a coincidence, but I noticed someone I hadn't seen in years also watching the man. When he got to the doors, I stood, left cash on the table, and followed him. So did the other man, which meant my gut was right, and this was the guy.

Getting to the front door, I watched the man get into a gold Audi and leave the same way I knew Evan and Jeff had gone.

I waited at the door until the other tail got there. "Matteo, what are you doing here?" I clasped his forearm as he clasped mine.

"It looks like the same thing you're doing here. What's your interest in Ryan?"

"The man with the tattoos who recently left?" Preston looked toward the main door.

"Yeah, Ryan Daniels, a racist POS."

"I believe he may be the man I'm actually here for. If he is, I know where they're going if you want to tag along. You can let me know why you are interested in him on the way."

"Let me call Leilani and let her know I'm going with you. She's upstairs, and I think she has a spa treatment soon."

While he was on the phone, I asked the valet to get one of the company cars for me. As I waited, a young Hispanic man approached.

"Are you Mr. Wessex?"

"I am, and who are you?" I had a hand on my handgun. You can never be too careful, even on the property of one of the most feared men in Las Vegas.

He offered his hand to shake. "I'm Todd. Mr. Abarca told me I'm to meet with you."

Shaking his hand, I looked over at Matteo, still on the phone. I'm sure this trip with me was going to cost him a piece of jewelry or something. He would buy it anyway. He worshiped the ground Leilani walked on. I would too if I was married to a direct descendent of the Hawaiian royal family.

"Okay, Todd, plans have changed slightly. Matteo over there on the phone is coming with us. If you repeat anything you hear, you'll be right alongside Ryan when all this is said and done. Do you understand?"

I saw the fear in his eyes, but it was quickly replaced by resolve. "Yes, sir. I would never do anything to disrespect Carlos."

Matteo walked over, sizing up Todd.

"Matteo, this is Todd. He's dating one of Carlos' daughters. Todd, this is Matteo, a friend of mine from Hawaii." As Todd looked up at Matteo, I could see the fear in his eyes was back before he offered his hand to Matteo, who shook it.

"Todd, I asked the valet to get the car, but apparently it hasn't happened yet. Can you please have a word with him?"

"Absolutely." Todd walked over to the valet and spoke to him.

"Todd is security here. Carlos has him watching Ryan."

"Is he coming with us?"

"Yeah, I already warned him." I laughed. As much as Matteo looked to be more dangerous than me, I was definitely the one Todd should fear.

"So, Leilani's here with you on business?"

"Do you really think I could come to the ninth island without her?"

"True. Are the kids here, too?"

"No, they are home with Malakai and the animals."

"How is Malakai doing?"

Matteo's younger brother, Malakai, was the reason I knew Matteo at all. Malakai and I attended school together before he got himself into trouble, and I bailed him out, literally. He's a good guy, so I had my father help clear things up. Matteo had come to the mainland to get his brother, and we became close. He was also the head of the Kau syndicate, an organized crime group controlling most illegal things going in or out of Hawaii.

"He's good. I think being in jail and having to have his friend bail him out made him get his head on straight. He's my number two now. Well, and a babysitter when we need it."

I could imagine Malakai watching Matteo's three sons. They were a handful, but good kids.

I saw a black Audi pull into the valet area, and a driver jumped out.

Todd raised his hand, and Matteo and I walked toward the car.

"Do you want me to drive?" Todd asked as Matteo and I looked at each other.

"Do you know where you're going?" I didn't know how much Todd was privy to, so I wanted to feel him out before I gave him too much trust.

"Yes, Mr. Evan is planning to show Mr. Martin all the family businesses, and he and Carlos have a meeting."

"Then yes, you can drive while Matteo and I speak. Thank you." Both Matteo and I went to the back doors and slid in while Todd ran to the driver's door.

As we left the casino, I turned to Matteo. "So why are you following Ryan?"

"About six months ago, Ryan and his two brothers, Kyle and Dillon, arrived in Hawaii. At first it was small things, like a gun would go missing, or one of our drivers would get somewhere slower. Initially, I blamed my group, but you know some of them. When one of our girls was kidnapped at the bar, we learned about Aktion; It's their name, apparently.

It was a group of about 15, mostly young, white men who thought they were doing something. We took out five of them a week ago, and we heard they left the islands hoping to find more recruits and money here in Vegas. One of the men thought telling us about how Ryan said Las Vegas would be easy pickings because a Mexican ran it would get him out of dying."

"Do they not realize Carlos isn't even Mexican?" I laughed as the wheels turned in my head. Hopefully, they didn't gain many new followers in the week they'd been here, or else things just got a lot worse.

"They don't care. It's all about them being white and in power."

"So, Todd, do you know anything about this group?"

"Some, Mr. Wessex." Todd looked in the rearview mirror as he drove.

"Well?" I knew he was trying to be respectful, but I would rather he speak. I wasn't huge on the tradition where you're not to speak unless spoken to.

"Ryan was staying at The Zephyr to make it seem like Aktion had more money than they do. One of the girls was complaining about him only leaving her a dollar tip last night. Apparently, the rest of his group are in a hotel in Henderson waiting on a deal to go through, which will set them up to move product in."

"Matteo, are you here alone?" I asked as a plan formed in my mind.

"No, I brought six of my guys. What are you thinking?"

"Let Ryan think he's in the clear. Let him watch Jeff and Evan go to a few businesses, and then we have a conversation. Evan has a couple of locations he can stall long enough at for us to grab him up. I have a warehouse we can take Ryan to have a conversation where no one can hear what's going on. If you want to take your men to the hotel to take care of the others, you're more than welcome to come back and help with Ryan."

"I appreciate that. The girl they kidnapped? She's dating Malakai, so this is personal for our family."

"Okay, let me give Evan a head's up on what's going on. Todd, can you pull over?"

"Yes sir, is here good?" He pulled into the parking lot of a pawn shop. It was one of the pawn shops Carlos owned and Evan would be showing Jeff.

Getting out of the car, both Matteo and I got on our phones.

I called Carlos first. "Hey, so change of plans. Do you remember me telling you about Matteo? Arms dealer out of Hawaii?

"Yes, why is he here in Vegas?" Carlos sounded wary.

"Well, he's here because our mutual friend tried to home in on Matteo's area, too."

"Is this Ryan who you suspect of wanting to get the deal with Jeff?"

"From what Matteo said, they are looking at moving up and think their group can offer better terms than ours."

I could hear the clicking of Carlos' pen, something he did when he was thinking. "How many of Ryan's group are here?" Carlos asked.

"I guess they're all here in Henderson."

"Is your friend alone?"

"Never." It was the truth, and I wasn't going to lie to Carlos.

"Are they planning to help? What do they want in return?"

"Nothing as far as I know, but I can work it out with Matteo. Yes, we plan on making the entire problem disappear."

"Thank you for the update. Please let Evan know I look forward to seeing him and Mr. Martin later this afternoon."

"Will do." I hung up and called Evan.

"What's up?"

"We're at Ace Pawn. Plans have changed slightly, but Carlos says he's looking forward to seeing you and Mr. Martin later, so can you make your visit at Ace a little longer than planned?"

"Will do. Oh, you know about the gold Audi, right?"

"Yup, I'm waiting for him, actually."

"Perfect. See you in about an hour."

"Okay, I'll let Matteo know."

"Matteo's there? With you? What?"

"I'll explain later, but play your part." Evan didn't need to know the specifics. Most of the time, he liked being in the dark about things, especially when it got bloody.

"Okay, see you in a bit."

Matteo and I finished our calls at the same time.

"Everything good?"

"Yes, the men can be ready in about an hour. Do you need more time?" Matteo scrolled through his phone, looking at messages.

"Yes, Evan said he and Jeff will be here in about an hour as well, so we have time. Now to figure out exactly what hotel they're in. Todd, come here, please."

Todd jumped out of the car and all but jogged to where Matteo and I were standing.

"Do you know what hotel they're staying in?"

"No, but I can figure it out in no time."

"How?"

"There are only two places in Henderson where a group of men like Ryan could stay, and my cousins work at both of them."

"Can you call them and ask without putting them in danger?"

"Absolutely." Todd immediately got on his phone, speaking in rapid Spanish. In less than five minutes, he returned with a grin.

"They're at the Roadside Motel, and they took up most of the place. I guess they ran off some long-term renters, and Analise says they're gross."

"Tell Analise thank you from me next time you see her."

"I will. Do you need directions on how to get there?" Todd asked Matteo, who was already on the phone.

"No, I'm sure they can find it. Analise doesn't work tonight, right?"

"No, she's a dancer at one of the big shows at one of Carlos' other places. She works at the motel in the early afternoon."

Hanging up, Matteo replied, "The guys are set and will be at the motel in about an hour."

"Perfect, now we wait."

Less than an hour later, Evan pulled into the parking lot with Jeff. We waited in the car as they entered the building. Just as Todd went to say something about no one showing up, a gold sedan pulled into the back of the parking lot and the driver got out.

"That our guy?" I turned and asked Matteo.

"Yup, how do you want to play this?"

"I don't want him in the pawn shop because I don't want innocent people hurt. By the look of how many cars there are, it's probably pretty full. Let me call Evan and have security stop him."

I watched Ryan walk around the parking lot looking at the different cars. He was probably making sure there were no federal or state plates before he went inside. I couldn't tell if he was carrying, but if I was him, I would be.

"Hey Evan? Yeah, he's here. Can you have security lock the door for a minute while Matteo and I escort our guest somewhere quieter?"

"Yeah, one minute." I heard Evan call over to Rudy, a former army special forces officer who now was well paid to protect the store from theft. "Okay, it's locked. I'm going to take Jeff through the shop but away from the windows. He doesn't seem like he's smart when it comes to criminal enterprises."

"We sure he isn't a cop?"

"Absolutely. I think this is his first job, so he's a bit flighty."

"Gotcha, we're going to wait until Ryan goes to his car, then Matteo will drive a newer Audi for a while." I smiled at Matteo as we had already discussed the plan.

"Okay, I'll let Dad know you won't be home for dinner. Be safe." Evan hung up, and I sat and watched Ryan try to get into the building.

After a couple minutes of him yelling and kicking his feet, he stormed back to his car.

Seeing the signal, Todd drove up, effectively blocking the car from the pawn shop's cameras.

I stepped out of the car while Todd stayed behind the wheel, and Matteo stayed in the back seat. The tint on the windows was so dark no one could tell who was sitting in the back. We needed to be able to get away quickly if needed, and having Todd outside of the car put him in danger.

"Hey man, what's up with you blocking me in?"

"You Ryan?" I asked.

"Yeah, what's it to you?" I saw him reach toward his back, where he most likely kept his gun.

"I want to talk about a business proposition. Heard you and your crew were in town and wanted to get off on the right foot."

I saw him relax, and he smiled smugly. "Oh yeah? What you got? We may be able to make some sort of deal."

"Oh, you know, guns, money, girls, drugs. I heard you were the guy to talk to. If I'm wrong, I can leave you be."

"No, we can handle it, but do you want to meet somewhere else? We've taken over a hotel down in Henderson. It's a good place to meet. If you want to follow me."

"Nah, I have a place closer and definitely more secure than any hotel in Henderson. Do you want to follow me or…?"

"Yeah dude, I'll follow you. Do you want to meet my crew?"

"No, we can talk about the specifics later. Let's head out. It takes about 30 minutes to get there. It's right outside of town, but you know how traffic can be."

"For sure, okay, let's go."

I couldn't believe how stupid this man was. If someone approaches you on the street, you don't follow them. This was going to be easier than I thought.

As I sat back in the passenger seat, Todd motioned to Ryan as he got back into his car.

I turned to Matteo. "Well, is it me, or was that much easier than expected? He was practically eating out of my hand."

"Let's hope the rest of the evening is this easy."

I was hoping for the same thing.

After driving through town, we ended up in the warehouse district outside of town. The area was quiet, and Carlos owned most of the buildings. One of them he used to store gaming machines and if he needed a quiet place to work. I had used the same building a few times in the past and knew exactly where I wanted to take Ryan.

"Go to building 102." I instructed Todd as he drove through the buildings.

102 was a standard warehouse with a loft inside. The large bay doors allowed vehicles to enter and leave without people driving by the industry park. It was also toward the back, so even fewer cameras were watching us as we drove in. It didn't matter. Most of the cameras were Carlos' anyway. Even so, it was better to do things with less visibility in case the police came sniffing around.

"Wait here. Let me open the bay door." I got out of the car and tapped out the code for the smaller door. When I walked in, I turned on the overhead light and punched in the code to open one of the bay doors. It slid open, and Todd drove in with Ryan close behind. I also chose this building because I knew Carlos was in the middle of a money and gun job, and so the warehouse had racks of weapons and bricks of cash.

I closed the bay door once Ryan was inside and typed the code to lock it along with the door.

Ryan got out of his car with his eyes glued to the weapons and cash. So entranced by what he saw, he didn't even notice Matteo get out of the car and walk toward the door below the loft.

I walked over to Ryan to ensure his focus was on what it needed to be on while Todd stayed in the car.

"So, is this what you want to talk about?" Ryan turned to me.

"Sort of. We're building additional warehouses like this, and since some other organizations have come into town in the same business as we are, if you know what I mean, we're having issues moving merchandise."

"It's that damn Mexican, isn't it?"

I bit my tongue to keep from saying something. I had to play the part until I knew Matteo was ready.

"There's a Samoan group stepping into our territory as well. We can't have those outsiders come in, now can we?" I knew Matteo was listening to everything I said.

"Not at all. We took care of some Samoans in Hawaii before coming here. They were weak compared to my men, and we had no issues taking them out."

"Are you going to be stretched too thin working both Vegas and Hawaii?" I acted like a concerned seller who didn't want to lose.

"Nah, I'm currently recruiting even more men to the cause."

"Good to hear. Okay, so here's what I'm working with. Tell me if it's something you can handle." I went on to explain how we have 1000 guns come through every month which needed to be sold to buyers, both legal and illegal. The more I spoke, the bigger his eyes got, as if he thought he'd won the lottery. "Is this something you could handle?"

Ryan paused for a bit, as if he was thinking. "Definitely, what else you got? I have a big operation in Hawaii, and so if this is it, I don't know if it's worth sending all my men for."

Agreeing with him this may not be enough for him and his entire group, I set the bait a bit more. "Well, I think it's a comfortable starting point for us to ensure it's worth our collective time."

"Nah, I want to see it all first. I have other obligations for my men, and need to know how many to bring in for it."

"No, I want to start small because I need to know if I can trust you." His nose flared as if what I'd said upset him. My fingers were itching to pull my knife, but I wanted to wait a little longer.

"How do I know you're not asking a bunch of people to do this?"

I resisted the urge to roll my eyes.

"You don't. But let's go into the office, and I can front you some cash to help. Okay?"

I could tell part of him wanted the money, but the other part wanted to see everything.

"Sure."

I turned my back on him as I walked toward the office. As I got close to the door, I heard the slide of a gun and felt it press into my back.

"What we're going to do is go into the office. I will take the money, and then I'll take the guns and cash out in the warehouse. You feel me?"

Acting nervous, I stuttered, "P-p-p-please don't hurt me. I'm doing what I was told to do."

"You won't have to worry if you keep quiet."

Reaching the door, I intentionally fumbled the handle to give Matteo notice before I opened the door to the office and went in.

Hopefully, Matteo had moved the stuff like I'd asked. As I moved further in, I realized he had, so I waited until we were both inside.

"Where's the damn light?" Ryan asked as the door closed. "What the hell?"

I closed my eyes as the light came on.

"Well Ryan, you see, I didn't expect you to be this much of an idiot, but here we are. I'm Preston Wessex, and this here is my friend Matteo. You've already met, though, right?"

Seeing Ryan's eyes widen as he waved the gun back and forth between us made me chuckle. "Back up. I have the gun. Don't try anything. I have men outside."

"No, you don't. All your men are at the hotel. Don't worry, our guys are keeping them company."

"Wait, who are you?" Ryan paced, holding the gun in one hand while his hand ran through his hair as if he was trying to think.

"I work for Carlos, the man you so rudely called a Mexican. He's the head of this area, and you're stepping into his territory. Trying to set up a meeting with Mr. Martin? To what? Start leveraging for jobs here in Las Vegas? Tsk tsk." I paced as I pulled out my knife and twirled it.

"See, first you went and stepped into Matteo's area and took a woman hostage. What were you thinking? Then you came here thinking you could get a couple jobs and take away from someone who has been here for decades and is truly a good guy?" I kept twirling my knife and could see Ryan's eyes follow the sharp weapon.

"So, here's what's going to happen. Your men are free to leave as long as they leave Nevada and Hawaii." I looked over at Matteo, who wanted to say something, but I shook my head.

"What about me?"

"Oh, well, as the leader of your little group, we have to set an example for your men. I mean, it wouldn't be right if we let you walk away, now would it?"

I sprung when his stance faltered. I sliced his wrist with my knife, causing him to drop the gun, which Matteo quickly picked up. As Ryan screamed, I pushed him back into the chair.

"Matteo, can you please tie him up? We want him to see what's about to happen."

Matteo walked around and handcuffed his hands to the chair and zip-tied his feet to the legs of it.

"Now that you're comfortable, remember how I said your men could leave?"

Ryan's head bobbed as I turned on the tablet screen, showing the footage from the hotel. While we had waited to get Ryan alone, Matteo's men had paid for all the remaining customers to leave and stay in nicer hotels. Then they turned the cameras so we could all watch what they did to Ryan's men.

"I may have lied a smidge. I know it's a bad habit, but here's the thing; you thought you were better than Matteo and Carlos. You thought you had the men to come into another territory and someone would hand you a job?"

On the screen, Matteo's men were dragging Ryan's men out of their rooms and into the center of the parking lot.

"So, what we do is make an example out of them to show other groups you don't step into someone else's territory. Also, you're a piece of shit, so it really is like taking out the trash."

There was no volume on the screen, but I could imagine the screams as Matteo's men cut down every single man, first by cutting behind their knees, then their ankles, and finally at the hips. After they bled out for a bit, they lifted each man's body by the hair and slit their throats before dropping them back on the ground.

With only one man left, I turned to Ryan.

"Isn't he your baby brother? Did you get him all wrapped up in this? It's a shame you can't be there with him as he dies, isn't it?"

"Please, stop. I'll do anything. Please don't kill him."

Matteo was on the phone, and I motioned to him.

"Oh Ryan, do you think I care? No, you brought this on yourself, and you and your racist ass family end now."

Matteo told the person on the other end of the phone to do it, and Ryan's brother was killed on screen.

I could hear Ryan crying.

"Now you did this, and you're going to pay. Don't worry, they're going to light the hotel on fire, so no need to claim the bodies or anything." The screen lit up as the fires began.

I turned off the screen and kneeled in front of Ryan.

"You, on the other hand, are going to be the example for others. But it won't be as quick for you. I think I'll start with the fingers. What do you think, Matteo?"

"I think you should start with his *boto* and balls. What kind of man kidnaps a woman?"

"You know, you have a point. Do you want to take first cut?" I held my knife blade out to Matteo. I didn't usually let others use my knives, but I trusted him and had seen what he could do with a knife.

Taking the knife, he slowly sliced away Ryan's pants before dragging the blade down his thighs. I liked watching someone get cut almost as much as I liked being the one doing the cutting, but I was growing bored. Taking out my other knife, I pulled his hand toward me.

"Now Ryan, how many people have you killed?" I asked as a stabbed between his fingers.

"None. I never killed no one. We were into drugs and stuff, not killing."

As he finished, I slammed the blade into his middle finger, separating the finger at the second knuckle.

"Oh well, such a shame. Matteo, how many have you killed?" I asked as I saw him slice open Ryan's nutsack.

Ryan screamed as he watched his blood pour onto the floor.

"Shit, at least 15, probably more like 20. What about you?"

I stabbed between Ryan's fingers again.

"You have an advantage over me, Matteo. You can feed bodies to the sharks. I have to get creative with it." We laughed as I stabbed the knife into his ring finger.

Between the screams, Ryan sobbed.

"Naw, you have, like, mountain lions and stuff." Matteo stabbed Ryan's thigh right above the femoral artery.

"True, so my count? Are we counting officially dead or everyone?"

"Let's do officially dead." Matteo stabbed Ryan's other thigh.

"33." I sliced Ryan's arm from his wrist to his elbow.

"Damn dude, you're like five years younger than me, too." Matteo stabbed Ryan's stomach.

"Yeah, I'll let you have this one if you want it. Start to even the numbers."

"Well, that is mighty kind of you." Matteo looked Ryan in the eyes. "Are you ready to die?"

Ryan shook his head as Matteo stabbed the blade into his heart. "I was getting bored."

My phone rang as he spoke.

"Shit, I hate getting blood on my phone," I complained as I pulled it out of my pocket.

Seeing it was Seth, I answered. He rarely called me, especially on a job.

"What? I'm bloody busy at the moment."

"Sorry for calling, but she's gone."

"Who's gone?"

"Carlie's gone. I came by the house, and she wasn't here. I went by her mom's, and she wasn't there either."

"FUCK, how long has she been gone?" I cleaned my hands on the towels sitting on the desk.

"Victoria said she saw her a couple days ago, but she was busy with an event your father was putting on, so she didn't check on her."

"Okay, I need to clean something up, and I'll call you back." I hung up and threw the phone on the desk.

"You okay?"

"No, my fucking wife disappeared." I was pissed. Who did she think she was, leaving without letting anyone know?

"Wait, you're married now? Congratulations." Matteo was cleaning up the blood pooling around the body.

"Don't worry about the blood. We have people we pay well to take care of it. Yes, I'm married. My father arranged it."

"Oof, why did he do something so stupid? Can I help at all?"

"I don't know yet, but if I do need your help, I'll call, okay? Let's head out of here. I'm sure Leilani wants you back at the hotel."

"She does. She's been texting me for a while now, asking for a time frame. What are you going to do with his car?"

"Carlos will figure it out. Thank you for helping." I clasped his forearm as he clasped mine back.

"We may not be blood, but I consider you family, Preston."

"I consider you my family as well, especially since my own family is the way it is." Matteo knew a little about my family, so he smiled.

Looking back at Ryan's body one last time, I turned off the light. Todd was waiting for us in the running car.

"All done?"

"Yup, thanks for driving. I need you to work with the cleaners to send a piece of two of him to send a message. Let's head back to the hotel and drop Matteo off. I also need you to take me to Carlos' place, please."

"No problem." Todd turned on the radio, and we rode in silence. My mind was racing with where she could have gone, why she left, and what I was supposed to do now. I swear if I found her, I would make sure she never left the house again without an escort. The ride to the hotel wasn't long, and when we stopped, Matteo and I got out.

"Please tell Leilani hello from me. The next time we're both in town, we should get together, assuming I find my *wife*." I can't believe those words just came out of my mouth. The voice on my shoulder was worried about her, but the other voice didn't really care.

Matteo laughed. "I'm sure you will. I'll let Leilani know. She'll be sad she missed you." He held out his hand, and I grasped his forearm. We slapped each other on the back in a quasi-hug, and I got back into the car. This time, I sat up front with Todd.

"So, I heard you're engaged to Maribelle." I looked over as he drove.

He looked like he was in his mid to late 20s, so right around her age.

"Yes, we're getting married next summer. We want to wait until I had enough money to buy a house."

"Carlos would have bought you a house, or at least bought a house you could live in."

"True, but I want to do it on my own. It makes a difference to show Mari I can do it, that I'm worthy of her."

"Having drive is important, and I respect that. So, if Carlos retires, what do you want to do?" Seems like he is a good man and I liked him. He kept his mouth shut, but I don't know how much he'd been told, so I wanted to feel him out.

"Right now, I like what I do. Not only am I a security guard at The Zephyr, I do odd jobs for Carlos. Nothing bloody or technically illegal, mostly driving. I'm good at paying attention to small details. You still have blood on your wrist, for example."

Looking down I realized there were three small flecks of blood on my wrist near my palm.

I wiped it off. "Thank you. So, if Carlos retires and someone takes his spot, you would work for him or her?"

"Depends on who they are and what they offer me. Carlos pays really well, and he's respected in the community, both with his businesses and how he treats others. I wouldn't want to work for someone who isn't as ethical as he is, you know?"

"I absolutely do know what you mean. Well, let's hope whoever takes over for him is as good as he is." I hoped I was. I tried to be a good person, even when doing bad things.

We pulled onto the property, and I saw Evan was already there, which meant Carlos and Jeff were meeting. Looking at my phone, I realized it was almost five. That gave me time to step into the meeting before changing for dinner.

Instead of leaving, I saw Todd park the car. The meeting must be close to being over because Carlos and Nancy have a set time for dinner every night. I'd like to have him on my payroll if he wanted to be. I wouldn't push him because I've learned when you push people, they're more likely to lie to your face.

Looking in the mirror by the front door, I rearranged my hair and looked for any remaining blood. Not seeing any, I straightened my jacket and walked into the office.

Carlos always believed in having the office near the front door, so business never interfered with family time.

He and Jeff sat facing each other at his desk. Evan leaned against one of the walls near the door.

Walking in, I nodded at Carlos and moved closer to Evan.

"How's the meeting going?" I asked.

"Almost done. Jeff saw enough today to all but put Dad in his will. Well, and I think my conversational skills probably helped."

"Yeah, I need you to do something for me. Kind of high priority."

Evan's eyebrows rose in question, and I waved him off as Carlos called my name.

"Preston, can you please come over here and join the conversation?"

"Of course." I sat next to Jeff.

"Jeff I know you met Preston earlier, but I wanted to have you speak with him as well. I'm planning on handing over the businesses to Preston at the end of the summer. Assuming he still wants them."

I shook Jeff's hand. "Yes, still the goal as of right now"

"Great, Jeff's in business with a group out of the east coast, but they're looking to get their money cleaned outside the area. The heat has been too hot lately, and they don't want anything coming down on them."

"Completely understandable. How often do you plan to make the trip out here?" I asked Jeff as he straightened his glasses.

"We were thinking quarterly, but to avoid suspicion, we felt half the trips should be Carlos or a surrogate of his traveling."

"I agree with that assessment and would have suggested the same thing. You may want to move up your timetable depending on your cash flow. If some months are busier than others, you don't want the authorities to notice a pattern."

"Thank you. I hadn't thought of that, but you're right." Carlos smiled as Jeff complimented me.

"Well, I need to attend to a pressing matter. Do you still need me, Carlos?" I asked as I stood.

"No. I just wanted to introduce you. Is everything okay?" Carlos looked concerned by my comment.

"Yes, nothing I can't handle, but I need to take Evan to help me. We aren't leaving the property, and we'll be available for dinner."

"Okay, I'm glad. Please make sure to attend dinner. Nancy has been cooking all day." Carlos went back to talking to Jeff.

Leaving the room, Evan was right behind me.

"What's so important that you need my help?"

"Carlie has apparently disappeared." We went up the stairs toward Evan's office/bedroom.

"What do you mean, she disappeared? She isn't a rabbit in a hat."

"I guess Victoria and Freddie had to help my dad with some fundraiser, and Seth was running security, so no one noticed she'd left."

"Shit, how can I help?"

"I want to check to see if she took the credit card or the phone, and if she did, maybe we can track her down through one of those."

"On it." Evan sat at the computer and asked for the number of the phone and if I could get the credit card number.

I had the piece of paper with both pulled out before he finished his question.

"You randomly keep your wife's credit card number on a piece of paper?"

"No wise ass, I knew you'd ask for it, so on the way back to the casino, I called the credit card company, and they were more than happy to give it to me."

I paced as Evan did his magic on the computer. In less than five minutes, he straightened. "Got her."

I looked at where he pointed on the screen. "What am I looking at?"

"You're looking at a small town right outside Vancouver, British Columbia."

"She's in fucking Canada?"

"Apparently. Do you want to know more?"

"What else do you have?"

"She's at the residence of Matthew and Margaret Bartone."

"Who the hell is that?"

Evan tapped a few keys, and a photo of a middle-aged couple appeared on the screen. "It looks like Matthew Bartone is a business owner, and his wife stays at home. They have two grown children who are out of the house. They moved to Canada about fifteen years ago from..." he started typing again. "Sisters, Oregon. Wait a minute. Isn't Carlie's last name Bartone? Do you think they are—"

"They are absolutely related, but how? And why would she go there? I need you to find out everything you can about them while I call Seth and get a flight to Vancouver as soon as possible."

"Don't forget Mom made dinner."

"Evan, have I ever left before dinner?" I went to my room to pack and call Seth.

"Hey boo." Seth almost sounded timid as he answered.

"Boo? I didn't think we were that close."

"Sorry, I thought you were Marie. Carlie was at your place, and the door alarm should have been on. I thought I covered all the bases, but then I had to do something for your father."

"No need to apologize. I figured as much and thought it was funny. I need you to schedule me a flight leaving Las Vegas in a couple of hours to Vancouver, British Columbia, and I need someone to drive me to a house right outside town."

As I was explaining to him what I needed, it hit me. "Seth, how did Carlie leave?"

"Oh, um..."

"Tell me."

"She took the Supra."

"Fantastic. Have Freddie get the tracking information from my father, and I want you to keep an eye on it. Let me know if it moves."

"Your father has a tracking device on your Supra?" I could hear Seth telling someone something about security.

"No, he had it on the Mustang, but I switched it. Can you get everything sorted out?"

"Yes, your plane will be ready in four hours at the private airstrip near Carlos' house. I have a driver who can pick you up. Do you also need him to drive you back to the airport?"

"No, my wife and I will be driving back home together. Have the plane return to Redmond."

"Will do. Preston?"

"Yes, Seth?"

"I'm sorry. I didn't think she would leave."

"Like I said, it's not your fault. How's the construction going, anyway?"

"They'll be done tomorrow."

"Perfect, right in time for my return with Carlie." I couldn't believe I had spent money on a pool, when I could just move back in with my father if Carlie was to not come home. We were going to have a nice, long drive to discuss how nothing of the sort will happen again. Hanging up the phone after saying goodbye, I realized I wasn't upset. It was my fault for taking a job so soon after getting married, even if I had to. Carlie wasn't to blame, neither was Seth. If anyone was to blame it was me, and I could accept that.

I showered and put on casual clothing for dinner and the plane ride. On my way out of the room, I saw Evan coming out of his and holding a tablet.

"You have something?"

"I do. It looks like Matthew is Carlie's uncle, her father's brother. When they moved to Canada, he started up his businesses."

"Are those businesses legal?"

"Gambling mostly. There's some money laundering. It looks like he did a little gun running between Alaska and Washington, but not enough to be on anyone's watch list."

"Good, I want to know what I'm walking into. Anything else?"

"No, they seem like your run-of-the-mill family. Smaller house, two cars, some debt, but not a lot. If they're doing more than I can find, they've kept a low profile and have for a long time. One of their kids lives in Quebec and is a banker, and the other…" Evan slid some windows around on the tablet. "is a model in Europe. Comes home twice a year, all expenses paid by the modeling company."

"Interesting. If you find anything after I leave, let me know immediately, okay? I owe you."

"You don't owe me shit. It's not like you have a bunch of other computer geeks at your beck and call."

We headed down the stairs to the dining room. "How do you know? Maybe I'm keeping them away from you? Gotta protect my interests."

"You would never." Evan looked shocked at even the thought of me having other computer literate people in my inner circle.

"You're right. One computer geek is enough for a lifetime." I laughed as we rounded the corner into the dining room.

Nancy came up to me. "Carlos said something was wrong. Do you have to leave?"

"I do, but I wouldn't dream of missing your dinner. I heard you spent all day on it."

She smiled. "Not all day, but yes, I made a special dinner for you. Carlos said some business issues were cleared up, but everything was back on track."

"Yes, we were able to fix the issues pretty quickly." Evan winked when I looked over at him. Nancy knew what I did, but sometimes I thought she pretended not to.

"Great, go ahead and sit for dinner. The girls are helping me bring all the food in from the kitchen."

Right on queue, Mari and her younger sister walked out of the kitchen with platters.

I sat across from Evan and next to Carlos. "So, what's going on?"

Carlos offered me wine.

"No, thank you. I have to leave after dinner. Apparently, sometime over the last two days, my new wife, Carly, decided to leave. She got all the way to Canada before anyone noticed she was gone."

"Interesting. Do you know where she is?" Carlos poured a glass of wine for Evan.

"Yes, she's at her uncle's house. A Matthew Bartone."

"Good guy. I was sad to see him leave the States."

"Wait, you know him?"

"Yeah, he and his brother were big into gambling and money laundering in Oregon years ago. I learned some of my best tricks from them. When I finally got enough money, we moved down here and started buying businesses."

"He and his brother were in the life?" I didn't realize Carlie's father had been part of our world.

"Oh, they were the best. The issues started because Matthew wanted to start running guns, but his brother didn't. He was happy with what he had and didn't want more. He also had a young daughter and didn't want her to grow up around guns and such."

Shit, I wonder if my rooms were the reason she ran. Could she have gotten into it?

"Interesting. Thank you for the information. Do you want me to tell Matthew hello from you? I plan on seeing him tomorrow morning."

Carlos smiled as Nancy served the food. "Nancy, you don't need to go to such lengths. You cooked. We guys can serve ourselves." Carlos stood to serve. "Yes, Preston, I would appreciate it, and you may not get shot. I've missed him over the years."

The next two hours were filled with food and laughter. All too soon, I realized it was time to go, so I asked Evan if he could drive me to the airport.

"No, Todd's still out there."

"Todd has been sitting out there for hours?"

"No, he came back to take you to the airport. We aren't into torturing our employees." Evan laughed as I gathered my bag.

"Please tell Carlie hi for me and tell her she can come swim in my pool anytime she wants." Evan waggled his eyebrows.

If I didn't love him like a brother, I'd think he was being serious, but I knew he wasn't.

"Nah, she can stay in my pool."

"Spoilsport. Have a good trip, and I'll talk to you in about a month unless something comes up."

I hugged him. "Sounds good. You be careful down here."

"Always." Evan shut the door.

Todd was waiting at a black SUV with the door open.

"Thank you. Do you know where we're going?"

"Yes, Evan filled me in. We're going to the airport up the road. Your plane is all fueled and ready to go."

"Thank you, I'm glad you're marrying Maribelle. You'll be a good addition to the family."

"I hope so, Preston."

We drove to the airport with the music on.

My mind filled with what I was going to say to Carlie the next time I saw her.

"We're here. Do you need anything else before I go?"

"No. Thank you, Todd. Have a good night." I got out of the car and climbed the stairs to the plane. Settling in, I heard the pilot say we would be taking off in ten minutes as after we'd been cleared.

I closed my eyes and tried to sleep, knowing the next 24 hours were going to be stressful, at least emotionally.

Three hours later, the pilot woke me up to announce our landing. As the plane came to a stop, I stepped into the colder temperatures, looking for my ride.

A dark-colored Chevy Trax came skidding in and parked near the plane. A man in his 40s stepped out and leaned against the front of the car.

"You Preston?"

"You my ride?" I stepped closer to the car with my hand on my gun.

"Yeah, Seth sent me. Told me to tell you, 'Your mother's favorite duck was a Speckled Eider.'"

I relaxed my hand from my gun. Not even my father knew what duck my mother had loved, so it had been the code Seth and I had used off and on during my work.

"Nice to meet you, I'm Preston." I approached him and held my hand out to shake.

He firmly gripped my hand. "I'm Erik. Where to first?"

Knowing it was too late to impose on Carlie's relatives, I directed him to a hotel a half mile away from their house. I hadn't told Erik, or anyone, but I planned to walk there from the hotel. This way, no one could connect me, or Carlie for that matter, with them if things ever went bad. I knew I had made dangerous enemies over the years, but I didn't want Carlie's family to suffer because of it.

At the hotel, Erik gave me his number in case I needed him to take me anywhere.

I thanked him and checked in. Getting to the room, I called Evan to see if there was anything else I should know before I walked up to a random stranger's house.

"You have anything useful?" I could hear Evan typing in the background.

"Nothing other than no one knew Carlie had left until after she was gone. She stopped four times on her way north, twice to gas up, and it looks like twice to eat and rest. She stayed at a hotel in Mount Vernon last night. Phone doesn't have any calls in or outgoing."

"Okay, so she left and didn't tell anyone she was leaving. What else did you find?"

"She hasn't used much money since she left your house, and she doesn't have a bank account. I found her name listed as a trustee on an account, but that's all. I didn't know if you wanted me to dig more."

"Interesting. I don't think there's anything else right now, but if it changes, I'll let you know."

"Okay, sounds good. Have a good night."

"You too." I hung up and laid back on the bed. There wasn't much more I could do until I confronted Carlie in the morning. Hopefully, me mentioning Carlos' name would smooth the edges with her uncle. Or I could get shot.

Chapter Thirty

7 Days After the Wedding - Carlina

I didn't realize how tiring driving could be, so I needed to stop multiple times. I thought I could get to Vancouver by the end of the first day, but by the time seven rolled around, My eyes started to flutter shut, and I knew it was time to find a room. There was no way I'd be able to stay awake for the rest of the trip.

I pulled into a hotel in Mount Vernon and parked close to the front door, hoping there were cameras. I didn't know what Preston would do to me if something happened to his car, especially since I mostly stole it.

"Welcome! How can I help you?" the cheerful lady behind the desk asked.

"Hi, can I get a room, please?" Looking around, the place was nice, but I hoped it wasn't too expensive. I suddenly realized I'd never stayed in a hotel before, which I wasn't sure was a good or bad thing. This whole situation made me feel like I hadn't had many of the life experiences others had in life, as I watched a family with two young kids going to the pool.

"Yes, Ma'am. We have a king bed with a large tub. Will that work for you?"

"Um, maybe. how much is it?"

"$122 a night, ma'am. How many nights will you be joining us? "

Unsure if it was a good price, it registered that it didn't really matter if it was or not because I needed somewhere to stay as soon as possible. I pulled out the credit card Preston had given me to use. "Only one night, please."

"One moment." She walked away to run the card, and I looked around again. There was a restaurant where several people sat at the bar.

"Thank you, ma'am. Your card is tied to a frequent visitor, so your room was only $92 a night." She handed me the room card. "Your room number is on the card, and the elevator is to your right. The restaurant is open until nine pm, and the bar is open until midnight. Our pool, down the hallway there, is open all day but closes at 10. There's also a hot tub and a sauna, which is open until 11. There's free breakfast in the morning from 7-10 AM. Is there anything else I can help you with?"

"No, thank you. I appreciate your help." I took my bag and walked to the elevator while looking at the room number on my card. The card said 715, so I went to floor seven, hoping it was right. I saw a plaque with an arrow indicating rooms 700-716 were to the right. I followed the arrow and stopped at room 715. Tapping the card against the door lock, the light turned green, and I pushed it open. I flipped on the lights, and the room was huge. It was larger than my room in my childhood home. I checked out the bathroom, and there was a sink opposite a large tub. The tub was larger than anything I'd seen. Even the one in my new house wasn't this big.

I wanted to take a bath, so I started the water and went back to the bedroom. Putting my suitcase on the top of the dresser, I pulled out my PJs before walking back into the bathroom.

Relaxing in the tub, I stared at the ceiling. How did I get into this position? Not necessarily the bathtub of this nice hotel, but in general, married at 18 almost 19, about to have more money than I ever thought.

As I laid there, my hand ran down my chest, cupping each breast before running down to my core. I thought of how Preston looked in his suit. Laying my head back on the edge of the tub, my finger found my clit and I circled it, speeding up.

Sliding one finger inside me, I used my thumb to push on my clit. Closing my eyes, I thought about him kissing down my body. While I was inexperienced, I knew what I liked and read enough stories to know what I wanted Preston to do. At least what I wanted the hand I was pretending to be Preston to do. I flexed my finger while I tapped my thumb on my clit. Feeling the pressure build, I sped up the motions of my finger and thumb.

Imagining what it felt like for him to be running his tongue up and down my slit as his finger entered me, I tensed up more. Starting at my feet, a shiver ran up my legs until it exploded in my core. I continued to shudder as the after tremors of my orgasm coursed through me. It was the first time I'd ever thought of a specific person as I played with myself, and it was the first time I came this hard.

Relaxing in the tub, I realized water had spilled all over the floor. It must have happened when I came. Laughing, I laid back and relaxed in the tub. Having nowhere to be and no one waiting for me, I thought about staying in the tub all night.

As I lay there, I thought about starting this next journey in my life. It was doubtful life would include Preston, even though it may have been fun. No, I wanted something more stable, maybe one with my aunt and uncle. I should at least get to know them before I decided.

An hour later, I was out of the tub and snuggled into bed. I was both excited and nervous about tomorrow and hoped they were home when I got there. If not, I guess I'd be exploring the greater Vancouver area. I can't worry about what I don't know yet, and tomorrow is a new day.

The next morning, I woke up at eight and stretched. Today was the day I would meet some of my dad's family. I had breakfast and checked out.

As I got into the car, I thought about what I would say to them. The drive to Vancouver was an hour and a half, so I should be there by 11 am. The rest of the drive to Vancouver was uneventful.

Arriving at the house at 11:02, I looked at it for a moment before parking the car in front of the house.

It was a modest two-story, blue house with white trim. There was a two-car garage attached to the house. I absolutely loved the native garden out front. It was full of plants and flowers I was sure local birds, insects, and animals loved. The garden was alive and colorful.

Walking to the front door, I saw a small path ending at a tiled circle with a table and two chairs. If I ever had a garden of my own again, I wanted it to look like this. The door opened as I approached the steps.

A woman my height with brown hair and a nice smile reaching to her eyes stood waiting for me to walk up.

"Hello, Can I help you?"

"Hi, my name is Carlina Bartone, well supposedly it is now Carlina Wessex."

"Carlina! I thought that might be you. I'm Margaret, your aunt, but please call me Marge." She stepped back so I could enter the house.

"Hi, how did you know it was me?"

"I have seen photos of you since you were little. Your father mailed pictures until he passed away. You look a lot like your uncle, which isn't surprising because he and your dad were twins."

"Wait, my father had a twin? I knew he had a brother, but didn't know he was a twin. Is he here? I have so many questions."

"I'm sure you do. Let's get you set up in one of the guestrooms. Matthew is on a business trip, and I expect him to be back early tomorrow morning. You should rest. I'll get lunch set up, and we can sit in the garden and have lunch if you're hungry by then."

"Thank you. Are you sure you're okay with me staying? You don't seem surprised I'm here, and I don't want to impose."

Margaret put her arm around my shoulders. "If our family records are correct, your birthday is today, so I knew eventually you would come up. There's no imposition. This is what we do for family."

I'd been scared she would turn me away or tell me I wasn't welcome, so I was filled with relief. "Let me get my bag, and I'll meet you back here."

"Sounds good. I'll be in the hall."

I pulled my bag and purse out of the car before making sure I'd locked the doors. Back at the house, I looked around the garden again. It felt peaceful and was exactly what I needed to calm my racing mind.

"You have everything?" Margaret moved up the stairs, expecting me to follow. The hall was dark, but when she opened the door to the bedroom, light filled the hallway.

Pale yellow with flowers painted along the bottom trim of the room. The bedspread was light gray, and there were two pillows. While not as large as the bed from the hotel, it was large enough for one person to spread out.

"This is beautiful. Thank you."

"Why don't you relax for a few minutes, and I'll call you down when lunch is ready?"

"Sounds good. Thank you."

Margaret left the room, so I laid down. I wasn't tired, but I also didn't have anything else to do.

Less than 20 minutes later, I heard my name being called.

Downstairs, Margaret was by the front door with two plates. I took one as I opened the door. I followed her out as we sat at the table on the tiled circle.

She went back inside and brought back two drinks. "How was the drive up? I saw the nice car you drove up. Is it yours?"

"The drive was good but long. I guess the car is kinda mine? It's owned by my husband."

She put down her sandwich.

"You're married?"

"Yes. Long story short, and I can give you the longer version later, but I was forced to marry Preston Wessex a week ago."

Marge bolted up.

"Does he know you're here?"

"No. He was on a job in Las Vegas with his friend, Evan. Everyone else who's usually around the house was helping Preston's father with an event he was putting on, so I took it as my opportunity to leave."

"Will he be angry you're here?"

"I doubt it. Let's say the marriage isn't starting off on the best foot. We don't know each other at all. He's already on a 'job', and I was kinda rude to him before he left."

"So, why did you get married?"

"My mom's husband made me."

"What do you mean, he made you?"

Sighing, I took a drink before answering. "My dad put the house in my name in his will. Well, my stepfather, Baron, somehow leveraged the house without my permission to pay for his business or something."

"How? That doesn't seem legal."

"I don't know, but allegedly they're six months from paying off the mortgage, and then it'll go back into my name."

"We need to let your uncle know about this as soon as he gets home."

I could hear a phone ring from inside the house.

"I'll be right back."

As I waited, I could hear her talking on the phone but couldn't make out anything she said. I watched a bee buzz from one flower to another while a bird hopped along, picking up seeds. If I stayed with Preston, maybe we could get a garden. There was enough land, and I would love to have a place to sit and relax during down times of managing the house.

I was paying so much attention to the animals I didn't hear Marge come back. "Your uncle was on the phone. I let him know you're here, and he said he's looking forward to seeing you again."

"Are you sure you're okay with me staying? I don't want to bring any danger or anything to your house."

"No, at all. Our security team comes around during Matthew's trips, and I can handle myself. I noticed you admiring the garden. Do you like gardening?"

"Yes, my father and I built a garden at my old house before he died. The last time I was there, one of my stepsisters,

Beatrice, was taking care of it. I miss it though. It was something my parents and I did together before my dad died."

"Matthew and your father really enjoyed gardening during their younger years. They learned from their parents how to garden and had a large one on their family property. We moved up here, so it was the first thing Matthew really put time into other than work. I asked him for this table and chairs because I wanted to sit out here since I don't work, and since the kids are gone, I don't have much to do during the day."

"How many kids do you have?"

Marge looked at me strangely.

"Surely you've seen pictures, right?"

"No. After Dad died and Baron and his daughters moved in, all the photos of his side, and even my mom's as well, were taken off the walls. Maybe I should ask my mom where she put them. Well, if I decide to go back."

"After we've sat here for a while and enjoyed the sun, I'll take you inside and show you pictures of the family. We have two kids. Mira is a model and business owner in Europe. I think she's in France right now. She's the younger of the two. You turn 19 soon, right?"

"Yes, today actually."

Marge's eyes lit up as she talked about her children. "So, Mira is a year older than you. Jason is 23 and is a banker on the other side of Canada. He went to college out there and fell in love with both the geography and the people, so he stayed."

"You must be proud. Do you see them often?" I wish my mom talked about me the way Marge was talking about her kids.

"I've very proud of them. They're wonderful kids. They come home twice a year, and we go visit them if business takes us up their way."

"What type of business does Matthew do?"

A cloud passed over at the same time I asked, so it looked like a shadow passed over her face. "You really don't know anything about your father's side of the family, do you?" She put her hand over mine.

"No, I remember my dad would make us dinner almost every night, and we would spend a lot of time in the garden, but he went away for business sometimes. We always had what we needed, and I was only 10 when he died."

"I think it would be best if Matthew explained to you in the morning about your legacy and what your birthright is, especially since he was in business with your father."

Frustrated, I shivered. I knew so little about my family, but I was also wary of what Matthew was going to disclose.

"Do you want to go inside? It looks like a storm might be coming in from the coast." Marge looked at the clouds.

"Sure, you'll still show me the pictures, right? And I can help cook dinner when it's time."

"Thank you, and yes, we have albums of photos for you to go through."

We stood, and I picked up my plate and cup to follow her inside.

After putting the dishes into the sink, she led me to the living room doubling as a library. The walls were dark and cozy. Marge walked up to the bookcase along one of the long walls and pulled a photo album from the shelf. "This is probably where we should start. We lived next door to you." She sat next to me on the couch and opened the first album.

The first picture was of both families.

I traced my hand over my dad's face before looking at Matthew's. They were identical twins, or at least looked like it from this picture. My mom and Marge were standing near each other with all three of us kids in front of them. Both Jason and Mira had red hair and pale skin like me.

"We look so happy."

"We were. Your father and Matthew were in business together, and we built houses next to each other. You and your cousins would play, but you were young. I think you were about to turn four."

"I don't remember at all. All I remember is the lady with the cats who lived next to us." I said as I kept trying to remember them being next to us, but I couldn't.

"Is her name Adele?" Marge asked.

At some point growing up, I think I remembered hearing her name. "I think so, but I don't interact with her much. Her cats are in the windows sometimes." Marge didn't need to know I thought she was weird, having cats and never having guests over as far as I knew.

"Probably. She moved in after we left. She's nice and takes care of the house since we live up here now, but we still own it." Marge smiled as she looked at the pictures.

"Why did you end up moving?" I asked Marge.

"Sisters is a really small town, as you know, and Matthew wanted to expand the business, but it was difficult from Oregon, so we moved up to Canada." Marge answered.

I flipped through photos showing the two houses and the gardens. My father's had brightly colored flowers, and Matthew's had more of his native plants.

"This garden is still there. It's more overgrown than in this photo, but Adele has kept it up."

"I'm glad. Matthew loves gardening."

For the next four hours, Marge showed me her family as well as Matthew and my father's family's photo albums.

I learned about relatives and where we came from. Standing and stretching, I realized I was getting hungry.

"I can help you with dinner if you're getting hungry?"

"I am. All this talking has given me an appetite. Let's go figure out what we want to cook."

We walked into the kitchen, and while she rummaged through the pantry, I asked, "So, how do you know so much about the family? By being married to Matthew?"

"Your dad and Matthew were already working together when I married Matthew. Your mom and I didn't have to work. We got pregnant first and when Jason, and then Mira, napped or went to school, I found I had nothing to do, so I started doing genealogy. I did it for other people sometimes, but mostly for our families. Because the businesses were successful, there were times I was able to travel to archives to get more documents."

"You didn't mind being at home all the time?"

"I wasn't at home all the time; I was a part of several charities and did volunteer work, but I enjoyed it. Why do you ask?"

"Part of the agreement with me getting married was I'm not supposed to have to a job. I get an allowance, but I'm expected to stay home and take care of the house. We have a housekeeper, she's one of the best things to come out of the marriage. She's a wonderful woman by the name of Victoria."

"Did you work before you got married? I can see it being hard to give up."

"No, I didn't really know what I wanted to do after graduating high school a month ago. I was thinking about going to college or moving somewhere and doing something once I get my inheritance. I never had time for work because I did most of the chores at the house. My stepsisters were useless."

"Were?" Marge started piling up food on the island.

"How can I help? And yes, were. Well, Annabelle is still useless, but Beatrice, like I said earlier, has started working in the garden and seems to be helping my mom around the house. Before I married, they were both spoiled brats who did nothing but tell me to do more chores."

"We're making roasted vegetables and Lemon Sesame Chicken. You eat meat, right?"

"Absolutely, and I can help by cleaning and cutting the vegetables."

"Thank you. I'm sorry you're going through this."

"It is what it is. I didn't tell anyone I was coming up here, especially after what happened with my mom essentially giving my house to her husband."

"Yeah, it never should have happened. So, tell me more about Preston?"

I debated how much to tell her. I didn't mention the guns at all, but I told her what kind of person Victoria thought he was, and what type of person he had portrayed himself to me.

"What does his father do?"

"Charles Wessex, owner of most of the businesses in town, seems to know everyone and everything."

"I don't know if I know him, but Matthew probably does, especially if they lived in town the same time we did."

"They did, and I'm sure he does. He seems like an okay guy other than making me marry his son. But now, the more I think about it, I don't think he's the one who made me do it. I think it was Baron's doing."

"Your stepfather, right?"

"Yeah, he married my mom less than a year after my dad died, and he moved in with his daughters even before then. I don't remember them ever even having a wedding, so they must have gone to the courthouse or something."

It felt like she wanted to ask more but didn't.

I didn't have more information to volunteer, so we both worked silently as I cut up the vegetables and put them on a baking tray while she pan-fried the chicken. The food was ready just as I heard a clap of thunder and raindrops hitting the kitchen window.

"Do these storms happen often?"

"Not really, but if they do, they're usually pretty bad. We aren't in danger of flooding, and because of the rain, we don't tend to have many wildfires, so it's nice to watch the lightning sometimes."

Removing the vegetables from the oven, I checked to see if they were done with a fork while nodding in agreement. Placing the tray on the small table in the connected dining room, Marge brought the chicken. Going back in, I set the table while she brought in the pitcher of lemonade and glasses.

"Thank you for dinner." I poured myself lemonade.

"No, thank you. If you hadn't come, I would've had something not nearly as healthy as this. I think I still have the bag of popcorn somewhere I had planned to have for dinner."

"You don't cook if Matthew is gone?"

"No, not if I can help it. Matthew doesn't really care if I cook for him or not, but I try to anyway."

"Well, I'm glad I'm here then." I smiled as I piled food onto my plate.

"I am too. I hope this isn't a one-time visit, but we shall see what tomorrow brings." She fixed her plate and returned my smile.

Dinner was filled with trivial conversation about music, books, and what our favorite colors were. It was nice to have dinner with someone and not be glared at or otherwise ridiculed the entire time.

After cleaning the kitchen as much as she would let me, Marge turned to me. "I'm going to go lay down. It's still early, I know, but I have to be at the airport by 3 am to pick up Matthew, and if I don't sleep now, I worry I won't be up in time. Are you okay being here alone? Make yourself at home, and you can watch TV or read if you want."

"Thank you, I think I'll watch some TV since I've been mostly reading the entire week Preston has been out of town. There wasn't really anything else to do at the house."

"Okay, the remote is by the couch, and if you press 'info', it'll show you all the channels and stuff. Don't worry about the noise. Once I'm sleeping, I'm out. I'll try to be quiet when I leave. Matthew will want to sleep in, so let's say breakfast at 10?"

"That sounds great. Thank you again." I moved to walk out of the kitchen toward the living room.

Marge came up and hugged me. "No, thank you for coming. I know Matthew will be excited to see you. He's been worried about what happened after your dad died. With everything going on up here, and the fact the last time he saw you and your mom was at your father's funeral, he didn't know if he should reach out. He did try to a couple times. I think the third time, your mother yelled at him, told him you were moving on, and he needed to as well."

Hugging her back, I teared up. "Don't feel bad; It'll be okay. I'll figure out what's going on with my life, and then I'll be great."

"I know you will."

She went upstairs to their bedroom as I made my way to the living room and turned on the TV.

After spending five minutes going through all the channels they had, I settled on a cartoon channel and curled up on the couch and watched TV until I fell asleep.

At 2:30, I heard soft footsteps on the stairs, and I sat up, initially not remembering where I was.

I saw Marge using the flashlight on her phone to guide her.

"You leaving for the airport?" I asked, and she jumped. I tried not to laugh, but she dropped her phone as she jumped.

"Yeah, it takes about 30 minutes to get there, and his plane lands at 3:10. You should go to bed. I'm sure Matthew won't be as quiet as I am."

"Thank you, I will." I got up as she turned on the lights so I could see where I was going.

As I reached the guestroom door, I called out, "Have a good drive."

Right before the lights went back off, she responded, "Thank you. Sleep well."

Smiling, I entered the bedroom and changed before sliding under the covers. Even though I didn't think I felt tired, the minute I closed my eyes, I could feel myself falling asleep.

Chapter Thirty-One

8 Days After the Wedding - Preston

I was up by seven but thought showing up at Matthew and Margaret's house so early would be impolite. Instead, I hit the gym, spent an hour doing cardio, and thirty minutes lifting weights.

Back in the room, I took my time deciding what to wear. Since I'd come straight from Vegas, I'd only brought everything I'd needed for the trip there, so I didn't have many choices. This detour was unexpected. I didn't want to come off as too black tie, so I chose a polo, slacks, and my tennis shoes. While I felt a little underdressed, I thought it was a good look for what I was there to do.

Taking a shower, I considered how I was going to approach not only Carlie's family, but Carlie. Storming in there and throwing her over my shoulder like a caveman wouldn't work. From what Carlos told me about Matthew, it probably wasn't the best decision if I walked in and did that. First, I wanted to talk to Matthew before figuring out how to get Carlie back to Oregon.

Downstairs, I had breakfast in the connected restaurant. All the families eating made me wonder if I ever could ever have something like that with my own family. Instead of vacations, I took jobs, which usually ended in blood. Depending on who I eventually decided to spend my life with, I don't know if she would be willing to accept me with all my flaws.

Thanking the waiter, I left a tip and checked the time. It was after 9:30, so I figured I would get there before 10, which seemed like a good time. No longer breakfast, but not quite time for lunch.

I asked the hotel if they would mind holding onto my bag while I did some sightseeing around town.

They gladly tagged it and put it in a back room so I could get it later. I didn't want to show up on the Bartone's doorstep with luggage. It wouldn't be a good look. I checked the directions Evan had sent me late last night and took off walking.

Less than five minutes later, I saw my Supra parked in front of a small, blue house. Checking the directions again to make sure this was the right place, I looked over my Supra to make sure there was no damage.

Not seeing any, I made my way up to the door through a garden and rang the doorbell.

A blonde-haired, green-eyed man about my height answered the door.

I could tell he was related to Carlie, so this must be her uncle, Matthew.

"Can I help you?" He eyed me with one hand behind his back.

I knew he probably had a handgun, but I didn't reach for mine at all. This was his house, and I was a stranger.

"Hi, this may sound strange, but I believe your niece, Carlina Bartone, is here. I'm her husband." I offered my hand, and he shook it while laughing.

"So, you're Charles' son, Preston, huh? My wife was just telling me all about the fiasco you and Carlina seemed to have found yourselves in." He turned so I could follow him into the house.

Looking around, I saw photos of family and wildlife. Sitting at the dining room table, Matthew offered me a seat.

I sat and continued looking around, expecting something, anything, to happen.

"Don't worry, this house is safe for all who enter it, as well as safe from those who try to enter it without permission."

My shoulders relaxed a bit, but I kept my knife close.

"Mar, can you please get Mr. Preston here a cup of coffee?" Matthew asked over his shoulder to a tall brunette woman standing in the kitchen.

She raised her eyebrows at me for confirmation I wanted coffee. I nodded, and she came over with a cup. "Cream and sugar are on the table. Are you hungry? I made scones this morning."

"No thank you, ma'am. I ate at the hotel this morning."

"Okay, but please call me Marge. I'm not old enough or gray enough to be a ma'am." She placed the coffee on the table in front of me with a smile.

I smiled at her before Matthew cleared his throat.

"Good, let's talk before Carlina comes down." Matthew turned toward me.

"What would you like to talk about?"

"I'd like to know what the hell is going on. Why she was married to you, and what is happening to her inheritance?"

"I can explain some, but before I do, I need to tell you hello from Carlos in Las Vegas. I don't want to forget, or Carlos will find out and skin me."

"You know Carlos?" Matthew cocked his head.

"Long story short, I'm good friends with his son Evan, and I plan to take over the business when he retires."

"So, he trusts you? Mar, can you get my phone?"

"Yes, I have dinner with him and Nancy anytime I'm in Vegas, and Evan was my best man at our wedding."

Marge returned with the phone, and Matthew ran through the contacts. Picking the one he wanted, he clicked on it and put the phone down on the table on speaker.

"Hola?" I heard Carlos's voice questioning the call. I assumed he didn't have Matthew's number saved.

"Carlos, this is Matthew. I have a young man in front of me who is claiming to know you."

"Is he a punk, with brown hair, tall, thin, and looks like he couldn't hurt a fly?" Carlos laughed, knowing he was on speaker.

"Yup, exactly like that." Matthew looked me up and down.

"Yeah, that's Preston. He saved me a lot of money and time this past week. He's the best there is for a certain kind of work." While outwardly stoic, inside I was grinning like a loon. I knew Carlos liked me, but to call me the best? It made me feel good.

"What does he do for you? Especially since he married into my family."

I opened my mouth to say something, but Marge held up her hand.

"He's a killer, but I think he wants to get out of that line of work. He's next in line for my businesses down here."

I concurred with his assessment. I would kill if I had to, but I didn't want to be a gun for hire anymore.

"Sounds good. It's been too long. Please give Nancy my love, and the next time we're in Las Vegas, I'll be sure to come visit with Mar."

"She's still with you? I was sure she'd have left you by now." Carlos laughed.

"Carlos, you know the only other man I could ever love is you, and there's no way I could beat Nancy in a fight," Marge replied before Matthew could.

Both men laughed while I sat there, unsure of what to do.

"True. Okay, well, Nancy is calling me for brunch, so I best get off here. Take care, Matthew. Preston, Matthew is good people. You hear me? You tell him everything."

"Yes Carlos," I heard the click before I could say anything else.

"Well, you're vouched for, so let's get down to business."

"So, my father, Charles Wessex, owns most of the businesses where Carlie, I mean Carlina, and I live. Her stepfather, Baron, is a piece of shit and owes my father a lot of money. Instead of taking it out on Baron's skin, my father decided I needed to get married. I did need to get married because I have money coming from my mom's family if I can stay married for a year."

"Okay, so Carlina, the heir to the Bartone businesses in Oregon, was forced to marry you?"

"She was yes, but Bartone businesses? I don't think I know of any businesses owned by the Bartone's."

"You wouldn't. They used to be in our names, but we moved up here, and Carlina got older. Mike didn't want the businesses to come back on his family at all, so we put everything into shell corporations. I run all the operations in Canada, and there are assigned managers who run all the businesses in Oregon and Washington."

"I don't know if my father knows about any of this. He was going to have me marry one of Baron's daughters, but at the last-minute Baron got my father to change his mind, and I married Carlina about a week ago now."

"What are the stipulations?"

"We have to be married for a year, and she has to stay home and essentially be a housewife. We have a house, she has a car, we have a housekeeper, and I gave her a credit card. I would have been there, but Carlos needed me for some business in Vegas right after the wedding."

"Your Supra she drove up here?"

"Seeing as she put a pink steering wheel cover on it, and it has a Bath and Body works air freshener, I'm guessing it's hers now. Which is fine. I have others."

"Okay, what else?"

"I'm expected to give my father some of the money I'm getting for his businesses."

"Are you going to?"

"No, I'm going to take over Las Vegas and the entire western coastline with my friends from Hawaii. Stateside coast."

"Why?"

"I have killed, and I'm sure I'll kill again, but I don't want to be involved with anything highly illegal anymore. No trafficking, no drugs, no questionable imports. I want to run clean businesses that are not currently clean, if you know what I mean." It was the first time I'd told anyone other than Evan and Brandon, another classmate, what I wanted. It felt nice to finally get it off my chest.

"I respect your desire to clean things up. Mar, can you get us more coffee, please?" Matthew made kissy faces at his wife.

"Yes, if you stop making duck lips." She laughed as she stood to get the coffeepot. Returning, she poured more coffee into our cups before setting the pot on a coaster in the middle of the table.

"It was kissy faces, not duck lips." Matthew mocked offense.

I wanted a marriage like this with someone who I could joke around with, but we loved each other.

"Anything else?"

"Why are you here?"

"To get Carlina and take her back to Oregon. She needs to be in Oregon, so we can continue being 'married', and I can get my money." There was no point in sugarcoating things.

"Yes, she does need to go back so she can get her money," Matthew replied.

"Her money?" I didn't understand what he was saying.

"Why are you telling him all this? He doesn't need to know any of it." I heard Carlie storm down the stairs into the dining room.

"Carlina Antonia Bartone, you will not use such a tone in this house; do you hear me?" Matthew stood, facing her.

I sat back and watched her face turn red before she burst into tears and ran into Matthew's arms.

Chapter Thirty-Two

8 Days After the Wedding – Carlina

The sun was shining through the windows, and the sound of voices filtered up the stairs when I woke up. The bedroom door must have been left open last night. I could hear Marge's voice, and two men speaking. Laying there and listening, I realized one reminded me of my dad's voice while the other — was that Preston? How did he find me? I jumped out of bed and put on leggings and a long T-shirt. Brushing my hair and putting on slippers, I went downstairs.

Near the dining room, I could hear them talking about me and my family. I heard who I thought was Matthew tell Preston I needed to go back to Oregon so I could get my money, and I couldn't stand it any longer.

"Why are you telling him all this? He doesn't need to know any of it." I screeched.

Turning the corner, I saw Marge and Preston sitting at the table as Matthew stood.

"Carlina Antonia Bartone, you will not use such a tone in this house; do you hear me?"

The stern warning came from eyes identical to my father's. Or at least what they would have looked like if he had lived. Breaking down in tears, I rushed to him, throwing myself into his arms as he patted my head and told me it was going to be okay.

Seeing movement to one side, Marge was getting a plate of food for me and a cup of coffee. Backing away from Matthew, I stopped crying and sniffled.

"I'm sorry. I shouldn't have thrown myself at you." Stammering, I sat at the table where the food and coffee were.

"Why?"

"Because you don't know me, and I threw myself on a relative I don't remember." I was embarrassed Preston had seen the whole thing, but he didn't say anything.

He stared at me as I ate. Or it felt like he was staring at me the whole time, anyway.

"I'm sure I resemble your father, and it's been what? 8 years since he passed away? It's okay. I have no issues with you crying into my shirt." Matthew smiled.

"Thank you. I don't know what hit me."

Marge patted my arm. "Emotion, it's okay."

In between bites of scone and sips of coffee, I looked at them. "So why did you share everything with Preston?"

"Because Carlina, you turned 19 yesterday. A lot of things are about to happen, and you need to be prepared."

"Like what? I know I get money, and I'm supposed to get a house, but what else?"

"Even though we didn't call or try to visit, we sent letters. Have you not been getting any of the letters we've mailed?" Marge frowned.

"What letters? I only got one before I was married. Well, I had to steal it from Baron's office."

Matthew and Marge looked at each other before responding. I couldn't tell what the look was, but it wasn't a good one.

Marge held my hand while Preston sat forward.

Matthew sighed. "You gain control of all of Oregon and Washington for the Bartone family because you're the only child of Michael and those were the territories he controlled. You're also to receive your inheritance and the house he built, along with the one next door."

I looked between the two. "No, what? Seriously? But what about Adele? What about your children?"

"She's a caretaker. You can allow her, and or her children, to live there forever if you want. You'll still become the owner. Our children aren't involved in the business, and they wouldn't want the houses. They have their own lives."

"Then how was my mother able to leverage the house?"

"What are you talking about?" Matthew stood.

"Baron told me I had to marry Preston because he and my mom had gotten a mortgage on it, and it was still six months from being paid off. He said if I didn't get married, he would stop paying for it, and we would lose the house."

"You know it shouldn't have happened, right? He shouldn't even know about the house unless..." Marge looked at Matthew, who agreed.

She rushed out of the room.

"Where's she going?"

"Going to get the copies of all the letters we mailed to you we've saved in the event didn't get them for some reason. Preston, this may turn into something in your wheelhouse if you're willing to take on a job."

"Wait, what? What would he need to do? And speaking of Preston, did he tell you he has a room full of guns and knives?"

Matthew rubbed his temples as he looked at Preston, who shook his head and leaned back, enjoying his coffee.

"Carlina, my niece. Your father and I, and Preston are in 'the business'."

"Well, yeah. I know you all have businesses. So what?"

Preston snorted as I turned to him. "Don't laugh at me. This probably would never have been an issue if you hadn't left the door unlocked, and I found your fun little room of torture devices."

"Those aren't torture devices, but I have some of those too, if you want to see them." Preston winked at me as I huffed and turned toward Matthew.

"No, we're kind of like the mafia. We have legitimate businesses, and we also do some not so legal things. The Bartone's have what's known as a syndicate."

"What do you mean? My father didn't do anything illegal."

"Have you been in your basement?" Matthew asked.

"We don't have a basement." I crossed my arms defiantly. If there was a basement, I would know about it.

"Yes, there is. The passage is in the garden, and the code is your birthday, like the code to the basement at your neighbor's house is Jason's birthday."

"I have worked in the garden my entire life and don't remember ever seeing a door."

"It's there, I promise. I'll have Mar find the blueprints for your properties."

Marge came back with a stack of paper. It looked like they had sent me a letter at least three times a year every year since my father died.

"These are all the letters we mailed you." She handed me the stack. "I made copies in case you didn't get the ones I sent. Yesterday was your birthday, so you still have time to get everything straightened out."

"Well, what if I don't want to take over the businesses? What if they don't exist anymore?"

"They do, and you will. Read the letters, and Preston, I assume you'll help her?" Matthew looked at Preston.

"Yes, sir. If there's anything going on with the banks, I have some friends and a computer program I have been working on with them to figure it out."

"Good, Carlina, you need to go. I'll have Preston carry you out to the car if I have to, but you have to go." Matthew hugged me.

I didn't want to go. I wanted to stay here with them. It felt like home, not like with the pompous smirking jerk standing between me and the door.

"I know you don't want to, but right now it's the best thing, okay? Here, take our number, and if you need anything or if Preston needs to disappear, let us know." Matthew looked at Preston, and I swore he paled a bit.

"I don't want to, but I will. I need to figure this out and figure out what I'm going to do."

"Good. Preston, Carlina will get her stuff ready. I need to speak to you privately for a minute."

"If it's about me, I want to know about it. No more secrets, and I mean you too, Preston." I stabbed my finger into his chest.

"No more secrets. We have a nine-hour drive, so we'll have plenty of time to talk."

"Wait, we're driving back? In what?" I looked out the small window to see if there was another car out there.

"The Supra. You think I was going to leave it up here? That's a negative, Ghost Rider."

"Oh, makes sense. Let me go get my stuff, and we can leave." I slowly walked upstairs. I knew it was the best thing, especially with my inheritance, but I didn't like how Matthew and Preston seemed to know stuff I didn't.

In the guest room, I put everything together and switched from my slippers to my shoes. This was utter bullshit. I felt like I was being handed from one man to another, and I didn't like it.

Downstairs, I gave the keys to Preston as he reached for them.

"You get all of your conversations done?" I asked with disdain.

"Yes, we did. Are you ready to go? There are a couple stops I need to make before we can get on the road home." Preston took my bag and walked outside.

I hugged Marge first. "It's too bad I can't stay longer."

"I know, dear, but once everything is figured out, we'll come visit."

Turning to Matthew, I hugged him. "Are you sure this is a good idea? We don't even know this man."

Matthew looked at me with my father's eyes. "Yes, Carlos trusts him, and we talked. He may seem like a jerk. We all do, but he isn't. You need to trust him."

"I don't trust easily."

"Nor should you, but if the women in his life tell you to trust him, then he's safe."

I pouted as I turned around and walked out the door. From the porch, I waved. "I hope to see you again soon."

"You will, Carlina. You will," Matthew said as Marge closed the door.

Sliding into the Supra, I tried to sit as far away from him as I could get. I looked at him, and he laughed as he put the car into gear.

"So, nine hours home? Then what? We pretend we're all married and happy and shit?"

"I have to make a couple stops, and I'm thinking we should stay in Seattle or Portland tonight. I've had a long week, and I think we could use the time to get to know each other better before going all the way home."

"Stay as in, like, a hotel room?" My eyes widened at the thought of us being in the same room.

"Yes, like in a hotel room. I know you know what a hotel is because you stayed in one in Mount Vernon."

"What? How did you know?"

"Carlie, you used the credit card I gave you. You didn't think I couldn't trace it?" Preston smugly reclined as he drove.

"Oh, I may not have thought that far ahead."

"Was this first time you've ever stayed in a hotel?" Preston asked.

It wasn't worth lying about, especially since I was told I could trust him.

"Yes, we've never gone anywhere, especially after my mom married Baron."

"Well then, I'll have to fix that. So, first stop is to get my stuff from the hotel I stayed at last night and then lunch."

I sat back. There wasn't really anything I could do unless I wanted to jump out of the car, and we were going too fast. I closed my eyes as Preston turned on the radio and connected it to his phone. The sound of hard rock filled the air around me as I lost myself in thought.

Within minutes, we slowed in front of a hotel.

"Why are we here?"

"I need to get my bag I brought with me from Vegas. Now, be a good princess, and stay in the car."

"I'm not a princess. How long will you be?"

"Like two minutes. Why? You thinking about taking the car again?" Preston smirked as he took the keys and locked the door before going inside.

Even though I wanted to revolt, to push his buttons, I stayed in the car because I knew my aunt and uncle were right. I pulled out the stack of papers they'd given me and read through the letters. I'd gotten through three of them before Preston unlocked the door and slid into the driver's seat.

"Getting some reading in?"

"Yeah, if I'm supposed to be this boss of a large syndicate, then I should read up on what I need to know, don't you think?"

"True, if you want to. It's a lot to take in if you haven't lived the lifestyle your entire life." Preston put the car in gear and pulled away.

I turned to him. "Have you been involved for your entire life?" Ever since he arrived at my aunt and uncle's house, he seemed different. Not as much of a jerk.

"Yes." He stoically looked ahead.

"So, where are we going now?"

"My dad has a business associate in Vancouver I need to see."

"Are you going to..." I didn't want to finish my sentence.

"No, I'm not going to kill him. I just need to pick up a package for my father."

"Wait, are we going across the border with something illegal? I don't want to go to jail."

"Princess, even if it was illegal, you wouldn't be going to jail. There's a reason criminal organizations get away with what they do. They pay people off."

"Oh. I guess I have a lot to learn." I sat back with the letters, debating whether I wanted to keep reading them.

"You don't have to take it over. Like I said, I'm sure there can be concessions and such."

"No, if my dad was involved, I want to know what he did. He was a good man." I crossed my arms, waiting for him to disagree.

Instead, he said nothing and kept driving.

I watched as we drove through Vancouver and ended up at a warehouse.

Stopping the car, Preston turned to me. "Listen, you need to stay in the car, okay? This isn't a good part of town, and I'll be in and out in no time."

The seriousness in his eyes told me he wasn't joking, so I sat there and agreed.

"Good. We'll get food after this if you're hungry." And then he was gone, again locking the doors behind him.

Instead of going back to reading the letters, I glanced around at our surroundings. It looked like an old section of town with many business warehouses. In contrast to some newer ones, the one we were in front of was in disrepair.

I saw what I thought were cameras, so while it looked rundown, there was at least some security. I also saw four men walking around, and at least two of them had guns in their hands.

Sliding a little further down in my seat, I watched them as they walked from warehouse to warehouse. Right before they approached the car, I saw Preston exit the building with a bag in his hand.

Seeing the men, his free hand went to the back of his jacket. As he got closer, I unlocked the door so he could get in. He threw the duffle in the back seat and got in.

Preston had started the car and was moving before his door was completely shut.

"Is everything okay?" I asked, even though it was obvious it wasn't.

"Yeah, those guys want what's in the bag, and we don't want them to have it."

"What's in the bag?"

"I didn't ask, and he didn't say, nor do I think I really want to know."

I looked at the bag, briefly debating if I wanted to know. "So, are you telling the truth? You want out?"

"Yes and no. I want out but not out of the life all together. I don't want to be in the stuff my father and others are into."

"Like my father?"

"From everything I know, your father wasn't into anything highly illegal."

I felt a small weight lift off my shoulders. "I don't know if I should be happy or upset. My mom knew all along and never said anything."

"I'm going to have Evan do some digging, but I think it may have something to do with Baron."

"Well, he's an abusive prick, so I'm not surprised."

"Has he hit you?" Preston looked over from driving.

"No, I mean technically, yes. He slammed me into a wall, but he hasn't hit me, hit me. But he's acted like he was going to. I'm sure he's hit my mom, though. I've seen bruises and stuff. She's also changed since she met him. She used to be outgoing and happy. Now she almost never leaves the house and is always moping around."

Preston nodded.

Not knowing what else to say, I went back to the letters. Preston turned the music on again, and we rode the rest of the way to Seattle in silence.

***

I finished reading the letters as we arrived in Seattle.

Seeing me put them away, Preston looked over. "Learn anything?"

"I got a list of all the businesses the Bartone syndicate owns in Oregon and Washington. I have some of the names of managers, the ones Marge and Matthew knew could help me and some information about the businesses."

"Do want to tell me? You don't have to."

"I do, because I could use your opinion."

We drove up to a nice hotel with a valet. "Are we staying here?"

"Is it okay? We can go somewhere else if you don't like it." Preston looked worried something was wrong.

"No, it's... are we staying in Seattle? I thought we hadn't decided. And this is a really nice hotel. I mean, we don't have to stay somewhere this nice." I stammered, not really sure what to say.

"Have you been to Seattle before?" Preston asked as he grabbed the duffle bag. He didn't wait for me to answer as he walked around to the passenger door and opened it.

He offered me his hand, and I took it because there were people watching, and I didn't want to be rude. His hand was smooth and warm, and I wanted to keep holding it, but the minute I was outside of the car, I moved my hand away.

He walked toward the back of the car to get the two other bags.

"Here, let me help. I can take my own bag since you have two of your own." I offered as he tried to juggle all three.

"Thank you. So, you didn't answer my question. Have you been here?"

"No, I..." I looked away.

"You what?" Preston grabbed my chin and forced me to look at him.

"Before driving to Matthew and Marge's, I had never left home."

Dropping his hand, he stared at me. "You're saying you've never left the tiny town we live in? And then you drove my car all the way to Canada? Wait, how did you get through the border?"

"I've had a passport since before my dad died. When I turned 16, I renewed it. It wasn't hard."

"Interesting, but more importantly, you've never been to Seattle?"

"No, nor have I been to Portland."

"Portland is a short drive for us. We can make the trip anytime, but Seattle? So, the Space Needle? The Pier?"

"Nope, I mean I know what they are, but I've never seen them."

"Oh, we're going to have so much fun. Seattle is one of the places my mom and I loved to visit before she got sick." Preston's smile died a little at the mention of his mom.

"I'm sorry. The way everyone talks about her, she seems like she was a great person."

"She was. She helped make me the person I'm today. Well, the non-work side of me." Preston turned to the valet driver. "Here are the keys. I want her away from all the other cars. Do you understand?"

The Valet driver looked at the car and back at Preston. "Yes, sir. We'll put it in our special reserved area. Please let the front desk know you valeted your car."

"I will, thank you." We walked into the foyer and up to the counter.

"How can I help you?" the young man behind the desk asked.

"We would like a room for one night please, preferably a higher floor, facing the water if possible."

"Perfect, so one bed or two?" the man asked Preston, and I froze.

What if he only says one? Am I going to have to sleep in the same bed with him?

"What do you have available?" Preston looked at me, and I'm sure he saw the fear in my eyes.

"Well, if you want something above the 10th floor on the waterside, it'll need to be a single king. I could get you on the 9th floor, but other buildings obscure the view."

Preston looked at me for guidance. It made me feel good, like he wanted my opinion.

"I want above the 10th floor?" I said, not recognizing the words until they left my mouth.

Preston hinted at a smile before turning back to the man.

"The wife wants an upper floor, so an upper floor we shall get." He pulled out his wallet and pulled out a black card.

"Oh, you're a member?" the man asked, seeing the card.

"Sure, we'll go with that." Preston slid the card over.

Running it through the machine, the man's eyebrows rose before he handed over the key inside a little envelope. "Sir, it's a pleasure having you stay with us. Your room number is on the envelope. I hope you have a pleasant stay. Is there anything else I can help you with?"

"Yes, can you please have a driver ready for us in 20 minutes? We had our car valeted." Preston looked at me again.

I agreed, not knowing what was happening.

"Yes, do you have a place you wish to be taken?"

"Yes, I'd like the driver to be available for the next —" Preston looked at his watch, "four hours for us."

The man picked up the phone to make a call.

I had so many questions. "Why do we need a driver for four hours? Also, why was the man surprised?"

"We have 20 minutes to get to our room and get ready. About that? My family owns a controlling portion of the hotel." Preston guided me to the elevator.

"You what? No. You know what? Never mind. What do I need to get ready for?" My brain couldn't wrap itself around everything that had happened in the course of the last week.

"Dress casual but with good walking shoes." He said nothing else as we got into the elevator with two other couples. Preston pushed the 15 while the other two pushed lower numbers.

After the other couples got off, the elevator took us to our floor. The floor had the same little signs as the hotel I'd stayed at, but instead of many numbers, there were only four.

"Why are there only four numbers?"

"Because there are only four rooms on this floor." He chuckled as he followed the arrow pointed for rooms 1501-1502.

"We didn't need something this nice. It must be awfully expensive."

Preston stopped right in front of 1501. "Princess, for as long as we are married, you will not need to worry about money, so stop."

"For as long as we are married, huh? You're saying I won't have to use my inheritance at all?"

Preston didn't answer as he unlocked the door and pushed it open with his hip.

"We shall see how you play your cards." He smirked, yes there was the old Preston. The hot but annoying man I married.

I didn't know what to expect when I entered the room, but a whole suite was not it. There was a tv and a couch, and a full kitchen along with a dining room table. There was a door I was sure led to the bedroom.

"This is expe—" I started before he pushed me against the wall and put his head next to mine, resting his forehead on the wall, his whole body pushing against mine.

"What did I say?" he whispered in my ear, his hot breath tickling the small hairs on my neck. I let out a small gasp.

"To not worry about money?"

"Yes, now be a good girl and go get changed. We have somewhere to be in less than 20 minutes." He kissed the crux of my neck as he stepped away.

"What if I don't get ready?" I snarked....

"Then you'll miss out on seeing Seattle, my Princess, but if you want, you'll see a lot of me." He smirked as he went into the bedroom with his bag and the duffle.

I wanted to see Seattle, but there was a small part also wanting to see more of him. Pulling my bag onto the couch, I opened it. I pulled out jeans and a tank top.

It was a nice night and since we had a driver, I figured if I got cold, we could come back. I heard the shower start and so I quickly changed. Looking at myself in the mirror, I fixed my hair and sat to wait for Preston.

Soon, he was out of the shower and dressed in a tight black T-shirt and a pair of slacks. I knew he was a jerk, and I should stay away from him, but seeing him in the T-shirt made my brain short circuit.

"You like what you see, Princess?" he asked as he walked in.

"What? No, I was wondering how such a big ego fit into such a small T-shirt." I blinked and stood.

"Well, you look really nice."

Now I felt bad for being a jerk when he was being nice. "Thank you, and you do look nice."

"Oh, I know. I mean, this ego did fit into the T-shirt, but it was a tight fit." He opened the door for me with a grin.

Rolling my eyes, I followed him into the hallway.

"Are you going to tell me where we're going?"

"If you must know, I'm going to take you to dinner on the pier. There are a lot of really good places to eat."

"Am I dressed okay?"

"Princess, in these places, you could be wearing a burlap sack, and they would serve you. You'd likely look just as good in a burlap sack, too."

"Are you staring at my ass?" I put a little extra sway in my hips.

Chapter Thirty-Three

8 Days After the Wedding – Preston

"Well, you're swaying it in front of me, so what's a man to do?" I knew she knew exactly what she was doing, and I was going to take advantage of it. I was really excited about showing her around town.

In the foyer, I approached the counter. "Is the car ready?"

The woman who hadn't been there earlier looked at me before flitting her eyelashes at me. "I don't know. Should I check?"

I couldn't believe she was trying to flirt with me, especially right in front of my wife. "Yes, my wife and I have places to be. Can you please look into it?"

She glared at me before making a phone call.

Hanging up, she looked at me and leered at Carlina before sneering. "Yes, your car is out front. It's a gray sedan, and your driver is Michel."

I was still figuring out what to say when Carlina stepped up to the counter. "Trying to hit on a man with a woman obviously right next to him? And then sneering at the woman after the man said, 'his wife'? Real classy. Not exactly how I would conduct myself, but to each their own. I mean it isn't like you are disrespecting a majority owner's wife or anything." She turned and walked toward the front door.

It took me a second to catch up with her.

"Really?" I asked as we walked outside.

"What? I may have been your last choice as a wife, but we are married, and her behavior wasn't okay." Carlie answered as she walked up to the car.

Shrugging, a little impressed, and turned on, I opened the door for her before I got in on the other side.

"Hi, I'm Michel. Where am I going first?"

"Please take us to the pier. Anywhere is good since we plan to walk for a bit before dinner."

"Perfect, I'll drop you off by the most restaurants." He pulled out of the hotel.

"So, what are you thinking you want for dinner?" I asked, realizing I knew nothing about her, so this was more like a first date, even though we were married.

"I don't know. Why don't you pick since I don't really know what my options are?"

I looked at her.

"What?" she asked.

"I don't want a wife who is indecisive. I want you to have a voice."

"Considering I've never been here and haven't eaten the variety of food you have, I have no idea what I could even imagine wanting, so I want you to pick. Trust me, I'll tell you when I have an opinion."

I heard Michel cough back a laugh.

"You make a good point. I'm sorry."

We rode the rest of the way in silence, which was only about 10 minutes to the pier. I appreciated he dropped us off farthest away from the Ferris wheel because I wanted to surprise her with it at the end of the night.

When we stopped, Michel rushed out to open Carlie's door as I opened mine. On the sidewalk, I handed Michel three 100-dollar bills. "I'm going to take her to the Ferris wheel and then we'll go to the Space Needle. Could you call and get us two tickets for each, please?"

"Absolutely something I can do. What do you want me to do with the change, sir?"

"Keep it if there's anything left. We should be at the Ferris wheel in about 90 minutes. Can you make it work?"

Grinning, Michel answered, "Yes, I can. You can pick them up at will call. Thank you." He got back into the car and took off, probably to find a parking spot near the Ferris wheel or somewhere nearby.

"Ready to go?" I offered my arm to her.

"What did you talk to him about? I saw you give him money."

"Yes, a tip for him waiting for hours for us."

"I'm realizing there's a lot I don't know, like how do you know when to tip someone?" I could see her frustration.

"You won't need to. It's not a woman's responsibility."

She spun around toward me. "What do you mean, it's not a woman's responsibility?"

"I mean, as long as we're together, I'll always be the one doing it, so you don't have to worry about it, but if you want to learn, I'm more than willing to teach you."

"Oh, makes sense. Sorry, the last week has been a lot." She slowed down to walk next to me.

"I get it. It's been a long week. Okay, so seafood? Or American?"

"Let's do seafood since we're literally on a pier."

"Perfect. I was hoping you'd say that. I know this place. It's in the next building, but if you want to go through this one first, we can."

We were standing in front of a building with restaurants and a candy shop.

"No, I'm hungry, but maybe if I want candy later?" She smiled as she waited for me to tell her where to go.

"There's a better place for sweets down the way. We'll go there after dinner. They also have ice cream."

"Well, why didn't you say so? Let's go to dinner."

"You only want to go to dinner now because you want ice cream later." I genuinely smiled as she shimmied at the mention of ice cream.

"Maybe. It doesn't matter. Let's go."

The Crab Pot was a fun place with seafood and other local options. We got the sourdough starter with butter.

"What are you thinking for dinner?" I asked as the server brought the bread.

"I don't know. Everything looks so good. You've been here before, right? Why don't you choose for me this time?" Carlie looked over the menu.

"I have, and is there anything specific you don't like or you're allergic to?" I knew what I was thinking about getting, but I wanted to make sure she wasn't going to have an allergic reaction or something.

"No allergies here." Carlie put the menu down and buttered a piece of bread.

I watched her eyes roll back as she tasted the bread along with a soft moan.

"It's good, isn't it?" I forced myself not to moan myself as my cock reacted to her sounds.

"It really is. I love sourdough, but this is so good."

The server returned to our table to get our order.

I ordered the Pacific for two. The assortment of seafood, along with sausage, corn on the cob, and red potatoes, seemed like a good choice for a new diner.

"Anything else?" the server asked.

"I'd like a diet coke. Do you want something, Princess?"

I saw Carlie's face redden at the name.

"No, water is great, thank you."

The server smiled and left with our order.

"Do you have to call me Princess?" Carlie asked after the server was far enough away.

"No, I like to, but I don't have to. Is there something else you'd like me to call you?" I rested on my hands on the table.

"You like calling me Princess? I thought you were being sarcastic." Carlie's eyes widened.

"No, I mean at the beginning, yes, but now? I kind of like it, and you're the heir to the Bartone throne, so you really are a princess."

"Let's not get too bougie. Do you want to talk about all my family stuff now?"

"No, we can talk about it in the car on the way home tomorrow. Let's talk about you."

The server dropped off my drink.

For the next hour, Carlie and I talked. Talked about our childhoods, what we enjoyed, what we didn't like. I was surprised how easy it was to talk to her, and it felt like we'd known each other a lot longer than a week.

After our meal was done, I paid the bill. "You ready for ice cream and the Ferris wheel?" I asked, offering my hand to her.

Chapter Thirty-Four

8 Days After the Wedding – Carlina

"I'm so full, I don't think I could eat ice cream, but I think we should still go there and see what they have." I took Preston's hand as I stood but quickly dropped it. Dinner was good, but I wasn't at the holding hands stage.

"Of course, but if we want to take some back to the hotel, we should wait until after the Ferris wheel."

"Oh yeah, where's the Ferris wheel?" I asked.

Preston turned me around and pointed behind the restaurant. In the darkening sky, the Ferris wheel brightened up the surrounding area with all its lights.

"Wow, I don't know how I missed it." I said as we walked toward the Ferris wheel.

"I'm sure it's because you were so enamored with me, you couldn't look away." Preston said, and I rolled my eyes. He was good looking, but not so much I didn't pay attention to my surroundings.

"Yeah, I'm sure." The line for will call wasn't long as we waited to pick up the tickets, and we got into the next available gondola. I wasn't a huge fan of heights, but I didn't want to tell him, so I steadied myself in the gondola as it rose.

At the very top, the gondola stopped and swayed a bit. "Is something wrong? Why did we stop?" I looked around, trying not to panic.

"Haven't you ever been on a Ferris wheel? It stops at the top so you can see the view."

"No, I haven't." I breathed heavily through my mouth, but I didn't think Preston realized I wasn't enjoying myself.

"Oh no, I should have asked before I bought the tickets. Are you okay with heights?" Preston put his hand on my thigh near my knee.

"Yeah, I'm not used to it, but I like it. It's pretty." I looked at him, and he leaned in and kissed me. The kiss was soft at the start, and I liked it. I moved closer as the kiss deepened.

One hand stayed on my thigh while the other pulled me in by the back of my neck. We weren't in the most comfortable position, but the kiss was nice. I didn't know what to do with my hands, so I put one on his leg. I wanted to be closer to him. Even though we were next to each other, I wanted to be closer. As I was about to move to sit in his lap, the gondola started up again, and I moved away from him.

"Are you okay?" Preston asked as he left his hand on my lower back.

"Yeah, I didn't want to be making out when the car gets to the bottom." I could feel my face flush.

"Makes sense. My goal is to *not* make you uncomfortable."

"Thank you. Nope, not uncomfortable."

I sat with my hands in my lap for the rest of the ride.

When the wheel stopped, we quickly got off, and I walked a few feet away from him. I took a deep breath to clear my head. The more time I spent sitting next to him, the more I wanted to be with him.

"Do you still want to go get ice cream? There's one more place I'd like to take you tonight." Preston caught up with me.

"No, I don't think I'm feeling ice cream right now. Where are we going?"

"Do you want to know, or do you want it to be a surprise? If you don't want to go, we can go back to the hotel." Preston looked at me under the streetlight.

"Don't tell me. I want to go, and I'm excited for the surprise." I was really excited. This was the first time someone had done something for me in a long time. It made me all warm and fuzzy.

"Okay then, let's go." Preston walked toward the parking lot where I realized the car we'd ridden to the pier in was parked.

As we approached, Michel got out and opened the door for me while Preston went around to the other side of the car.

"Thank you." Preston accepted the papers.

"What do you have?" I tried to read the writing on the pieces of paper, but he quickly put them into a pocket.

"Our next stop. Remember, you wanted it to be a surprise."

Even though I wanted it to be a surprise, I still huffed at him for not telling me where we were going.

We rode in silence as I watched out the window at the buildings and lights. I enjoyed living in a smaller town, with dark nights and quiet streets. There were times I wondered what it would be like living in a large city, especially one which never slept.

I felt the car turn and slow, and I looked over at Preston, who was looking out his own window. He looked like a kid admiring something. From my angle, I couldn't see what he was looking at.

"What are you looking at?" I asked as his eyes reflected the lights.

"Our stop," he said as the car stopped.

Michel was out of the car and opening my door as Preston got out on his side. As I turned around, I saw a metal frame high rising in the air. Looking up, I could see the building continued on for what seemed like forever.

"Thank you. It should be about 40 minutes," Preston told Michel before Michel got back into the car.

I hadn't realized Preston had come around to my side of the car until I felt his hand on my lower back.

"Are you ready?"

"Am I ready for what?" I looked around.

"The Space Needle, I had Michel get us tickets while we were at dinner." He walked toward the building.

"We're going there?" I asked as I caught up with him. Even though I wasn't much shorter than he was, his long strides forced me to walk faster.

"Yup, all the way to the top."

I looked up and realized just how high it was. It was much higher than the Ferris wheel, and I was a little worried about getting sick while we were up there.

When we walked in, there was a person taking tickets, and we were ushered into the elevator. We rode up with a group of people, so I stood close to Preston. The elevator was on the outside of the center metal structure so I could see how high we were getting. The outer rings appeared, and the elevator dinged. The door opened behind me, and as we turned, I saw the observatory along with a couple of food places. I stepped off the elevator and looked around. The walls were all slanted glass, and toward the outer walls, the floor was glass.

"There's a pie place here. Do you want to get a piece of pie on the way down?" Preston asked, but I couldn't respond, as I was enthralled by everything around me.

I had never been up this high. Feeling a bit lightheaded, I reached out and grabbed Preston's hand.

"Are you okay?" Preston made me look at him.

"Yes, I needed to hold on to something." I felt more confident holding his hand.

"Hold my hand. I won't let anything happen to you," Preston whispered in my ear.

I didn't even respond as we walked around the observatory level. There were people taking pictures of their family members against the glass wall.

"Can we get a picture?"

"Of what?" Preston asked as he gazed out over the buildings.

"Us, here." I thought it was obvious, but then I realized I hadn't really wanted to behave like a couple until now.

"Oh, yeah, Let's get one." Preston pushed me back toward the glass wall. Right before I touched it, he turned me around. With one hand, he held me around my waist while he took a picture on his phone with the other. Still holding me, he turned the phone and showed me the picture.

"I really like this picture. Thank you." The image showed the cityscape behind us. We looked happy.

"No, thank you, Princess. You made the picture good."

I smiled at his compliment.

"Okay, I'm ready for pie and the hotel now. Are you?" Preston asked as he moved his hand from my waist to my lower back.

It felt good there, like it belonged, and I started to wonder if maybe we could make this marriage work after all.

"Sounds good to me."

We walked over to the TipTop Pies stand and both got a slice. I chose Yakima Peach and Preston bought a slice of apple for himself. The clerk handed them to Preston, and he carried the bag as we walked toward the elevator.

"These smell so good; maybe we should eat them in the car." Preston and I rode the elevator down.

"Absolutely not. I don't want to get crumbs all over the car, and we didn't get a piece for Michel. It would be rude to eat it in front of him."

Preston kissed me on the temple. "You really are a good person, aren't you?"

I smiled as the door opened, and we got off the elevator. This time, however, I grabbed for his free hand.

"Oh, *now* you want to hold my hand? Is it because I bought you pie?"

"No, it's because you're being sweet, *and* you bought me pie." I laughed as I got into the car on the side Michel held open for me. I heard Preston huff as he got in on his side.

"Did you enjoy the Space Needle, Ma'am?" Michel got into the car and put it in gear.

"I did. Thank you for purchasing the tickets."

"It was my pleasure. My grandparents brought me here once a month when I was a kid. As I sat waiting for you, I realized I hadn't gone since they passed away. My son and I should go next weekend."

"I'm sorry for your loss. I think your son will love it, especially since they have pie at the top." Preston commented as he put the pie between us.

"I appreciate it, and yes, he'll love the pie." Michel drove us back to the hotel. "I hope you two have a good night." Michel returned to the driver's side after letting us out of the car.

"You too, Michel." I replied as Preston put his hand on my lower back and escorted me to the lobby.

The flirtatious lady from earlier was at the front desk again as we approached. She smiled at Preston, but then she saw me.

I finger waved at her while we walked past.

"Seriously?" Preston asked as we got into the elevator.

"What? I was being friendly." I blinked innocently at him.

"If I didn't have this pie..." Preston started as the elevator went up.

"You would do what? Nothing, because you're all talk." I don't know where the comment came from, but the look in Preston's eyes scared me a bit. I felt my panties get wet from his heated look.

"Pie first, always pie first." I didn't know if he was talking to me, or to himself, but either way, I was going to eat pie.

I went straight to the kitchen after Preston opened the door. "Do you want something to drink? I'll grab the forks."

"No, thank you. Where do you want to eat?"

"The table is fine. I don't need peach all over me." Walking around into the living room area, I saw Preston staring at me while he held the bag.

"What?"

"Peaches on a sexy peach? I'm here for it."

I wanted to be snarky and say something else, but the look in his eye was almost feral, and I wasn't sure I wanted to go there yet.

"Okay, I won't talk about peaches." I smiled as I sat. I heard him groan as he took his seat. This was fun. I knew I was probably going to be punished somehow.

The peach pie smelled so good I almost didn't want to eat it after opening the box.

"The peach smells amazing. I should have gotten that one instead." Preston reached over with his fork.

"You keep your fork away from my pie, or I will stab you." I raised my fork threateningly.

"Fine, I'll eat my delicious apple pie and won't share with you either." Preston made comments about how good it was as he lifted his fork to his mouth.

I shook my head and took my first bite and moaned. It was that good, but about halfway through, I was done.

"Do you want the rest? I'm full." I asked Preston as he grabbed my leftover pie and ate it. "You could have said yes, you know." I laughed as he finished off both pieces, and he took the forks back into the kitchen.

Leaning back in the chair, I realized it was time to go to bed, but I didn't know how the sleeping arrangements were going to be, and I needed to shower.

"What are you thinking about?" Preston asked as he brought me a glass of water.

"How the sleeping arrangements are going to work, and I need a shower."

"I need to catch up on some stuff with Evan, so if you want to shower, I can work out here."

"Okay, I'll be fast."

"Take your time."

Grabbing my bag from the couch and going into the bedroom with the connected bathroom, I put my bag on the huge bed taking up much of the room. Preston had put the duffle we'd stopped to pick up in the closet along with his bag.

Shrugging, I grabbed what clothes I needed and took my shower.

After stepping out of the shower, I put my hair in a towel and got dressed.

I found Preston in the living room with his laptop at the table and on his phone. With one hand, he was playing with a small knife like a fidget toy.

I silently watched him as I walked around the table and sat in front of him.

He looked up for a second before looking back down.

"Yes, I don't know if we'll need to use the full program, but I'll know within a couple days." He paused to look at me with a slight smile. "Yeah, we're staying in Seattle. It wasn't too bad of a drive." Preston typed something on the laptop as he listened.

"Okay, well, tell your mom her favorite son says love you." He looked at me and rolled his eyes.

"Yes, Evan, I'm talking about me. We both know it."

I watched as Preston smiled during the conversation. His eyes lit up when he truly smiled, and I could tell he cared about Evan and Evan's mom.

"Okay, talk to you tomorrow." He hung up and shut the computer down. His hand never stopped playing with the knife.

"Everything okay?"

"Yeah, Evan and I have been working on a program with a friend of ours that could come in handy, depending on what we find when we get home."

"What do you mean?"

"Are you sure you want to talk about it now? It can wait, and I'm getting tired."

"It's ok. We can talk about it later."

Preston ran his hand through his hair and laid the knife down with his other hand. "If it pertains to you, or to our marriage, I will always tell you. There is more if you want to know, but if it'll upset you, then there are some things you don't need to know."

Thinking about what he said, I could feel myself starting to have feelings for him. "I appreciate it, and but for right now, let's start slow. But if I'm going to be a part of this life, with or without you, then I'll need to know more. Does that make sense?"

Preston smiled as he stood. "It does. Ready for bed?"

"Um what? We didn't discuss where you're going to be sleeping." I stayed sitting because I had a bad feeling I knew where this was going.

"Well, since I've been driving, and I paid for the room, I should get the bed, right? But of course, you're welcome to join me."

"You want me to sleep on the couch?" I stood and walked toward him. "I thought I was a princess? Shouldn't I have the bed to myself so I can get as much beauty sleep as possible?" I smugly smiled.

"No. If you're in that bed, you will not be sleeping." He raised an eyebrow.

Instead of responding, I walked toward the bed.

"Did you hear me?"

"I heard, 'Yes, Princess. You can have the bed all to yourself because you're my wife.'" I made it through the door before he picked me up around the waist from behind.

"Not what I said," he growled in my ear. Trying to squirm out of his hands, he carried me over to the bed and tossed me onto it.

I crawled up to the pillows and sat up slightly.

"Fine, we can share the bed, but you have to sleep on top of the covers on this side of the pillows." I pulled the pillows down and built a wall, giving myself the majority of the bed.

Preston silently walked over to his side of the bed.

I watched as he took off his shirt and worked on unbuttoning his pants.

"Um, what do you think you're doing?"

"I sleep nude. I hope you're okay with skin." Preston grinned as he paused, taking off his pants to put a gun and knife on the side table.

"Can I have the knife on my side?" I asked, not really wanting it, but wanting to see if he would give it to me.

He picked it up and handed it to me by the blade so I could grab the handle.

Feeling the knife in my hand, I lightly played with it. I watched Preston and watched his eyes glimmer.

Wearing his boxer briefs, he got onto the bed.

"What do you plan on doing with my knife?" He laid on his side, facing me.

"Nothing. I just wanted to see if you would give it to me." I handed it back.

"No, we aren't playing a game." He took the knife and ran the knife point down my chest and stomach over my shirt, and I sucked in a breath. I didn't look at him as he continued playing with the knife and ran it down my thigh.

"If you feel uncomfortable, you tell me to stop, okay?"

Instead of responding, I raised my shirt a bit higher.

"You are beautiful. You need to stop right now before I can't stop." I heard Preston stammer. The power I felt making this man, this killer, tremble pushed me on.

"Stop doing what?" I lifted my shirt more as he ran the cool tip of the knife against my stomach again. The cold metal against my hot skin felt nice.

"What. You're. Doing" Preston motioned to my shirt, which had slid up to show the bottom of my breasts. Preston's words were not a request but a demand, so I stopped lifting the shirt. He placed the knife on the side table next to the gun and rolled back over. He was closer this time, on the pillows versus on the other side of them.

"Okay, time for bed." Grinning, I scooted down the bed so I was lying flat. Pretending I hadn't stirred up something in Preston, I couldn't tell if he wanted to ravish me or push me out of bed. It was time to find out.

"Not going to happen." Preston rolled so he was on top of me so fast I squeaked. His legs were on each side of mine, holding me in place, but I could feel his hard dick against me. He lifted himself so he was above me, looking down.

"What? I didn't do anything."

Preston took one of his hands and ran it through my hair as he held himself up with the other.

"Oh, you didn't do anything, huh?" He grabbed my right hand and held it above my head, holding it with his hand as he grabbed my left and put them together, holding them both in one hand. His other hand caressed my face as he lowered himself.

"Nope, nothing," I said as he kissed me. What started off as soft soon turned heated. My hands were still above my head, so I couldn't touch him. I felt his tongue run against my lips, and I opened them slightly to grant him more access.

His tongue darted in before he bit my lower lip gently.

I wanted more, needed more. I met his kiss with my own energy as I arched my back to press further into him.

Holding himself up with his hand holding mine, his other hand ran up and down my side, lifting my shirt to caress under.

As his hand brushed my breast, I sucked in a breath.

He let go of my hands to remove my shirt. I laid back down with him looking down at me. I insecurely felt the urge to cover my chest

"You're beautiful." He kissed down my neck, lightly nibbling as I squirmed.

I needed release as I tried to rub my legs together.

"Not yet." Preston pushed my legs together again with his knees, so I couldn't rub them together. As he got to my breast, he sucked in my nipple between his lips and lightly bit it.

I groaned at the feeling.

"You like what I'm doing?"

I couldn't form words, so I moaned as he continued kissing and biting across my chest and down onto my stomach. I felt like I was going to explode if he didn't touch me soon.

"More, I need more."

He looked up from where he was kissing my stomach.

"Oh, and what do you want?" He looked at me.

"More. I need you to touch me. I need you to be inside me. Now!"

"My, you're a greedy little princess, aren't you? Well, with your mouth being as snarky as it is, you're going to have to wait."

I almost screamed in frustration as he went back to lazily kissing up and down my sides.

Suddenly, his weight was off my legs, and he lifted my hips to remove my shorts and underwear. He ran kisses and bites along my thighs. Every time he got close to my center, he would start over. I tried to close my legs. Even though it felt good, I was unsure. This was the first time someone else touched me there.

"Carlina, are you okay?" Preston looked at me with concern.

"Yes, it's just new."

"Well, we'll go slow then. Just tell me if you want to stop." His fingers lazily ran up and down my inner thighs and core.

Just as I was about to take matters into my own hands, he kissed across my mound and slid his tongue in between my folds.

"Oh, you're wet for me. Now what should I do?"

I was feeling everything and knew if I told him what I wanted, he would do something else instead, so I stayed quiet and watched as he kissed, licked, and bit.

He spread my legs and licked up my entire center.

I almost screamed; the feeling was so intense.

As he focused on my clit, he gently pushed one of his fingers into me, sliding in and out slowly at the same speed as his tongue. I grimaced when his finger moved, not having anything inside me before.

"Are you okay? Do you want me to stop?" Preston paused to look up at me.

"No. It feels good, but also new and a little uncomfortable."

"Like new, new?"

"I've played with myself before, but I've never been with anyone. So yes, new, new."

"Oh shit, I didn't know. If anything becomes painful, let me know, and I'll stop." Sliding up to kiss me, he then went back to my clit.

I could feel myself getting close, but didn't want to come yet. It felt so good I didn't want it to be over so soon. It was nothing like when I played with myself under the covers.

Looking up at me, he smirked as he made a come-hither motion with the finger inside me at the same time he sucked on my clit. I came so hard, my entire body shuddered around his finger as he lapped and sucked on me. He gripped my hip so I would stop thrashing around. After the last shudder, I laid there while he climbed slowly up to my face, kissing me hard. I could taste myself on him.

"You ready?" he asked.

I realized the head of his dick was pressing against me. I hadn't noticed him take off his boxer briefs.

"Wait, protection?"

"Princess, we're married." His hips rocked forward, barely pushing into my opening.

"I'm not ready for kids, are you?"

He paused for a moment.

"You're right. Give me a minute." He left the bed and rummaged around in his bag before going into the bathroom. Coming back to bed, he had a condom and carried a towel in his hand.

"Do you want to put it on? I'll show you if you're not sure how to do it." He tore the edge of the wrapper and held it out to me.

"What's with the towel?"

He handed me the condom. "You're a virgin, right? This is to make sure that if we make a mess, it won't be on the bed."

"Oh, I hadn't thought about that. Thank you." I reached out and wrapped my hand around his member. My hand fit comfortably between the bottom edge of the head and the base, and with my fingers touching, gripped him firmly. Slowly, I stroked as I watched his face.

"Princess, you need to stop, or I won't be able to get this on in time."

"Then you should hurry." I continued stroking. I paused for him to put the condom on and laid back.

He rose onto his knees between my legs. Grabbing my hips, he gradually pulled me onto him. Slowly at first, and I could feel every inch as he entered me. The stretch burned and gave me an uncomfortably full feeling but was pleasurable at the same time.

He watched me intently as he slid in and out, rocking to where my clit was being rubbed against.

"You doing okay?"

"Yeah, I'm just adjusting." I wanted more and deeper, as I felt myself getting close again.

"Harder." I told him as he looked at me with surprise.

"You sure? I don't want to hurt you."

"Yes, harder."

He lifted my hips with both hands and slammed into me. Screaming at how great it felt, he continued pounding into me. My climax continued to build higher and higher.

"I'm getting close." I gasped as he pounded into me. As he thrust into me, I felt myself fall off the cliff and my body tighten up before releasing. It felt nothing like when I made myself come. Coming, I looked up at him as he sped up, a look of concentration on his face as he came deep inside me.

He laid me back down and collapsed on top of me, breathless.

"Amazing," he whispered in my ear.

I could still feel him inside me and didn't want the feeling to go away, so I whimpered as he pulled out.

"Don't worry, if I could, I would stay inside you all the time." He kissed my forehead before going into the bathroom.

"Do you want to take a shower?" I stood to find my clothes.

"Only if I can fuck you in there," he responded from behind the door.

"Do you have enough condoms?"

"I'll buy stock in condoms if I need to, but no, I only had the one. We could order more and have them delivered."

"I'm so tired I'll be asleep by the time they get here. No sex, but I think you should probably buy more." After getting dressed, I crawled into bed. As much as I would love to have sex in the shower with him, I didn't want to get pregnant at 19.

Preston came out of the bathroom and turned off the light. "You're right, I should." He crawled into bed, throwing the extra pillows off the bed and holding me from behind. "How are you, Princess?"

"Sleepy, sore, but oh so good." I meant it. Even though I still had my reservations about Preston, he seemed like a decent guy, and I needed someone to help me over the next month with everything going on. Who knows, maybe we could learn to like each other.

Chapter Thirty-Five

9 Days After the Wedding – Preston

Waking up, I felt along the bed where Carlie had been the night before, but it was cold. I sat up and checked my side table to see if maybe she had taken the gun or knife, but both were still there. I laid back down and listened while I thought about the night before.

"Are you ready for breakfast?" Carlie walked into the bedroom.

"Breakfast?" I sat up, looking at her wearing a pair of leggings and a tank top.

"Yeah, I had breakfast sent up and let you sleep. It's on the table and getting cold, so you should get up." Carlie returned to the sitting area.

I got dressed and walked in to find a full breakfast spread on the table, and she was rereading the letters she'd gotten from her aunt.

"That's a lot of food." I said looking over the table.

"I didn't know what you liked so I got a bit of everything." She looked sheepish before looking down.

"Thank you for getting breakfast. Learn anything new?"

"Not much. I'm just fed up with this whole thing." She tossed the letters on the table. "But I guess let's talk about it if you want to. We should eat first, since we have a long drive ahead of us."

I couldn't tell if her attitude was from the letters or if she was bothered by what happened last night. I sat and took her free hand.

"Is everything okay? I know last night may have been a lot, but I don't want you to be upset by what we did. If I went too far, please let me know."

Carlie looked up at me. "Last night was great, and I have no regrets. Sorry, I'm trying to figure some stuff out and getting frustrated."

"Frustrated by what?"

"The fact my mother never told me any of this. Does Baron know about it? I mean, I assume he's read the letters from my aunt and uncle, so everything I know, he knows, and it pisses me off."

"Why does it upset you?" I lathered butter and jam on a biscuit.

"Because I don't trust him. I never have, and there's a lot of information in these letters. At least, there seems to be."

I thought about what she said as I ate. Knowing she would let me know what was in them if I asked, I didn't feel the need to read the letters. The first thing we should probably do when we get home is get this figured out. Well, after I showed her what I'd had built for her.

"How about we enjoy the rest of the drive home instead of stressing over all this? I'll take you by Mount Hood, and after we get back to the house, we can sort the letters and work from there?"

Carlie looked up at me hopefully. "You'll help?"

I may not be the best guy in the world, but I wouldn't sit by and let her flounder her future, especially since I kind of liked her feisty nature. She was so different from any of the women I'd dated before. They'd all treated me like a spoiled rich kid. Carlie knew I was rich but didn't treat me differently.

"Of course I will. Let's eat, okay, and we'll get home and get to work."

"Okay." She put the letters away and started eating her breakfast.

I would have left straight for home if I didn't want her to have the opportunity to experience new things along the way. Part of me wanted to get home sooner rather than later, but I wanted to give her new opportunities.

After breakfast, we packed up and went down to the lobby.

"How was your stay?" the man behind the desk asked.

"It was very good, almost like a honeymoon." I winked at Carlie, who blushed.

"I'm glad you had a good time. Here's your receipt, and we hope you visit again." The man handed me a piece of paper.

"Thank you. I'm sure we will, right Princess?" I asked Carlie.

"Absolutely." Carlie smiled as she put her arm through mine.

"Perfect. I took the liberty of calling the valet as you checked out, so your car should be ready soon."

"Thank you." I walked with Carlie outside where the Supra was parked in front, waiting for us.

The valet handed me the key after I put the two suitcases into the trunk and the duffle in the back seat. He helped Carlie into the car, and I felt a twinge of jealousy when she smiled after him after he held the door open for her.

"Ready to go?" I asked as she got settled in her seat.

"Yes, but let's go straight home. I want to get going on these letters and maybe help you increase your stock prices." Carlie winked.

"Whatever you want, Princess." I envisioned her under me naked again, only this time it could be anywhere in our house.

The drive home didn't take long as I thought it would, since we spent the entire time talking. We stopped in Zigzag, Oregon for lunch. After that we pulled into the parking lot for Mt. Hood so I could show her the mountain. It was early evening by the time we got home.

"I need to drop this off at my father's before I can do anything else. Okay?" I motioned at the duffle in the back seat.

"I almost forgot. Yeah, I don't want the duffle with us any longer than it needs to be, especially since I don't know what's in it." Carlie shuddered.

Honestly, I had no idea what was in it, and while my father was into a lot of things, the duffle wasn't large enough for most of it. So, it was either money, drugs, guns, or something I didn't even want to consider. I didn't like transporting for my father. It was usually for something illegal. This was one of the last transports I would do for him.

"Sounds good." We drove through town and went straight to my father's house. I could see the light in his office was on, so I knew he was home. "Stay in the car. I don't plan on being here long." I kissed her temple as I got out with the duffle.

At the door, I saw Seth standing inside. I walked in, and he stood straighter, looking sheepish.

"Knock it off. You're not in trouble. An asshole maybe, but not in trouble."

"I know Preston, but I still feel bad about it. I mean, something could've happened to her." Seth was groveling, and I hated it.

"Nothing did, and we're good. If something had, then we would've exacted revenge. Is Father in his office?"

Seth eyed the duffel. "Yes, he is."

"Thanks. Carlie's is in the car if you want to say hi," I called over my shoulder as I stepped into my father's office after knocking.

"You're back. Was the trip successful?"

I'd told him I was going to Vancouver for business for Carlos, which was why he'd asked me to get the bag from an associate of his. I hadn't wanted him to know Carlie had taken off.

"Yes, I finished the job and was able to acquire the duffle bag for you. There were some men with weapons scoping out the place. They started to come after me like it was the reason they were there after seeing the bag."

"I'm sure it is. This is worth a lot of money." My father came over and took the bag before putting it on one of the two chairs facing his desk. "Do you want to know what it is?"

"Is it business or personal?" I didn't really care either way, but if it was personal, I didn't want to know.

"Business." He unzipped the bag and inside were bags of white pills. "This is 10 million dollars worth of ecstasy we can supply the entire Pacific coast with."

I hated drugs, hated my father being a part of it and hated what they did to people. "Why did you have me pick up pills you can get anywhere in the US?"

"Because these are different grade than what you can get nationally, and because they're from Canada. They aren't on anyone's radar yet. The faster we sell these, the less likely we'll have issues. I'll start calling the dealers."

"Well, I'll leave you to it. I want to get home and see Carlie." I lied about where she was, but I didn't want my father to know she was with me.

"How's married life going? You've been home, what, one day since the wedding?"

"Yes, but I hope to stay home more now the jobs are done. I'm going to get going. If you need anything, give me a call." I left the office and closed the door behind me.

I could see Seth talking to Carlie outside. Outside, Carlie noticed me and smiled. I smiled back as I made my way down the steps and got into the car.

"Okay Seth, we're going to the house. If Father asks you, Carlie wasn't here, okay?"

"Whatever you say, Preston. Have a good night, Miss Carlie."

"You too, Seth." Carlie smiled as I put the car into gear.

"How was your father?" Carlie asked as we left the property.

"He's fine, just dealing drugs, which is horrible." I didn't look at her. From what I could tell, she was as upset about it as I was.

"Were the drugs in the bag? I think I'm going to be sick." Carlie's voice washed away some of the nerves I'd had about telling her.

"Yeah, he's into a lot of stuff, but I don't deal with drugs, and he knows it. Which is probably why he didn't tell me what it was."

"Huh," Carlie said as we drove the rest of the way to our house.

At our house, I parked right by the front door. Turning off the car, I got out and opened Carlie's door before grabbing the two suitcases.

After she typed in the passcode to the front door, I dropped the suitcases and picked her up before she could walk inside.

"Why are you carrying me?" Carlina asked as I carried her across the threshold.

"While we may have gotten married over a week ago, we are only now starting our lives together." I put her down in the hall. I didn't let her go, though, my hands resting on her shoulders.

"What?" Before she could say anything else, my lips crashed into hers. I held her around the waist as she wrapped her arms around my neck. I ran my tongue over her lips as she moaned. Taking her bottom lip in between my teeth, I bit down gently while pulling.

Finally, Carlie leaned back, breaking our kiss. "I love when you kiss me, but what was that for?"

"What? I can't kiss my wife?" I asked smugly.

"Of course you can, but the kiss seemed to have intent behind it."

"You're right, it did. I was afraid to tell you about the drugs because I was afraid you wouldn't be as upset about it as I was." My arms were still around her waist.

"Oh." Carlie then hugged me with her arms around the back of my neck, standing on her tiptoes to be almost my height. "I'm still learning, but I'll never be comfortable with anything as destructive as drugs."

"Keep saying sweet nothings to me, and we'll never get to the letters." I held her close.

"Oh yeah, why don't you pull them out while I find something for us to eat." Carlie stepped away from me, my body already missing her heat.

"In the formal dining room would probably be best. I'll also grab a notebook and pen so we can make notes if we need to." I took the letters and went into the dining room.

"Great idea." I heard Carlie say on her way into the kitchen. Within minutes, she was back with two plates of assorted fruits, crackers, and cheese.

"We had a late lunch, so I figured we should have a lighter dinner."

I stood to take the plate from her and kissed her temple. "This is perfect. Thank you. Okay, where do you want to start?"

"Let's start with the businesses the Bartone group owns and who manages them. The business names are written out, but the managers aren't. I didn't really pay attention to the business names while I was reading the letters. I was more focused on everything else."

"So, if someone were to intercept these letters, they would know the names of the companies, but not who actually runs them, protecting both the companies and the managers." I wrote out a list, but after three, I noticed not only a pattern, but businesses I recognized.

I kept going through the business names, and I could feel my forehead wrinkle over what I was seeing.

"What's wrong?" Carlie asked.

"Some of these businesses are ones I know about." I pointed at some of the list with the pen.

"Sure. I mean, some of them are local businesses, right?" Carlie reached for the paper.

"Yes and no. Some are ones I thought my father owned. I wrote down the entire list and starred the ones I thought were his." I handed the list to Carlie with the 42 businesses on it.

"This is a lot of businesses, and you're saying these..." Carlie counted the starred ones. "six are owned by your father?"

"No, I *believed* he owned them."

"Are all his businesses on here?"

"No, he probably has 15 or 16, but of some of those are on this list."

Carlie sat back in thought.

"Well, maybe we should ask him about it. Do you want to call him now?"

"Not yet. I want to see what else there is before I call him. I'm not ready for him to know you know about these yet."

Carlie took the list and looked over it again, slower this time.

I watched her eyes widen before closing to slits.

"What did you find?"

"These two?" Carlie pointed at two toward the bottom of the list. "These are businesses Baron said he owned or bought right around the time he met my mother."

"Does he only have two?"

"No, he has four businesses, but two of them are on this list. What the hell is going on here?"

"I don't know, but we'll figure it out." I moved my chair to sit closer to her.

"What else is in there?" I asked as I rubbed circles on her thigh with my fingers. She didn't say anything, but I felt her move closer to me, so I kept going. Each circle I got closer and close to her core.

"Initials for the managers, basic information about the house, but nothing about the next-door neighbor's house. I wonder if they'd suspected someone was reading the letters." I heard her moan as she finished her sentence.

My finger had brushed against her pussy, and I could feel the warmth.

"Preston, I thought we were working on this." Carlie moved closer still, draping one of her legs over mine.

"We are. I thought you were tense, and a massage would help." I grinned as her eyes rolled back when my hand ran up and down her slit.

"Well, then keep going." Carlie moved the papers back into a stack and leaned forward to push it into the middle of the table.

"Why did you move them?"

"Because I think we both know we're done working with the papers." She moved to sit fully on my lap, her back pressed against my chest. I moved my hands to the waistband of her leggings and pulled them down, only to realize she wasn't wearing panties. She stepped out of her leggings before sitting back down.

"No panties?" I glided my fingers between her lips and found her clit.

Her gasp told me I was in the right place.

Carlie's head fell back on my shoulder as she whispered, "Figured I wouldn't need them today."

My thumb rubbed her clit as I slid my fingers down. My middle finger entering her as I kept a steady pace with my fingers.

She rubbed her ass against my penis.

"Careful or I'm going to come in my pants," I mumbled in her ear as she laughed and continued to rub.

One of her hands reached up and massaged her breast.

I grabbed the hand and pulled it behind her. "No, I'm the only one who gets to do that. Do you understand, Princess?" I added a second finger, stroking in and out.

"Uh huh, you're the only one." She was practically bouncing on my dick, and I knew I needed to be inside her soon.

I removed my fingers and moved them to her clit, wet with her juices. Pausing every time I heard her suck in a breath, I slowly moved back and forth. I felt her clit tremble and knew she was getting close.

"Are you going to come for me, Princess?" I asked as she rubbed against my hand.

"Yes, I'm so close, please."

With one finger, I held her clit in place, while the other rubbed over it. I felt her tense and then come. I wasn't done with her yet, though.

"Stay here. I'll be right back."

"Wait, where are you going?" she asked as I quickly left the room.

Running up the stairs, I grabbed a condom from my nightstand. When I returned, I found her in the same place, her hair hanging over her shoulders.

"I had to grab something." Lifting her gently, so she was standing, I moved behind her. Bending her over the table, her feet were on the floor, but her chest was on the table.

"What if someone—"

"This is our house. If I want to fuck my wife on my dining room table, I can and will."

Leaning over, I kissed her neck before I bit softly and licked my way down to her shoulder before kissing down her back. I straightened and put the condom on before I bent back over her. "Are you ready?"

"Yes, please."

Those words were enough for me to come unglued. Gripping her hips with my hands, I slid into her wet opening. I dug my fingers into her hip bones as she moaned, and slowly stroked in and out as she laid on the table, bracing herself.

"This good?" All I heard was a muffled 'uh huh' from the table. Looking down at her, I realized something.

"This won't do." I took my belt and grabbed both her wrists. Bringing them behind her, I wrapped my belt around, holding them together. "It's not too tight, is it?" I asked.

"No," I heard her mumble from under her hair.

"Good. Are you ready?"

Instead of saying anything, she pushed back, arching her back and taking in all of me. That was all I needed to know as I held her hips and picked up the pace. I pounded into her as she thrashed under me. I knew her hips would have bruises on them, but the thought made it even hotter.

"Harder, Preston. Make me come."

I pulled her closer and used one hand to grasp her hip while the other hand found her clit. As I stroked hard into her, I teased her clit with my finger.

"Fuck yes, so close." I heard her say as I felt my pressure build.

"Are you going to come for me, Princess? Come for me all over my hard cock." I bit into her shoulder while I played with her clit. Pushing all the way in, I felt the sides of her vagina pulsating while she screamed. I leaned on her and as I came. I tasted blood and realized I'd bitten her harder than I realized. Not stopping until I heard her say, "Okay, enough. No more, please," I removed my hand from her clit and slid out of her.

"I'm sorry." I pulled the condom off.

"For what?" Carlie looked confused by my comment.

"For biting you so hard." I pointed to the small drop of blood on her shoulder.

"The pain was fucking amazing as I came. Don't apologize." Carlie got dressed.

I couldn't believe what I'd just heard, and it made me want to bend her over all over again. This was a woman I'd been forced to marry but seemed to be into some of the same stuff I was, or at least it appeared like it so far.

"Well then, consider the apology revoked." I grabbed her by the back of the neck and pulled her into me, kissing her hard as her hands found their way to my back.

"Shower?" I picked up the clothes not put back on along with the condom wrapper.

"As long as you have another condom." Carlie grinned before jogging toward the stairs.

Following her up the stairs, I laughed. "I'll meet you in your bathroom in a minute. I have to grab some stuff." We split at the top of the stairs. She went to her bathroom while I went to my bedroom to get the box of condoms, since I had a feeling we'd need more than one. A brief thought about what it meant to have my father's businesses on the list passed through my head as I walked back to Carlie's bathroom, but I pushed it back. Tonight was not the night to be worrying about business.

Chapter Thirty-Six

9 Days After the Wedding – Carlina

Opening my eyes, I could see it was late in the morning, which isn't surprising because Preston and I had been up late. Reaching over to wake Preston, I found the bed empty. As I got out of bed, I realized how sore I was.

After going to the bathroom and putting on a robe, I walked out of my room. I could hear Preston talking from the open door to his office. He wasn't worried about closing the door since he knew I was aware of the guns.

Instead of walking into his office, I went downstairs and got two cups of coffee from the full pot. I didn't see anyone else around, but there was a plate of fruit and another plate of muffins. Victoria must have come and cooked breakfast before leaving again.

Upstairs with the two cups of coffee, I tapped one against the door, realizing Preston wasn't meeting with someone. He was on the phone.

"Yes, can you? I think the program will be great for it. Okay, keep me updated." I heard as Preston paced the room. Seeing me, he smiled and walked toward me and took the cup I offered. Mouthing, thank you', he nodded along to whatever was being said on the other end of the line.

"How long do you think it'll take? I want to bring it to my father today, if possible, but we may go to the bank first."

He must be talking about the businesses and my inheritance. I sat in the chair at the desk and looked at the letters stacked in neat piles around the monitor. Holding a letter up and looking at him, I mouthed, "Why?"

He held up a finger.

"Great. Thanks Evan, I owe you. Yes, I'll have Victoria make cookies for you. Okay, I'll talk to you later." He pushed a button on his phone and stalked toward me. He put his coffee mug on the desk and picked me up from the chair before sitting down and putting me on his lap.

"How's Evan doing?" I picked up my coffee cup again.

"He's good. I'm having him do some research for me before we talk to anyone about anything. Especially with your birthday having passed. I don't want to tip anyone off that we know more than they think we do."

"What program were you talking about?"

Preston slightly turned in the chair so he could look at the computer. "At the academy, I made friends with Evan and Brandon, mostly. They're both brilliant, so I used some of my money and knowledge to team up with them to make this program. It's still in beta testing, but I figured with your situation, it would be the perfect test."

"Okay, but is it?" I watched as he clicked through things on the computer.

"Essentially, it's a program you can use to follow money or business lines quickly. If someone deposits money, it can trace the money if they move it through different accounts. If a business is owned by another business, it can go and backtrack to individuals. It's a way to sniff out illegal money and shell companies."

"Doesn't the government already have something similar?" It sounded interesting, but I didn't know how practical it would be.

"Kind of, but this isn't for government use. This is to track dark money and dark businesses and expose those who own them. For instance, let's say Evan's dad was going to buy a business, but it's owned by a shell company owned by another shell company. The shell company is owned by someone who's a drug dealer. This program would let him know in a matter of minutes, and then he would know if he still wanted to buy the business or not."

"What will you do with this information?" I could see how it would be useful if you're buying and selling businesses, but I didn't know if it was useful in other ways.

"Influencing business deals, blackmail, I'll even turn it over to the authorities if it's something needing to be done. The other thing is internet searching. We can use it to find the IP addresses of someone who is, for instance, selling another human online, even on the dark web."

"That sounds like it will help, right? Stop criminals from selling people?"

"Exactly. All three of us come from money. Some of that money was made illegally, and we want to make the underworld less dirty."

I kissed him as he finished.

"Thank you, but why?"

"You're a good guy."

"No, I'm not, but I try to do some good to balance out the bad. Speaking of which, I have two things to show you." He stood and grabbed my hand.

"Where are we going?"

"You'll see." He walked down the stairs and to the back door. "Close your eyes."

I did as he asked, and he guided me through the door onto the back patio.

"Okay, open your eyes."

Opening them, my jaw dropped. A pool and a large garden now occupied the space where the backyard lawn used to be.

"Do you like it? It's your birthday gift. Well, one of them." He guided me down to the pool.

"How did you get this done?"

"The construction when I left was the pool, and when I flew up to get you, I had Seth get his uncle's yard crew out to create the garden."

"It's beautiful." I strolled around the pool, observing the garden.

I couldn't put my finger on why the garden looked so familiar

"Do you recognize it?" Preston put his arms around my waist.

"There's a familiar feeling about it. Like welcoming but different."

"It should. It's a replica of your garden at your childhood home with the addition of wild native plants."

A gasp escaped my lips, realizing why it was familiar but not.

They had recreated the garden from my dad's house but added in native plants to make it more natural.

Turning, I jumped into his arms. I even saw several monarch butterflies flitting around the milkweed.

"I love you," I said before I realized it was out of my mouth.

"All I had to do was build a garden for you to fall for me?" A smug smile played on Preston's lips as he kissed my forehead.

"It just slipped out. Meaning, I love what you did, but not necessarily that I love you." I tried to step back from my admission.

Preston hugged me. "No takesies backsies," he said, holding me.

I was sure my face was bright red.

"Do you want breakfast?" I had to change the subject as soon as possible. I stepped out of his hug and went back toward the house.

"Sure, then we can get ready and go to the bank."

"Oh, I remember you mentioned going. Why are we going to the bank?"

"Because your birthday was two days ago, and we need to prepare for you to take your power."

"Why are you so interested in me taking over? What do you get out of it?" I asked as we stepped into the kitchen. I'd been thinking about it. Why was he pushing me so hard to take over the Bartone Group? I knew nothing about it yet and didn't even know if I wanted to be part of it.

I sat while Preston brought over the food and two plates. "There are a couple reasons, but one is purely selfish."

I looked at him as he filled our plates with food.

"Continue?" I sat, still wanting to know where he was going with this.

"If my father is on the list because he's a manager, which I believe he is, then it'll be easier for me to take over this area and remove him from power."

"Why do you want to remove him from power?" I wasn't opposed to the idea, but I didn't know enough about it to be on board, especially if he expected something from me to accomplish it.

"He's not a good man, and he owns businesses that import things he shouldn't. Not to mention he owns people in many different ways. Some aren't right. There are good things he does, but I don't know if it's enough to balance the scales."

"So, you want to take over the businesses he manages? But wouldn't you take over the bad things at the same time?"

"No, I don't want to take over his businesses. I want to slowly put him out of business. I plan on taking over Carlos' entire network, which extends from the Mexico border to Oregon. Which, now I know why he never moved into Oregon or Washington. It was because of your father and uncle."

"You plan on taking out Carlos? I thought you liked him. Wouldn't your father try to have you killed?" I was worried about how he seemed to be ready and willing to backstab his best friend's father.

"No, Carlos is going to retire in a year. I'm buying him out. His wife, Nancy, is tired of the life and wants to travel. Evan doesn't want the company, and none of his sisters could run it. So, over time, I've talked to Carlos about it. He's decided he wanted me to take it over, but I'll pay him for it. My father could try, but I have more resources than him now, let alone in a year when I control everything south of the Oregon border."

I let out the deep breath I was holding. "Okay, I thought..."

Preston looked at me and laughed. "Wait, did you think I was going to kill Carlos? He's more my father than Charles ever has been. No, it's in the works, but I have to stay married for a year to get the money to do it."

I looked away, not knowing what to say. I felt like an idiot thinking he was going to kill Carlos.

Preston grabbed my chin and forced me to look at him.

"I only kill when I have to. My preference would be to never, but I'm really good at it. Have been for a long time, so I'm the one called on to do it. I don't like doing it and don't usually relish the fact I took a life, but there have been a few exceptions."

"Oh, I'm sorry." Looking down at my food, I wasn't hungry anymore. Pushing it away, I stood. "Well, let's go to the bank, I guess. I'll go get ready."

Preston stood and grabbed me before kissing me hard, his arms holding me tightly against him. "You have nothing to apologize for, and I won't hurt you. Will you trust me?" He looked down into my eyes.

I smiled before he kissed me hard again and let me go.

"We can go after I call Evan."

Making my way upstairs to get ready, I thought about my life. Was I really going to be the wife of someone who kills other people? Was I ready for this life? Did my mom know what my dad was into before they were married? I had so many questions and not enough answers.

After I was dressed and ready to go, I sat in the library waiting for Preston to come downstairs.

We were silent on our way to the car.

I didn't know what to say. Sitting in the passenger seat of the Supra, my mind kept running through all the information I'd learned and questions I had.

"You okay?" Preston asked as we drove toward town.

"Yeah, I have a lot on my mind."

"Want to talk it out? I promise I'm a good listener." Preston put his hand on my thigh, and I looked at it, zoning out.

"Maybe later. Let's do this and figure out what's going on." I wasn't sure if I was ready to talk to him about what I was thinking. Things were moving so fast, and everything was a blur. What if I made the wrong decision?

"Ready?" Preston asked as he parked the car.

"I guess."

He opened the door to the bank, and I took his hand. I held my head up high as we walked into the bank, even though I didn't feel like it.

I stood in line with Preston, waiting for the next teller. I approached the window after the first person left. "Hello, I need to speak to someone about a trust account and a safe deposit box."

The teller acknowledged with a slight bow of the head before leaving to talk to a manager. He briefly listened to the teller before coming over.

"What can I do for you two?"

"My name is Carlina Bartone Wessex, and I'm here to claim my account and safe deposit box as per the terms of my father's estate." I sounded a lot more in control than I felt, but having Preston's hand on my lower back helped.

"Can I please see some identification?" the manager asked.

I handed over my driver's license.

"Thank you. Please take a seat at the desk." He motioned toward an empty desk with two chairs on one side. Sitting, I felt impatient but also excited. I had learned about the safe deposit box from the letters.

A few minutes later, the manager returned. "There seems to be a problem. I found the safe deposit box, but the account is not solely in your name."

"No, it should be in my name, my father's name, and my mother's name, as she was the trustee."

Looking down at a piece of paper, he paled. "What are your parent's names?" he asked.

Looking at Preston before I answered, "Celeste and Michael Bartone."

"Um, there seems to be an issue. There is someone else on the account."

"That can't be right. Who's on the account?"

"I'm sorry, ma'am, but I'm unable to tell you as it states the account shall not be given to you until the other party signs off. I can take you to the safe deposit box, however."

We followed the man to the room where they kept all the boxes.

He unlocked mine and placed it on the table. "Let me know when you're done. I'll be outside the door and will lock up the box for you after."

"Thank you." I waited until he left to ask Preston, "Who the hell is on my account, and why can't I get my money?"

"I don't know, Princess, but I'm about to find out."

As I stared at the box, wondering what was inside, Preston was already on the phone with Evan. Drowning out their conversation, I opened the box to find stacks of paperwork, jewelry, money, a picture of me, and some random items. Sorting through the documents quickly, I saw they were business agreements and deeds to houses. The paperwork went into my bag, and I left everything else in the box.

"Ready if you are." I looked at Preston.

He glanced at what remained in the box, looked at me, and I shook my head. Nodding, we left while he was still on the phone.

The manager was standing at the desk and came over as he saw us coming out.

"Are you ready for me to lock up the box?" the manager asked as he approached.

"Yes, thank you." Following him, I wanted to be sure he locked it without looking inside.

He picked up the box, placed it back on the wall, and locked it before turning to us. "Is there anything else I can help you with?"

"No, thank you. I will—" I was going to say more, but I saw Preston approaching with a dark look on his face.

He took my arm by the elbow.

"Thank you. Let's go, Princess." He looked at the manager before ushering me outside.

"Everything okay?"

"I just got off the phone with Evan. Guess who's on your account?"

"Who?"

"Baron, your stepfather."

I immediately froze, ready to turn around and go back inside the bank. "How the hell is he on the account? My father set it up before he died."

"Evan is doing some digging, but is Baron at work right now?" Preston opened the door to the car.

"Yes, he should be. Why?"

"Let's go have a conversation with your mother first. We'll get this straightened out."

"We'd better because I'm pissed." I slapped my hand down on my thigh.

Driving to my mom's house, I couldn't imagine how he'd gotten himself added to my account, but the more I thought about it, the more concerned I was about my money than my house. Peering over at Preston, I wondered what he thought about this whole thing.

Right as I was about to ask him, we pulled up to what was supposed to be my house. Seeing it now through open eyes, it felt different. It wasn't home anymore, but damned if I'd let Baron have it. I'd burn it to the ground first.

I knocked twice on the front door, waiting for someone to answer. Finally, my mom opened the door with a rag in her hand. There was a bruise around her left eye.

"Hi Carlie. How are you? I wasn't expecting you. Nice to see you again, Preston," she said without real emotion. I noticed she tried to cover her eye with the rag, but we'd already seen it.

"I'll be honest, I've been better. Is anyone else home right now?" I walked into the house.

"No, it's just me. What's wrong?" She scurried after us as I entered the living room.

Preston never left my side as I looked at her.

"So, my birthday was two days ago now. Thanks for messaging or calling me, you know."

"I'm sorry, it's been so busy around here. Annabelle has been working full time with Baron, and Beatrice has been in school. I've had to do everything around here by myself"

I put my hand up to stop her.

"Spare me. I don't care. I went to the bank today, and a funny thing happened. Do you know what happened, Mom?" I watched her eyes shift back and forth.

"No, what happened?" She feigned ignorance, but I could tell she was lying.

"Oh, apparently Baron is on my trust account. Did you know? Yeah, I went to get my money out, the money my father left for ME, and they said I couldn't because there was another person on the account who had to sign off in order for me to get it."

"Oh, how did you know it was Baron?" She wrung the towel in her hands.

"It doesn't matter, especially since you not only confirmed it, but confirmed you knew as well. What the hell, Mom? How is he on my account? I want him off, immediately."

"Honey, you don't understand. After your father died, I was all by myself. Baron came along, and he treated me really well. He just needed a little money for his businesses."

"How did you even change my trust? Everything I know says he shouldn't have been able to."

My mom looked at the floor. "He had a good friend at the bank who changed the paperwork for him."

"You used my money, MY goddamn money, for YOUR husband? Absolutely the fuck not." I was pissed, and I wanted to rage and throw something, but Preston's hand centered me. At my outburst, my mom slumped onto the couch, but I continued standing.

"So, how much has he spent? How much do I have left, if anything? Why did he steal the letters Marge and Matthew sent me?"

Her head shot up. "What letters?"

"Oh, he didn't tell you either, huh? Apparently, they've been sending me letters since dad died, telling me about the Bartone Syndicate, about the house, about the safe deposit box." I let the last words hang to see if she even knew about it.

"No, I didn't know. What have I done?" She cried, but I had no pity for her. She chose a man over her own daughter, and I didn't care anymore.

"You put yourself and that *man* above me, above my dad, and above the family. There are no emotions I have left for you now, and I would suggest you start packing." As I walked to the front door, I could hear her wailing and calling my name, but I didn't turn around.

Preston quickly caught up to me as I walked outside and stood by the car. He opened the door after kissing my temple and got in on the driver's side.

"Are you going to kick them out?" Preston asked as he drove back to our house. "We have a house. We don't need yours."

"I understand, but I would rather the house burn to the ground than let them live in it after what they've done to me. Yes, I *am* kicking them out. She chose Baron and his daughters over me. I bet his daughters were spending my money this whole time while I was going without. He spoiled them all the time but never seemed to have money for necessities, so we had to use my mom's stipend from my account." The more I thought about it, the madder I became.

"Do you think she knows Baron is running some of her deceased husband's companies?" Preston asked as we turned into his father's property.

"I don't know. I doubt it. Why are we here?" I realized we weren't at our house.

"It's time for everything to be out in the open, at least with my father." He got out of the car and opened the door for me. I put my bag under the seat and got out, holding his hand as we walked into the house.

I stayed slightly behind Preston as we walked into the house, and he knocked on the office door.

Chapter Thirty-Seven

I wasn't nervous walking into my father's house. I was more annoyed that he wanted me to be a part of his businesses but didn't want me to know anything. With Carlie holding my hand, I knocked on my father's office door before opening it. He was on the phone and held up a finger as we got close to his desk.

"I need to let you go. My son and his wife walked in. Yes, I'll plan for next week. Thank you." He hung up the phone and came around the desk toward us.

I subconsciously put myself in front of Carlie, but not so much so my father noticed. Or if he did, he didn't say anything.

"Preston, Carlie, it's nice to see you. How's married life treating you?" He reached out to kiss Carlie on her cheeks.

"It's going well, Father, but as you may know, Carlie turned 19 over the weekend. Well, today we received some news."

"Oh, and what news do you have?"

"I thought you would know, since you're the manager of a couple of the businesses she now owns."

Instead of responding, he walked around and sat behind his desk. Steepling his fingers, he looked at me. "So, you think I'm involved with some of your *supposed* businesses?"

Carlie put her hand on my leg, telling me to stop.

I didn't say anything, and she spoke up.

"Yes, and they aren't 'supposed' since I have the list from my aunt and uncle. Since you're a manager for several of them, you should know now I'm 19. I *will* be taking over the businesses with Preston's help. If you could please provide any paperwork or contacts regarding the businesses you have, I'd appreciate it. I have some other things to attend to, but I look forward to touring the businesses next week and setting up a schedule to transition leadership."

She looked at me. "Are you ready to go home? I want to swim in our new pool."

Looking between her and my father, I paused before answering, "Yes, but before we go, I have a couple of other questions to ask, okay?"

She sat back in the chair after I kissed her forehead.

I turned back toward my father. "Did you know?"

Looking at Carlie, he answered, "Not until he said your name during the ceremony, and even then, I didn't think you'd want to take back control of the businesses. Honestly, you didn't seem like the type of person who would be able to. Is this your doing, Preston?"

I felt Carlie grab my leg. Putting my hand on hers, I gripped it firmly. "No, I had nothing to do with it. She received a letter from her aunt and uncle, and she's been doing a lot of research. Speaking of which, what do you know about Baron?"

"Carlie's stepfather? Not much other than he showed up right around the time Michael died, and he got into the business. He isn't very good at it, so now he's indebted to me. Why?"

"If it comes down to it, will you side with me and Carlie or another party?"

"Preston, I will always side with you. You should know by now. I may not be the best father, but I will never disrespect either of us by choosing someone else."

"Baron is also the manager of a couple of Bartone businesses, as well as the owner of his own."

My father's eyebrows shot up.

"Are you sure?" he asked.

"I have someone digging into the list we have now, yes, but there's more."

"What?"

"Apparently, Baron has somehow managed to not only leverage Carlie's house for money but also place himself in charge on the trust her father created for her."

"He shouldn't have been able to. Not knowing your father the way I did."

"You knew my father?"

"Yes and your uncle. We went to high school together. After he married your mother, and I married Preston's mother, we lost touch, at least as much as you can in a town this size. Right before you were born, he and Matthew came to me and asked if something was to happen to either of them, if I would agree to manage the businesses in their place. Since I already had a few of my own, I said yes."

"What do you get out of managing them?" This was all new territory for me.

"Since it was your father who passed, the businesses were based in the United States. Every year, managers have to pay a certain percentage of the profits to two different trusts. One was in Carlie's name, for you at 19, and the other is for the Bartone Syndicate to continue to grow."

"What happens to the rest?"

"We're allowed to keep it. Managers are paid through the small remaining amounts. The years the businesses do well, we do well."

"Thank you, Father. We need to go see Baron." Carlie and I stood.

"Carlie, whatever you decide to do with your businesses is up to you, but if you need a manager, I would be happy to stay on."

"I'll think about it, Mr. Wessex." Carlie reached for my hand, and we made to walk out of the room.

"Preston, don't go see Baron without being armed. He could be dangerous if he sees his world falling apart."

"Thank you, Father. I'll be sure to be prepared." We left the office and went to the car.

Getting in, I waited until Carlie buckled her seatbelt before I started the car.

"So, what do you think?"

"About what?"

"Everything so far?"

"I trust your judgement regarding your father, but if the managers were also responsible for maintaining and growing the Bartone syndicate, how would anyone know if they were buying businesses but not reporting them? Is the list Matthew had accurate, or could there be other businesses that have been bought but aren't on there?" "I was thinking the same thing. Before we arrived at Father's house, I texted Evan and had him search for what the Bartone Syndicate owns in Oregon and Washington."

"Good thinking. I also think it's strange Baron showed up out of nowhere and took over as manager. I think we should go see him." Carlie sat back as we drove.

"Do you know where he'll be?"

"Middle of the day, yeah. He'll be at the warehouse."

"Okay, let's go pay him a visit."

The drive to the warehouse took about 10 minutes, and we didn't talk, both lost in our own thoughts. I was worried about what we may find when we get there, or what truths Carlie may learn while confronting Baron.

Arriving, Carlie pointed at his car. "He's here. Let's go see him."

"Okay." I reached across the car and opened the glove box where I stored my pistol and knife.

"Do you think we'll need them?"

"I don't, but my father doesn't give warnings often, so we should probably be prepared."

In the office, I saw a few staff, but I could see Baron at his desk on the phone through the glass windows. He didn't look happy, and I hoped my father wasn't on the other end of the line, because if he was, I would not be kind in my takeover.

Finally seeing us, he disconnected his call and came to the door. Opening it, he plastered on a smile as though he were happy to see us.

"Carlie, Preston, to what do I owe the pleasure?"

"Hi Father. I wanted to come by and see the warehouse since I haven't been to this one yet." Carlie smiled sweetly.

It worked because the tension in his face had ebbed away.

"Yes, this one is new. The old one is still in use, but we needed more space. Here, let me show you around." He went to another door and put in a code to open it.

"This is the main docking area where the trucks arrive to pick up the products," he explained as he walked through the large open bay, waving at people.

"This is busy. Is it always this busy?" Carlie asked.

"Yes, we're a major distribution hub for most of the goods coming in from Portland to Idaho, Nevada, and further east."

He walked us through another large bay with floor to ceiling racks and boxes filling most of them.

"And here's our storage area where we hold stuff for customers awaiting pickup." He beamed.

"Great. So, is this the company Annabelle has been helping you with? Mom told me she's been going to work with you."

His eyes grew dark for a second before he smiled.

"No, she's helping with one of the hospitality businesses." He smiled as we went back to the front office.

"Well, thank you for the tour, Father. I have one more question for you." Carlie turned and held my hand.

"What is it?" Baron leaned on one of the desks.

"Is this one of my businesses, or did you start it with my money you've been taking from me?"

He sputtered as he stood. "What are you talking about? Did you mother send you?"

"No, I know you're the manager of at least two Bartone businesses. I know that Charles was giving you money to keep businesses afloat. I went to get my trust today. Imagine my surprise when I found out your name is on it. Why do you think that is?"

Baron turned red in the face. "I don't know. It must be a mistake."

"Stop lying. I want everything you have. I want contacts, details, and I want them by tonight. Do you understand me?" Carlie stepped closer to him.

"But—"

"No buts. I will be back at 10 pm to retrieve what's rightfully mine. And don't worry about your friends at the bank. I already have someone working on it." Without looking at him again, Carlie turned on her heel and stomped toward the door.

Baron's face showed he was debating going after her or going back into his office.

"If I were you, I wouldn't try it." I looked at him before taking steps backwards toward the front door, keeping my eye on him.

Instead of coming toward us, he ran back into his office and grabbed his phone.

Getting into the car, I turned to Carlie and grabbed her by the back of her neck, kissing her deeply.

"I could get used to this. Any specific reason for the kiss?" she asked when she came up for breath.

"You were amazing in there. Do you think he'll show tonight?"

"Absolutely, but in the meantime, I need to get everything I can because I have a feeling he's taken a lot more than just my trust fund." Carlie sat back as we drove home.

***

Getting home, I hugged her. "Carlie, I'm going to get with Evan and find out what we can. Why don't you get into the pool and relax for a little while, and I'll meet you there before dinner."

"Okay, sounds good." Carlie kissed me before going up to her room to get changed.

Following, I watched her. Once inside my office, I called Evan.

"I need help, and I don't have a lot of time." The minute the phone connected, I was speaking.

"Hello to you as well. What do you need?"

"Has the program found anything out?"

"Yes, a Mr. Smith is the one who put Baron's name on the trust. A total of five million has gradually been taken out over the years. All of it has gone into businesses Baron owns or to pay off two large credit cards he has. The house was also mortgaged with Mr. Smith being the bank signatory."

"Great, can you—"

Evan interrupted, "I've already corrected the deed and moved what money was left into her account. I also told the FDIC about Mr. Smith, along with the corporate offices. They should be removing him from the bank right... now." Evan sent me a picture of a short, pudgy man being walked out of the bank in handcuffs and followed by two men who looked official, likely federal police officers.

"Thank you. What else did you find?"

"Well, this is where it gets interesting. Should Carlie be on the line with us for this?"

"No, I told her to go swim in the new pool. She did great standing up to her stepfather today."

"Okay, well, the Bartone Syndicate owns 57 businesses between Oregon and Washington. Some of them are umbrella corporations for others. Their yearly revenue is over a billion dollars."

"Interesting. It sounds like there are more businesses than Matthew and Marge knew about. They only knew about 42 of them." I tapped my pencil on the desk.

"I'll send you a list of the businesses with who the manager is for each."

I could hear Evan tapping on his keyboard.

"Okay, what else?" I looked at the time and wanted to be down in the pool with Carlie, not stuck up here.

"Carlie's father's death may not have been an accident."

"Wait, what?"

"I had the program going, so I figured I could look into the circumstances of his death. It looks like it may have been intentional. The police could never prove it, so it was closed as accidental, but there were some red flags thrown up the last time I looked into it. I'm sorry if I overstepped. You know how I get when there's a puzzle to solve."

"No, I appreciate it. You didn't overstep. I think I know who assisted Carlie's father in his death, though."

"Was it your father? Because holidays are going to be really awkward if it was." Evan laughed at his joke.

Holidays were already horrible. Finding out my father killed my wife's father would not make them worse.

"No, but I need to let you go. Hey, listen, I need you to email everything you have to me and the details about Michel's death to Matthew. I'll give you his number."

I rattled off the number Matthew gave me and told Evan bye. In less than five minutes, I had changed and was jogging down the stairs. I needed to go over everything and let Carlie know what Evan had found, but I didn't know how to tell her.

"Hey, nice of you to finally join me. Here I was thinking I would have the entire pool to myself." Carlie taunted as I approached the pool.

Without answering, I jumped in and swam to her. Putting my arms around her waist, I pulled her in tightly and kissed her.

"How was your call?"

"Informative. How long did you want to stay out here? I was thinking about ordering dinner and then planning for tonight."

"Sounds good. Will you tell me what was so informative?"

I wanted to lie and tell her we'd found nothing. Lying wouldn't make it easier, though, especially since the truth always came out in the end.

"Of course I will." We swam side by side.

After doing five laps, she moved to the shallow end while I continued and did another ten.

I felt nervous about tonight, not about what I thought would need to be done, but the fact Carlie would be there.

Slowing, I swam up to her as she floated around. "Ready?"

"Yeah, I brought out two towels because I didn't know if you would remember to bring one." She walked up the steps toward two rolled up towels.

She handed me a towel. "We don't have to order food. There's a bunch in the fridge. Why don't I get something in the oven while you go upstairs and get ready, and I'll join you in the shower?" Carlie put on her slides and started toward the house.

"I'll be in your shower." I winked as I jogged up the stairs, and she went toward the kitchen. Everything had been going well, but I was afraid of what the information I had would do to her.

Chapter Thirty-Eight

9 Days After the Wedding – Carlina

In the kitchen, I knew something from Preston's call wasn't good. His body language said it all. I turned the oven on to pre-heat as I went to the fridge and pulled out the salad fixings and pre-prepared casserole with instructions on how to cook it. I cut up the vegetables for the salad while I waited for the oven before putting it back in the fridge. The oven hit the right temperature, so I put in the casserole and went upstairs to my bedroom.

I could hear the shower going and stood in the doorway watching Preston rubbing his hair under the showerhead.

I stripped out of my swimsuit and slid the glass doors open.

"Can I join you?" I asked as he turned to me.

"Always." He smiled and pulled me close to him.

I felt his hands go to my ass and pull me against him even tighter. Looking up, I kissed him before stepping back.

"Let's get ready. Dinner should be done in about fifteen minutes, and we can go over the plans."

"Sounds good." He got the shampoo to wash my hair.

As much as I wanted to relax and get lost in the feeling, there was doubt creeping in.

While he washed and conditioned my hair, I thought about all the things he could have found out. Maybe I wasn't really the Bartone he thought I was. Maybe it was all a mistake. Bartone couldn't be a unique name, right? I shook my head at my thoughts, knowing full well it wasn't a case of mistaken identity, and I was who everyone said I was.

We took turns washing each other, and Preston got out to dry off while I stayed under the water a minute longer.

"Everything okay?" Preston hung his towel.

"Yeah, I'm thinking." I turned off the water and got out.

He handed me a towel and peered at me, waiting for me to elaborate.

It was hard to concentrate with him standing there naked.

"We can talk about it over dinner. Go get dressed, and I'll meet you down there." I dried off before wrapping myself in my towel on my way to my room.

He walked to his room holding his swim trunks and pool towel in front of him.

I was so preoccupied I didn't even see his bare ass walk away from me.

After I dressed in black leggings and a black tank top, I went to the kitchen to take the casserole out of the oven and to pull the plates and bowls out. I pulled out the salad and two types of dressing from the fridge and put them onto the table, along with the salad bowls and plates for the casserole.

Preston came in as I was putting glasses on the table.

"Yes, I understand. We're seeing him tonight." He moved around the table on his phone.

"No, I don't think you need to come down, but we'll call you after it's done."

Smiling at me, he continued, "Yes, I talked to my father. He suggested the course of action. Do you know how many of the managers would be up for a new arrangement?"

He looked at me. "I'll talk to Carlie about it."

He clicked his phone off right before sitting.

I put a jug of lemonade on the table along with a pitcher of water, not knowing which Preston would prefer.

"Okay, we'll talk to you later." Preston put his phone on the table. "Matthew says hello. I had Evan send him something before I got into the pool, and he was calling me to confirm it said what I thought it did."

I absently dished up the casserole. "What did you think it said?"

He put his hand on my hand holding the spoon. "I need your full attention for this."

Laying the spoon down, I turned to face him completely. "You have it."

"Evan found some information about your trust and the deed to the house. It's being fixed, and the man at the bank who's responsible was taken into custody."

"So, the house is truly mine now?"

"Yes, we'll go in whenever you want and put the deed entirely in your name, so not even your mother can touch it unless you say so."

I breathed a sigh of relief. I didn't realize how much the house meant to me until Preston told me I didn't have to worry about it being sold or destroyed by Baron.

"Seriously? I didn't realize how much hearing those words would make me feel good. What else is there?"

"We got the autopsy findings of your father, and it doesn't look like it was an accident." As Preston finished his sentence, the world started to fade to black.

"Carlie, don't faint," I heard Preston say as I watched him get up and come over to my chair. It was all in slow motion, or at least it seemed like it.

I woke to Preston sitting on the floor next to the table, holding my head in his lap.

"What happened?" I asked, vaguely remembering what he'd said right before I'd fainted.

"You fainted because I told you something upsetting." Preston looked concerned. "Maybe you shouldn't go tonight."

"Absolutely not, I'm going. What did you say?" I stood and sat back in my chair.

"Promise me you won't faint again." Preston smiled as he sat and poured me a glass of water.

"I promise." I took a drink.

"Your father's death wasn't an accident."

"That doesn't surprise me unfortunately. Who knows about this?" I couldn't believe someone would have killed my father.

"You, me, and Evan."

"And whoever killed him."

"True." Preston started eating.

"Anything else I need to know?" I picked up my fork. I wasn't overly hungry, but I knew I needed to eat.

"Not really. Everything will work out, I promise." He picked up my hand and kissed it.

The rest of dinner was silent as we were both lost in our own thoughts. I picked up the plates and put them into the dishwasher while Preston put away the dressings and leftover food.

It was almost mundane. The heir to a vast network of businesses, and a killer having dinner like all was right in the world.

Shaking my head, I turned to him.

"Now what?"

"Let's go up to the office, and I'll pick out a weapon for you."

"I need a weapon?"

"Yes because I have a feeling Baron won't want to meet with both of us, so you may have to go in alone."

Shuddering at the thought, I realized Preston was probably right.

"Princess, I'll be outside, and nothing will happen to you. I'll make sure of it." Preston hugged me.

"Okay." I followed him up to the office, where he pulled things off the wall and out of drawers.

"Have you ever used a gun?" He looked at the assortment he had pulled out.

"No, and I'm not comfortable with a gun, at least not yet." Silently, he put away the guns. Looking at the counter, there were five sharp-looking knives.

"Not everyone has to use a gun. I don't specifically like to unless it is absolutely necessary. Here are the knives I think you'll do the best with." He showed me the five and explained their strengths and weaknesses.

I pulled open one of the drawers.

"What about these?" I pointed at the stiletto knives I'd seen the first time I'd come in.

His face turned red, and he looked down before hesitantly looked back up. "Those are more for fun than for tonight's purpose."

"What do you mean?" I pulled out a thin one and watched his pupils dilate.

Walking close to me, he gripped the hand holding the knife. "Remember how I played with the knife before we had sex the first time?"

I nodded and realization hit. "You like playing with knives?" I grinned as his face turned red.

"Yes, but can you put it away? We don't have time for fun right now."

I smirked as I ran my hand over the other small knives. I heard him suck in a breath before I shut the drawer. Looking over, I could see he was hard through his slacks. Walking up to him, I slowly ran my hand over his erection while pretending to look at the knives.

"Please stop. I want to fuck you on this floor right now, but this meeting is more important."

"Promise?" I grinned as I rested my hand on the knife that felt the most comfortable when I picked it up.

I didn't hear him as he approached, but he whispered in my ear, "Pinky swear." His hot breath on my neck sent tingles all the way to my core.

"This is the one I want." I showed him.

"Okay, we have about an hour. Let's go over the plan."

For the next hour, I taught her how to effectively use a knife, and where the best places to cut were. We talked about all the things that could go wrong, what to do if they did, and the distress signal in the event Baron wouldn't meet with both of us.

***

The drive was quiet. The warehouse was dark except for the one light left on in his office.

I walked up to the door with Preston and knocked. I saw Baron pick up something from his desk before stalking to the door and unlocking it.

"Did you get everything together like I told you?" I asked as he held open the door. I didn't step in yet, waiting for him to answer.

"Yes, of course I did. I don't know what this attitude is about. I've been nothing but good to you," Baron mocked offense as we both entered.

"No, just a little abuse here and there, right?"

Baron sneered. "Why don't you and I talk about this privately? You can send your lap dog back to the car." He shooed Preston away like you would shoo a bug.

I looked back at Preston while pretending to be nervous. In reality, I wasn't.

"Very well. I'll stay out here." Preston nodded to Baron and took a step back.

I walked toward his office as I heard the click of the door being relocked.

It was a glass door, so one shot or a hit from the baton I know Preston had would break it if necessary.

Sitting in the chair facing the desk, I watched Baron move to the corner of the desk and sat on it.

"So now that he's gone, what did you really want, you little bitch? You come in and demand files you're not privy to."

"Baron, you know as well as I do some of the businesses you 'own' are actually owned by my family. I'm 19 now, and your entire empire is about to collapse."

He reached out to grab my shoulder, and I jumped up and out of my chair.

"Listen you tramp, I don't know what Preston Wessex has been telling you while you're fucking him, but you don't own shit. You don't even own the house you lived in until I married you off."

I made my way around to the other side of the desk to be further away from him. "Oh, you're sorely mistaken. It doesn't matter that you got to the letters first. I met my uncle Matthew, and he gave me *all* the information. As for your little friend at the bank, you won't be seeing him for a long time, probably 20-30 years, depending on what else they find out he did during their investigation."

Baron paled slightly. "Yeah, but if you die, then what? The money will go to your mom, which will then go to me because she's a broken bitch who will do whatever I say."

Anger at him calling my mom names flashed before I became numb to his words. I'd heard him call her things in the past, but I was done with him, and her if she wanted to stay with him.

"Okay," I said with a shrug, and I could see he was getting mad. "What? You going to hurt a little girl? One you said you loved, cared for, and raised like your own daughter?"

"I raised you long enough to get what I wanted. You were a means to an end."

"Well, this means to an end is done with you. Now, where are the things I asked for?" I looked at the desk and saw nothing.

Before I could do anything, Baron rushed forward and grabbed me.

"Now I'll do what I've wanted to do for years but couldn't because you were my *stepdaughter.*"

I could feel his breath on my cheek as he licked the side of my face.

"Ew, get away from me." I tried to push away from him, but he held me against the wall.

His mouth came down to my throat while his hands started pawing at me.

Trying not to gag, I brutally raised my knee and connected with whatever I could.

He fell back, and I rushed toward the office door.

He pushed a chair into me as I ran past him, and I fell. I felt him grab at my legs.

As I tried to crawl to the door, hoping Preston would see me, he pulled me back right before I could see the door. I opened my mouth to scream, but he held his hand over my mouth.

He straddled me and punched me in the face. "No one will want a used bitch after I'm done with you. I hope you had fun being married while you could."

I could feel myself slipping into unconsciousness as I felt him lift my shirt. While one hand was pinned between my hip and his leg, my other was free. Sliding my free hand up to my hip where my knife was, I gradually pulled it out of the sheath. He was too preoccupied with trying to tear off my shirt to notice me quietly getting the knife.

He ripped off my shirt and leaned me over, trying to undo the front clasp of my bra. Feigning unconsciousness, I slid the knife up and stabbed him in the side.

Baron screamed as he looked down at the knife handle protruding from his ribs. Due to how high up the knife was and his position, he couldn't pull it out himself. He moved, shifting some of his weight off me.

I scooted back and tried to get on my hands and knees to get out the door. I heard the knife clatter on the floor and felt him grabbing at my legs again.

"Where do you think you're going? I'm going to kill you like I killed your father, you filthy bitch."

I saw red as I thrashed around as much as I could. My screams shrill after hearing him say he'd killed my father.

He put his hand over my mouth and nose, and I felt myself passing out.

Suddenly, I heard a scuffle and the weight pressing down on me was gone. My brain cleared, and I saw Preston pulling him off me, blood running down Baron's side.

Preston kicked Baron twice and checked to make sure he was out before rushing back to me. "Princess, are you okay? Answer me."

I could hear he was nearly hysterical.

"I'm okay. Let me breath."

He sat me up, and I took a deep breath.

"Did he hurt you?"

I could feel him touching my ribs and side.

"Yes, but I'm okay. Can we finish this?"

Baron was moving, and before I could warn Preston, Baron jumped onto his back. Looking around for the knife I'd stabbed him with, I found it leaning against one of the walls. Crawling over, I grabbed it before facing them.

Preston had slammed Baron into the wall near me, but Baron had his hands around Preston's throat.

"When I'm done with you, I'm going to fuck her until she bleeds and then kill her," Baron spit as he tightened his hands.

"You will do no such thing." I stabbed Baron in the middle of his back, next to his spine. I kept stabbing as he fell. It wasn't until Preston grabbed the hand holding the knife did I slow down.

"He's gone, Princess."

Looking down, all I saw was the knife and my arm covered in blood. I didn't even look at Baron or what was left of him.

Preston sat next to me and pulled me onto his lap.

"He told me he killed my father. He admitted it. Why?" I sniffled as Preston hugged me.

"Money and power, more than likely, but we'll know for sure soon. I'll have Evan look into everything. You're safe now Princess."

I sat silently for a moment before I fell into tears. I could hear Preston calling someone for cleanup, but I cried as he rocked me.

Four men came to the office.

After talking to them for a minute, Preston picked me up and carried me to the car.

I didn't remember the drive back to the house, but he carried me into the shower and washed off all the blood before putting me into bed.

He shut off the light and crawled in next to me, holding me as I fell asleep.

Chapter Thirty-Nine

365 Days After the Wedding – Preston

"Are you ready?" Carrying the bags, I called for Carlie.

"Preston, let me take those. I'll get the car ready," Seth said as I handed him the bags.

Carlie walked down the stairs in a sundress. "Let's go, I'm ready. Why are you in such a hurry? It's a private plane. They won't leave without us. We're going to be in Vegas for a week. I don't think being a couple minutes late is going to kill us."

Rolling my eyes, I offered her my hand. "No, but I have so much to show you."

"Okay, then, why are we still standing here? Let's go." She grinned and skipped out to the car.

The flight to Las Vegas wasn't long, and I ushered Carlie off the plane the minute we touched down.

"First, you rush me at the house, then you don't want to become part of the mile high club, and now you're rushing me again. Seriously, Preston, what's going on?"

"Nothing, Princess. I'm just really excited to show you the city." I was, but I also had a surprise I couldn't wait for her to see.

"Afternoon, Sir Wessex. Where are we going?" Todd asked.

"To the casino first to drop off the bags and then to the house, please."

Todd tipped his head while Carlie looked at me through narrowed eyes. "What house?"

"Don't worry about it. Relax." I told her.

Dropping us off in front of The Zephyr casino, Todd removed the bags from the trunk and handed them to the porter, who followed us inside.

Checking in with the front desk, I watched Carlie taking in all the lights and sounds.

"Thank you, Mr. Wessex. Your room number is on the card. We hope you have a nice stay. Let us know if you need anything else." The lady behind the counter smiled as she handed me the key.

"Thank you, and we will." I gave the porter the room number to drop the bags off in, and took Carlie's hand. "Do you want to see the room first or go to the house?"

"Let's go see this mysterious house you keep talking about." She sounded annoyed, but her smile said otherwise.

"Perfect, let's go." We walked back outside to Todd, leaning against the SUV. "Ready?"

"Absolutely."

We got into the SUV, and he drove out toward Carlos' house. Todd was almost to Carlos' driveway, but he bypassed it and proceeded to the next, where a gate swung open.

Carlie took in the view. There was a lush garden with trees and a fountain as Todd drove them around the circular driveway and stopped near the apex. "This is beautiful. Whose house is this?" Carlie watched the birds and bees flit between the plants.

"You'll see." I said as we came to the front door.

Todd stopped the car and let Carlie and me out. Instead of going directly into the house, I turned to Carlie. "Want to check out the fountain first? I think you'll like it."

"Sure." She held my hand as we approached the fountain where a statue of a mother duck and her ducklings swam across the pond the fountain fed into. Milkweed plants surrounded the fountain with yellow, pink, red, white, and purple flowers.

"This looks like—" She turned to see me down on one knee with a group of people coming out from behind the car toward us.

"Princess, will you marry me...again?" I opened the ring box to show a sapphire ring with two diamonds on either side.

"Of course I will." She pulled me up and kissed me as she threw her arms around my neck.

Letting her go, I turned around. "Everyone, please meet Carlina Wessex, my wife. Now, let's go inside our new house."

Everyone clapped before going back toward the house.

"Wait, what? Our new house?" Carlie turned to me, shocked.

"Yes, I'm going to be taking over Carlos' business soon, and I figured we needed a house in the area. It's not completely ready, which is why we're staying in the casino, but consider this an early housewarming party."

Inside the house, I introduced her to everyone.

Matteo, Leilani, and their kids were there with colorful leis.

Carlos and his entire family, minus Evan, were also there.

Going around the corner, Carlie squealed and ran into the arms of her aunt and uncle.

I had called to make sure they could come down, and this was the first time she'd seen them since we'd left their house the day after she'd turned 19. She had talked to them a few times, and Matthew and I had spoken frequently to make sure all the businesses were being properly taken care of.

We spend the rest of the day meeting with and spending time with people we cared about.

As it got dark, Matteo hugged us before saying it was bedtime for the kids, and he and I agreed to meet up to talk business later in the week.

As it got later, more people said their goodbyes until Todd was the only left to drive us.

"Princess, are you ready to go?"

"Yes, I'm getting tired."

"Todd, can you get the car ready? I think it's time to go back to the casino."

"Great, I'll have it ready in a few minutes." Todd walked out the front door.

Carlie turned and hugged me.

"What's the hug for?"

"This house, the fountain, the proposal, everything." She smiled up at me.

I kissed her. "Well, you're welcome." I heard the horn honk. "Time to go."

She leaned against me in the car as we rode to the casino, and I practically had to carry her to the elevator because she was so tired.

I unlocked the door and led her inside.

"Let me get changed, and we can go to bed." Carlie went to her bag and grabbed some clothes.

"Sounds good." I stripped off my suit and got into bed.

Carlie came out of the bathroom wearing nothing but a body chain with her hands behind her back.

"I thought you were changing?" My cock was instantly ready.

"I did. Don't you like it?" She pouted as she rotated out a hip, making the chain flash in the light.

"Oh Princess, I love it. What do you have behind your back?"

She pulled her hand out and showed off a thin stiletto knife. "Oh, you know, it's our anniversary, so I thought this may be useful."

She crawled up the bed before straddling my thighs.

"Oh, and what do you want me to do?" I pulled her close and kissed her throat, my mouth running down to her nipples, slightly nibbling them while her hand ran softly over my dick.

She began to stroke me harder before she lifted herself and sat on my hard organ, easing herself onto it.

I grabbed her ass as she settled and rocked against me.

"What about a condom, Princess?"

I placed one of my hands between us as I rubbed her clit, and she gradually picked up speed.

"Not unless you want one." She said as I rolled her over onto her back.

Watching her, I looked at the knife again. I took it and slid out of her, dragging the knife down her chest and leaving a scratch mark. I ran it from hip bone to hip bone before I slid the tip over her clit.

She gasped at the cold metal, but I wasn't done.

I put the knife down and rolled her over onto her stomach. Picking up the steel again, I ran it down her back.

"What do you want me to do with this, Princess?" I asked while she moaned.

"I want you to mark me and take me."

"Your wish is my command." I pulled her up to her hands and knees before I took the knife and slowly pierced the skin on her lower back. Slowly, I drew a small letter above each cheek.

As she started bleeding, I licked away the crimson droplets.

"Still doing okay?"

"Yes, are you done? I want you inside me."

"Patience, Princess, patience." Looking at the letters and happy with what I'd done, I lined up my dick with her opening and pounded in while I held onto her hips. One of my hands grasped her hair, and the other went to her clit as I slammed into her. I pulled her hair back so she was looking at me.

"Harder. Fuck me harder." She put her hands on the headboard while looking back at me.

I placed my hands back on her hips as I slid in and out. Looking down at the P and W, raised and oozing blood, I stroked harder, my hip bones slamming into her ass cheeks.

When I slid out and rolled her over, she looked up at me, questioning. "I want to see you when I come inside you." I slid back into her, one of her legs around my waist as I held the other one higher. With my free hand, I rubbed her clit.

"I'm getting close, fuck," she said as I watched her eyes roll back.

I sped up, and as I felt her tighten around me, I leaned forward. "Come for me." I felt her whole body tighten.

"So good, so good," she muttered as she shattered around me. I stroked one more time before kissing her hard as I came and resting my head next to hers. Turning, I whispered in her ear, "That's a good girl."

"Always for you," she said as I rolled off and laid down next to her. Kissing me, she rolled onto her side and got up to go to the restroom. I followed her to help her treat the cuts, so we could minimize the blood on the sheets.

Getting back into bed, I pulled up the covers. Within minutes, she was asleep as I laid there watching her.

Right before falling asleep, I turned to her. "I love you, Princess." I didn't think she heard me until she sleepily replied, "I love you, too."

About Author

Flo Journey is the pen name for two authors who have come together to write in a variety of genres they enjoy. Look for more short stories and novels in the future from them. They genre hop among the genres they love. They write non spicy books under F.L. Journey.

Follow us on Facebook, Goodreads, Bookbub, and Amazon. Look for announcements about future projects. Please review and share.

If you read this far, please leave a review on your favorite platform

By signing up for our newsletter, you will be sent exclusive content.

Website: https://fljourneywrites.com/
Facebook: https://www.facebook.com/FLJourney
Tiktok: https://www.tiktok.com/@f.l.journey

Other books by Author

As F.L. Journey

Ancient Resurgence Series

Ancient Resurgence: Daniel's Story

Ancient Resurgence

Cerberus Brothers Series

The Cobalt Warrior

The Crimson Scholar

The Jade Commander

Matching Galaxies

Princess and the Pirate

Once Upon A Midlife

TBD – Book One (Coming 2025)

Anthologies

Illusions – "Death Awaits" – July 2024

Little Witches – "Growing up Teen Witch" – October 2024

Dark Descent: Whispers from Beyond – "Night Terrors" – (Coming June 10, 2025)

As Flo Journey

PNW Syndicate Series

Carlina

Beatrice (Coming 2025)